DOWN RYTON WATER

ALSO BY E. R. GAGGIN

An Ear for Uncle Emil

ILLUSTRATED BY KATE SEREDY

RYTON WATER

By

E. R. GAGGIN

Drawings by Elmer Hader

THE VIKING PRESS · NEW YORK

1941

FIRST PUBLISHED OCTOBER 1941

SET IN GARAMOND, EMERSON, AND TRAFTON TYPES
BY WESTCOTT AND THOMSON, INC., AND
PRINTED IN THE UNITED STATES OF AMERICA
BY THE COUNTRY LIFE PRESS

PUBLISHED ON THE SAME DAY IN THE DOMINION OF CANADA BY
THE MACMILLAN COMPANY OF CANADA LIMITED

TO

My Mother

whose secret Pride was an ancestress who fled before the King down Ryton Water, not forgetting to take along, however, plenty of seeds, slips, and simples for the planting of a new garden in another land. Truly an artful, competent, and noble lady, my mother always said.

TO

My Mother

whose manifest Pride was the fringe of small fingers that edged her apron where'er she walked. "Children draw their need from me" (and she might well have added, their sweetness!) "as a bee draws bread and honey from the opened flower!" she boasted gently.

TO

My Mother

whose dignified Pride was in the complete knowledge of the use of simples—"wort-cunnynge." It might well be written of her, as of one who lived and died long before her time, " 'Tis the truest grace of every female, be she dame of the Manor House or humblest goodwife, this knowledgement in the growing and drying and brewing of simples."

Contents

PART ONE

An Old Country

/

THE STRANGER IN MY MOTHER'S GARDEN

"THE elder is a cursed tree!"

I looked above to where the pleached boughs allowed a pleasant pattern of sunshine and shade to fall upon the pansy-studded turf of Elderblow Lane. And then I lowered my gaze as far as the coral top of Giles Kerry.

"No tree is cursed!" I argued hotly. "When the world was God's garden, He planted all green things that are—and all have their use."

"Thistles, too, I suppose!" yelled Giles, stooping to pull a thorn from his bare leg. And glared as though the fault of its prick were mine. "What are thistles good for, smarty?"

I did not know, but I was willing to guess. "For punishment!" I told him. "For the wagging of an untruthful tongue!"

"Dear lud, look at who knows so much!" jeered Giles, forgetting his leg and making a frogface at me. "And yet does not know about the elder tree! Listen, Titmouse—Judas, the sinful one, was hanged upon an elder bough! And the Cross was made of its wood! So, forever, is the tree accursed."

It was smothering sweet in Elderblow Lane in the June-time. Buff honeysuckles, rambling roses, and wild grape vines walled the place thickly on either side and the elders roofed its entire length. It buzzed with cockchafers and locusts, chirped with titlarks, and rustled in the ditches with tiny, busy harvest mice all red-brown fur above and soft white underneath.

I knew where there was a linnet's nest and five brown-spotted blue eggs, I knew where a harvest mouse had tied his round ball of a grassy home to a stout stalk under the hedgerows, I knew where there was a fat green locust. It was in my pocket. I had found it on a blade of grass, washing its face and ears as thoroughly as Old Tab, our cat, after a fish dinner. But I wasn't telling Giles Kerry about any of these treasures. Anybody who made a frogface at me would have to be satisfied with lesser finds.

"There's a Tiger Beetle under that elder tree," I told him. And marveled at the space of turf he covered in a jump.

"Step on it!" he howled. But I only stirred the Sparkler with a twig.

"He smells like a leaf of—of verbena from our garden," I said.

Giles didn't care about any Tiger Beetle's smell. "Kill it!" he urged wildly.

But I only kicked the beastie under the hedgerows and lifted my small nose to a lovely amber tassel that hung just above my head. "Wild grape blossoms smell just exactly like reseda, did you know that, Giles?" I asked.

"Smells! You and your smells!" he scoffed. "If we're going to get any eels today, it's time we climbed down into Scrooby Waters! Come along, Titmouse!"

The hedgerows at my right parted slightly just then and Goodman Brewster stepped out of the Manor House property into Elderblow Lane. "Scrooby Waters, Young Matt?" he warned. "I didn't suppose you were allowed down the bank into Scrooby Waters, lad!"

"Not before today!" I told him proudly. "Even yesterday I was too small. But tomorrow I have a birthday."

"A birthday—no! 1603—1604—and now we have 1608!"

"Yes, sir—June 1608!" I exulted. "Yesterday I was no more than 'going on five,' and so I had to keep to Elderblow Lane, from St. Wilfred's corner to the Old Mill House."

"And tomorrow you'll be five years old!" Giles looked at me and sniffed. "And still you are no bigger! You're like a block of oak, Young Matt—you don't lengthen out like a growing tree!"

I was satisfied with my growth. "I am like my mother's kin," I boasted. "The Brodes of Austerfield are all small and wide—but smart! We broaden in the skull, my Uncle Samuel Brode says, instead of thinning in the legs."

"And so you are to be trusted by Ryton Ford, eh?" Goodman Brewster looked at me doubtfully. "There are some pretty deep bog holes by Ryton Ford, Young Matt!"

"I'm not to go that far," I made haste to assure him. "Only below the bank at the end of Elderblow Lane. Ryton Ford is on the Great North Road, and my mother fears that. She trembles at the pounding hoofs and shudders at the cries of the plunging horsemen; and when she hears a whistle, when the King's Men are being summoned, you know, she calls it the 'King's Voice' and grows pale at the sound."

I noticed a sprig of mugwort growing at my feet in the lane and, stooping, broke off its spire of green seeds and tucked it inside my blouse.

"There you go!" Giles jeered. And yet there was nervous curiosity in his eye. "Such a lad for simples! What's the mugwort for?"

"My mother had the word of a wise man who wrote, long before she was born," I told him solemnly, "that 'the wayfaring man who hath this herb tied about him feeleth no wearisomeness at all, can never be hurt by poisonsome medicine, nor by any wild beast, nor yet by the sun itself'!"

"And you fear a wild beast down beside Scrooby Waters?"

"The King's Men are worse than any wild beast hereabouts!" I told him. "Even as the Tiger Beetle snaps up other beasties, either innocently passing by, or out of their quiet homes, and drags them into dark places for devouring—Goodman Brewster" (my thinking was broken), "Piet Billing said that a rider came down the road last night and turned in at the Post. He was wrong, wasn't he?"

"Piet was right. It was one who brought news from Londontown."

"Not a King's Man, then?"

"No. Quite different."

"Oh! Goodman Brewster," I continued, haunted by a sharp memory, "my mother said not more than a week ago that the Great North Road was the worst thing that had ever happened to Scrooby Village. What did she mean?"

"Why didn't you ask her?"

"That damp woman child who has lately come to swing in the cradle beside our hearth wailed at the moment and all was forgotten until she should be comforted."

" 'Memby, eh? You find a baby interferes, Young Matt?"

"Aye. When she is awake, my mother has little time, now, to prattle with me. She has to sing to 'Memby. Only, she makes up words to the lullaby and the words are for *me,* you see, and that damp one gets the tune that I don't care anything about. When she sings:

"Master Hugo Chillingsworth
Climbed up a monstrous hill,
To pick a fagot, sir, of thyme,
And rue, and sage, and dill!

I know that she wants me to pluck and bind a bundle of soup greens for the evening pot. And when she hums:

"Master Hugo Chillingsworth
Says he who eats in May
A twig of sage shall have good luck
For aye and aye and aye!

I know that the goose is ready for the roasting pan and only awaits his garden dressing—his pudding grasses."

Goodman Brewster laughed and vowed that it was a clever trick, but Giles tugged at my doublet and said if we were ever to spear that fat eel for supper it was time to be about the business.

"Wait!" I begged. And pulled free from his clutch. "What about the Great North Road, Goodman Brewster?"

"Ah, the Great North Road!" He stooped and marked with his long thin finger in the pansy-studded turf of the lane, pressing deeply so that the picture remained on the sod for as long a time as we stood beside it. "This, Young Matt and pink-topped Giles, is Scrooby Village—this great Y which I draw here upon the sod. Only it was the Finger of God that drew it, long ago, upon the green earth of Nottinghamshire in the midst of swamp and mireland. The long line to the left is the one sure crossing of all that dangerous mireland—the safest passage from Londontown, over Ryton Ford, to the country of the Scots in the misty north. The line to the right, springing from it, ending at the water above, is Elderblow Lane. Together, they make the Y. In between is the flurry of cottages that makes Scrooby Village, you see."

"Where's the Manor House?" I wanted to know.

"The Manor House? Ah, yes—the Post and Inn!" He made a great swirl with his finger at the right of Elderblow Lane. "Here we have it," he explained, "attached to the lane by the bit of pansy-studded path, like a great bubble hanging to Scrooby Village by a thread!"

We nodded, stooped above the pressed sod. "And now we come to Scrooby Waters," Goodman Brewster continued. "At the top of the Y lies the Ryton, at the east, the Idle; by a merging of the two, we have the Trent. And the Trent, rambling eastward, finds the Witham, and the Humber, and finally the open sea! These be the waters of Scrooby, lads—rivers that are ever too full, rivers that spill their wetness about our lanes, a protective cloak of mire, fen, swamp, bog, and marshland. Quicksand and bog holes, lads! Scrooby Waters are dangerous to cross for those who know not their secrets. With them spread about us, we of Scrooby Village could live our lives, think our thoughts, talk of our beliefs among ourselves and fear no one."

"But then, the Great North Road was laid!" I reminded him. "A curse, my mother calls it."

"It has been so for us, Young Matt! When we got a Queen who found so much business in the country to the north of us, then must a means be found for the safe carrying forward of that business in the speediest possible time. The one stretch across these marshes was discovered—the one safe stretch. The road was laid, Ryton Ford was crossed in comfort, Yorkshire, beyond, was easily reached, and the country of the Scots opened to daring riders."

"The pity of it is that *we* are opened up, too!" I complained.

"Aye." Goodman Brewster turned and gazed thoughtfully in the direction of the Old Mill House. "Still," he reminded us then, "still, we have Scrooby Waters, Young Matt! A pathway between us and the open sea."

Jon Brewster came running down the bit of pansy-studded path from the Manor House just then, saw us, and shouted from afar: "One has come who would speak with you, Father!"

"In warning?"

"I think so. He rode like the wind!"

With no other word, the two turned and left us, hurrying back to the Manor House, which was Scrooby's Inn and Post in these days.

"Well, how about it, Titmouse?" cried Giles. And sang mockingly:

"Master Hugo Chillingsworth,
He cast a spear—oh, my!
He then stewed fennel with some plums
And made a grand eel pie!

How's that for getting an idea into your broad head?"

I went forward with him then to the Old Mill House and the grassy bank at the end of Elderblow Lane. Scrooby Waters steamed in the hot June sunshine. Here and there, upthrust patches of plowed land greened prettily with peas, beans, scarlet poppies, hops, and rye. On other islets, lush and boggy, the cows of Scrooby grazed in rich contentment.

A short distance beyond were the forest and warrens that provided the gentry of Londontown with venison and hares for fine eating and beyond that, as far as the eye could reach, the sky met earth in a thin line of golden gorse.

A flock of waterfowl settled in the reeds below, chittering. One loon, and then another, dived into the bright ripples and they were gone for so long a time that it seemed, surely, they must be gone forever—only both Giles and I knew that they would reappear in the reeds farther along when they had pulled their fill of water grass, showing no signs of distress from their long stay under water. Gulls dipped and shrilled above our heads, feeding their young on the wing; larks trilled, cuckoos called from wet meadow to wet meadow, and everywhere was the noisy wrangling of rooks.

We sat upon the grassy bank to pull off our boots and soon were busy treading mud in the shallows with our bare toes. I got my mettlesome eel out to the sod without assistance, and soon Giles was astride his, holding it fast.

"Woosh!" he gasped. "We'll never get them up the—up the bank—all alone!"

"*I* will!" I replied. And chased mine this way and that as he coiled and uncoiled. "Let him wear himself out—only keep between him and the wash, Giles! This is the fattest eel ever speared from Scrooby Waters—and I did it! He'll not escape me *now*—and that I tell you!"

He almost did, though. Until I thought to cast my doublet upon his slippery length and so, snared, I was able to drag him up the bank into the shade of the Old Mill House and so, sitting upon an outflung sleeve, keep him within bounds and catch my breath at the same time.

Giles followed my example as soon as he had witnessed the success of my maneuver. "I'll guard them both," I promised him, "while you slide back into the shallows and fetch a coil of sedges. We can wrap them about the beasties, you see, and so grip them like a pot by the handle and fetch them home alive. I should like my mother to see the strength of this one of mine!"

He nodded. And was gone. And my eye would never have wavered from the writhing doublets had it not been for a puff of whiteness that suddenly appeared in the distance above the Great North Road.

"Riders!" I said to myself. And stood up to see. "King's Men, from the dust they make! And yet—and yet—King's Men go forward into the north, or backward toward London-town. They don't kick up a puff of dust just to hang it in the air above St. Wilfred's Church!"

"Giles!" I called, leaning far down the bank. "There are horsemen on the Great North Road!"

"What of it? There always are!"

"But these *go* nowhere! They make a dust that hangs in the air."

He scrambled up the bank, both hands full of trailing sedges. "Where?" he asked. And then, "Dear lud, is that aught to make a fuss over? I almost had a tortoise—we could have kept him in Jon's fish pool over at the Manor House. And now he's gone—on account of what?"

"A puff of dust."

"Is that anything to lose a good tortoise over?"

"But, Giles, where's the rider? He neither went forward nor backward."

"Disappeared, I suppose, like a moor hen under water! Such a crazy lad! Likely the dust out there is what is left hanging in the air from the courier that came with messages for Goodman Brewster."

"Look *out!*" I shrieked. And Giles's leap surprised me. "Under your heel—you almost mashed him!"

"Mashed him—mashed—what *are* you talking about, Young Matt Over?"

"My eel. Think I want to get him home to my mother with his tail slit?"

"Blazes! I thought you were talking about a rider."

"I was. But he is gone, now. Giles," I boasted, "do you know that not even my Uncle John Brode, and he the better of me in age by three years, ever speared a fatter eel than that out of Scrooby Waters! It's just like my Uncle Samuel says, 'Life gets better and better with the living!' Today a fat eel—tomorrow a birthday—the next day——"

"Yeah? What about the next day?"

"School."

"What's good about that?"

"We Overs desire learning."

"Lud, I'd rather rove the Seven Seas with Sir Raleigh, like your Uncle Samuel."

"Yes, my Uncle Samuel is pretty wonderful!" I boasted.

Giles was sorry he had given me the chance. "Pooh! You and your uncles!" he scoffed. "You haven't seen your Uncle Samuel for so long you wouldn't know who it was if he came striding across Ryton Ford this minute!"

I was unabashed at the charge. "Yes, I should!" I told him calmly. "Because if anything was wrong, and we of Scrooby in need of help, and if a man should come striding across Ryton Ford, that would be my Uncle Samuel Brode! Wherever there is great need, there is my Uncle Samuel—always!"

"Hey!" Giles eyed my contortions with disfavor. "You can't get that eel down the lane that way!"

"Why not?"

"It slaps your heels and scuffs the sod. Hoist it a bit!"

I made the attempt and failed. "You're too small, Titmouse!" he cried. "Coil the thing about your neck!"

I opened my fist and the beastie dropped to the sod. Only for the sedges he would have slipped down the bank and been lost. "No!" I rejected the proposal loudly and curtly.

"All right, figure out your own trouble!"

And so I did, wrapping the doublet about the sedges and carrying the whole thing across my shoulder by the knotted sleeves.

We parted at the gnarled pear tree in the lane outside the Kerrys' garden. "Let me know if you ever see that rider, Young Matt!" chuckled Giles, with a last mocking wink.

"Well, there *was* one!"

"Yeah? There was a black cat astride a besom once, journeying above Scrooby Waters. I saw it. Only when I woke up, it was gone!"

"If you think I was napping on the bank beside the Old Mill House——"

He was gone too, laughing loudly. And so I went forward to the next break in the hedgerows of Elderblow Lane and, looking in, saw my mother on her knees digging soot about the roots of the white digitalis plants. She was a bit smudgy, with a dab of black on her nose, but her coif was pushed back so that the breeze played with a cloud of soft brown curls and her cheeks were pink as the wild roses in the lane.

Goodwife Fentry, who lived on one side of us, was funny and kind but she was as big as a man; and Giles Kerry's mother, who lived on the other side, had a mole on her chin and hair like that tuft of coral my Uncle Samuel once brought us from the Seven Seas.

My mother was like a blossom, tiny, bright, and sweet.

I knew that she saw me as soon as I turned in through the hedge out of Elderblow Lane although she kept busily at work, never, so far as I could make out, cocking her head my way. But she dug her spud into the soil briskly and hummed:

> "Said Master Hugo Chillingsworth:
> 'There's quite a chilling breeze!
> Let's brew a bowl of thoroughwort
> Before we start to sneeze!'"

"I needed my doublet for my eel," I began.

And then we both fell silent, facing the stranger who had just entered my mother's garden from the Great North Road. He was a tall man, reed-like, and he rippled with satin fringes like a golden poppy. A golden plume sprang from his velvet cap to coil about his neck, and there was a lash with a golden head thrust through the knot of his silken sash.

Unmindful of paths, he walked as he chose, crushing ferny milfoils, dusty sages, spicy mints, rosemary, savoury, tarragon, and thyme beneath his heel. He doffed his cap, as to a great lady, though it was easily seen the act was mockery.

"A very good day, my beauty of the weeds!" he said. And smirked unpleasantly.

My mother had no word for him. She knelt where she was and waited. And, at her back, I stood silently watching.

The stranger sniggered and flicked a caterpillar from his golden sleeve. "Once," he said, as though we had been brightly chatting together this long while, "once, oh, some quarter of a score of years ago it was, I was strolling about the churchyard of St. Paul's in Londontown—and there at the Sign of the Angel I purchased a certain delightful quarto. 'Twas writ by a very good friend of mine, one Will Shakespeare. Do you count him among your friends also, beauty of the salads?"

Hearing no reply, he came a step closer and said: "I must tell you about it. You will appreciate its charm. 'Twas about a 'garden full of weeds, her fairest flowers choked up.' And, by the rood, if it didn't tell of 'wholesome herbs, swarming with caterpillars'! There's a coincidence for you, my beauty of the beasts!"

"I am called," said my mother with stiff dignity, "Goodwife Over, wife to Matthew Over, yeoman. If you have business with the Over family, put it in two words!"

"God bless us, a cockchafer of the lanes!" smirked the stranger. "And this, I suppose, is your grub! Let us hope that his jaws are less biting!"

I was shocked to discover from his leer that the man meant me.

"This be my son, Young Matt Over."

"A swinish ragamuffin of the first quality!"

Now, treading the mud of Scrooby Waters was never a redolent business, and what lad hasn't a burst spot about his garments somewhere—but "swinish," and "ragamuffin"! My lips flew open, but a fluttering of my mother's fingers beneath her linen apron warned me to close them on nothing more than a strangled gulp.

"We be as we be, simple folk of Scrooby Village," replied my mother coldly. "*Free*men, however—servants to none!"

"Oho-o!" The stranger fingered the lash at his belt and a red wave washed his cheek. "So, these be the courteous ways of Scrooby folk, eh? We in Londontown have heard rumors of—well, all in good time! Insolence, rebellion, blasphemy, too much freethinking—there be punishments to fit all crimes. They will be meted out later, never fear! Just now, we have to consider a certain garden of Scrooby—a garden of simples."

"Simples are grown in every garden in Scrooby."

"Probably. I said a *certain* garden, however. This!" The man turned and looked coolly all about. "Ague-weed and mandrake, arnica, aconite, heal-all, agrimony, ale-hoof, felt-wyrt, borage, and fewmitary—a veritable paradise for a witch!"

My mother stood then, and drew the bucket of dampened soot nearer to her buckled boot. "The man suffers from cramps, Young Matt!" she said lightly. "Pluck him a sprig of mint that he may gnaw and begone!"

"No mint, grub!" he said, and laid his hand again to the lash.

"Then crack your intention!" my mother told him boldly. "As I said, this be yeoman's land and you trespass!"

"I, my sweet? But what about your King?"

"The Stuart?"

"Have you another?"

"I will know how to speak to my King when he stands before me."

"The foot of a trusted messenger is the foot of the master himself."

"I am to understand that you bear orders from the Stuart? To *me*—a humble woman of Scrooby? What does he wish?"

"A welcome for his trusted messenger. Nothing more than admittance to your scullery, pretty cockchafer!"

"To my—to my scullery? Why, the Stuart must be a fool!"

"Have care to thy words, Goodwife!"

But my mother wouldn't. She never would, when her anger was aroused. Others, bigger folk, she always said, could do battle with their brawn; but she must learn to weapon herself with a sharp tongue and quick wit.

"The Stuart, did I say?" she cried hotly. "And he be not the only fool! *All* of you in Londontown must be maggoty-headed to think that *any* woman of Scrooby would fail to see the trick in opening her door to those who would spy upon William Brewster and trap him to his undoing!"

"Was mention made of one William Brewster?"

"No need! Since the only good of my scullery to you would be the window, shaded by honeysuckle vines, that looks upon the orchard and the bowed window and the three fish pools of the Post and Inn. William would feel no need to hide himself from the window of a friend—and so, you think, I would betray his trust and——"

"Not so loud, dame!"

"Loud? I haven't yet begun to shout the charge against you and the rest of William Brewster's enemies! When I do, every door in Scrooby Village will burst open and the King's Foot, as he calls himself, will find himself tossed to the quicksands below Ryton Ford! God's truth, thou *art* a fool to entrust thyself, alone, to the wolves of Scrooby!"

"Not alone, sweet! Plenty will rise to my aid when I call!"

"Do you speak of the dead?"

"I speak of the living! King's Men who lie hidden in the weeds beside the gray church at the crossroads. You didn't really think that I would be sent to pull the rat from his hole without assistance, did you? I have but to blow once." He twiddled a golden bauble that hung about his neck on a slender chain and, seeing it, my mother turned pale for the first time.

"The King's Voice!" she gasped.

"Aye." The stranger loosed the pretty whistle. "One breath blown into this, and it is as if the Stuart commanded! His men will come to learn his orders and——"

"So *that's* why the puff of dust neither went forward to Ryton Ford nor backward toward Londontown!" I cried, finding words for the first time. "Giles Kerry said that I dreamed. Dreamed—huh! But I never would have thought to look in the ditch for riders. Wait until Giles hears of that!"

The stranger's fist dropped to the golden knob in his sash and this time the lash came forth with a cruel hiss. Without waiting for further knowledge on what I sensed was the purpose of the gesture, I hoisted the burden I was carrying, swung it once for luck, and let go with a sureness of aim that had been envied by Piet Billing himself, who, it was known to all, could kill a swift on the wing with nothing more than a bit of sharp rock and a leathern thong.

The eel slipped from its sedgy jacket in mid-flight, slapped the stranger's chest, and then, finding a break between tassel and bow, moved inside the golden doublet, downward, and so was lost to view.

But not to feeling, it seemed. The man leaped straight into the air again and again. I had never before seen anything like such hops and bounds. In my mother's garden, where only cicadas and frog-hoppers were wont to perform, a King's Man was playing at their game and outdoing them!

At first he soared above the dusty sages and pounded back upon their greenness until the air was spicy with the odor of bread dressing; but after a time he left the sages, and leaped above the mayweeds, the felt-wyrts, the savouries, and the woad-waxens. The man was moving forward, vaulting in my direction. Soon, at this rate, I would be within reach of that swinging, hissing lash.

Once, Giles Kerry and I had happened on a water serpent swimming the ripples below the Old Mill House. Giles hit the evil thing with a bit of rock, and for the flick of an eye it stood upon the tip of its tail on a wave and looked for us. Then, like a flung black staff, it slapped the water, heading for our grassy bank.

I remembered the water serpent today while this man was heading for me across my mother's garden of simples. He cried that he would slice the ears from my poll with his lash. But just when he might have done so, something twisted within his doublet and he forgot. He clutched at whatever could be torn loose from his front and cast it wide into a bed of ruddy-stemmed hyssops. I was on it, like Old Tab lighting on a harvest mouse in the ditch of Elderblow Lane.

But it wasn't my fat eel! I was foolish, I felt then, to expect anything so decent from this stranger. The thing I held in my grubby fist was the King's Voice—on a slender, broken chain. A whistle, think of that! In return for the fattest eel ever speared out of Scrooby Waters.

And then the lash lifted a flap of skin neatly from my bared neck and a maddened voice shrieked: "Hand back that which thou hast stolen, rat of the boglands!"

My mother bent to her bucket of dampened soot, and when she straightened she held, gripped in both hands, the ladle, full and dripping. "We have no thieves in the Over family!" she said coldly. "Nor rats! Mouths that slaver dirt must be plugged with dirt!"

Before the man could utter another rageful cry, while his lips were still fully parted, however, she heaved the dripping scoop full at him and thus sealed his lips, gullet, eyes, and ears, for all I could see. "So!" she said. And spatted her hands delicately. "I lost my temper, Young Matt! It is my custom to count five simples and their uses before allowing my temper freedom to take its own course. And so I tried, today. 'Mandrake for bile—one,' I said to myself. And then, 'Monk's rhubarb for the blood—two! Howsleke for fever—three! Borage for courage—four!' But when I came to 'Borage for courage,' I knew that I was becoming more irritable with each count, and if I am going to stop, I said, let it be with 'Borage for courage'! And so I did. God's mercy, Young Matt, where has the King's Foot got to?"

"He's gone down the path, over the lane, and down the road, like a Water Wagtail."

"Good!"

"Good? When he's taken with him the fattest eel ever speared out of Scrooby Waters!"

She straightened her coif and hummed gaily:

"Fie, Master Hugo Chillingsworth!
I cannot help but feel
You'll never wrap your fists again
About that toothsome eel!

He'll be shaken out into Scrooby Waters once more, but he'll hardly be the same beastie after what he has been through! Our golden friend is probably by Ryton Ford, cleansing himself from soot and muck and the thought of common folk like us."

"Ryton Ford?" I stared at her, amazed. "But his men are hidden in the ditch by St. Wilfred's Church—quite in the opposite direction."

"Of course they are, lad! He won't let them glimpse him

again until he is pert and fresh and sparkling once more. Nor will he risk himself, alone, in Scrooby lanes where he would *have* to be if he were to join them."

"He could summon them to his side, Mother!"

"Without the golden whistle—the King's Voice? Where *is* the thing, Young Matt? I grow weak at the thought of it!"

I patted my doublet and grinned—grinned crookedly, as did all the Brodes, herself, my uncles, and the damp woman child who swung in our cradle. "He can summon no aid to his side as long as this hides inside here!" I comforted. "The King's Foot without the King's Voice is more like a rabbit's foot than not! But what *will* he do, Mother—stay down by the ford until he is missed and searched for?"

"None will search for him, lad. The men have their orders to remain hidden until they hear his whistle or his very voice. So he will bide his time among the willows until dark and the night mists fall, and then will he creep his sneaking way thitherward and down Elderblow Lane to St. Wilfred's."

"And then return to harry us?"

"Not him, Young Matt! He knows, now, that we are warned and he knows that, when warned, Scrooby folk can handle more than his small company. He will return to Londontown for more men and then, it may be, two days from now the Great North Road will be filled with pounding hoofs and plunging horsemen and—ah, well!" She grasped the dibber, spud, and ladle and motioned me toward the soot bucket. "Fetch it, Young Matt, and we will go inside!" she said. "We have done enough damage, you and I, for one day! Although I won't say that the doing of it wasn't pleasant!"

2

A KING FROM OUT OF THE NORTH

INSIDE, a mewing from the cradle indicated that the woman child was damp again, so while my mother got out the basins and fresh linens I crossed to the scullery and stood on an overturned tub to peer through the tiny window.

There was nothing worth reporting. "Nobody is about the Manor House," I called back across my shoulder.

"I felt sure there wouldn't be!"

"Goodman Brewster was working in the orchard, but he isn't now. He isn't in the bowed window, either. And Jon's nowhere around the fish pools! We could have laughed at that golden one, Mother, if he had come inside and wasted time staring at plum trees and rooks and the beehives beside the first pool!"

"I would rather laugh at him under the willows!"

I climbed down from the tub and went to stand beside her while she fed a brew of warmed milk and nep to the gurgling woman child on her knee.

"How did you happen to know so quickly what the stranger wanted of our window, Mother?" I asked.

"Men such as that one never leave the Great North Road to stroll through Scrooby's gardens except for one purpose. They seek what they must never find, lad—our good friend William Brewster!"

"The King hates him, doesn't he? I wonder why."

"Because of the King's arrogance, my lad. The King would be surrounded by slaves, and the folk of Scrooby are slavish neither in their thinking nor in their acting. The Stuart claims to be divine; we know that there is only One who is divine: God! To the Stuart we offer obedience in all earthly matters, since he is master of our land; but to God alone do we offer obedience in spiritual matters. We claim the right to pray to our God in words of our own choosing."

"The King writes our prayers for us, doesn't he?"

"He proclaims what we are to say. We pray as our souls order."

"And he won't let us worship at the Manor House any more. We are to go to St. Wilfred's or suffer punishment."

"It is the new law. The Stuart forgets that, though humble folk, we be still freemen here in Scrooby, dwelling on bits of land of our own. We do a powerful lot of thinking, my lad! Some call us Independents—and 'tis an evil title, as our enemies mouth it. I don't wonder at that way of looking at the matter, though. To be independent, in the eyes of James Stuart, is to be disobedient to his will! And one who is disobedient to the King, they say, is a lawbreaker."

"But we *aren't* disobedient, Mother!"

"Not in earthly matters. Only when our dealings with God be touched upon. Our first obedience, we feel, is owing to the King of heaven and earth. If the Stuart would only stop meddling in our churchly life——"

"And leave us alone to Goodman Brewster's teachings—hey, *now* I know why Jon came running down the lane this morning!"

"Jon? Jon Brewster?"

"Giles and I were speaking with Goodman Brewster in the lane when we were going eeling, you know, and Jon came out and said a rider was come from Londontown in warning. And with that, Goodman Brewster was gone like a locust over the hedge."

"Thank God that those who watch over William in high places learned in time of this newest plan of the King's, to send this golden one to our garden to practice his trickery!"

"They barely got word to him in time!"

"One moment to spare is enough for William Brewster! Nobody knows the secret hiding places in the swamps hereabouts as does that one."

"What do you suppose the other rider wanted?"

"*Other* rider? Have *three* come from Londontown today, lad?"

"Not today, Mother!" I assured her. "Only the one from Goodman Brewster's friends, and the golden one from the King. But Piet Billing said that a courier came riding posthaste last night and turned in at the Post."

"God's word, you frightened me, lad!" She turned 'Memby frontwise across her knee and spatted her briskly to make room for more of the brew.

I snickered. But not because of the damp woman child's noisy sprawling. I hardly noticed her, with the thoughts that crowded my small head. "Mother," I said, "the King sends his Foot to Scrooby to do his evil will, and the King sends his Voice to protect his Foot in the doing of that will, but the King never sends *himself,* does he?"

She snapped 'Memby upright and reached for a basin. "He did, once!" she said. "Once is quite enough, my lad!"

Blazes! I had forgotten about that. James Stuart—he was the very one! The King who came to Scrooby, for a fact! I drew a stool nearer and seated myself. "It was when he came out of the north, wasn't it, Mother?" I remembered. "Tell me about it."

"Oh, lad, with so much else to think about——"

"You saw him, didn't you?"

"Aye."

"Was he golden and splendid and sparkling?"

"He was more like James Billing."

Lud! James Billing kept an odds-and-ends shop down by the crossroads and was lean, sour, and shifty.

"*Him!*" I regretted. "I thought he would be summut like my father, with a plume to his cap and tassels on his breeches. I didn't know gentry looked like James Billings!"

"There's no law, my lad, that puts drab plumage on the tiny, humble bird nor color in the wings of the Jer-falcon. Fine drapings do not make the gentry. For the matter of that, William Brewster is gentry and he wears no tassels on his breeches. He lived at the court of the Queen who is dead, in Londontown, and was more than once of great service to her."

I nodded. "Begin with her!" I urged. "The Queen who is dead—the tale of the King who came out of the north rightfully begins with her, doesn't it, Mother?"

She laid the woman child in the cradle and covered her with a bit of woven cloth. "It was in the year 1603," she said, "and that was full five years ago!"

"The very year I was born."

"The very month!"

"When I was little—but not so little as 'Memby, eh, Mother?"

"Littler!"

"Well, not so damp, anyway!"

"Damper!"

Blazes! This was getting nowhere! "Well, anyway," I reminded her, "you were standing outside next to the borages, looking down the Great North Road."

"Toward Bawtry and Austerfield," she added. "Your grandmother was to bring John over to Scrooby for the day, to see the new baby."

"Me?"

"You! . . . Suddenly I heard hoofbeats at my back. Riders were coming down from Londontown."

"And you trembled, didn't you, Mother?"

"Shuddered, more like, when I saw only one horse—with two men astride."

"But there *had* been two horses!" I could have told the old tale as well as herself, after these years of listening to it. "Only the fine gentleman and his courier had ridden so hard and so fast that one horse had been done to death and left by the roadside down beside St. Wilfred's Church."

"A pity, too!" she agreed. " 'Twas a fine beast. The other only lasted as far as the Post and Inn, but that was far enough. William Brewster furnished both men with fresh mounts, and they were off again like terns on the wing."

"Goodman Brewster told you who they were, didn't he?"

"Aye. The important one was Sir Robert Carey. He was on his way down into the north to fetch a King!"

"Because our Queen was dead on her royal couch in Londontown—with no son to wear the crown after her. And that's bad!" I concluded, as though wise in matters such as these.

"Bad!" My mother pushed her coif awry and allowed the soft brown curls to cloud her brow. "Almost always it means misery and bloodshed, there being so many ready and anxious to stick their polls under a crown that has been laid aside. The prize generally falls to the first one to grasp it, and so haste was necessary, you see. Sir Robert Carey could lose no time along the Great North Road, horse or no horse. There was one who awaited him at the border of our land and the country of the Scots."

"James Stuart, son of our dead Queen's cousin Mary!" I cried. "Himself a Scot!"

"Aye, but willing to become King over English blood, remember! He was waiting at the border for Sir Robert and the Queen's ring which Sir Robert was bringing from the dead finger to the hand of the living. The King received the ring impatiently, put it on his own lean finger, proclaimed himself ruler over all of England, and, placing himself at the head of a great company of fine ladies and gentlemen, set forth on the long journey from the misty land of the Scots up the road to Londontown."

"And so, with the Sheriff of York leading the way, they swept merrily onward until they were stopped by the wide expanse of Scrooby Waters!" I was close to making a song out of the tale at this point. "And there must they bide their time for the Sheriff of York to take his leave, since Yorkshire ends beside the waves and Nottinghamshire begins on the other side. There, by Scrooby Waters, did the Sheriff of Nottingham then step to the head of the merry company, and so he conducted them safely across Ryton Ford, and so he led them, the Stuart and his court, to the Post and Inn for a night's rest and refreshment. And so you saw the King!"

"And so we saw the crooked legs of him, the leanness of him, the sour face, and the mean eyes. We saw him take, so he said, his pleasure in hunting the deer of Nottingham Forest, but the greatest pleasure he took was in ordering a poor soul who crossed his path to his death on Gallows Hill.

We saw the arrogance of the Stuart then, and the inner cowardice."

"And that is when he saw *us!*"

"Aye. He saw us. He saw William Brewster, and those of us in Scrooby whom he called disobedient lawbreakers, because we desired to worship God in our own fashion. He would have no noble, free, independent thinking men like William in his kingdom."

"And yet he won't let us go away!"

"Well, no! We be good tillers of the soil in Scrooby and of value to him. Too, it would seem as if we had defied his will and escaped punishment if we were to leave English soil unharmed. And that he will never permit. Some tried to leave Scrooby last year—Goodwife Fentry was among the number, you remember. But they were caught and driven back after bitter trials."

"We didn't go, did we, Mother? Why didn't we go with Goodwife Fentry?"

"The reasons were many, Young Matt, many!" She jogged the cradle with her outstretched toe and sighed deeply. "You were so little—and 'Memby was looked for. And your Uncle Samuel urged patience for yet a short time, and—and, well, this was the home of Matthew Over, yeoman, from the days of his grandfather's father. The leaving of such a home is no light matter, my lad! Still, if it had gone well with that company who made the attempt to escape last year——"

"It didn't, though! They all came back to Scrooby."

"They all came back—to the planting of peas, beans, barley, and hops, to sheep-shearing and cheese-making. Almost as though nothing had happened. Almost! Except that oftener and oftener, now, riders pound down this way from Londontown; oftener and oftener William Brewster is obliged to slip away to hide among the bogs until they be gone; and now comes one from the King, bold enough to demand entrance to the cottage of a freeman, there to spy upon a friend and betray him to his death!"

'Memby flailed the air just then with her balled fists and wailed testily, so I left her and my mother to the basins and, going out through the scullery to Elderblow Lane, turned my attention to Jon Brewster, who was just come outside from the Post and Inn to seat himself on the rim of the first fish pool.

I made no more than two jumps of Elderblow Lane. "Hey, Jon!" I cried. "Wait till I tell you what happened to my eel!"

"I know. I saw you throw it."

"Where were you?"

"Out by the Great North Road, waiting for William Bradford; he and your Uncle John were coming from Austerfield to spend the night. But when I saw that lone King's Man hopping from garden to garden, right after our own messenger had come and gone, why-y, I thought it would be better to watch *him* than William Bradford. So I came back to Elderblow Lane through Kerry's gooseberries and hid in the hedgerows by your garden gate. My father will be proud to hear about your eel—and your mother's scoop of soot!"

I grinned crookedly. "Where did he go?" I asked, never expecting a direct answer.

But Jon replied simply: "Toward Londontown."

I cleared the distance between us with a rush, all but pushing him into the pool among the startled fish. "Toward Londontown!" I yelled. "Why, don't you know, Jon, that the King's Men are on the Great North Road, Londontown-way, seeking him?"

"Nobody'll find him on the Great North Road! He went his way through the marshlands, hidden by reeds. He's not gone *all* the way, either, lad—just far enough to meet one who has sent for him, wishing to converse with him in a secret place. A rider came to summon him to the spot."

"The one who came when Giles and I were on our way to the Old Mill House?"

"No. That one brought warning of the golden stranger who came to your garden. The one I mean came last night."

"The one Piet Billing saw!"

"Piet doesn't miss much! Maybe he knows what happened to the maid."

"What maid? He mentioned no maid. A woman child—like 'Memby?"

"Well, not quite that small. Small enough, though. She rode behind the courier on the horse and clutched his mail pouch like a cocklebur—but never a yelp out of her, though she was weak with fear. That much could be seen. Father wanted to feed her, but she would have naught to do with us. She was sent, so the courier said, to Dame Cotter's Free School. And he added that he had been told she was kin to a witch."

"Blazes! And clinging to the back of his coat all the way from Londontown! He must have been glad to shed her."

"He was. I've been down the lane by Dame Cotter's more than once today to see what the kin of a witch looked like by daylight, but no sign of her!"

"Maybe she rode away at dawn on a besom."

Jon grinned. "Hardly likely!" he said. "If she could have ridden a besom she wouldn't have stuck to a courier's mail pouch all yesterday and had the bones 'most shaken out of her skin!"

The air was suddenly cut by such crazy laughter as the loon makes when a storm is on the way, followed by the trill of a lark and the call of a cuckoo, both sweet and faint, as from far-away, wet meadows. My father was coming homeward from his rye field and he was signaling me to meet him in Elderblow Lane. I left Jon on the instant, crossed the orchard of the Post and Inn, and so came out through the hedgerows opposite Kerry's gnarled pear tree.

Matthew Over, yeoman, mattock across his broad shoulder, was swinging down the lane, whistling merrily. "Ho, lad," he shouted, "so this is where you have been hiding, eh! Under the wild grape tassels with the titlarks! A father has powerful worries when his son is no bigger than a hedge bird! When you're by the water, I fear a bream will leap forth and drag you beneath the ripples; when you're in the lane, I think of hawks!"

I grinned crookedly. "I'm big enough!" I told him. "Well-nigh as big as my mother."

"And she as long as my nose!" he roared.

"Still are we *able*—having broad heads and quick wits!" I told him simply.

He stood still and eyed me curiously. "I should hate to have given a coxcomb to the Over family!" he said.

I knew what he thought and made haste to assure him that I was something more than an empty boaster. "Few twice our size," I explained, "could have done what my mother and I did today!"

"Yes? What powerful mountains have you two grains of sand moved?"

"All alone, I speared the fattest eel that was ever pulled from Scrooby Waters!"

"Well, brave enough! And what of Goodwife Orris?"

"All alone, she routed a King's Man and sent him scuttling to the willows by Ryton Ford with his mouth full of wet soot."

"She—she—dear God!"

"The worst of it is, though, he took my eel with him! In his breeches."

My father lowered the mattock to the pansy-carpeted sod and leaned heavily upon it. "Now then, Young Matt," he begged, "let's have the tale in full!"

And so I told him all, beginning with the moment when I entered my mother's garden from Elderblow Lane and found her digging soot into the foxglove clumps. I told him of the insolent stranger, of his trampling our simples carelessly under his foot, of his claim to the right to act as he chose since he was "the King's Foot"! He had been sent to use our scullery as a spy-hole for the trapping of William Brewster.

"He was alone, Young Matt?" my father interrupted my rush of words.

And then I told him of the King's Voice and the men hidden in the ditch by the crossroads. And the swung lash. And the eel that plopped against a golden doublet before disappearing inside. I told him of the golden whistle that was cast aside. And the scoop of choking, blinding soot. And that my mother said we had done summut, we two, this day!

"Done summut! Dear God!"

"Few twice our size could have done more!" I concluded thoughtfully.

Now, the Brodes of Austerfield were a small folk, but my father Matthew Over, yeoman, of Scrooby, Nottinghamshire, was a mighty man with hands like another's thigh. There was ever a trembling in his powerful fingers when he laid them on my mother, on the wee child 'Memby, or upon me, as though he feared to break that which he fondled. I marked that trembling now, as he laid a hand upon my shoulder.

"None in Scrooby, no matter what their size, would have done as much!" he said solemnly. "Come with me to get some balsam of thy mother's brewing for that wound!" His hand slid inside my torn doublet and came forth clutching a sprig of mugwort and the King's Voice. "What is this?" he asked.

"Blazes! Either a King's Man is no wild animal, or there is no power in the stuff!" I complained. "Maybe fewmitary —to drive off evil spirits—maybe that would be better!"

"This bit of gold, Young Matt!"

"Oh, that! That's the whistle to blow upon in time of need. Only the one who came to our garden waited too long before blowing."

My father turned the bauble on his great palm and a scratched side came uppermost. "What is it?" I asked him, in turn.

" 'Tis writing, lad! It says: 'THE KING SPEAKS, RE-MEMBER!' " And he made a gesture as though he would throw the thing far out across Scrooby Waters. I rescued it in time.

"Let me see!" I begged. "Show me the letters!"

Letter by letter, he showed me the message scratched upon the golden whistle. Clear to the last word, RE-MEM-BER.

"Re-mem-ber," I repeated it after him and stood on my tiptoes the better to see. "Why, that's the name of the woman child who swings in our cradle!"

"So it is, so it is, lad!"

"We shouldn't throw it away, Father—with her name upon it!"

"We shouldn't keep it, lad!"

"It's pretty."

"And dangerous to hold!"

"But if we were in need, and should have it to blow on——"

"And should summon King's Men to our cottage! Would that be good?"

Lud, no! I couldn't think of anything worse. "We'd better not blow upon it!" I agreed. "Never! Just keep it to look at —and tell 'Memby about when she is woman grown."

"I'll have to speak with Goodman Brewster about the matter!" my father decided at last. "What he says, that will we do. And until then, we will hide it and speak of it to no soul! Does Giles Kerry know of the bauble, lad?"

"Nobody—not another soul but you and my mother and the golden stranger and me."

"Then three will try to forget it—pray God that the fourth does the same!"

We turned out of Elderblow Lane into my mother's garden and, crossing it, entered the scullery through a narrow rear door. Dried simples were hanging from the rafters in odorous bunches, fagots of twigs with healing bark, clusters of brittle leaves and powdery blossom heads, knots of tubers and pungent roots. Reaching high above his head, my father concealed the King's Voice in a bunch of rustling ague-weed that filled the darkest corner.

"So!" he said. "I've no doubt the thing would better be under Scrooby Waters. But it has value, being gold, and it fell into your hands on the eve of your birthday—mayhap it is a token of something. Whether of evil or good, we'll soon know. Meanwhile, it is forgotten! Is that understood, Young Matt?"

"Aye!" I told him. He knew well that, being a Brode of

Austerfield and an Over of Scrooby, I could be trusted to hold to my word.

And so we entered the kitchen and took our places at the long table opposite the open door. We ate heartily of thick barley slices and dark rye bread, of fresh cheese, of spicy radishes, and thickened jam from a deep blue mug. Only my mother would not sit and sup with us.

She stood uneasily at the farther end of the table, scraping skirrets, slicing greens, and preparing roots for the stew pot. Once she went outside to the garden and plucked a fagot of green herbs: thyme, savoury, sage, fewmitary, and dill.

"Wear a sprig of fewmitary,
Wave a twig of dill,
And so prevent the witches
From the doing of their will!"

I chanted. And licked at the jam on my thumbs, thoughtfully.

My mother laid down her knife and tugged at her coif. "Witches, Young Matt?" she said. "I do not like the word!"

"That golden one," I reminded her, and fetched the memory of his words out of the back of my mind, "that golden one said that our garden was a veritable paradise for witches."

"He said much that was foolish."

"But maybe he *knew*, Mother!" I clung to the thought unduly. "Maybe the witches of Londontown like simples."

"Witches of Lon— There are no witches anywhere, Young Matt! Goodman Brewster has told you that over and over again. 'Tis a wicked belief that is going the rounds of ignorant folk."

"Jon Brewster said that we have a maid in Scrooby who is kin to a witch."

"Jon said that?"

"Aye. She came from Londontown last night, riding behind a courier, clutched to his mail pouch like a bur on a woolen hose!"

"Still is it a wicked and senseless word!" my father interrupted the argument sternly. "We'll hear no more of it in a godly household! Sit thee down and sup, Goodwife!"

My mother went, instead, to stand in the doorway and look out upon the garden, wrapped quietly, now, in the last long rays of a setting sun. Soon there would be a mist and the fragrance of dew-drenched blossoms would fill the room. "The lavenders are opening!" she said. And then, "I'll have my tea, Goodman, when I am more able to shift my mind from the happenings of this day."

"God grant the others will be able to shift the burden from their minds as easily!" groaned my father.

My mother threw back her head at that, and the kitchen rang with her merry laughter. "They'll have their trouble shifting the smut from their pates!" she told him. "The battle of the soot bucket, Matthew!" she added. And wiped her eyes with a corner of her linen apron. "I shall have a word to say to William Brewster about this new setting to an old tale. I shall tell him that the Overs needed *two* Davids for one Goliath, being extra-small folk—one to swing an eel and one to swing a soot ladle. But they, between them, did surely overcome the giant! Only this golden Goliath did not fall dead of his wounds! My word for it, he did not drop at all! He squeaked like a Musk Beetle, he squirmed like Old Tab in a fit, he leaped like a cricket, and he scuttled for Ryton Ford like a water spider. A conquered giant, but nimble to the end!"

I choked and giggled, and my father roared with laughter.

'Memby awoke, mewed for attention, and was drawn from the cradle to my father's shelf-like knee, where she was spatted gently back to slumbering while my mother got herself a trencher from the cupboard and a cup from the shelf and seated herself at table.

"I'll eat now," she said. "My appetite is returned. Cut me an end of the barley loaf, Young Matt, and shove the jam mug nearer!

"Master Hugo Chillingsworth—
No matter what comes after—
A meal is relished best when spiced
With lots of merry laughter!"

Somebody swished along Elderblow Lane past our scullery window and my father, rising with 'Memby under his arm, was just in time to see through the little window that Goodman Brewster was returned, hurrying up the path beside the three fish pools. He entered the Post and Inn, and Jon closed the door behind them both.

3

KIN TO A WITCH

THERE was a scratching against the window lattice that awakened me the next morning, and I jumped from my straw pallet at the far end of my parents' sleeping chamber to investigate.

It wouldn't be Beggar, Jon's pet dove who took his barley crumbs where he found them, because the morning was still dark with fog and Beggar preferred sunshine. I mounted a stool and came nose to nose with Giles Kerry.

"Hi, Titmouse!" he whispered. "Get into your doublet and wiggle out through the lattice!"

"Why should I?"

"Don't you want to watch Piet Billing shear sheep?"

"Where?"

"On Goodman Fentry's island."

"How would we get there?"

"Piet said we could go with him. He's got an old wherry down by the ford and——"

He said no more, but vanished from the lattice in a flurry that I knew was not of his making alone. I stuck my head outside the window and saw my father with a milk bucket in one hand and Giles in the other. And, from the open kitchen door, my mother was peering out into the fog.

"Matthew!" she cried. "Goodman Matthew! Over against our wall—there was a noise."

"Don't fret!" he comforted, coming to where he could be more easily seen. " 'Twas merely a curious beastie attempting to crawl about the lattice. I plucked it off." He shook his fist and all but spilled Giles out of his doublet. "Fetch a timber, Goodwife, and I'll crack the grub so he'll be no bother to our vines in the future!"

A shrill howl pierced the morning and my father gazed downward in mock surprise. "Eh, what's this, what's this?" he demanded. "*Giles Kerry?* Merry Andrew, but you howled barely in the nick of time to save that clover top of yours! What's the reason for climbing our honeysuckle before daybreak?"

"I—I was but calling Young Matt."

"Have you forgotten the path to our kitchen door?"

Giles would find trouble in explaining his visit, I knew, but he was spared the effort, for my father did but loosen his grasp for the small part of a second and Giles was gone into the fog like a swift after a moth.

There was a chuckle below the lattice and a ripple of laughter from the open doorway; and then the rushes crushed and rustled beneath my father's heavy tread as he entered the other room and joined my mother beside the hearth.

"You shocked the lad, Matthew!" she told him.

"I hope so. 'Tis quite proper for Young Matt to learn to stand boldly against temptation in his early years, but there is no kindness in allowing every tempter the run of the place."

"You know what day this *is,* don't you?"

"The middle of the week."

"Plague on you, man! You know what I mean! This be the only day in his whole life that our son can say: 'Today, I come five years of age!' A memorable day, Matthew! You should know, having enjoyed just such an occasion."

"I do. After twenty years, I remember the day well! And so shall Young Matt, I promise you! Today, within the hour, he will be handed over to the gentle mercies of Dame Cotter!"

"Oh, Matthew, not school, today!"

"Why not? A son of mine should be able to write his name in full and read a psalm with his betters as soon in life as possible."

"I know. And Young Matt is eager for learning. But, today! God's love, I was for making this day a happy holiday! John was coming over from Austerfield yesterday to spend the night at the Manor House, but I got word to him to wait until today, to surprise Young Matt. I thought the lads could do a bit of eeling in Scrooby Waters to make up for the disappointment of yesterday, and I was planning a rich hare pasty for supper, and——"

The damp woman child let out a shrill wail just then and the kitchen rumbled with my father's laughter. "Six of the clock, Orris!" he said. "The sun might mistake its rising time, but that lass never could miss the hour for her breakfast."

"Six of the clock—*six!* Why, it can't be!" My mother must have crossed the room nimbly because I heard the rushes murmur under her swirling skirts. "It can't be, but it *is!* And if Young Matt is to begin his schooling today, he must be at Dame Cotter's within the hour! Rap on the wall, Goodman! Rouse him thoroughly, and tell him to draw on the brown doublet with all the buttons and his best buckled boots!"

Blazes, she never held out for her way against his when it had to do with me or that damp woman child in the cradle!

My father said school, and so she forgot all about eeling! I sighed and reached for the buckled boots.

"Coming!" I shouted. And eased myself through the door into our other room, fastening the brown doublet as I went.

"Well, Young Matt, very, very nobly arrayed!" My father greeted me with beaming approval. "Dame Cotter will think that gentry has come knocking at her door. Stand here against my thigh, lad!"

And when I had done so, he smiled with even greater satisfaction. "Not bad! Not bad at all—for one who has only been five years in the family, and who is part Brode, at that!" he shouted. "You're climbing up my breeches, lad! Not speedily, but enough. When I think of where your poll hit last year—well, just keep it in mind that you are an Over, Young Matt! And the Overs all stand better than six feet, with their bared heels on the ground!"

I stared upward at the length of him and was discouraged. It would be easier, I felt, to keep in mind that I was part Brode. And moved over beside him to the table, where we all stood for grace, 'Memby even, bouncing in the crook of my mother's arm. I hoped that God was taking notice of my new brown doublet and my best buckled boots.

And then Beggar squeezed through the lattice and shared my barley slice with me, and some bees from Jon's hives in the orchard of the Post and Inn followed and found the mug of thickened jam, and then—and then—and then it was time to go. For the first time in my life, I had to leave this breakfast table and start forth alone upon the business of growing into manhood.

Blazes! This wasn't like going outside for a morning of

pleasure along Elderblow Lane! I choked over the last bit of crust and wondered how much 'Memby would be grown before I saw her again, how my mother would carry her soot bucket about the garden without me, what I had done with the locust in the pocket of my other breeches.

My father and mother rose from the table with me and walked along, one on either side, through the fragrant, dewy garden of simples. When we were come to the clump of silvery artemisia by the lane, they stopped and my father reached forth his hand, clasping mine as man to man. And suddenly the feeling of banishment left me and I was proud to be started on the business of becoming an Over like himself. I felt pity for my mother and the damp woman child left behind beside the hearth, and when she plucked a sprig of borage for my pocket I would have none of it. I needed no simple to give me courage on the day that I came five years of age.

Dame Cotter's Free School stood at the edge of Scrooby Common, close to the stocks, the pinfold, St. Wilfred's Church, and the Great North Road.

Looking ahead down Elderblow Lane, I could see Giles Kerry, Olin Hughes, and Joseph Roberts stop beside the little gray church and stick their heads inside a partly opened door. Doubtless, Giles made his frogface and the others yowled like tortured cats, for soon the three stumbled backward on their heels and an angry sexton brandished a frowzy besom about their ears. They waved their arms, shouting derisively; and after the door was closed upon their nonsense, they shoved one another around the common, tripping what hurrying lads came their way.

And so, although he was started on his way so much

earlier than myself, it happened that Giles entered the Free School no better than just ahead of me. "Hi, Titmouse!" he snickered, turning to waggle his ears in a frightening grimace. "Still looking for that rider who came thus far and no farther, last night? Maybe he's hid in Dame Cotter's cheese box."

And then he leaped forward through the door with a yell as Dill Cotter's limber rod caught his heels, leaving me quite in the open in the narrow, shadowy passageway.

"You're late!" said Dill, swishing his birch with the utmost satisfaction. And then, seeing me, "You're later!"

Yesterday I had seen a rod lifted against me for the first time in my life; today, I was looking at another. I liked one as little as the other.

Not that I feared the hurt, nor that I felt like cringing and whimpering, but I was Young Matt Over, son of a freeman, and I had been reared to know right from wrong in other ways than through fear of a rod. Dill Cotter should never see tears in *my* eyes, I promised myself, nor gloat over my yelps and capers. I passed him with head high and scorn blazing from the north, south, east, and west of me. And so I missed all except the agonized howl.

It was Dill who howled! I stopped and couldn't believe my own ears and eyes. But certainly the shrieks were coming from Dill Cotter down there on the floor among the boiling rushes! Through a side door, Dame Cotter appeared and gazed upon the rushes with an equal astonishment. She had been breakfasting, to judge from the specks of egg that still clung to the hairs of her upper lip; her frilled cap was untied, and her little eyes glittered meanly.

"Dill!" she squeaked. "Dill Cotter! Come up to light and stop that clamor! Who's that you are fighting—*eeeek!*"

Whoever it was down there in the rushes with Dill succeeded in catching hold of his rod just then, and cut loose with it. I knew what must have happened when I saw Dame Cotter hop about the passageway on one foot.

And then the knot on the floor uncoiled and a small maid stood up out of the dust, with one last sharp kick for the still prostrate bully. She shook her skirts and looked about, pleased. She had been wearing one of Dame Cotter's frilled coifs, but that was gone now, clenched in Dill's mean fingers, and the dimness was lit by the brightness of her tousled head. Her hair was not like the Kerrys', pink. It was a fiery, lively, burning red. I had never seen anything like it. It was too bright to be entirely godly, I felt.

"So-o, 'tis *you,* eh, Winnifret?" Dame Cotter squalled fiercely. "I might have known! Nothing but uproar and trouble can ever be expected from a witch's brat like——"

"That'll do, Dame!" piped the maid, entirely unruffled and firm. She shook her skirts once more and reached out with another sharp kick when Dill's lank shin showed signs of moving. "We'll hear no more of that, if you please!" she warned. "Unless you wish the folk of this village to learn that it is not *I* who am kin to a witch!"

"Hush, brat!"

The maid nodded. "That's better!" she agreed. "Stand off—I'm going to snap this rod!"

"Not in my house."

"Well, outside, then!" She stepped unhindered to the open door and cast the splints over the sill. "I'll not have Dill Cotter lie in wait in the darkness and spring forth to lash at children who come to this place. Little ones, too!" she eyed me with a pity that was not entirely pleasing. "Do you know what I have been told little children were, Dame Cotter?"

"Pests!"

"No. They be souls lifted like cups to be filled with fair learning."

"Odds blood!" Dame Cotter wiped her chin, but it continued to tremble.

"It is a cruel shame," the maid added, looking about the passageway, "that the pitcher of this place is so empty. There is naught to pour into the cups here, you see! There must be fair learning in the teacher before it can be shared with a pupil; and though I have been here but a short time, still is it long enough to understand that the pitcher is dry."

"Thou—thou—thou witch's——"

The maid lifted her foot and stamped once. And Dill's yell silenced all other sounds. "She mashed my finger, now!" he bawled. "Before, she sank her viper's fangs into my wrist."

"How far in?" asked the maid. And sniffed when she saw the mark. "Only *that* far—dear, dear! But you've got to remember I've a loose tooth that must be spared. Only for that I could have gone to the bone——"

"Ow-w-ooooooo!" cried Dill.

"—and likely have crushed it!" concluded the maid with pride. "I have gnawed bones before this."

Dame Cotter sprang forward then with a cry of fury. Even I, who was very nearly ignorant in such matters, realized that, having been forced to contain her rage for a time, this mean old woman would be all the more terrible once she began to let herself go.

"Fetch me another birch, Dill!" she snarled. "From behind the stairs. This brat doesn't know that our supply of rods is ample. Haul the lad aside."

She meant me. I was not to be beaten. I was to make room for the cutting lash that would fall upon a maid hardly taller than myself and half as thick, a maid with hair like a blazing pile of fagots, a maid who had fought for me.

Before Dill could find his feet I dropped broadly and heavily upon his head, whacking it back into the rushes, and sat there, spread out as wide as could be managed, looking up into the ugly face that trembled now shockingly. I was thankful that we Brodes were broad and heavy. My only worry was for the seat of my best brown breeches.

"You shall not beat this maid!" I told Dame Cotter calmly. "Nor shall Dill—ever!" I added, with a slight jounce. "I, Young Matt, son of Matthew Over, yeoman, say that you are to have a care about beating this maid!" To this day I do not know where I found such a curious array of words. "*I* will not allow you to do it! Nor will my father! Nor will my Uncle John, son of John Brode, freeman, of Austerfield! Nor will my Uncle Samuel, who sails with Sir Raleigh! Neither the Overs of Scrooby nor the Brodes of Austerfield will allow a maid who has no more meat on her bones than the tongs in our fireplace to be beaten! Dare to lift that rod, and for each blow an eel shall wriggle coldly down the bosom inside that blouse!"

The maid Winnifret jerked me to my feet and dusted my doublet with the coif she took from Dill's lax fingers. "Say no more, little boy!" she warned. "Between us, we have given this family much to think upon! Did you come here to school, this morning?"

"Aye. It is my first day."

"I thought I didn't see you yesterday."

"I went eeling in Scrooby Waters yesterday."

"Yes-s? Well, come on in and I'll show you where you are to sit."

We entered an inner room, where the children who had arrived earlier were huddled about the door watching, horrified, the excitement of the passageway. They made way for us without comment, and Winnifret seated me in the choicest place beside the latticed window. I could see a slice of Scrooby Common, the stocks, the shadow of St. Wilfred's Church, and a bit of the Great North Road. She found herself a stool and drew it close to my back.

When Dame Cotter and her bulging basket of mending appeared in the room, the older children reached hastily for their hornbooks and the place droned like Jon's beehives beside the first fish pool. A-b ab, e-b eb, ib, ba, beb, bi, and bob, over and over again.

It made me sleepy. I thought of the lovely morning mist over Scrooby Waters, the call of cuckoo to cuckoo across wet meadows, my mother on her knees among the sullendines and felt-wyrts in her garden of simples, and I wondered, drowsily, why I was here in this strange room. To learn to write my name in full and read a psalm with my betters, of course. But how did one learn to write and to read? There was a cold breath down my back, and Winnifret, leaning too close, whispered: "There aren't enough hornbooks for all, little boy! Later, we shall have our turn at them—I'll see to that, don't worry!"

I didn't doubt her word. "I could run this school better than that old woman!" she continued under her breath. "You see, *I've* had some schooling—and she hasn't!"

"Here?"

"Lud, no! I've only been in this place a day!"

"You aren't old enough to keep a school!" I told her.

But when she asked me how old I was and after I told her that I had come five years of age that very morning, she snickered into her apron corner and my ears reddened.

"Five?" she said. "My goodness! *I'm* going on eight!"

Blazes! Almost the better of me by three years—almost as grown up as my Uncle John! Old enough for anything! I wished that she would change stools with Giles Kerry, but she didn't.

"Who's the man in the stocks?" she asked after a time, her chin on the sill and her eyes flitting about Scrooby Common.

"Goodman Colson—from Londontown."

"Glory, *Londontown! I* was in Londontown two days ago!"

Before I was done with this thought, her curiosity was afire once more. "What evil did he do?" she whispered eagerly.

"He did no evil."

"But he *must* have, little boy! Else why is he fastened in the stocks where everybody can pelt him with stones and rubbish?"

"Nobody will pelt Goodman Colson!" I assured her. "He is a Puritan. Like Scrooby folk. The King put him there to scare us. He thinks we'll see what will happen to all of us if we don't stop thinking inde—independently, that's what my mother says! Some things the King tells us to do, we *don't,* you see—church things. Like going to St. Wilfred's instead of praying in our own way with Goodman Brewster in the Manor House. You don't call that being evil, do you?"

"No."

"Well, then! We don't pelt Goodman Colson. We don't worry about the stocks, either!"

"Only a Puritan, eh? I thought he might be a witch!"

A witch! I turned and stared full into the sharp little face. "There aren't any witches!" I told her firmly. "My father says so."

"Maybe not here in Scrooby, but there are plenty in Londontown, little boy!"

I looked at her again. She wasn't jesting. "How do you know, Win—er—er—Fox-tail?" I asked.

"Fox-tail!" The maid snapped her chin from the sill and for a moment I thought she was gone. But she had only drawn back to think. "Is that a good name hereabouts?" she asked.

"For you, it is!"

"Better than Winnifret?"

"Easier to think of. A fox's tail is comely—and red, you know."

"I never saw one. But if you like it, call me Fox-tail. Only nobody else shall, if I have to bite out all my teeth to keep them from it! And when I tell you that there are plenty of witches in Londontown, well, you wouldn't doubt the King's word, would you?"

"Yes! What did he say?"

"He said that once he was on a ship sailing far into the north and two hundred witches set upon him and tried to drown him and——"

"Pfft! *Two hundred*—and they didn't do it!"

"Well, something happened! Anyway, they have their way with illnesses in Londontown! God's mercy, the fevers and plagues that those witches do cause!"

"They don't!"

"Oh, yes, they *do,* little boy! My mother died of the plague they brewed—and my father—and all my kin! And I myself was sickened unto death of it. While I was pepper-hot with the fever and out of my wits, I wandered from the dwelling where my folk lay dead and roamed the highways, not knowing where I went nor what I did."

"For—for long?"

"For long enough, let me tell you! Until I was exhausted and could go no further. Then I dropped to a doorstep, so they told me afterwards, and was hauled inside by a dirty, frowzy old dame. She let me bide in a corner on a pallet until the fever was spent. Then I found out she was a witch."

I tumbled from the stool and should have occupied Dame Cotter's attention by such unseemly conduct, only it was plain to be seen that Dame Cotter meant to ignore me for a time until she could concoct a safe and fitting discipline. She never lifted her head from her mending and I was abandoned to the mercies of the fiery-headed maid, who dusted off my breeches like a mother.

"Let be!" I snapped. And then, "Are they harmed in the rear? These be my best brown garments. Let be, though! I can see for myself!"

"Why shouldn't I clean you from the rushes?"

"You! You who have dwelt with a witch!"

"I had to have a crust now and then, didn't I?"

"Now I know who you are!" I told her, shocked as the truth broke over my own consciousness. "You are the maid who came down from Londontown with the courier, night before last, clutched to his mail pouch like a cocklebur!"

"So would you—if you had bounced the way I did!"

"And you wouldn't let Goodman Brewster care for you."

"Who is he?"

"And Jon said you were kin to a witch."

"He lies. She was no kin of mine. I but fell at her door when fevered."

"How do you know she is a witch, Fox-tail?"

"*Was*—not is! She isn't living any more. And as for being a witch, she said so herself—she boasted of it!"

Dame Cotter laid aside her mending just then and the wild mob in the inner room rose to jam the doorway. "Nine of the clock!" announced the maid at my back. "Recess for fifteen minutes. Come outside and sit by the church with me!"

"Weren't you frighted of her?" I asked, when we were seated, our heels in the sod and our backs to the ivy.

"No! Never! Not even when she tried to make me shudder! She said that she could turn herself into a rat without a tail and *would,* if I did aught to displease her!"

"Blazes! Did she?"

"You don't think I waited around to see, do you? She was gone most of the time, anyway! Off to the Playhouse."

"Playhouse! Oh, Fox-tail!"

"What's wrong with that?"

"A place of sin, so Goodwife Fentry says."

"Is it? Well, my old dame sold oranges there. She said that is how she earned our crusts, but I think she would have gone there, anyway. To listen to the actors. Especially when they were playacting the writings of one William Shakespeare. Him she liked best of all. She knew much of his poetry by heart and used to tell it to me—as good as any actor in the Playhouse."

I must have shuddered, for the maid ceased speaking to eye me curiously. And then she said: "What's the matter, little boy? Do you know Will Shakespeare?"

"Did he write about a garden choked with weeds?" I asked.

"Why, you *do* know him!"

"And about wholesome weeds dripping with caterpillars?"

"And about a witch who boasted that she could lurk in a dame's bowl in the form of a roasted apple, and when the dame drank, then she'd bob against her lips, you see? How do you know Will Shakespeare, 'way down here in Scrooby?"

"I don't. I know his friend!" I replied. And sighed at the memory of a golden stranger in my mother's garden. "I don't like either of them!"

"Well, Dame Dill did!"

"Dill!"

"Of course, Dill! She was sister to this old Dame Cotter, it seems. I didn't know it until she was dead."

"Who is dead—the witch?"

"Of course! Witches die too, you know, just like other people. Sooner, when the King's Men get after 'em! Something had to be done about it when so many people sickened of the fever and plague, and when it began to be told about that the witches were at the bottom of all that trouble, why, the witches had to die, don't you see? Some King's Men came last week and led old Dame Dill away to be tried for the sin of causing a plague. She died. And then the King's Men found *me* in a corner of the room."

"And they led you away to——"

"Don't be silly! They had to do something about me, so I wouldn't starve."

"Why didn't you?"

"Oh, there's ways to eat if you watch the cats and do as they do. All I wanted was to be let alone—for the King's Men to keep away. Only they wouldn't. They came back."

"Again?"

"And again! They tried to find some of my kin, only there were none left. So they pretended, as soon as they learned of this sister of the witch's, that I belonged to Dame Dill and this Dame Cotter was my kin. And they said she must care for me."

"And they sent you with the courier."

"Yes. Lucky thing they happened on one who was just starting for Scrooby with messages for the Post and Inn. He said to toss me up behind his mail pouch, and I can tell you we stopped for nothing!"

"Jon said your courier got here just in time."

"A funny thing, sending word of ships to Scrooby!"

"Ships!" I stared at her, open-mouthed. "What do you mean, ships?"

"Why, I only heard a word or two while the courier was at the Post, before he took me on to Dame Cotter's, you see. But I did hear him tell the man there at the Post and Inn——"

"Goodman Brewster."

"It might be. The courier told him that the ship awaited according to plan. And that it was close to Hull. And that he was to meet somebody in a secret place in the marshland at once—and to watch out for himself since the hue and cry was on again—and—and I don't remember what else."

Dill Cotter came out of the Free School just then, swinging a great bell. "Three minutes more of recess!" Winnifret told me, watching him.

But my thoughts were not for Dill Cotter. "You, Foxtail," I said, "where did you say that ship waited?"

"Off the Boston strand. What is it to you?"

"My Uncle Samuel comes in ships, from far places. And when he comes, he brings me gifts."

"He does? What?"

"Well, once he brought me a box of sweet spice buds from the Islands of Spice in the Seven Seas. And once he brougnt a crystal from the Mountain of the Winds in Arran, where the crystals stud the mountainside like plums in a Christmas pudding. And once he brought a herring, dried and salted as only the folk of those parts know how to season herring."

"Glory! I hope he brings you another herring! Is that all?"

"And once he brought me a bowl with a hollow stem to it, and some dried herbs. These he brought from the colony of the Virgin Queen in the New World, where men are red. He put the herbs in the bowl, as do they, and the stem in his mouth and kindled the herbs—and smoke came out of his nostrils!"

"God's mercy! Was he afire inside?"

"No-o."

"Well, I'd rather have the herring!"

Dill Cotter appeared with the swinging bell again and this time I marched inside well ahead of the others and, finding my stool beside the latticed window, accepted a hornbook from the fiery-headed maid.

"This is what you study," she explained. "But only the a-b abs at the top!"

"Why not what's below? I know the a-b abs."

"That below is the Prayer of Our Lord. It is not for sinners like you and me. We fought Dill, you know!"

"But I know the Prayer of Our Lord already."

"So do I. But it's just as well not to tell Dame Cotter everything."

Dame Cotter, it seemed, had just come to a conclusion on

the matter of my discipline. She was across the rushes and beside me before I knew it. "Among the sins of childhood hardly one can be counted greater than idleness!" she squeaked. "Goodman Brewster has said the same thing, Young Matt Over! And so punishment is deserved. Your mind has been everywhere but on learning this morning!"

She reached forward and cracked my skull with her metal-thimble-tipped finger until it rang like a hollow nut, and I saw stars in the full daylight.

I saw something else, too. I saw a maid like a straight, thin rush-torch well flaming at the top end step forth from a huddle of children to face a horrible old woman.

"I told you," piped the maid, "that you were never to hurt the children again while I was here—the *little* children—especially this little boy! You knew that it was a bargain between us—if you stopped hurting the children, I would hold back that which you feared to have known in this village. But you broke your bargain. And so I tell boldly where all may hear and carry the word to their homes at this noon hour, that you are——"

"No such thing! It's a lie—a lie!" screamed Dame Cotter. But she couldn't lay hand on Fox-tail. The maid was too quick.

"It's the truth! Everyone in Scrooby shall know within the hour that you are kin to a witch!"

The children surged from their stools with popping eyes and made for the door, stopping there, however, to hear what more the maid might be saying.

"You are kin to a witch by the name of Dame Dill, who was hanged for her sins by the King's Men in Londontown no more than a week ago!"

"It's a lie—a terrible lie!"

"It's the truth. I know because—because I lived with the witch!"

"Ha-ha-ha!" Dame Cotter's cackling laughter was more frightening than words. "So you were forced to confess, eh? *Now* let it be judged who had traffic with evil spirits—*I,* who know naught of any Dame Dill, or *you,* who dwelt with her! What kind of brat are you to come, unasked for and unwanted, beneath my roof and tell me what I shall do in my school and what I shall not do! When was there any mention of bargains?"

"Not in so many words, but we understood each other, you and I!" The maid was as calm and undaunted as ever. "And none knows better than you, who were her sister, that I am no kin to the witch who was Dame Dill! Still—still—" The maid's eyes left Dame Cotter's face for the flick of a breath and switched to the latticed window, where, as usual, bees were curiously pushing their way in and out. One, bolder than the rest, was about to leave the sill and set forth on a winged flight about the room. Dame Cotter noted the bee and fluttered her apron, nervously.

"Still," the fiery-headed maid continued, "a body can't be expected to dwell with a witch without learning *something*! And if I am to be kept in this place by order of the King's Men, you may as well know now that it will be better to look twice before you leap once in my path, hereafter."

And then, deliberately turning her back on Dame Cotter, she grinned at me impishly and pointed a spike of a finger at the blundering bee.

> "Come, *come!* I call thee, plaguing bee!
> Come pester this old dame for me!"

she ordered shrilly.

4

THE SHIP OFF BOSTON STRAND

LATER, much later, I discovered that nobody in that Free School was more shocked or disturbed over what followed than was Winnifret herself.

"I saw she was cowardly," the maid explained to my father, "and I wanted to keep her at a distance from me, through fear of me, if need be. And I saw the smear of honey on her lip where she had been feasting during recess time! But I didn't expect the bee would see it so soon!"

The bee, however, zoomed down a streak of sunlight into Dame Cotter's horrified face; and when she let out a blood-curdling shriek and beat at it with one of Dill's torn doublets that she had been mending, the beastie buzzed to her flapping cap frill, crawled inside, found an ugly yellow ear in the way, and stung it thoroughly. I doubt if one of us could have told of a door that opened and shut behind Dame Cotter. She was simply before us one instant—and the next she was gone!

"Odds blood, she *is* a witch!" howled Giles Kerry, leading the way down the passage to Scrooby Common. "Did you see her vanish?"

"Right through the roof!" howled Joseph Roberts. "I saw her! Saw smoke all around her, too!"

"Come, little boy!" said Winnifret, reaching for my hand. I followed her outside, dazed with all that I had seen and heard. "There'll be no more school this day! Where do you live?"

I pointed toward Elderblow Lane and we entered the lovely tunnel of shadow and fragrance without another word. Nor had much more to say, one to another, until we stood outside the Over hedge, beside the clump of silvery artemisia. It was an exciting smell inside that set us to chatting.

"It smells savory in there!" said Winnifret. And stood closer to the artemisia.

I nodded. "Gooseberries!"

"What about them?"

"They're stewing into jam, silly! Don't you know gooseberry jam when you smell it?"

She shook her head.

"Well, *I* do!" I cried. And pranced joyfully on the pansy-studded turf. "Everybody will be making jam now, but my mother is always first! There'll be a crust of fresh bread with a smear of hot jam for my supper and—and—and, blazes, she's making a hare pasty, too! That's because this is my birthday!"

"Do you live here, little boy?" the maid asked. When I assured her that I did, she said: "It's nice!" And followed me down the path between the beds of fennel, sage, and hyssop.

My mother was at the fireplace stirring something in a black pot, but she whacked the rim with her ladle as soon as my step sounded outside and sang:

"Oh, Master Hugo Chillingsworth,
I like this season lots,
When every stool and bench is filled
With jam in little pots!"

But my father, who was seated at the only bare spot of the

kitchen table, put down the knife with which he was spreading a barley loaf and looked out our door without a word.

"You'll have to fetch a trencher and carry your bread and cheese to the top step, Young Matt!" warned my mother, still with her head bent to the boiling pot. "I can't leave the jam at this point, and there's only room inside for your father! I missed your nimble fingers with the picking this morning, lad. I never saw finer berries!"

"Giles Kerry says there are no ripened berries on his bushes."

"I believe him. And I can guess at the reason for it, too! It's a trial for Giles to wait for jam to get at the enjoyment of his fruit. Take care that the hot juice makes no stain on your best brown doublet, lad!"

She turned with a scoop of the hot sweet for my bread. But, turning, she saw me and stood still, ankle-deep in the rushes, and said no more than "God's mercy!"

And then, "Goodman Matthew, be that a cloud of steam that troubles my eyesight, or—or——"

My father beckoned gently with his mighty hand and said: "Thou art welcome, wee lass! Come into the home and speak your name."

The fiery-headed one put her claw of a hand on his knee, confidently. "My name is Winnifret," she said. "But this little boy calls me Fox-tail. I don't mind what—what—what friends call me."

"Nor should you, since they speak only in love. Thou art a stranger in Scrooby, Win?"

"Since yesterday, Goodman. I was brought from London-town by the courier."

"When the witch died!" I cried. Who should have held my tongue.

"When the—oh, Matthew!" cried my mother. And pushed her coif awry, as was her custom when frighted.

"Easy, lass!" my father comforted. And then, "Have a care to thy words, Young Matt! There be no witches!"

Winnifret came to my rescue. "Oh, Dame Dill was a witch, all right!" she told him firmly. "The King's Men said so and they led her away to die for her sin in causing the great plague that has made so many to sicken and die in Londontown. I myself was fevered and fell on her doorstep."

"And the witch let her stay!" I shouted, disliking the thought but eager to share it with my family. "She sold oranges in the Playhouse and was acquainted with the actors."

"God help us, Matthew!" cried my mother.

"And she knew that playwriter William Shakespeare—the friend to that golden King's Man, Mother, don't you remember?" I added, heaping crime on crime. "All about the garden choked with weeds, and the herbs that dripped caterpillars!"

"He wrote nice things, too!" Fox-tail interrupted, most unexpectedly. "About daffodils that come before the swallow dares." Blazes, I didn't know about this! "And about banks where the wild thyme blows. Only Dame Dill didn't care so much for Will Shakespeare when he got among the gardens!"

"Goodman, what have we done to our lad, sending him forth in search of learning?" asked my mother weakly. And sank upon a stool with the jam trickling about the rushes.

"Well, he has found it—after a fashion!" my father told her, chuckling comfortingly. "And this Will Shakespeare—I have heard of him from William Bradford and Goodman Brewster. His father is a respectable yeoman of Stratford, a wool dealer. Something of good must be in the son of such a worthy man—it is not for us to judge, Goodwife. Only something else has come up here today that we *may* judge, we of Scrooby who know the truth of the matter!"

He stretched out his free hand and drew me against his knee; and so we stood, Fox-tail on one side and I on the other, each held firmly by the fist. "This I solemnly swear to the two of you, having had the truth from Goodman Brewster, who had it from the Word of God Himself—there be no poor, evil spirits in this world, such as are commonly called 'witches'!"

"But—but in Londontown—" faltered the maid.

"I know. In Londontown poor folk are dying, falsely accused of this terrible thing. In Londontown there be plenty of sin, of one kind and another. That we cannot help. We of Scrooby can only try to understand God's love and keep our own hands and souls and minds clean. This witch-hunting is a madness that pleases the cruel hearts of some in high places; we will have none of it in Scrooby. Especially will we have none of it in the household of Matthew Over, yeoman! Is that understood?"

I nodded. And repeated after him: "There are no witches!" And so, to my utter astonishment, did Winnifret, adding: "I only repeated what I had been told. I never did believe that Dame Dill was a witch—she couldn't ride a besom more than another! It was her jest, to keep folks in fear of her. I promise, Goodman, to carry the report no further!"

"I accept thy word, lass!" replied my father.

"You—you might call me Fox-tail."

"You honor me greatly, small one!" my father told her gently. "But we might find even a better name, in time. Just now"—he turned and faced my mother with a smile—"it would seem to me that a spot *might* be cleared at this end of the table where the lass, Young Matt, and I might break bread together in friendship."

My mother gazed across the maid's blazing head in silence. But then she stood and fetched a stool and, placing it between my father and myself, motioned Winnifret to be seated. For the first time since I had set eyes upon her in the passageway of the Free School, the maid showed diffidence. She drew away from the table and would have fled into the garden but for the firm hold upon her wrist as my father urged her nearer the board.

"I—I wouldn't take the little boy's rightful food!" she stammered.

"God's love!" cried my mother, her pretty head reared in pride. "You take nobody's food but what is to spare, my lass! The Overs' larder is filled and running out at the cracks! Eat, and put some covering on those bones!"

"I—I eat very little, Goodwife! Only that which might not be wanted."

"I believe you. There's naught before you that is wanted, then! And if Young Matt lifts a fat fist to more than his share I'll fetch him a crack on the knuckles! Take barley bread, my dear, and a bit of the pickled eel. Here's cheese—and fresh jam—a crisp radish from my own garden outside."

The damp woman child wailed just then, and Winnifret leaped from her stool to meet the sound. "Oh-h!" she said. And looked about, bewildered. "Was that a baby? I didn't know you had a baby, little boy!"

"It's a new one," I told her. " 'Memby. She's in the cradle by the hearth."

Fox-tail crossed the rushes and bent above the damp

woman child, her blazing strand swinging free of the confining bands of Dame Dill's enormous coif. "We had babies in Londontown," she explained eagerly, "and you wouldn't believe the wetness of them! I know just how to stretch a baby along the settle, Goodwife, and make it sweet and dry. Babies love me—you'll see that this wee lad——"

"Our baby is a lass!" I interrupted indignantly. "Her name is 'Memby!"

"What difference, lad or lass? They get wet the same, don't they?"

I felt suddenly that in some mysterious way her interest in me was fading, was being transferred to the woman child in the cradle, and I drew back to my bread and jam, abashed.

"Such a sweet lass!" she said, bending once more above the cradle. Her colorful strand swung enticingly within reach. 'Memby grabbed at it, caught it, and her lips parted in bubbly, gurgling laughter.

"Oh, she laughed!" cried my mother, crossing the room with a swirl of her skirts. "Her first laugh is for thee, Winnifret!"

"Crooked, too!" I discovered. "Like all the Brodes of Austerfield!"

"Hurray!" shouted my father. "Don't forget the Overs of Scrooby, my lad!"

"Let go the lovely hair, 'Memby!" urged my mother then.

But 'Memby wouldn't.

"Make her let go!" I insisted. "Fox-tail's got to go back to Dame Cotter's!"

Without moving, the maid looked at me curiously then, her eyes upside down. "I shall never go back to Dame Cotter's!" she said.

"Well, to Londontown, then!"

"Neither to Londontown."

Blazes, here was a rare tangle! "Where *will* you go, then?" I probed.

My father brushed me aside and once again he reached out for the maid and drew her close to his knee. "You had a true home once, lass," he said gently. "Where is it?"

"The—the King's Men ordered it burned—when the plague came. I—I don't even know where it stood, now."

"I see. And what was your father called?"

The maid trembled like a reed in the wind. It was not easy for her to speak of her kin, but she slipped her little claw inside his mighty fist and took courage. "My father was Hugh," she said, "and my mother was Alicia. They died in one night. We dwelt in a fair place, with lilacs in tubs in my mother's room, and roses in glass stems everywhere. Each morning there were fresh roses—and always a little red bud for me!"

"God's mercy!" cried my mother. And hid her face among 'Memby's covers.

"Gentry!" I yelled. And laid my bread and cheese aside to await a less impressive moment. "I'll wager your father could sign his name in full and read a psalm with his betters!"

"Read? He *wrote* that others might read!" She tossed her blazing strand proudly. "And after he had written, he made paintings on the parchment with red and blue and green and gold colorings. And he taught me more and more each day. Not a-b abs, but to read and write and why little children come wandering into this world to bide with grown-up folk. But—but he never said what children should do when —when the King's Men burned their home."

"Some things take a deal of time to the telling, dear lass!"

said my mother then, briskly coming up out of the woman child's cradle. "And the great sickness got to him first! But he was a wise man, don't forget! He would have told you that when evil destroys your home, God will lead you to another! And today, I venture to believe, Hugh and Alicia walked, one on either side of God our Father while He led you up Elderblow Lane to the cottage of Matthew Over, yeoman. 'Tis a happy home, my dear!"

My father bent to look keenly into the thin little face at his knee. "Does it seem a pleasant home to you, lass?" he asked.

"Oh—oh—*yes!*" She trembled again, like the reed in the bog. But suddenly her sharp eyes fell upon me and she stiffened. "Look to that jam, little boy!" she warned. " 'Tis trickling on your best brown doublet!"

"Would you be content to call the Over home *your* home, too?" my father asked then. "To be a sister to Young Matt and the wee 'Memby? To be kin to our kin? To be 'Winnifret Over'?"

"Oh—oh—Goodman Over—" Fox-tail could say no more. But it was enough. Already her eyes glowed with pride in the home that had become her own.

"Then the matter is settled for all time!" announced my father. "I shall have word with Goodman Brewster and Dame Cotter this afternoon, and Goodwife Orris will see if she can't find a more sizable coif in her chest for a comely daughter almost as large as herself already! God love us!" he roared with laughter. "There'll be many a goggling eye in Scrooby when it is learned that the Over family has been enriched by another sweet maid within the hour!"

"Come!" said my mother briskly, throwing no more than a merry grin in our direction. She flicked the great, ugly, frilled thing off Fox-tail's fiery head and tossed it among the embers in the fireplace. "The gown will follow," she promised, "as soon as we are alone and can have a basin and bucket in the scullery for a good clean-up. There's a dove-gray frock at the bottom of the chest wrapped in lavender buds that will need but a tuck here and a pleat there to fit as if it were known that a lass of your size was soon expected. And a linen apron with lace edging. And here"—she threw back the lid to her precious chest and lifted forth a small, snowy, stiffened coif of her own. She tied it beneath Winnifret's chin, and the difference it made could not be expressed in words.

"Odds blood, a beauty!" howled my father. "A true Over!"

"My own dear lass!" said my mother proudly. And then:

> "Oh, Master Hugo Chillingsworth,
> There's nothing quite so fair
> As folded buds, and lily bells,
> And maids with blazing hair!"

But I cocked my ear and whispered: "Traffic, Father! On the Great North Road. Coming this way!"

"From Londontown-way?" gasped my mother. "Oh, Young Matt—that golden one! *So* soon?"

"Not from Londontown!" I told her, standing to catch the confusion of distant voices. "Some are coming from Ryton Ford, from Bawtry or Austerfield."

"Thank God!" She patted the maid's shoulder and shoved her toward the cupboard. "Fetch another trencher, dear love!" she begged, moving about the table busily. "Young Matt's (and *yours,* now!) Uncle John is on the way from Austerfield to make merry on the lad's birthday. Like as not

William Bradford is with him. And there's a hare pasty in the oven."

"Only *two* lads outside there!" puzzled my father. "And a clamor fit for a herd!"

I threw wide the kitchen door.

And there, crossing my mother's garden of simples, was my Uncle Samuel Brode!

With him were the Fentrys, Goodman and Goodwife Kerry, my Uncle John, William Bradford, James Billing, who kept the odds-and-ends shop beside Scrooby Common, and many another. Many another! The garden swarmed with Scrooby folk. Giles Kerry was in and out, everywhere at once.

"Here he is, Young Matt!" Giles shouted, reaching the door before anyone else. "Here's your wonderful Uncle Samuel! 'Wherever there is great need, there is my Uncle Samuel!' you told me yesterday. Now then, where's the need?"

"Samuel!" My mother stood beside the table and grew pale as though she had heard the King's Voice on the Great North Road. "Oh, no! You must be mistaken, Giles! Samuel Brode is far away at sea with Sir Walter Raleigh!"

"Samuel Brode is coming in at the door for a sight of the sweet face of his sister!" a great voice boomed from the sill.

"God's mercy, my jam pots!" cried my mother, seeing what was to follow. "Quick, Winnifret! Into the scullery with them! And help me push 'Memby's cradle to a more sheltered corner!"

"One is coming in at the scullery door—from across the lane!" Fox-tail warned shrilly.

"It's Goodman Brewster! Make him welcome beside the hearth—the room is full to bursting!"

She sank to a low bench beside the cradle and drew Fox-tail and me close, one on either side. Giles watched with popping eyes. "What's Dame Cotter's maid doing here?" he wanted to know.

"She isn't Dame Cotter's maid—she belongs to us!" I told him indignantly.

"Isn't she the one who was said to be kin to a—" began Jon Brewster. But never finished.

"This be my sweet elder daughter!" announced my mother with dignity. "If she be kin to anybody, let us say that she is from now on kin to the Brodes of Austerfield!"

"Well, scrape my barnacles!" boomed my Uncle Samuel in the voice that roared with all the hurricanes of the Seven Seas, as he maintained. "How your family does grow, Orris! What might your name be, my fiery-headed lass?"

"Winnifret."

"Winnifret *Over!*" added my father, proudly.

"Go on, Samuel!" squeaked James Billing suddenly. "Tell Matthew Over what has brought you to Scrooby this time! Let's hear the rest of the tale you were unwinding as we came from the Great North Road!"

"Trouble, Orris!" said Goodwife Fentry in a loud aside. "The sour Stuart is curdling milk again with thoughts of Scrooby!"

"Dear God, if we were only beyond his reach!"

"Well, we aren't—nor like to be! I was with those who tried to flee last year, remember! No more of that for *me,* I can tell you! There we were, stranded in Boston, our men held as criminals in the guild hall and we women left to find our way back to Scrooby the best way we could. They stoned us as we passed through some villages, and there was a she-hawk in Bawtry who emptied a pail over my head while I was resting under a tree. I'd give a good deal for the chance of cracking the beak of that one before——"

"Hush!" whispered my mother. "Worse trials may be before us."

"—and so," My Uncle Samuel's voice lifted above the hubbub, "and so, when I heard the rumors that were flying about thick as gulls before a storm, I knew that the hour had struck at last. I disembarked at Londontown, hired a ship to await further orders off Boston strand, and sent for William Brewster to meet me."

"That was *my* courier!" said Winnifret to me across my mother's apron.

I nodded, but kept silence, for Goodwife Fentry was speaking. "*What* rumors, Samuel?" she asked. "Wherein have we of Scrooby sinned this time?"

"You have been ordered to attend worship at St. Wilfred's Church."

She agreed, with a loud sniff.

"And you chose to ignore the command of the King and to meet with William at the Post and Inn on the Sabbath Day."

"Where one or two are gathered together in His Name, there is a church!"

"Men are dying for talk like that, Goodwife!" my Uncle Samuel warned her quietly. "If the law says worship at St. Wilfred's and you obey it not, then are you lawbreakers in the eyes of the King and worthy of extreme punishment. That, in fact, *is* the new law: death for those who fail to attend St. Wilfred's in Scrooby!"

"Well, I never heard the like!" howled Goodwife Kerry, exasperated beyond endurance. "Has it come to where the Stuart must feed us religion by hand, like snail-oil? Can't we choose our own doses of God?"

"We can't choose anything any more, it seems!" shouted

Goodman Hughes, angrily. "Whether to go or whether to stay."

"The Stuart says that we stay!" interrupted Goodman Fentry.

"I know. And then he proceeds to lay out the week for us. We must do so and so on the Sabbath Day. We must do thus and so with our own farms on Monday, Tuesday, Wednesday——"

"What do you mean by that, Oliver?" asked my father quietly.

"Haven't you heard? We of Scrooby are to till no more than a quarter of our land from now on, because the moors, forests, fens, and warrens must spread to provide the gentry with fine eating!"

"Even though we starve for it!" howled Goodman Roberts. "Look at the land they steal from us so that their sheep may graze undisturbed."

"Laws, laws, laws!" shrilled Goodwife Fentry above the din. "Soon the Stuart will be saying: 'Cabbage on Tuesdays, or a shilling to pay! Skirrets on Wednesday, or the stocks! Cheese on Friday, or death!' A pretty pass the Scrooby freemen have come to!"

"Strange that it should be that way!" Goodman Brewster agreed, speaking for the first time. "Since England herself knows what it is to desire freedom of worship. Bare twenty years ago, horses were plunging inland from the coast by here in a continuous stream, bringing news of the great conflict that was to decide whether England should be free or bow beneath another's yoke, worship in another faith."

"I remember those days!" sighed Goodman Fentry. "I was young then like you, William, no more than one and twenty. You hadn't settled down then at the Post and Inn."

"No. But I was back and forth a good deal. I can close my eyes now and see the signal fires flashing, warning that the powerful Armada of Spain was sighted in English waters. England knew, then, that she loved freedom better than life. She fought and conquered the invading foe, hounding their ships the full length of the Channel to the sea! She won, then, the right to worship God in her own fashion—a right that, seemingly, is to be denied us of Scrooby today."

"Is freedom of worship to be found anywhere, sir?" asked William Bradford of Austerfield.

I was in awe of William Bradford in those days. He was son of a yeoman long dead, and was being reared by two grandfathers and three uncles, all men of wealth. One grandfather was a tax collector, one a leading shopkeeper. And the property of all three uncles would come to William in time.

That counted for nothing in my judgment, however. It was the lad's age—there was a matter of thirteen years between us—his dignified demeanor, and his general bearing. His breeches and doublets were always brushed, tied, and well buckled; the cleanliness of his fists and features was incredible. He was distinctly not the type of lad to sit on a bully's head and jounce it into the rushes, nor could you fancy him slinging an eel down the neck of even his worst enemy.

When William Bradford spoke out among men, I listened and swelled with pride that such a one took pleasure in the friendship of humble Scrooby folk. Nothing, probably, would have surprised William more than to learn of my childish estimation of his young manhood.

"Is there any place where we might find freedom of worship, sir?" asked William a second time. And I kicked Giles Kerry's shin that he might hold his clack and hearken to wisdom.

"Yes-s. Yes, William, I think there is!" Goodman Brewster hesitated and looked about the room. "But with so many frail women and tender children——"

"Wasn't the hardship and failure of last year's attempt due to the bad faith of a rascally skipper, sir?"

"In part, lad. We trusted in the word of an Englishman—it was a mistake. He took our money, and betrayed us. He turned us over to the King's Men."

"So I understood. Couldn't such a mistake be avoided?"

"It could, lad!" boomed my Uncle Samuel. "And has been! *This* time I have made arrangements with a *Dutch* skipper. He will keep faith."

"Then," said William Bradford earnestly, "let us make a new attempt to find freedom! If this one fails—well, then, we will bide our time and try again. And again!"

"Hurray!" shouted one noisy lad, I couldn't see who. Olin Hughes, probably. "I'll go with you, William!"

"And I—and I—and I!" The place crackled like a rookery. Men and children shrilled together.

"I'm to till but part of my rye fields, am I?" roared one who owned a larger patch of rich land out in Scrooby Waters than most of the others. "I'm to raise ducks for the King and lift no hand when his swans fight my own fowl! I'm to be overrun with hares and not allowed a meal out of them for my hungry children! Why, that is the treatment accorded slaves! This be *my* land—I and my father before me——"

"We're freemen!" somebody else agreed harshly. "We'll handle our bits of land as it pleases us!"

Goodman Brewster was unable to still entirely the storm

of words. "You worry about your bodies and properties becoming enslaved," he protested. "My worry is for the enslavement of our souls. It is freedom of worship that we demand."

"They are bound closely together, sir!" William Bradford spoke gently, as though to himself. "Living in freedom—worshiping in freedom—we must have both!"

"So we must!" agreed Jon Brewster. "I've had enough of sitting on the rim of the fish pool, hearkening to the pad of hoofbeats along the Great North Road, waiting for them to mean mischief to the rebels of Scrooby."

"Not rebels, lad! Independents, if you will, but not law-breakers!"

"Whatever we are," Jon concluded, and went to stand beside William Bradford, "there are those amongst us who are kindling against the treatment of the Stuart. The longer we bide in Scrooby, the fiercer will that flame of anger glow. Let us leave while we are able to go in peace."

William Bradford was eighteen years of age that year, Jon Brewster but fifteen. But there were other lads, younger still, who realized what was being decided that day and wished a voice in the matter: Isaac Fuller, who might have been ten, a sober lad, stepped out of a dim corner and stood beside William. And my Uncle John Brode, eight years of age, but with an earnestness and wisdom that gave him a rightful place with the older lads. And John Alden, who was visiting kin in Scrooby at the time. And Young Matt Over, son of Matthew Over, yeoman, who was a bare five years of age at the moment.

Fox-tail thrust forth a thin leg as I sprang from my stool and all but overturned me upon the rushes. "Sit back, little boy!" she hissed. "Why should *you* want to leave a home like this and wander forth with a batch of wild lads! Watch your mother's face for orders, boy!"

I stumbled backward upon my stool, hoping that nobody had noticed my shame, but suspicious about Giles Kerry, who stooped to peer at me between my father's legs and grin. Fortunately James Billing lifted his squeaky voice just then and attention was turned from my corner of the hearth.

"Are we *all* to leave Scrooby at one and the same moment, Samuel?" he shouted.

"Except those who would prefer to remain behind and deal with the King's Men."

"But—but my shop——"

"Oh, *you* aren't wanted with the rest of us Scrooby folk!" sniffed Goodwife Fentry, who was on bad terms with every member of the Billing family. "You bide by the odds-and-ends shop and squeeze shillings out of the noses of all who pass along the Great North Road. And good riddance to you, my man!"

Goodman Brewster lifted his hand for peace. "If we go," he said, "all Scrooby folk who desire freedom more than life are welcome to go with us."

"But, God's mercy, William, we of Scrooby be honest folk!" It was plain to be seen that Goodwife Fentry was vexed beyond endurance. "Must we burden ourselves with the care of a shopkeeper who trades a copy of Holy Writ with fifteen pages missing for an iron pot with a lid to it?"

"The pot was cracked, William!" James Billing piped shrilly. "And the crack hid under a mud smear!"

"You're right, it was!" Goodwife Fentry exulted over the memory boldly. "And that's the first time in my life I ever got ahead of that weasel! I only wish I could have seen your face, my man, when you filled the pot and set it to boil!"

"If you have a ship waiting for us, Samuel—off Boston strand, didn't somebody say?—what are the skipper's orders?" Goodman Roberts asked suddenly. "Where are we to go?"

"William Brewster has had that in mind this long time!" my uncle told the suddenly quiet assemblage. "When he was on service for our Queen—the one who ruled in Londontown before the Stuart came up out of the north—he had occasion to travel hither and yon, studying foreign folk and foreign places. Tell them of the place you have chosen for a new home, William!"

"Not far from here," replied Goodman Brewster quietly, "there is a land where unhappy fugitives have always found a generous welcome. The folks yonder are calm, studious, with pleasant habits. They are a God-fearing folk——"

"Are you speaking of the Low Country, William?" asked my father.

"I am, Matthew."

"But—but—well, calm they may be, as you say—but of a profound stubbornness, so I have been told. A trait which makes dwelling with them exceedingly difficult."

"They are devout, Matthew. They will understand our desire for freedom of worship—and they will be kind."

"But will they be pleased to see an assemblage of beggars come to their shores, looking for means of livelihood?"

"Beggars!" It was a roar of displeasure that filled the room. "We of Scrooby be no beggars, Matthew Over!"

"Beggars of peace and freedom only, Matt!" added Goodman Brewster. "We shall be a congregation to merit respect. Perhaps you have not heard that John Cotton of Londontown will join us in the Low Country—as well as Samuel Fuller, the wise physician, and Nicholas Danforth."

"Not that Nicholas Danforth who was to be knighted!" squeaked James Billing. "Why-y, that one has large properties."

"That same one, James!" My Uncle Samuel nodded proudly. "He is ready to leave wealth and honors for freedom!"

"There, you've got it!" my father insisted. "Willing to leave wealth, you said. We will have to leave everything behind, as I see it, and what does that make us but beggars when we land across the water? Can we find work among strange folk—strange work? We be farm folk, remember! I shouldn't want Orris and the children to suffer."

"Orris might not be so happy in Scrooby, come tomorrow, when that golden one that I saw flying from her garden yesterday returns!" sniffed Goodwife Fentry. "Eh, Orris?"

My father looked to her also. But my mother did no more than push her coif backward until her brow was clouded with little brown curls and whisper: "It is for you to decide, Goodman Matthew! The children and I bide by your will."

"How do we go, Samuel?" cried Goodwife Kerry. "All together? To perch along the Boston strand like rooks on an oak bough? Won't the King's Men see us and hale us back for a second, and sorrier, round-trip?"

There was silence as my Uncle Samuel began to explain the manner of our flight from Scrooby. "All who decide to go with us are to meet by Ryton Ford while the bogs and fens are veiled in morning mist," he said. "There, boats will be riding, sheltered beneath the willows, for all the women and children."

"What about the men?" cried Goodwife Kerry.

"The men must walk through the bog, fen, swamp, and marshland to Grimsby—'tis only a matter of forty miles. It has been reckoned that they should arrive there just as your boats come riding out of the river to the sea."

"God's mercy, are *we* to pole the boats alone?"

"I end the journey right here and now!" cried Goodwife Fentry. "It is all I can do to hold my stomach inside my bodice when I'm on the waves, without attempting to pole a boat!"

"You won't have to, Submit!" grinned my uncle comfortingly. "Each boat is to be poled by a skilled boatman. They know the course down the Ryton to the Idle, from the Idle to the Trent, to the Humber, and so to the open sea."

"These be the waters of Scrooby, lad!" I heard the words again as though it were but yesterday when Goodman Brewster stood beside me in Elderblow Lane, pressing upon the sod with his thin finger. "A pathway between us and the open sea!"

5

FAREWELL TO SCROOBY

"You make it sound as easy as a stroll along the Great North Road to Bawtry!" cried Goodwife Hughes suddenly. "But I'm one to suspicion my radish until I have examined all sides for worms. Suppose the men be *not* waiting on the strand when we come floating out of the river to the sea—what then?"

"That mishap has been considered—and orders given!" my uncle told her promptly. "The boatmen are to drift along the coast between Grimsby and Hull, and the skipper is to wait offshore until the men appear. There are two things, however, for you women to bear in mind, and one is that you are to take with you as little gear as possible. And that must include what will be needed for your men! They can carry nothing, having forty miles to walk across bog and moor."

"Dear lud, I don't know *what* to take—or what to leave!" Goodwife Kerry wailed. "All I've got is needed!"

"What you leave will be sent on as soon as you are settled in the Low Country."

"Settled in the—I don't know as I care much about becoming a Dutchman, Samuel Brode! I'm English and——"

"And must remain English!" Goodman Brewster interrupted grimly. "We must hold together, always remembering our English blood. This can't be repeated too many times! We are not to become Dutch! I shouldn't want to see the Scrooby folk scattered, become a part of the Low Country.

We must always bear in mind that we are English folk; we must live as an English community, transferred elsewhere for the time being. When times are kinder, it may be possible for us to return."

"What's the other thing we are to remember, Samuel?" asked Goodwife Hughes. "You said there were *two*."

"There must be silence in the boats!"

"You mean we mustn't talk? Lud!"

"I do mean that, Anne! What do you think would happen along the way if chattering in the boats called the attention of people on shore to such a gathering? An alarm would be sounded."

"That's enough! Mum's the word as far as I am concerned!"

"And how about me?" wailed Goodwife Fentry. "With an unruly stomach that gives no heed to the people on shore, once the waves begin to roll——"

"Get Orris to brew you some simples!" said 'Lissy Kerry sympathetically. "When I poured that trencher of hot stew down my leg last week, what *was* that stuff you gave me for the scald, Orris?"

"Howsleke, sweet clover, camomile, and the inner bark of elder simmered in fresh butter," my mother told her.

"Well, it's only a mess of simples in my hand, but it's a healing balm once you are through with it, Orris Over!" Goodwife Kerry praised, before all the listening women. "And there was that stuff you prepared for Meg Crosset's aching joints, that time she couldn't turn herself on the bed. What was that?"

"Yellow poplar, dogwood, wild cherry, and white ash barks brewed with the berries of prickly ash and spikenard root."

"Now then, hark to that!" Goodwife Kerry bade all who heard to look and admire. "Orris is as good a leech as the best in Londontown! 'Tis said that 'twig runes shalt thou ken, if thou a leech wilt be.' And there's nary twig hereabouts with a message that Orris can't read! She'll anchor that stomach of yours till it be as solid and steady as the Great North Road, Submit!"

"When do we meet at the ford, Samuel?" asked Goodwife Fentry suddenly.

"Tomorrow morning."

"Tomorrow! It can't be done!"

Every woman in the room joined in the loud cackle. One had her hands to the elbows in this task, the next one was bound by another. Only my mother, whose gooseberry jam was already simmering at the cool end of the log, added nothing to the din.

But when they were scattered, she stood to gaze slowly about her kitchen and then, her eyes coming back to me from where they had started, she grinned crookedly and hummed:

"Oh, Master Hugo Chillingsworth,
We leave so much, so much,
To hunt a freedom that has fled,
To dwell among the Dutch!

I wonder, when we have found it, if it will pleasure us as much as the thing we have paid for it! Goodman Matthew, your grandfather's father thatched the roof of this cottage! He planted these rye, barley, and hop fields. He hammered together these sheepfolds and byres."

"I know, Orris!"

"Scrooby is made out of the blood and brawn of the Overs, Goodman! Young Matt was to heir this."

"The Overs are freemen, my dear. If Young Matt heirs their desire for freedom, I shall be satisfied."

She looked at him curiously and nodded. "That, too, you got from your grandfather's father—and all the rest of the long line of Overs!" she said. "That, at least, you can take with you on the morrow and pass on to our son. But—but what can *I* take of Scrooby? Oh, Goodman, Goodman Matthew, my garden! My scullery! My jam pots and brewing kettle! My chest of fair linen in lavender buds! I—I could almost be a slave to the Stuart to keep those!" She grinned again so that we should understand that her words were but nonsense, to be taken lightly. But there were tears on her long, lovely lashes.

My father crossed the room and laid his mighty hand on her shoulder. "If you like, Orris, we will stay!" he said simply.

I do not know my mother's answer because I was turned toward the hearth, my attention caught by the breathless silence of the maid on the stool in the dim corner. She sat there, her thin little hands folded on her knees, motionless, lifeless as the maidens carved in the stone of St. Wilfred's Church. The firelight played about her shining hair, the sweet little coif that had been my mother's, and the shapeless garment that would have been large enough for Goodwife Fentry were the strings of the dingy apron that kept it within bounds once loosed.

A glistening ball of water was gathering in the cup of each eye; it swelled and grew until, at last, breaking free, it rolled swiftly down each pale cheek to splash off the peak of the maid's chin, making way for other bright balls to follow. Why, Fox-tail was weeping!

"Blazes! What's wrong, Fox-tail?" I asked, half under my breath.

"Go away, little boy!" she replied, as softly. "I must be alone when I sorrow!"

"Sorrow?" My mother heard that word and came out from under my father's arm to stare curiously.

And then she crossed the short space between us in a rush and gathered the grieving lass to her bosom. "Why, dear one, sweet one!" she crooned. And then: "*Brave* one! Never try to bear a burden of sorrow all alone when there are those who love you near at hand to share the pain! I think I know —but tell me, dear child!"

"I—I shall never return to Dame Cotter!"

"Of course not, Winnifret. That has been settled."

"Nobody wants me in Londontown."

"I hope not, because we in Scrooby want you so very much!"

"But—but you are going to leave Scrooby. And you should take as little gear as possible, and—and——"

"God love us, you don't think that *you* are merely *gear,* do you?" My mother reared backward and shook the maid tenderly by the shoulders. "No more than that damp woman child 'Memby! No more than that fen-widgeon Young Matt! You are an Over now for all time, since you would have it that way. The troubles and pleasures of the family be yours, as ours—but they are to be borne or enjoyed *together,* remember! No more sitting alone with grief in a dim corner! God knows what is before us, lass, but *you* go with us into the future! Does that comfort you?"

"Aye, Goodwife Orris. I'll take very little space."

"You'll take more," my mother promised her cheerfully, "by the time my good barley bread and creamy cheese are done with you. And now, while there is a bit of time, we'll have a look at that dove-gray dress in the chest, and the linen apron with the fine lace border, and a bucket of hot water in the scullery. And you, Young Matt, shove the oven back from the flare of the log! That hare pasty will do for tomorrow, I'm thinking! And then step along to Dame Cotter's with your father when he is ready for a word with her—Winnifret and I have business of our own, and would be undisturbed in the doing of it."

So did my mother create a pleasant stir in the room, and so in the carrying out of our assigned duties did each one of us lay aside for a brief while the dread of a dark day to follow.

Not until much later in the afternoon did the billows of consternation roll against me, threatening to break in foam above my head. It was when I returned from Dame Cotter's and my mother, meeting me beside the clump of silvery artemisia, walked with me the length of her garden of simples.

"Now, butter with a leaf of sage is good to purge the blood, remember that, Young Matt!" she said. And stood with me looking down upon silvery green foliage and lovely blue spikes of bloom. " 'Tis also, so they say, an excellent preservative of the memory—and the hair!"

We moved along to the marjorams. "The sweet marjorams," she said, "please the senses in nosegays and sweet powders, in sweet bags and sweet waters. They are a comfort when strewn among the rushes. As are also mints, lavenders, fennel, costmary, germander, hyssop, and violets. These be all strewing herbs. And thyme—smell it, lad! The Bed of Bethlehem was made of thyme! Ale-hoof, for the strengthening of failing hearing. Sullendine, for the eyes. 'Tis said that swallows bathe the eyes of their young in its orange juice for their better seeing. Ferny tansy, caraway, and dill. And St. John's-wort! Where will we be on St. John's Day, I wonder, and what will become of thee, lovely golden brush?" she whispered, bending low above the thriving clump.

"Last year, on the fifth day of July"—she grinned crookedly and shared the secret with me, now that the deed was likely never to be performed again—"I did as those of our blood were accustomed to do in years gone by, I hung a fagot of green birch, fennel, orpine, white lilies, and St. John's-wort above our door. There was a time when our English folk kindled bonfires of birch twigs in every village to warn off evil for the year that was to follow; and the lads and maids danced in every street, with garlands of motherwort and vervain on their heads; and they held violets in their hands and, lifting them, peered through to the flame, believing that whoever watched the flame through flowers on St. John's Day should feel no suffering in the eyes from that day forward. But—but, dear God, why should I bid you remember these English simples! We bid farewell to them tomorrow, lad. I hope the Dutch folk are wise in the growing of healing and comforting herbs."

She bent and plucked a sprig of borage and tucked it in her blouse. "Borage for courage!" she said boldly. "I shall plant borage wherever I make a garden, Young Matt!"

"Are we to have a garden in the Low Country?"

"Of course we shall—I have just decided it! 'Tis the duty of every woman that she be knowledged in the art of growing simples, of drying them, of distilling their healing juices, of compounding soothing unguents and tasteful conserves. I shall teach Winnifret to make conserves of rose leaves and violet petals sweet with dew. Ah, well, come, lad, and give me a hand with the jam kettle!"

I was shocked beyond measure to discover that what she meant to do with the fresh gooseberry jam was to dump it under an elder tree in the lane where the bees from the Manor House could find it and gorge themselves on its sweetness. Nothing brought to me such a complete realization of being cut loose from the land of my blood as that wasted confection soaking into the flowered turf of Elderblow Lane.

"Aye, lad, we have done with Scrooby!" My mother always knew by a glance at my face what my thoughts were. "But—but we have loved it well. Your father has said that he will take his desire for freedom elsewhere and, in the Low Country, build a new home for us upon it; I shall take my garden with me, no matter what happens, and plant it yonder, for no home is complete without well-known blossoms about the door; but *you,* what are you to take away from Scrooby, to bide with you all the years of your life?"

"What?" I asked, feeling helpless to choose.

"Memories, I think!" She stood and looked down the lane of pleached elders. "Walk down Elderblow Lane, *now,* and collect them—and never, never let them go, lad! Stand here with me and mark every beautiful thing—the loon on the wing, the lark's trill across bog and fen, the hedgerows, the buff honeysuckles and wild roses, and the amber tassel of the wild grape that's not to be told from reseda."

Blazes, she *did* know, then! There was nothing my mother didn't know about green things.

"And never forget," she concluded, crossing the lane to watch more closely, "never forget the sun-cast shadows of new leaves on the brick face of the old Manor House today!"

"I'll never forget what Goodman Brewster told Jon and me about the Manor House," I told her then.

"I hope not. 'Tis a splendid dwelling. No other building between here and Londontown can boast a face of brick, lad! It has housed the daughter of a King—*and* a King—and the great Archbishop of York."

"It was his hunting lodge," I added, assembling the tales of Goodman Brewster, bit by bit. "It has thirty-nine rooms—though most of them are sealed and given over to bats, these many years—and the refectory is ceiled and dressed in oaken wood without knot or flaw, and the window of it bulges into the orchard, almost as far as the first fish pool."

"Good!" she said. "I shall remember it forever. What more?"

"Whenever the fat old Archbishop of York would wish to run deer in Nottingham Forest, he would heap all the furnishings for nine and thirty rooms on the backs of two hundred horses and so would he come to Scrooby Waters, bringing with him all his soft couches, his carven benches, his chests, stools, bunched velvets, lace, and tapestry hangings, his mighty refectory table and all the golden goblets, bowls, and trenchers to set forth upon it."

"When he returned to York, he took everything back with him, to the last spit and trivet for the fireplace, I wager you that!" she grinned crookedly.

"He *did!* Jon and I used to hope he might have forgotten something, and we searched and searched through the nine and thirty rooms. But we only found bats!" I sighed.

"Well"—she moved back from the hedge toward our own garden—"even nine and thirty bat-filled rooms, just so long as they be Scrooby rooms, will be a pleasant thing to think back on in the years that are before us, my lad! And now I'll take the kettle back—I can manage it alone, since it is emptied—and do you go on ahead to the end of the lane, looking this way and that, hearkening to this and to that, filling your pocket with memories to take down Ryton Water on the morrow!"

Giles Kerry pounced out to the lane from behind his gnarled pear tree. "Hi, Titmouse!" he shrilled. "See what I've got in my doublet!"

It was a small, sad tortoise. "What you going to do with it?" I asked.

"It's the one I missed yesterday when you called, you know!" he explained. "I went back after it. I'm going to take it to the Low Country in my breeches pocket. Shall I go down the bank and look for another for you?"

I shook my head. "I'm going to take memories in mine—" I began, but then I stopped. Giles wouldn't understand the ways of my mother and me. "I'm going down to the Mill House to look for my father across the water," I said. And left him abruptly.

I sat down upon the grassy bank, my shoulder to a corner of the Old Mill House, and looked out upon the shallow, silvery ripples and the upthrust, lush islets before me. June time, gooseberry time, blossom and fragrance time. Soon it would be July time, time for getting in the crop of hay. Then August and barley harvest. Then September, and who would gather the fresh rushes for our cottage floor next September? For the matter of that, who, at the time for scattering Winter wheat in October, would run back and forth across my father's plowed land, swinging bundles of brush to scare away the thieving crows? Who would attend to Scrooby's November beef-salting? Would there be feasting and frolic, merry tales, songs, and games beside the hearths in the Scrooby cottages next Christmastide?

Well, Scrooby years would have to get along without the Over family from this day forward! We were going away! All these doings from June time to Christmastide were to travel with me, so my mother said, as dear memories. Soon they would become dim old tales, as when the King came up out of the north, when the Archbishop of York hunted deer in Nottingham Forest, when Margaret crossed Ryton Ford.

Margaret, daughter of a King! Of course I would never forget her as long as I dwelt in Scrooby, as long as I could sit upon this grassy bank and look off into the blue mists and gray fog along the Great North Road. But I was going away where there would be no Great North Road, where the mists and fogs, doubtless, would be different, where it would be nothing to boast about that the daughter of a King had once ridden the lane behind my cottage. I must hold to her memory against all the tide of strange events in the Low Country.

In the fragrant summertime of a certain far-off year, word got about Scrooby that Margaret, daughter of the King in Londontown, would pass that way on her journey down into the country of the Scots to become the bride of their King.

The word passed like a flock of swifts through all the bog, fen, swamp, and moorland hereabouts and soon all the folk from miles around began to surge toward Scrooby, to feast their eyes upon gentry.

They brought with them, the country folk, that is, hampers of fat capons, roasted wild fowl, partridges, and little baked pigs so that "none might want for food because of their numbers, but rather much be left behind for the poor of the neighboring hamlets," so the old tale said. And there, crowding the narrow lanes of Scrooby Village, they feasted and waited in patience for the coming of Margaret and her noble lords and ladies.

When she came—when she came, then, indeed, did they feel that all their effort had been worth while! For with Margaret came the noble Earl of Surrey with all his lords, knights, squires, and pages. And the lady his wife.

And with her, the lady his wife, came all *her* noble lords, ladies, knights, squires, and pages.

And the gentlemen, every one of them, rode upon prancing steeds of great spirit and beauty. And the ladies rode palfrey, with their squires before them.

The gentlemen of Margaret's train were most nobly arrayed in jerkins, doublets, and slashed hose of the brightest of satins, with fringes, cords, and tag ends of silver and gold until they glittered like shaggy poppies in the sun. They wore great plumes in their caps, too, plumes that swept downward, enfolding their shoulders like a cape.

But if the gentlemen were a treat for the eyes, what do you think of the ladies? my mother always asked me at this point. Not being able to tell her, she answered for me. "The ladies," she said, "were like the butterflies that haunt our parsley border!"

Their hair was curled, frizzled, crimped, dyed, and piled in drifts atop their pale, slender necks. Moreover, it was behung with sparkling wreaths of jewels!

Their ruffs were stiffened with forked wires until their mouths and noses were not to be seen for the smothering froth of delicate laces. Their gowns were of quilted brocades. And their shoes had heels of cork to tilt them forward when they should stand!

With Margaret, the noble Earl of Surrey, their lords and

ladies, rode also the clergy, each with a dagger beside his dangling cross of gold.

And behind the clergy rode minstrels who made sweet music as they traveled. And behind the minstrels rode the Sheriff of Nottingham and his gentlemen and squires to the number of two hundred.

And last of all, *walking,* came all the officers and lesser gentlemen like a herd of driven cattle.

And all this assemblage thought to pass the night in Scrooby! Why, the thirty-nine rooms of the Manor House were scarcely able to accommodate Margaret and her gentlewomen in comfort! As for the gentlemen and the rest of the escort, they were forced to remain outside when the drawbridge was lifted, and they crowded to the grassy banks above Scrooby Waters and prepared to spend the night in the open, on the very spot where I was seated.

There was a thread of new moon that night and the nightingales sang across the meadows; the minstrels made quiet music, the wild fowl twittered sleepily beneath the willows, the horses rolled and fed lazily in the lush stretches below the banks, and 'twas, I doubt not, the sweetest night many of them had ever spent. The gentlemen from Londontown were not to be pitied, resting in the open upon the peaceful banks above Scrooby Waters!

In the morning they were gone. With a flourish of trumpets, the drawbridge was lowered and out, like a cloud of pretty butterflies, came the ladies with Margaret, daughter of a King, at their head. They frisked along the pansy-studded lane, joined the waiting gentlemen in Elderblow Lane and the other quiet lanes of our sweet village, and so, prancing to the Great North Road, they reached Ryton Ford and crossed it in safety to Yorkshire beyond. And, beyond that, they were lost in the blue mists and the gray fogs of the north.

But never forgotten by the folk of Scrooby! On winter nights when the gales tore bitterly at Scrooby Waters and the fireplaces of Scrooby's cottages smoked and flared comfortingly, gaffers and crones with the household about their knees in snug, warm corners told over and over again three tales of Scrooby's glorious past. One was of the fat Archbishop of York with his two hundred horses laden with soft couches, costly hangings, golden trenchers, and rich food. And one was of the lean Stuart who came up out of the north to be King in Londontown. And one was of Margaret, daughter of one King and bride of another, who came to Scrooby with so many noble gentlemen and fine ladies that the Manor House was unable to contain them all.

And these who honored Scrooby by their mere presence were drawn here because of Ryton Ford! Blazes, what would be the good of filling my pocket with memories such as these to carry forth on the morrow unless we could take Ryton Ford with us to the Low Country! And we couldn't do that.

Ryton Ford would stay behind us. Scrooby would stay behind us. We were going to a strange place to dwell among strange folk who had never heard of the Archbishop of York or of Margaret, daughter of a King, and who did not care for what they *had* heard, like as not, about the lean Stuart in Londontown.

My mother couldn't have thought about that. I arose from the grassy bank and started homeward to talk this thing over with her. It was suppertime, anyway.

Winnifret was sitting on my mother's low stool beside the hearth, 'Memby on her knee, and for one brief moment I took her for my mother. The trim, dove-gray dress, the collar, cuffs, and apron of sheerest linen, stiffened, and edged with fine lace. And the snug coif. Not until I caught sight of the blazing strand hanging down from the coif did I recognize the maid who was said to be kin to a witch.

"Don't touch me, little boy, your hands are dingy!" she warned. "There's a basin in the scullery."

"Lud!" I stared, open-mouthed. "You're—you're an Over, all right!"

"Isn't she lovely?" cried my mother, proudly. "Aren't we pleased with this new Over?"

"She's not a Brode, though!" I replied, grinning crookedly. "Only you and 'Memby and I are Brodes."

Winnifret shoved back her coif as she had seen my mother do and let the remark go unanswered. It was not meant unkindly. It was simply that the grin that marked us of the Austerfield part of the family could not be assumed, I felt, as easily as a dove-gray frock from the linen chest, lace-edged collars, cuffs, and snug little coif. I had no thought of keeping any part of my family away from the lonely, brave maid. There had been a time when I might have felt jealousy of my mother's interest in another, but that time passed when the damp woman child came to swing in the cradle beside our hearth. Winnifret was an improvement on 'Memby, I felt.

"Clean your hands," she repeated, "your supper is on the table! There won't be any hare pasty, even if this *is* your birthday. We'll need to save that for tomorrow!"

"You come and eat, too!" I suggested.

"I already ate once today!" she told me promptly. "I don't have to eat *all* the time!"

"Don't urge her!" my mother shook her head at me and moved busily in and out the scullery. "Winnifret has had an exciting day for a little maid! If she wants to sit and enjoy her new frock and fineries, 'twill be as comforting to her spirit as bread and cheese. There will be plenty days to come for food to gain importance. When you have finished, brush your brown doublet and crawl under the plaid!"

She meant that I was to go to bed on my pallet in the far end of her sleeping chamber. There was a bed for herself and my father beside the window in the same room, and 'Memby's cradle would be pushed in from the kitchen at the proper time.

"Where—where will Fox-tail sleep?" I questioned.

"I—I need no pallet!" the maid interrupted hastily, fearful of finding herself a burden to our household. "In Londontown, at Dame Dill's, I curled up on the bricks in a corner of the hearth. And at Dame Cotter's, there was a dark closet under the stairs."

"And since you have come home, there is a big soft bed beside the window, under honeysuckle vines!" my mother concluded. "We'll try and forget those days when our little maid was lost outside in the world, if you please!

"And, Master Hugo Chillingsworth,
Suppose you fetch a chair
And lift me down that heavy Bowl
That's hanging over there!"

"But where will *you* sleep?" I howled, giving small heed to her song.

"I shall not sleep tonight, lad! There is much for me to do." She pointed to the peg beside the door. "Lift the Bowl down."

The Bowl was of shining metal and shone like silver when polished. It was as big as a tub and had handles on either side, and my Uncle Samuel, who had brought the thing as a gift to my mother from foreign parts, explained that it was a wassail bowl. But when he went further and explained the meaning of wassail, then did she tell him to cease his chatter. "Bowl is enough for me!" she said. "And there will be no mistake when I ask for the Bowl, since there is no other tyg like it in all Scrooby!"

My father was accustomed to peer into the polished bottom of the Bowl when his hair needed parting, my mother bound her coif neatly in place with its help, and both 'Memby and I had been bathed in its depths when the necessity was great.

"What do you want the Bowl for?" I asked now, dire suspicion making me slow to cross the room. "I can have a basin in the scullery as well as Fox-tail—I'm not as grimy as she was!"

"Hush, lad!" She nodded toward the stool impatiently. "There is no plan ahead to scour thee with sand and besom! I want the Bowl down."

"Orris!" It was my father, entering the room from the scullery. "You have no thought to carry the Bowl to the Low Country on the morrow?"

"But I *have*, Goodman!"

"Samuel said we must take no extra gear."

"Samuel does not know the heart of a woman! This, the most precious of all my possessions, is *not* extra gear—'tis a very part of me!"

"But—but, Goodwife Orris, what is left behind will be sent on to us later."

"The Bowl goes with me now! I must leave my pots and kettles, my linens, stools, and plaids—all the furnishings which have gone into the making of a home, it seems. That is like parting with a living arm, Matthew, but it *can* be done. When, however, I am told to turn my back on all the simples that I have bred and reared, that touches the heart, Goodman, and there is no parting with the heart if life is to remain in the body. My Bowl and as many of my simples as it will hold must go where Orris Over goes!"

"Take them, Goodwife!" said my father, going then to stand beside her. "And thank God for the strength he put in my back and shoulders! We'll manage the Bowl and the simples—and 'Memby on top of them, if need be!" he promised her quietly.

"My Goodman, my children, and my simples!" she whispered, lifting a corner of her apron to her eyes. "After all, I can build another home in the Low Country or elsewhere if *they* are left to me! With them, I take the best there is in Scrooby down Ryton Water!"

6

DOWN RYTON WATER

THE morning was still gray, heavy and solemn with fog, when I heard voices in the other room and hastily reached for my doublet, breeches, and buckled boots. Pushing out, I saw Winnifret and my mother, as like as two stalks from the same clump of silvery sage save for the fiery strand that swung below one coif; they were bending over the Bowl.

My mother straightened, with a cutting of buff honeysuckle in her hand. "It won't go, lass!" she despaired. "No use to look—we've hunted for and found so many last nooks and crannies!"

"But it *will* go—right in here next to the jug!" Winnifret cried triumphantly. "See?" And then: "Here's the little boy!"

"Not Master Hugo Chillingsworth!
Then now, my darling daughters,
The Pilgrim band will journey forth
By way of Scrooby Waters!"

my mother hummed merrily. "Call your father, Young Matt! He's in the scullery."

I hesitated, however. "What's a Pilgrim band?" I wanted to know.

"*We* are! Don't you remember what Goodman Brewster read us out of the Good Book last Sabbath Day? 'Strangers and pilgrims on the earth.' That's what we are from this day until—until—well, until we find a home somewhere and plant this honeysuckle against the door! Pilgrim folk—and a Pilgrim garden!"

"Why are we?" I was still in a daze.

"Because pilgrims, my lad, are strangers in a strange land. And so will we be—and my poor simples! Pilgrims wander about the earth in search of the blessed vision that keeps ever out of reach, just ahead of them. And that is like to be *our* fate! Our vision is a place to live where we may have freedom to think, freedom to worship, and freedom to dig in the muck once more. Call your father, lad, and take up your staff—or rather, take up one end of the Bowl."

But when I took hold of the handle, she ordered me curtly to let go. "You couldn't budge the thing!" she said. "We'll need to wait for that giant in the scullery!"

"What's in the Bowl?" I asked curiously.

"Everything! A home, my lad!"

She must have spent most of the night in her seed cupboards, in the lane, and in her garden. The Bowl was filled with tiny seed packets that had been folded and laid aside for another year's planting, with pungent roots already sprouting, with damp wrappings of slips, grafts, and greening clumps, and with fagots of dried simples. In one corner was a small jug, the kind she was accustomed to store essences in. And folded neatly atop was my father's clean shirt and best doublet.

"A nice place for 'Memby to lie!" she explained, patting the doublet smooth. "And now, my lad, for the last time, summon your father! The fog is thinning—and there's plenty of noise of footsteps outside hurrying down Elderblow Lane to Ryton Ford."

I pushed open the scullery door and came face to face with my father. "Remember!" I whispered in the nick of time.

"Remember? Remember what, my lad?" he asked, puzzled. "Have I forgotten anything?"

I nodded. "I was to forget it," I told him, "and I did—while we dwelt here. But if we are going away to wander about the earth, I want to take it with me!"

"Take *what,* Young Matt?"

"The King's Voice."

"God love us, you don't mean that golden whistle, do you?"

"Aye. 'Twas to blow upon in time of need."

"Not while we are in England!"

"No. But I must have it with me!"

"And suppose we are stopped, and the King's Men find the bauble around your neck, what then, my lad? *Then* will we all be in the greatest need of our lives!"

"They won't find it around my neck!" I promised him, and pulled the thing from its hiding place among the dried ague-weeds in the corner.

Back in the kitchen, I slipped it in among the seed packets, grafts, and slips and shook the Bowl until I heard a faint clink as metal met metal at the very bottom. Then I patted the doublet smooth.

"Put that damp woman child atop!" I invited. "No King's Man will ever search under *her!*"

Winnifret stared, wide-eyed, but she asked no questions. Neither did my mother, who knew the answers already. All she said was: "Up with the Bowl, Goodman—it grows late! And you, Winnifret, lass, have charge of the hare pasty. Young Matt will make shift with the barley loaf and the round of fresh cheese, and I will carry 'Memby to Ryton Ford!"

My father went first around back of the cottage, however,

to fasten the loosened lattice of the scullery window against a winter's gale. And then he found a rotted timber in the step and rubbed it with his thumb.

" 'Tis beginning to show signs of—" he began, choked, then continued bravely: "A day's labor will put it to rights when we return."

My mother wasn't deceived by his words. "Pilgrims never return!" she told him. "They go forward in search of that which is dearer than what has been left behind!"

And herself led the way through her dewy, fragrant garden without casting a loving, farewell glance downward to the purple pansies of Elderblow Lane; from our silvery artemisia clump to the Old Mill House and then, turning abruptly to the left, to Ryton Ford and the boat that was slapping beneath the willows.

The Fentrys were waiting for us. And my Uncle John Brode!

"John!" cried my mother. "I thought you returned to Austerfield with William Bradford last night."

"And came back to Scrooby with William this early morning!" he told her quietly. "With Jon, we will walk to Grimsby with the men."

"Walk! You do not mean that you and William are going to flee to the Low Country!"

"The lads have whispered of freedom in Austerfield, Orris, as well as in Scrooby!"

"But—but our aging father, John!"

"Samuel had a word with him yesterday, before coming to Scrooby. He bade us both go with God—and William Brewster!"

My father drew forth the boat then, and settled my mother in one end, the Bowl between her knees, 'Memby asleep atop, and myself clasped to one hip. In front of us, wedged against the Bowl to make herself as small and of as little trouble as possible, was Fox-tail.

The full length of the boat away was Goodwife Fentry. "Get in here, John!" said my father. "You'll be needed to steady our good Submit!"

"But the men are to walk, Matthew!"

"Man in spirit, you are after all but a frail lad, John!" my father told him gently so as to ease his pride. " 'Tis too long and hard a march for your legs! Besides, I should fret at leaving my household with no man of the family in charge of their well-being. See that you bring them to me in safety at Grimsby, lad!"

In the middle of the boat, standing or sitting as his work required change of position, was the boatman. My father stood back and waved farewell. The boatman dipped his pole into the mud and shot us forth from the shelter of the willows. Goodwife Fentry groaned: "Dear Lord, the rolling water! What a fool I was to hearken to William Brewster!"

And so we fled down Ryton Water from the tyranny of James Stuart.

We were well on our way when my mother, thinking no doubt upon the small duties left undone owing to the haste of our departure, half started to her feet with a cry. And then the boat *did* roll, for a fact. I could well understand Goodwife Fentry's shriek: "Orris, you'll have us in with the eels! Sit still, can't you?"

"But we have forgotten something, Submit!" my mother wailed in anguish. "We have left a friend behind to bear the full brunt of the King's wrath!"

"Yes-s? Who?"

"Goodman Colson—in the stocks on Scrooby Common. The Puritan from Londontown."

"God love us, sit still!" Goodwife Fentry clutched the rail. "Nobody has been forgotten! The seal of the stocks was broken in the night, and Goodman Colson was shown an unmarked trail across the bog to Nottingham Forest. He'll find shelter there and—and—can't you hold this craft steadier, boatman?" she demanded sharply.

"We're riding as steady as a duck on a pan of milk!"

"Oh, is that so! Well, keep your mind on your job, my lad!" she warned.

Nothing more was said for a time until she asked: "Can you see the other boats, Orris?"

"Not clearly. The fog still holds."

"I wish it would lift."

"But 'tis so beautiful, Submit!" my mother replied, contentedly. "It is like drifting inside a silvery bubble. We see nothing behind or before."

"That's just the trouble! Suppose we ride up on a sunken log. God's mercy, what was that?"

"A Water Wagtail!" I told her.

"That? The thing that swished me in the face?"

"Oh, that! That was only a reed. I know where there's a swan's nest in the reeds hereabouts."

"Well, don't get out and look for it! The way this craft rocks——"

"Look!" I cried. "A heron coming out of the fog!"

And then I noticed the stiffness of the blazing head in front of me, the paleness of the thin little cheek, the utter silence that was like the silence of yesterday when the frightened maid sat alone with sorrow beside our hearth.

"It's only a bird, Fox-tail!" I whispered. "Didn't you have birds in Londontown?"

She made no reply.

"Didn't you ever sit in a craft before?" I persisted. "Don't let Goodwife Fentry scare you—'tis her stomach that's pestering her!"

Winnifret simply dropped her head backward upon my mother's knee and sighed feebly. And my mother bent above her like a hovering moth. "Why, the lass is close to fainting!" she gasped. "And no wonder, with all this yelping and not a proper bite of food in mercy knows *how* long! Speak no more of rocking boats, if you please, Submit! Or if you must, pretend this is a steed and that we are jouncing along the Great North Road! And do you, Young Matt, get out the barley loaf and cheese—and unwrap the hare pasty!"

But Fox-tail would have nothing. "I ate yesterday!" she reminded us.

"Well, didn't we all?" inquired Goodwife Fentry, amazed. "I'll have a bit of that ripe cheese, Orris!"

"You'll regret it, Submit!"

"It might as well be cheese as anything else!"

She cut herself a wedge. And while we were getting it back past the boatman, along with the hare pasty that my Uncle John had dipped into, the fog lifted suddenly. And there was the Kerrys' boat, with Giles stuffing himself on a barley crust and salted fish; and the Hugheses' boat, with Olin carving himself a whistle out of a willow branch he had broken in passing; and the Robertses' boat, with Joseph fishing out of the back end. And many another.

It was more cheerful drifting down Ryton Water after that. The women gossiped softly, they even sang together in sweet, muffled tones when there was none along the banks to hear. And once, as the boats swung close together, they bent their heads and prayed for a safe outcome to this journey.

"We be only poor pilgrims," one said above the others, "wanderers in strange places. We seek the blessed state of freedom!"

And so I heard that word again, and came to know that Matthew Over, yeoman, was left behind us in Scrooby Village; that from now on we were of the family of Matthew Over, Pilgrim. Our roots were no longer deep in soil that had belonged to us from far-away times; we were cut loose, drifting on the future just as the willow branch that Olin had cut from the great tree was drifting now with the aimless waves. I did not like the feeling. I had been reared in pride of the Overs' bit of free land, in the cottage that tied us to it; it was a shocking thing to be stripped bare and cast forth, a wanderer on the face of the earth. The Overs were no wanderers by blood!

After a time we came to where the Ryton and the Idle met, both running into the Trent. And we followed the Trent for a matter of thirty miles until the boats began to quiver, roll, and toss this way and that regardless of the boatmen, who sought to hold them close to the strand. We knew, then, that we were drawing near the open sea.

Farther along, an oncoming mountain of water slapped clean over us and Fox-tail moaned. For the first time then since his eyes had fallen upon her in our kitchen at Scrooby did my Uncle John appear to notice the maid.

"Thou art wet to the bone, lass!" he said, kindly. "And frightened, because there is naught to steady thee where thou art sitting. Crawl along the bottom of the boat, between the boatman's legs, and thou canst brace against me and be sheltered from the waves by my coat!"

He stretched forth an arm as far as it would go to guide her passage, and without a word but with her first sob, the fiery-head slid along the boat and came to rest against his side.

"Don't fret, Win Over!" he said, giving her the name that was to last her through life, only changed to Winover for easier speaking. "There is no storm. The women wail and shriek because they are cramped and weary, but we only rock on the waves as 'Memby in her cradle."

"Cradle!" howled Goodwife Fentry. And then: "Cheese! John Brode, do you have to speak of rocking when—when—when—oh, Orris!"

"Don't blame John for his words, Submit!" My mother's voice was kind and unruffled. "Blame yourself for an appetite that is stronger than your judgment. I warned you that you would regret—there, that's right! You'll feel better, now!" She reached into the bowl and brought forth the jug of essence.

"Reach for it, John!" she said, sliding it along the bottom of the boat. "And see that she drinks of it freely. 'Tis the proper brew for tormented innards."

"Dear love, you brought it just for me!" Goodwife Fentry reached for the little jug. And then she cried: "What's in that brew, Orris Over?"

"Bayberry and hemlock barks, ginger root, red pepper, cloves——"

"—and eternal fire! The skin is gone from my gullet!"

"More will grow," my mother comforted her. "You need warmth in the spot that the cheese has vacated."

"That curd has ruined me for life!" moaned Goodwife

Fentry. And went to sleep with her head on my uncle's shoulder.

Twenty miles more of wild water! We came out of the rivers to the sea and our boatmen poled us wearily from Grimsby to Hull, keeping as close to the strand as was safe, but seeing nothing of the Scrooby men who were to be waiting thereabouts for us. The Dutch boat was waiting, but the skipper's orders had been to make no move to pick up passengers until the men had appeared. So he tossed idly upon the waves in his comfortable craft, and we most miserably in our smaller wherries.

The sun dropped low into a heavy cloud bank, the fog thickened, and the night that was before us became a fearsome thing to think upon.

And then, suddenly, the news spread from boat to boat that a sheltering creek had been descried ahead and the boatmen were entreated to pole us into this cove and up the quiet waterway for a measure of rest during the dark night.

"We have our orders," they protested, "to wait outside all inland waterways, in the open sea."

"And dump us under the waves when night has fallen, eh?" howled Goodwife Fentry, beside herself. "Maybe you're in the pay of that lean Stuart——"

"Hush, Submit!" cried my mother.

But Goodwife Hughes would not be stilled. "I asked Samuel Brode, what if the men await us not on the strand when we come floating out to sea!" she shrilled, over and over again. "And he said that such a mishap was considered —and taken care of! Foosh on the man!"

Blazes, she spoke of my Uncle Samuel!

"He'd be here if he could!" I piped indignantly. "Maybe

the King's Men caught him in Bawtry! Maybe the King's Men caught *all* of our folk! Or maybe they are trapped in quicksand in some bog."

"Oh, Young Matt, hush! Hush!" whispered my mother. And clutched at the boat rail frantically, as though about to leap outside and wade ashore.

I was silent then, realizing suddenly that I was bringing no comfort to any listening ears. The women wept, the children wailed, and the boatmen, frightened by their turbulent cargo, made for the peaceful cove and, of their own will, pushed our wherries into the haven and as far up the quiet water as possible.

"I've a mind to climb over the side and walk ashore!" grumbled Goodwife Fentry through the fog. "If I could only see the strand."

"Or know the depth of the water!" my mother warned.

"Or what was waiting on shore!"

"But, you see, we *don't,* Submit!" My mother shoved her coif to the back of her pretty head and sighed. "If we did, I'd be tempted to go with you. I'm cramped."

"I should think you would be, huddled behind that tub of greens. Toss the thing into the sea, Orris!"

"No!"

My mother said no more, but she leaned forward and laid her cheek beside 'Memby atop the damp sprigs of buff honeysuckles and took comfort from the bowl.

One by one, the black hours of that night passed slowly on. We dozed as we could. And woke to more darkness and the discomfort of a drenching fog. Morning came at last, however, and showed us, who had no knowledge of tide water, that the quiet cove had drained away to sea during the night and that we were stuck fast in mud.

We could draw no nearer the strand; we could draw no nearer the open sea. We could see the wild water in the distance and a stretch of strand, but nobody, not expecting to find us trapped where we were, would think of peering into the muddy cove to find *us.*

If the men should *now* appear on the strand, they would decide that we had been safely transferred from the small craft to the Dutch boat hours earlier and would lose no time in joining us.

And suddenly, the men did appear on the strand and, huddled in a little black group, they gave the signal to the skipper who was watching for them and anxious to be as far from the English shore as possible, since he had been delayed a night and day.

Gigs put out from the Dutch boat, the men were taken aboard, the skipper gave orders to sail at once and with full speed, and our menfolk could do nothing about it when they discovered that they were headed for the Low Country alone, that in some unaccountable fashion their women and children had been left behind.

Those in our boats were panic-stricken. They shrieked frantically after the disappearing Dutch craft. Goodwife Fentry, although as big as my father, blubbered helplessly and moaned: "I knew something like this would happen! Let me ashore! I don't care if a dozen King's Men wait for me there—I'll make the first one that lays hand on me sorry for the day he was born!"

"Aye. But how about the second King's Man?" my little mother asked. "And the third?"

And then, seeing Fox-tail, my Uncle John, and me staring at her in quivering terror, waiting to set our course of action by her mien, she grinned crookedly and tossed her head and never again shall I hear words as brave as the foolish little song she sang into the shrill din:

"Well, here we sit, Young Chillingsworth,
Quite safe—but stuck in dirt!
And there goes Goodman Matthew,
Without his Sunday shirt!"

"Shirt!" cried Goodwife Kerry. "Who cares about his shirt?"

"He will—by the time he's like to get into it again!" My mother giggled and lifted 'Memby out of the Bowl to her knee. "It's under this damp woman child!"

"Blazes, is she going to basin 'Memby right here, before everybody!" I gasped to myself. She was. She did! And the women in the other boats took comfort in watching her, busy with little homely duties, and they ceased wailing. One even laughed aloud. And then another. "Thomas might not worry over *me!"* somebody shouted from a distant boat. "But he will over his gear! Never was such a priggish man! He'll be sorry he didn't carry his own—God save us, look to the dunes, women!"

We turned, following her pointing finger with our eyes.

"The King's Men have found us!" said my Uncle John.

"With all the sheriffs and bailiffs in Yorkshire to help them!" Goodwife Fentry agreed. "Look at them, strung out across the moor like a black rope! They went to Scrooby and found us gone——"

"—and Dill Cotter showed them the way we went, I doubt not!" said Fox-tail, speaking for the first time in hours. "I would I had bit into his neck with a sound tooth, instead of into his wrist with a tooth that wobbled!"

"Come and get us!" howled Goodwife Kerry suddenly.

"If we can't get ashore through the mud, neither can you reach us!"

"Not until the tide turns!" our boatman said under his voice. Goodwife Fentry heard him, however.

"You're forgetting this cursed tide, 'Lissy!" she cried. "When the waves pound back from the sea, we'll be floated upon the strand and fall into those clutching hands like ripe plums from the bough!"

"What of it?" asked my little mother quickly, before panic could seize the women again. "After all, we be but helpless women and children who have done no harm."

"You weren't with us last year, Orris, when we were captured at Boston."

"No, but I am now!" My mother giggled and tossed her head. "And if you will but watch me and do as I direct, I promise you that if there is any pity to be wasted on the strand yonder it will be spilled over the capturers rather than the captured. You haven't shed *all* your tears, have you, Submit?"

"Tears?"

"You're a big woman, but you *are* a woman, aren't you? You can sob and faint, droop and require the support of a manly arm."

"And God have mercy on the manly arm that tries to support me in the direction I don't wish to take!" Goodwife Fentry sniffed boldly.

"Good!" giggled my mother. "Bear down all you can! But, women, offer no resistance! Be helpless and frighted as much as you will—wail and weep at the top of your lungs—drop weakly by the wayside as much as you can and require to be transported—do you get the idea? Above all else, be dumb and stupid as possible!"

"Well, the Lord watches over us still, I see!" cried Goodwife Roberts, who had been listening eagerly. "Joseph, prepare to blubber thy best! Never mind a cuff or two on the ear—'twill be a comfort to thee to know that thou art bearing punishment like a good soldier. Howl all the louder!"

"Hark to me!" Joseph promised stoutly. And to myself I vowed that, although undersized, an Over should outdo him in racket-making.

The tide turned and we were floated gently into the grip of the Law. Our Golden One was not among the King's Men present, but there were plenty of others, and a pompous bailiff, stepping forth from the throng on the strand, proclaimed that the crime, whatever it should turn out to be, was being committed in his shire and would have to be tried in the nearest town before his own judge.

Our women made no objection. They merely piled his arms with gear and stepped aside for my little mother to take the lead. She pointed meaningly to the Bowl.

"Odds blood!" howled the bailiff. "Leave it where it is—'twill be safe enough!"

"No!" my mother told him firmly. "I don't like the looks of your men. Of course, they *may* be honest, but my gear goes where I go! Either carry it—or me!"

"But a man can't lift it!"

"*My* man did! Up with it, weakling!"

He hoisted it to his shoulder and after that even I felt some pity for the man. His pomposity oozed from him with every painful step and he had my mother clinging to his doublet like a nettle.

"Come, hurry!" she urged when he paused for breath. "Your judge is waiting!"

And when he groaned at the weight of the Bowl, she commiserated with him and, patting his arm with her tiny hand, said that it was easy to be seen that the men of this shire lacked the brawn of Scrooby folk. She fretted, too, when his chops and cheeks blazed red as any cock's wattles with wrath, pretending that it was some inward fever burning through the skin, and she advised a bit of fair linen wet with a brew of hamamelis buds laid upon the heated surface. When he stumbled, she lurched forward to support him, reproving the watching women with a gentle shake of the head.

"Laugh not, friends!" she said. "The ox is not to be blamed for the clumsy hoofs with which he was born, remember!"

By the time we arrived at the guild hall, the bailiff hardly knew the crime for which we were to be tried. "Odds blood!" he groaned. "A wildcat, that one, if I ever heard tell!"

"The hussar?"

The bailiff turned about and stared at Goodwife Fentry's robustness indifferently. "No, not that one!" he said. "The sand-widgeon with the face like a flower. Don't let the face fool thee, man! There's a stinging brier behind the skin."

But the judge, when he saw us, beat the air in despair. "Scrooby folk!" he shouted. "Why have you brought me more of those waterfowl? Only last year—well, what is it now? Speak up!"

"The same thing all over again, I'm afraid!" my mother confided gently into his big ear. "We want no more than to be let loose of this land—like you'd shake yourself free of a caterpillar that had laid hold of your doublet. You'd feel all the better with the beastie gone for good—*look* better, too!"

"It is claimed that Scrooby folk are rebellious, irreverent, lawbreakers——"

"Oh, tut, tut, you know how people will talk!"

The judge gazed at her sweetness distractedly. "Who can argue with a woman?" he cried. "Bring me the Scrooby men!"

"Aye, bring them!" sniffed my mother and lifted a corner of her apron to her eyes. "Don't you hear the judge, my man?"

"They're gone, Your Honor!"

"Gone? Gone where?"

"Forth—by boat. Before we could head them off. We only caught the women and children."

"And very noble and brave of you, I'm sure!" added my mother meekly. "But clever of—of our Scrooby waterfowl, too, that they were able to escape from right under the big red nose of a bailiff!"

"Do you mean that we have only women and children in this guild hall?" roared the judge, turning furiously on his own officers of the law. "Why, women cannot be held for the crimes of their menfolk!"

"I heard something like that, once!" my mother agreed.

"It is for a man to command—and a woman to obey! These women did but their duty in obeying their men and following them in flight. The sin of the deed rests upon the men!"

"Who have gone," interrupted my mother. "Leaving their best shirts behind them! When Goodman Over discovers that baby 'Memby has been sleeping on his——"

"Clear these women out of my court!" roared the testy judge. "Clear them out of the town! Clear them out of the land! Find a vessel and send them to sea in search of their missing men!"

My Uncle John, the fiery-headed maid, and myself stood against the rail with salt spray cutting our cheeks, watching the wheeling gulls.

"Fox-tail—" I began. She stopped me.

"That's not my name any more, little boy!" she said.

"Winnifret——"

"That, neither!"

"What, then?"

"Winover!"

I accepted the change without comment. "Winover," I began, "do you know what I would do if I were a gull?"

"Fly back to Scrooby Waters and fish for an eel."

"Blazes, no! I wouldn't go back to Scrooby *ever*—with King's Men all over the place!"

"You'd be safe enough from them if you were a gull!" she giggled.

"These gulls are fleeing from something!" I told her.

"They are looking for food," my Uncle John told us both.

"Food! Away out here where the waves are like mountains?"

"There may be some cast-off food from the ship. Or it might be that we are nearer land than we think." And then, turning with his back to the way from which we had come, he pointed and cried: "Look yonder, Young Matt!"

"I see a thread of green!" shrilled Winover. "It *is* land!"

"We've come to the Low Country!" I cried. "Do we go ashore soon, John?"

"No," he explained. "A seaman was telling me that the

Low Country lies far below the ocean level—if it were not for high dikes on this side, the whole place would be drowned."

"How do we get into it, then?"

He made a mark like a hook on the deck with his finger. "Northward," he said, "there is a thin bit of land like this —the Low Country tapers off to a hook, up there. And in a certain place the hook is broken, leaving a passageway. Boats edge in through the passageway, between the mainland and a little island called Texel, into the Zuyder Zee."

"Into the what?"

"The Zuyder Zee."

"What's that?" asked Winover. "More water?"

"Aye. Plenty more water! The seaman said that not many mariners would dare to take a craft of this size through the Zuyder Zee because of powerful currents and hidden sand bars. But he said that our skipper was most skilled and in him could we put our trust."

Blazes! My mother would want to hear about this. I ran to fetch her. She was sitting on the boards, leaning against the Bowl.

"Young Matt," she sighed, "the ducks at home could sit in comfort on Scrooby Waters and doze, but I can't! Humans should keep off the waves, I'm thinking!"

"Get up and look over the rail!" I shouted. And when she did, she was as excited as I had been. "God's mercy!" she gasped. "Have we come to shore?"

"No. That's an island."

"An island!"

"Texel! John says we go in between it and the mainland— and so come into the Low Country by the scullery door, so to speak."

"I understand—but, oh, isn't Texel beautiful!"

It was. Soon we could look down upon lush green meadows, lazy kine, happily grazing sheep, and a lad in blue pantaloons and a maid in a lace bonnet. Never had anything seemed more beautiful!

But after a while we left Texel far behind and, rushing to the front of our boat, we saw a great city spread out before us like a half-moon. Amsterdam!

Great ships, their very planks still breathing forth the fragrance of the Islands of Spice, were drawn up at the docks. Some rested after a hard voyage, their sails furled; but other sails were unfurling, other voyages to unknown worlds just beginning.

It was a place of noise and confusion. Strangely clad folk, strange language, strange activity. Bales, kegs, barrels were tossed and rolled this way and that. We hardly noticed the extra uproar when Goodwife Fentry, joining us at the rail, added her shouts to the din.

"The ship yonder!" she boomed. "The one that is outward bound for God knows where! Samuel Brode stands upon the deck!"

"Samuel! Where?" cried my mother.

And then my Uncle John leaned far down into the clamor below and shouted: "Samuel! We have come—we are all here in safety!"

"He knows that!" Goodwife Fentry sniffed mightily. "He has ways of knowing, like the birds of the air, when his business in one place is finished and the time has come to move on. That lad can't resist a ship that is outward bound!"

"But he might have waited just until we—until we—" My mother sighed and held her peace. She knew that she had no rightful complaint against my Uncle Samuel Brode.

"He'll come again if we need him!" I told her proudly.

And then Winover cried out with a shrillness that turned many a head on the dock below upward. She pointed to a blur of menfolk who stood at some distance, silent in the midst of turmoil and confusion, faces toward the sea, patiently waiting. Their black doublets, breeches, and capes made a blot on the colorful picture.

"Scrooby!" piped the fiery-headed maid. "They didn't see us because we came in behind that ship with the great sails spread—they were watching Samuel Brode! But now that the ship has moved, I can see—I can see Goodman Over!"

"Goodman Over!" boomed Goodwife Fentry, spreading her long arms and wide cape above our excited heads. "Tell Oliver Fentry to come right over here and get me off this craft! I never want to step foot on a drop of water again as long as I live—even a puddle in the lane is going to be safe from me! Hurry, Oliver!"

And then, coming down off her toes and folding her cape primly about her, she spoke what was in the hearts of all of us. "Thanks be to God—and with the help of Orris Over," she said, "we made it, this year! We fled the Stuart and we have come to the Low Country! May we have peace and freedom enough here to satisfy every man of Scrooby!"

PART TWO

A Low Country

7

MY NAME IN FULL

"GIVE me a hand with the Bowl, John!" said my father. "I'll tuck 'Memby under one arm, and do you follow close, Submit! You are to be with us at the home of Stephen Clifton until we have found other lodgings."

"Clifton—Clifton? Wasn't his wife called Annice, Annice Fuller, as a maid?"

"That's the one! They fled from Scrooby some years ago to join the congregation here in Amsterdam, and now they have opened their home as a refuge for William Brewster's company. Watch out for that rolling keg, Submit!"

"I'm watching it!" she told him. "And the next time it bangs into me I shall kick it over the edge into the sea!"

"Odds blood, watch Submit, Oliver, and never mind the kegs!" laughed my father loudly. It was good to hear him again. "We want to get out of this tangle without trouble, you know!"

"Do the Cliftons dwell far from here?" asked my mother.

"On the St. Anthonies Way. A craft will be passing the curb here soon."

"A *craft!* Did you say craft, Matthew Over?" Goodwife Fentry pushed between six whirling kegs without even noticing them. "No matter how far it is, I'll go by way of the lane!"

"The lanes are waterways in the Low Country," my father told her quietly. "Here comes a flatboat that will pass close to the St. Anthonies Way. Step aboard, everyone!"

Blazes! The lanes are waterways in the Low Country, my father said. The lanes—the *lanes!* If that was so, how would I ever go eeling? My mother would not allow me near a waterway such as this alone! Didn't these people have any pansy-studded turf and tangled hedgerows? Must we hop a waterway every time we should desire to leave our own garden or enter a neighbor's?

It was a pleasant ride to the St. Anthonies Way. All about were flatboats, like our own. The canal was choked with them. Some were piled with vegetables, green and crisp; some were floating gardens, drifts of lovely blooms; some were heaped with curious little round cheeses; and some were laden with rosy-cheeked lads and lace-bonneted maids.

Nobody looked as if he were holding an ear cocked for the pounding hoofbeats of the King's Men!

Dusk was fallen by the time we had been welcomed at the Cliftons' and supped, and so we were taken to sleeping chambers. For the first time in my life I was helped by my father to rest upon a spread of fair linen on a bed. It was a strange experience, and not entirely a pleasant one.

"Who sleeps with me?" I asked nervously.

"Nobody. You sleep alone, like the Stuart himself—in grandeur!"

"What holds me in, then?"

"You'll learn the trick, my lad, after a tumble or two!"

"Don't they have pallets for little boys in this country?" I asked, thinking wistfully upon my straw and warm plaid back in Scrooby.

"I doubt it! The Low Country folk are much too clean—they wouldn't clutter up their corners with straw ticks!"

"What covers me, then?"

"This!"

Lud! It was a snowy bag filled with goose down and it was slippery as any eel! I spent the night napping, waking chilled, hauling the cursed thing back from the floor, and holding it fast until sleep loosened my grasp again.

Toward dawn, I gave up the struggle with the snowy bag. I found my doublet and breeches and crawled into their familiar warmth and, tucking my feet under a woolly rug on the floor, fell asleep on the boards.

A din outside the window wakened me. I thought it was Jon Brewster's dove Beggar, at first, but in a moment I knew better. Beggar wouldn't be here. This was the Low Country, and Beggar was back in the Old Country.

I shoved a stool against the window and tugged at the heavy tapestry hangings. Outside, the place was aswarm with yellow-headed men in baggy breeches with round black hats on their polls, and fat women in welling skirts and winged lace bonnets. With them were lads and maids, clad as like themselves as was possible. They clattered about the cobbles in wooden shoes.

And they were buying and selling at planks that dripped and smelled like—like—blazes, *fish!* What kind of country was this where people spent good money for fish, instead of hauling what they needed out of the water!

A woman stepped back from the planks and I saw what she held in her hand before she dropped it into a string bag. An eel!

Were my days of treading mud at an end? Must all our fish and eels from this day forth be selected from the piles on dripping planks? I wonder if Goodman Brewster knew about this when he praised the Low Country and chose it for our new home. I got down from the stool, buckled my breeches neater, and pondered upon the sacrifice we had made in leaving Scrooby.

My father found me sitting on a stool, head in hands, sunk in gloom.

"Up, my lad!" he roared cheerily. "We've all been bitten by the same bug this morning! Goodwife Fentry mourns for a pot of hot boiled tea, your mother for her dewy garden and the song of a cuckoo down the lane, and I for my mattock and bean patch. But we've all taken comfort in the thought that we have been led safely together, that the Stuart is far behind, and a long, sweet life ahead. And so must you, Young Matt!"

"Do you know that these folk *buy* their eels?" I asked him. "Outside, there."

"Aye. And very good they are, too. I just had a bite at one. What you need, now, is a trencher of proper food, my lad!"

But it wasn't. Or else the food was not proper. I felt no better after a bowl of hot, thick chocolate and sweetened white bread. I wanted tea and the heel of a barley loaf and a wedge of cheese.

"Well, anyway, we don't have to go to Dame Cotter's!" Winover whispered.

I would have gone to Dame Cotter's willingly, after this taste of the Low Country.

"Take him outside, John, and brighten him with a look at our new home!" my mother suggested when I pushed back from the table and would eat no more.

We went, Winover and John and I, hand in hand for comfort. "I thought there were no lanes, John!" I objected, once outside in the open place beside the dripping planks. "Just waterways."

"Well, there aren't any lanes like the elder tunnels in Scrooby. But there are cobbled walks alongside the canals—and some paved streets."

"And churches!" sniffed Winover, looking about. "The place is a-clutter with churches!"

"Here's one that I've heard about from William Bradford!" my Uncle John discovered suddenly. "It's called the New Church. William showed me a picture of it. The rulers of the Low Country receive their crowns here. Let's go inside."

"Go—go inside!" I stammered. And looked at him in astonishment. "Why, we aren't allowed to go inside a church. You know St. Wilfred's——"

"That was in Scrooby, lad!" he reminded me. "The King ordered Scrooby folk to attend St. Wilfred's, or suffer death for their disobedience. Here, where there is freedom, there is no disobedience—we may enter a church or remain outside, as we wish, with no fear of wrongdoing in either case."

Lud! Some people could think lightly of this freedom thing. It made me uneasy! I wasn't ready for it yet, and told him so. "I'll keep away from churches!" I said. "Let's go look at the Manor House."

"What Manor House?"

"Yonder. The brick dwelling."

"That's no Manor House!" John told me then. "There be many such buildings of brick hereabouts. Folk like us live in them!"

"Are they *all* gentry, in the Low Country?" I asked.

"They're all blithe and happy," Winover replied then. "And that's better than being gentry. The women are fat and smiling and the men are broad and kind. And everywhere bells are ringing, like the bells in Londontown on Fair Day.

Only it was gray and dirty in Londontown, and here it is sunny and clean!"

"*Too* clean!" I grumbled. "I couldn't eat my sausage at table and so I dropped it into the rushes under my stool. Only, when Goodwife Clifton drew back our stools after the eating was over——"

"There were no rushes!" howled the fiery-headed maid suddenly. "*Now* I know why Goodwife Clifton's kitchen seemed so different to me! Why hasn't she any rushes on her floor, Uncle John?"

John grinned at her crookedly. "You'd best call me John, like the rest!" he said. "And as for Young Matt's sausage, all I know is that it sat on the tiles like a grebe on the waves. And Dame Clifton was put to a sight of trouble to scrub away the grease spot afterwards."

"But what is one to do with unwanted eatings?"

"Leave them on the trencher."

"They are seen there, too!"

"Then must they be swallowed." And I knew that he would do just that. But not Winover.

"I'll give mine to you, too, John!" she said graciously. "How Goodwife Clifton gets along without rushes, though, puzzles me. Why, in Londontown ours weren't disturbed for the better of a year."

"Ours in Scrooby were!" I cried indignantly. "We changed our rushes often."

"You were close to where they grew—in the swamp at the end of Elderblow Lane. It was easy for you to clean out clear to the bottom of the room. When *we* got fresh ones, we tossed them atop the old. So, when they *were* changed, the things you found on the boards below!"

"And it was because of that very thing that you, in Londontown, suffered so bitterly last year!" John told her soberly.

"Because of our rushes?"

"Because of the filth that lay beneath them. Goodman Brewster was explaining the matter one day to Jon, and I listened. The rotting filth under all the rushes everywhere in Londontown is what caused the plague. Witches had nothing to do with it. There be no such evil spirits! Poor old dames were blamed and died for the great fever that spread far and wide, but all the time it was caused by the filth hiding beneath the rushes in every dwelling."

Lud! I foresaw an unhappy time in this Low Country. I didn't want to keep Goodwife Clifton busy with mop-cloth and besom and I certainly wouldn't want a hand in causing any plagues—but peppered sausage like the piece I had tasted that morning, and fish spiced with buds, seeds, pods, and pungent leaves such as we had been offered the evening before, and meat sauced with an unpleasant powder and scarlet buds that nearly burned the skin from my gullet!

We crossed a canal or two and so wandered back to the St. Anthonies Way and sat down on the curb before our house. Above our heads, over the dripping planks, there were some black letters painted on a wall and I asked my Uncle John if he could guess their meaning.

"V-I-S-C-H-M-A-R-K-T," he read the letters slowly.

"Like a-b abs at Dame Cotter's?" Winover wanted to know.

He shook his head. "It's to let folks know fish are for sale here," he explained. "Fish Market."

"What's wrong with their noses?" I grinned.

"Young Matt's going to learn how to read letters like that

some day!" Winover said suddenly. "He's going to learn how to sign his name in full, too!"

"Why not now?" John replied lazily. And fetched a bit of crayon from his pocket.

"Where did you get that?" I asked. But he waved aside my interest in the thing. "Out of Hanson's store in Austerfield," he said. "William Bradford gave it to me. Never mind about the crayon, lad; what you have to do is to watch what it does and learn from it. Now then, take a good look at those letters on the wall!"

I did. They hadn't changed.

"Some of them belong to *you!*" he said.

Blazes!

"We'll have them down," my Uncle John continued, "and then you will see what I mean. Give heed, now! Can you count six?"

"Aye. 'Tis one full fist and a finger from the other hand."

"Good! Begin at the first letter and count. One—two—three—four—five—six! Stop! That is an uphill, downhill, uphill, downhill letter, like this." He made another just like it on the cobble between us with his crayon, and handed the crayon to me. "I'm going to rub it out now," he warned. "You make a letter just like it, lad!"

"Why?"

"Because that is the letter M. And M is the first letter you have to learn if you are to write your name in full."

I bent, then, to the cobble and wrote M over and over again. Winover, too. I wrote M until I knew it forever and ever.

"Now, up there on the wall, right next to M, there is a letter with a bridge in the middle."

"A!" yelped Winover excitedly. "It *is* like a-b abs, John! Does A belong to Young Matt, too?"

"It's his next one—follows right along after M."

I made it. And then I had to look along the whole line of black letters on the wall until I came to the very last, the one with a cap on its head. And that was mine. I needed *two* of them, though, John said.

We put them side by side on the cobble, and there we had it, M-A-T-T!

"Is that all there is to him in writing, John?" asked Winover. And stood to walk around the cobble and compare it with me on all sides. "God's mercy, he's little any way you take him, isn't he?"

"He's got another name, of course—Over."

"Well, give it to him, then! He needs it. Is Over on the wall, too?"

"Part of it is. Not the first letter, but that is nothing more than a ring, like this. O!"

I could make that with my eyes shut.

And the next letter, it turned out, was half an M turned upside down, and was the first letter on the wall.

The third letter was the worst to make and to remember. Until Winover told me that it wore a cap and a shoe and had a bridge in its middle. And who could forget a letter like *that?*

And the last letter—R—was on the wall. But it meant more to me when I discovered that it was long and straight on the left side, like the Great North Road. And curling around the top was the Ryton. And the Ryton met the Idle in the middle, and so flowed downward and away. R was my Scrooby letter.

All together, then, I set my letters side by side on the cobble: MATT OVER. And so it was in Amsterdam that I first learned to write my name in full.

I was puffed with pride and leaped from the curb at the first call of the cuckoo from across the square, ready to show my father that my learning was beginning in fact. But one look at his face told me that he was too occupied with matters of his own, that I must wait for an easier hour, and so I followed him into Goodwife Clifton's kitchen and sat on a stool in the corner while voices buzzed about my ears. Some of the chatter of my elders escaped me, to be sure, but I understood more than they thought for.

"Goodman!" cried my mother, busy with 'Memby and the basins beside the shiny green stove. "Did you find a farm?"

"Farms—in Amsterdam! Orris!" Goodwife Clifton's rippling laughter filled the room. "What are you thinking of?"

"But Matthew Over is a farmer! How else is he to earn our bread, save in a barley patch? How am *I* to live with cobbles clear to my door? I need a garden."

"Stephen and I have managed well!" Goodwife Clifton said proudly. And looked about the bright room. "We chose a happy location for our small shop, to be sure. And we were able to make connections with the ships that ply between Amsterdam and the Indies, bringing spices, silks, ivories."

"The Overs were never shopkeepers, Annice!"

"I looked at a dwelling near the church—" began my father. But Goodwife Clifton stopped him at once.

"Church?" she asked. "What church? Amsterdam is full of churches."

"The Puritan meeting place," he explained hastily. "William Brewster wants us to hold together, clustered about our house of worship."

"Oh, la! 'Tis a long time since William Brewster has lived in the city, that much is plain to be seen!" she said. And tossed her pretty head. "Stephen and I have fallen away from worship lately; the congregation is too much torn with strife."

"Strife!" cried my mother. "When they have freedom to think as they choose?"

"They have too much freedom, my dear, if you ask me! Freedom to poke their sharp noses into our daily habits of living! Like whether or not we should stiffen our coifs and aprons with starch and——"

"No, Annice!"

"Yes, they did, Orris—it was made an issue in the congregation. A woman who stiffened her coif was no Christian, it was maintained. And some went so far as to try to force a certain garb on each and every one of us alike. We were to go about the streets like uniformed orphans."

"Annice!"

"It began to look as if every Puritan in Amsterdam would need a church of his own if he were to live in peace with his conscience—peace is as necessary as freedom, say I!"

My father stood and breathed deeply. "You have forgotten what it is to dwell where there is *no* freedom, Annice!" he said quietly. "I'll step outside and have another look at that place beside the church."

"Wait a minute, Matthew!" Goodwife Clifton looked at my father thoughtfully. "Have you sought employment?"

"That will come later. First I must find a roof to shelter my family."

"Matthew—Orris"—she spoke almost as though fearing to give offense—"since you are here, you see—well, what I am trying to say is that there are two or three tiny rooms in the loft of this house that we use as storerooms. They are small, but they are empty at the time and they can be scoured and scrubbed well in a few hours' time. It might solve your problem for the time being."

"Do you mean that we should live in your household, Annice?"

"In your own household—under our roof. Orris and I would be neighbors again, as we were in years gone by in Scrooby. Only there it was a fragrant lane that separated our homes; now it will be a staircase."

My father sighed gustily and I knew that his heart was rested of worry to know that my mother would be settled with friends for a time. "God reward thee for thy kindness, Goodwife!" he said simply. "I will speak with Stephen about the rental."

"There will be no rental, Matthew."

"We have not come to the Low Country seeking charity, my dear! There is enough in the money bag for our needs until I can begin filling it again!"

"Keep it, Matthew! You'll find use for all you have brought with you—seeing that you have brought four children as well as yourself and Orris!"

And so was the matter of our living in Amsterdam settled until my mother thought of her Bowl and upended 'Memby with a sharp cry. "How are my slips and grafts, my seeds and clumps of simples to be kept alive," she asked, "with our heads bumping the roof and our feet three flights above the cobbles?"

"Amsterdam can provide rich loam too, you know!" Goodwife Clifton reminded her gaily.

"A garden needs space for its roots. It can't flourish on a cobble!"

"It can flourish in kegs set on the cobbles!" Goodwife Clifton said firmly.

"God's mercy, a garden in kegs!" My mother looked about the room and shoved at her coif frantically. "My simples and my family, Pilgrims all! Just as I told Young Matt! Wanderers, atop the earth! And I and my savouries do so need a spot of deep loam to hold fast to!"

We were a year in Amsterdam. Not a particularly happy year for those of us who were trying to find that which would not be found.

My Uncle John and Winover were contented enough, taking pleasure in the city's fine school. But I, who sought for Scrooby in our living arrangements, continued to be bewildered and disappointed.

It was my need to look in through an open door any time of day when I was at play in fragrant lanes or dewy gardens and see my mother busy at the hearth. I knew then that my world was in order. In Amsterdam, however, to assure myself of my mother's serene presence it was necessary for me to climb three steep flights of steps. Too often, then, the kitchen would be still, empty. It was frightening to a lad who had known no other home but Scrooby!

Of course it would take but a moment to recall the garden of kegs and scuffle down the three flights to the inner courtyard. And there my mother would be, at work among her slips and grafts.

She did not know why I came running into the courtyard so often, to drop on the cobbles close to her side and press my head against her knee. I had lost my mother, but now she was found. I had *never* lost my mother in Scrooby!

It was only after Nicolas came out from among the eels

at the back of his father's stall in the Fish Market one day and showed me the longest one in the pile that these periods of lonely torment began to lessen. Nicolas boasted of the eel, and I told him of the eel I had caught in Scrooby Waters and boasted of *it,* and although we spoke in different languages we understood each other very well.

After that day, Nicolas and I were never separated for long, not while we remained in Amsterdam. We chattered together constantly, and it never occurred to me to wonder whether I was learning to speak in his tongue, or he in mine.

Nicolas made a game of running in from the cobbles to find my mother; he would race me up the flights and when the kitchen was empty he would shout: "*Dat is goed!* Now *you* beat me to the garden!" And when I did, we came upon my mother with merry cries and we all huddled on the cobbles to laugh together. And those were the only times that I learned to watch my words. My mother did not like to hear me speak as the Dutch did.

I remember one lovely day in early spring, April it was, that I came storming in from the Fish Market to find both my father and my mother in the kitchen. My father was there often that month and it comforted me, although he never looked as happy as in the days when I ran to meet him in Elderblow Lane.

"I'm going with Nicolas!" I shouted. "With Nicolas and his father!"

"Quiet, lad!" my father said sternly. "Where art thou going with the fisherman?"

"In his flatboat—out into the harbor. To see the *Halve-Maen.*"

"The what?"

"The *Half-Moon.* 'Tis an odd craft that lies beside the

dock of the Dutch East India Company. You can see it from the shore, but the dock is crowded, so many are going to have a glimpse at the queer thing. Nicolas says that we can see it better from the water."

"But what *is* the *Half-Moon,* lad?" my mother insisted. "A craft—but what craft?"

"'Twas built for one Hendrik Hudson, who is master of it—" I began.

My father interrupted me. "Henry Hudson, an Englishman," he explained.

"Aye. He sails any day, now, to the New World to discover the Groot River."

"The Great River?"

"Aye. He says there be a Great River that will make the passage to the Isles of Spice shorter and safer."

"He tried for that passage last year," my father remembered, "when the Scrooby folk made their first attempt at flight. We failed—and so did he!"

"But we didn't *this* year!" I reminded him. "And 'tis said that in the *Halve-Maen* Mijnheer Hudson will succeed in finding what he seeks in the New World."

"Go on, lad!" he said. And turned from me to resume the earnest discussion with my mother that I had interrupted.

Not many weeks later, I learned what that discussion was about; what that discussion which I interrupted each time I stormed in from play was *always* about. My father too, it seemed, was trying to find that which would not be found in all of Amsterdam.

It was June again—June, with another birthday for me! My mother had sent me forth into the marketplace on an errand, but I had not yet left the stool in a dim corner where

I was buckling my boot when my father came into the kitchen and sat down beside the table.

"Orris," he said wearily, "I begin to despair of ever making a home for thee in this city beside the Zuyder Zee!"

My mother stood 'Memby on her own two feet, giving her the table leg to grip to, and said quietly: "You *have* made a home for me, Matthew! Where you are—and the children and—and—and my kegs, there is home!"

"Two rooms above a fish market! For a yeoman of Nottinghamshire!"

"For a Pilgrim, Goodman."

"I am thankful that you can still be merry, Orris! But it seems that no labor is to be found in all the city of Amsterdam."

"It doesn't seem possible, Matthew!"

"So I thought a year ago, while we were in Scrooby. Mighty shoulders like mine, I said in my pride, will be in demand wherever labor is to be done. But it is not so. There are more than three hundred bridges in Amsterdam, and I have come to know them all. I have walked until my feet must have made tracks in the planks and cobbles—I have even today, as a last hope, gone into the Joden-Breestraat."

"God's mercy, dear heart, thou art no diamond-cutter! What kind of labor is trinket-making for a yeoman?"

"Any kind of labor would be fitting! But there is none. Amsterdam has been too kind and hospitable for its own good. Some five and twenty years ago, so they all tell me, there was war hereabouts and a flood of working folk poured into this place from the city of Antwerp. They were given shelter and protection, and they quickly took over the business of the place. 'No help needed,' is all I am told at every door. I am going to William Brewster this very night and tell him that, as far as the Over family is concerned—by the way, lass, where's Young Matt?"

"Gone to the shop for a smear of jam. This be his sixth birthday, you know."

"Jam!" I yelled. And leaped from my stool in the shadows. "*Ik heb iets vergeten!*"

"Watch your words, lad!" my father warned. "How could you forget jam?"

I grinned crookedly. "I was thinking of getting down into the Fish Market," I confessed. "Nicolas said that because of my birthday I should have the fattest eel on the planks for a feast, but *ik zal morgen om*——"

"Goodman Matthew!" My mother laid her tiny hand on my father's arm in warning. "Let it pass! The lad cannot help his tongue slipping when his only companion is that sweet little Nicolas. Nor is anybody to blame, unless it be ourselves who think that we can live, English folk, in a Dutch community without rubbing one against the other. Not even William Brewster could walk among my white lilies without being brushed by the yellow pollen! If we are to keep our thought and our tongues and our—our doublets entirely English, then must we move on. Pilgrims cannot bide too long in one spot, it seems!"

Move on! Leave the St. Anthonies Way, the Fish Market, and Nicolas! Leave the docks and the great white sails that came in from distant seas like homing gulls! I was shocked. But before I could spread my thoughts in fitting words, the door burst open and my Uncle John raced into the room with Winover at his heels.

"*Hoe laat is het?*" he shouted.

"Going on noon, lad!" my mother replied patiently. "You're a bit late."

"*Ja,* I met Goodman Brewster outside the school and he said to tell you that he would be here summut after the noon hour."

"Here? William Brewster?"

"Aye. But wait, I met William Bradford near the Oude Kerk and what do you think? His uncle has just died."

"Which uncle?"

"The one who was taking care of William's property in Austerfield. Now William heirs all from his father and two grandfathers and three uncles!"

"God's mercy!" My mother shoved at her coif and looked about the room at her own brood who would heir no wealth no matter who died. "And William still but a lad! How old is he, John?"

"Close to nineteen. I know that Jon Brewster stands between us, and Jon is sixteen. I'm nine."

"Young Matt's six years old today!" cried Winover, as if anybody cared then. "And we're going to have gooseberry jam for dinner!"

"Young Matt forgot the jam, dear!" my mother explained hastily. "I wonder what business Goodman Brewster is coming on. Was it about William Bradford, do you think?"

"No, it's still about Scrooby!" John tossed the matter aside and looked to see what was spread on the table.

"Scrooby? What about Scrooby, lad?" asked my father. And there was no ignoring those tones. "Drop the oily cake and tell us what was said!"

"Why, he said that there was no true happiness among the Scrooby folk," my uncle remembered then. "He said that they were either becoming one in tongue and spirit with the Dutch, or they were finding no labor for their hands and becoming discontented with life in the Low Country. He said that they were showing a disposition to scatter here and there, and *that* he did not wish to see. He said that a place must be found where all can live together and labor."

"Labor!" my father sighed. "Let him find a place where our labor is needed!"

"He *has*—that is just what he is coming to tell you! He has found a city that will welcome us, will give our men work, and set aside a section of land whereon we may build homes for one hundred, so Goodman Brewster says. He wants to know if we will be one of the first hundred families to go with him."

"Where, John?"

"To Leyden."

"Leyden? Is that far away, Goodman?" My mother looked about the cozy little kitchen and shivered. And then she grinned crookedly and added: "But never mind where it is, my dears! The simples and I are still in kegs as it were, we haven't rooted deeply, yet. We can be moved. When shall we start?"

"Start!" My Uncle John and I both cried the word in one voice. But after it was out, I had nothing to follow. This thing of being a Pilgrim was bringing me naught but upset, bewilderment, and grief.

John was able to shape his dismay in understandable language. "Leave Amsterdam," he exclaimed, "just when we are beginning to learn how to plot and lay out a village, in school! 'Tis wonderful, Matthew! Some day I shall lay out big cities and erect suitable buildings; now, we work only with little places of only one marketplace, a town hall, and no more than a dozen dwellings. But 'tis amazingly interesting! Even little villages like Zaandam and Huizen and Broek and——"

"Scrooby!" suggested my father quietly.

John was puzzled. "What about Scrooby?" he asked.

" 'Tis a little village—and English!"

"Foosh! Where's there any art in the building of Scrooby?"

"Matthew—Goodman Matthew!" cried my mother sharply. "Go to the door and see if William Brewster is on the way! 'Tis full time that we wander on—to Leyden, or wherever!"

8

THE COTTAGE ON THE DIKE

THE Bowl came down from its peg the next day, and within the week it was filled with cuttings, seeds, grafts, and damp clumps. "The thymes, mint, parsley, and sage I'll leave for you, Annice!" my mother told Goodwife Clifton. "The good English flavor of them will wipe away the taste of so much cardamom and curry. And the kales! 'Tis scarce a hundred years since the Dutch gave us cabbages, but we have had sallets of kale since the Romans invaded Britain! They'll keep Scrooby in your heart, Annice!"

"I don't need simples to do that, blossom!" Goodwife Clifton replied tenderly. "But what will you do without all of your clumps?"

"I shall have them—and more with them!" I drew near to hear how this was to be. "You know the lad, William Bradford of Austerfield, the one who has come into so much property?"

"Aye."

"Well, he is to make a hurried trip back to his old home to settle some business matters. And he has promised me to visit Scrooby while he is across the water, and to bring me all the simples that are still growing in the old garden, besides pink daisies and purple pansies from Elderblow Lane and cuttings from the gooseberry bushes in the Manor House orchard."

"That will pleasure you, dear!"

"Aye. If only—if only Matthew can find sufficient number

of kegs!" my mother laughed, and brushed her hand across her eyes.

It was a journey of never-to-be-forgotten beauty, that slow, gentle journey along the canals through the tulip fields from Amsterdam to Leyden.

There were meadows of lush green with lazy cows at rest, banks of fresh green with stretches of new linen whitening in the sun, tiny cottages with red roofs and a stork's nest huddled close to the warm chimney, lovely gardens, men in blue breeches, women in lace bonnets, maids and lads in both. And then the breath-taking fields of open tulips!

"Matthew, look yonder! Oh, Goodman Matthew, see *this* one!" cried my mother over and over again, always sure that no view could be more enchanting than the one she was looking at, at the moment. "Oh, if *we* could have a tulip field like the one just ahead!"

"I know naught of tulips," my father regretted, "but I'd like to try a bit of barley on that loam!"

"A farm, Matthew! With the children growing red and fat on good cheese and milk."

"William Brewster frowns on farms. He wants us to dwell together, as one community."

"God's mercy, who was it first made a garden for William Brewster to dare to frown on them!"

'Memby rose to her feet in the flatboat at just that moment and, clinging fast to a handle of the Bowl, steadied herself while she laughed like a chime of silver bells. She pointed to the moving wings of a great windmill, to the miller's house below, and to the wee lad who stood in the doorway watching us.

'Memby waved her small fist in greeting, and the wee lad

lifted both arms above his head. "Why, the darling!" cried my mother, forgetting the tulip fields completely. "Wide blue breeches, buttoned doublet, and round black hat exactly like the miller—and he can't be three years of age, yet! Boatman, what be this place?"

"The Weddesteeg."

"I mean, what city are we nearing?"

"Leyden."

"Leyden!"

"Strangers and wanderers on the face of the earth, I have a feeling that the Pilgrims have come home, at last!" said my mother under her breath. And looked as she did when kneeling beside Goodman Brewster on the Sabbath Day.

We passed the night with Goodman Stedman in Nun's Lane.

And the next morning, my Uncle John, Winover, and I went out together to see what manner of place this Leyden might be. Only this time we did not go hand in hand for comfort; we had no timidity before the kindly Dutch folk now.

We discovered a long, tree-shaded street with shops on one side and bookstalls on the other, and scholarly folk sitting beneath the trees in the open, quietly reading.

Canals and churches were no novelty to us by this time, of course, but a hillock with a fortress atop in the center of the city *was*. Likewise, a stadthuis with a tower and a chime of bells and "God Protect Holland and Bless Leyden" cut in the rock above the door.

It was good to know that the folk of Leyden, like those of Scrooby, boldly lived with God.

Coming to the end of the tree-shaded street, we made the

greatest discovery of all—a great sheet of silvery water that cut the city from east to west. "That's no canal!" Winover yelped. "When you stand here on the grassy bank and look out on it it's like looking out over Scrooby Waters!"

"It's a river!" John told us. "The Rhine!"

And then we saw them, the six markets that lay along the great river, side by side, backed to the waves!

"Six markets!" I gasped. *"Six!"*

We wandered through them, wide-eyed. One was a timber market, one a flower market, one a vegetable market, one a butter market, one a seafish market, and one a—one a—one was an *aalmarkt!* One whole market given over to eels! Leyden was too good to be true!

After that, I insisted upon returning to Nun's Lane to tell my mother, and so we crossed the Breedestraat and ran all the way back. Outside the Stedman door, I heard her talking.

"I found the exact spot, Mary!" she cried, in the happiest voice I had heard since the golden King's Man entered our garden of simples in Scrooby. "I followed the canal, as you told me, and I came at last to the old mill—and—why, it's wonderful, Mary! There's the mill, and the tiniest cottage on the dike in the shadow of its turning wings, and the canal at one side and a great silvery body of water spread out in front."

"The Rhine. I know the place," Goodwife Stedman replied. "The cottage has only two rooms."

"I have never had more! There is a tiny loft where John and Young Matt can stretch their pallets. And Winover shall curl on a settle beside the hearth. Mary, the miller's little boy came out to look at me! His name is Harmensz."

"I know. The miller is Mijnheer Rembrandt. But, Orris, that cottage on the dike is very old and has been vacant for a long time. The plaster has fallen from the outside, and I hate to think what it must be like inside."

"It has a garden."

"It has a weed patch."

"What may be weeds to you, Mary, may be simples to *me!*" my mother told her with dignity. "I shall treat that patch with respect until it has unfolded its secrets through the seasons."

"Are you really going to take the poor little cottage on the Weddesteeg, Orris?" Goodwife Stedman asked. And frowned over the plan.

"Of course I am—tomorrow!" I went inside the room to enjoy my mother's happiness. "I met James Billing in the Breedestraat and he is going back to Scrooby to see about some of his own gear in the shop there, and for a small sum of money he promised to attend to the packing and shipment of all that was left behind in our cottage when we fled down Ryton Water." She reached out and tapped me merrily on the shoulder, and sang:

> "So, Master Hugo Chillingsworth,
> We'll grub again in mire,
> And hang our pots and kettles, sir,
> Beside our own hearth fire!

No more nesting at the top of a building like a finch in the upper branches of a linden tree! We'll sit on our doorstep and scrape our heels along the sages and felt-wyrts. Dear God, I haven't been so happy since I traveled the Great North Road from Austerfield to make a home with Goodman Over in Scrooby, and that was—that was close to ten years ago, when I was naught but a foolish lass."

"You're naught but that *now!*" laughed Goodwife Stedman.

But when I asked: "Will Elder Brewster let us live in the cottage on the dike, Mother?" they both stopped laughing.

"*Let* her—what do you mean, lad?" Goodwife Stedman asked.

"Oh, 'tis an idea William has, that we of Scrooby should all dwell together," my mother explained nervously. "He worries lest we scatter among the Dutch and become one with them, forgetting that we are English folk."

"Nonsense! He wants you to dwell like bees in a hive?"

"Something like that. He has acquired a lot in Bell Alley."

"Bell Alley! Over against St. Peter's Church?"

"I heard that it was thereabouts. Do you know the site, Mary?"

"Too well! Think twice about locating there, Orris! The cobbles are always damp, no sunshine strikes the spot, and the very air is sour. And with Young Matt and Winover still snuffling from their last colds—and John growing thinner and paler than a lad of his years should look—and 'Memby's nose running like a brook——"

"You aren't trying to persuade me against Bell Alley, are you, Mary?" my mother interrupted the torrent of words. "I *told* you that I had already decided on the Weddesteeg! *I* know, better than many, that what children need is green grass under their heels and hot sunshine on their heads! And if there is a sheet of silvery water in front, so much the better, since we of Scrooby are accustomed to that! I've been hearing naught but freedom—freedom—freedom—for years on end, my dear! Our men have chased after it as lads chase pied wagtails across the marshes, but now that they have caught the thing in a foreign land, *I*, too, shall lay fist on a feather! I claim the freedom to make a home where I see fit!"

"If only the plaster weren't dropping away," Goodwife Stedman worried.

My mother brushed the thought of missing plaster aside. "There's a buff honeysuckle from Elderblow Lane in my Bowl," she said, "that will hide all bare spots on the wall, once it begins to clamber. When I get my pink daisies and purple pansies into proper soil, my basil, balm, sages, savouries, lavender, rosemary, howslekes, sullendines, and rue to greening the borders, the Scrooby folk of Leyden will be coming to stand outside the wee cottage on the dike and dream of English lanes."

We moved to the Weddesteeg the next morning: ourselves, our Bowl, and a besom and tub of scouring sand that were borrowed from Goodwife Stedman. My mother and Winover kilted their skirts above their little knees and set to work at once, scrubbing, sloshing, and scouring, for if there was one thing that they had thoroughly learned in the year that we had been in the Low Country it was just that. I had my hands full to keep 'Memby away from the slopping buckets.

"We aren't to have rushes on our floors, are we?" panted Winover once, stopping long enough to bind her blazing strand of hair tighter beneath her coif and then slapping at the boards with her wet cloth twice as briskly to make up for lost time.

"No rushes, lass!"

"Thank God!"

My mother sat back on her heels to look at the maid.

"They're filthy!" Winover explained. "John says so!"

"Well, as a matter of fact, they *are!*" my mother agreed.

"It's much better to have white scoured boards underfoot, like they do in this land."

"We could use the little larder for a scullery."

"So we could, lass! I'll have Goodman Matthew put up shelves there tomorrow for our jam pots, essence jugs, and cruets of fragrant oils. We'll knot the simples as they ripen, and hang them to the rafters, along with pungent roots and healthful barks."

"And I'll get about and see what the Leyden folk have for gear in their kitchens!" Winover promised, and sloshed a bucket of water the length of the room. "Maybe Goodman Matthew could make what we lack."

"We'll see that he does—although we'll not lack much when James Billing gets back from across the water! I'll be glad to get at my coverlets and chests of fine linen again, lass! And when I swing my own stew pot over the log, and spread my bed with my own woolen plaids instead of these bags of goose down, I'll be the happiest woman on earth!"

"It might be," I said suddenly, laying a firm hold on 'Memby, "that that is why Goodman Brewster doesn't want Scrooby folk to scatter about the Low Country."

They both stopped scouring and looked at me. "What might be?" Winover asked.

"It might be that he thinks they would make homes like this, on the dike and in the tulip fields, and grow to love them so dearly that they wouldn't want to leave when the time came—the time to move on again!"

"Move on again, Young Matt? What have you been hearing?"

"Back, I mean!" I corrected my words. "Don't you remember that he said that we were to keep ready to go back to Scrooby when times were happier."

"God's mercy, you had me scared, lad!" my mother shoved back her coif and bent again to the besom and sand. "There will never be any going backward, Young Matt! Pilgrims go on—and on—and on. Maybe, though, we have gone far enough!"

"Let 'em go if they want to—*we* won't!" Winover decided. And wrung her dingy rag fiercely. "We like this land, and Goodman Brewster could just keep out of our business! There, the walls and floors are clean—all they've got to do is to dry in the sun for an hour or so. You sit out in the garden, Goodwife Orris, while I step next door!"

"Next door? Where do you mean, lass, the mill?"

"Aye. I want to have a look inside Mijnheer Rembrandt's kitchen."

When her fiery head appeared once more above the green of the grassy dike, she was running. And shouting. "The Bowl, Young Matt!" she cried from afar. "Fetch the Bowl right out here in the garden next to the water keg and the scouring sand!"

"But, Winover"—my mother got off her knees among the weedy borders and stared at the lass—"the Bowl *is* out there—only it is still filled with slips and grafts. Young Matt couldn't lift it."

"Oh, I thought it was emptied by this time. Well," she insisted, "empty it! Dump the greenstuff on the sod!"

"But why? In such a hurry, too!"

"Go next door and you'll see! Pots, pans, and kettles on the wall until it makes you blink, the way they all shine! But just let me get at our Bowl with the scouring sand and *we'll* have something that shines on our wall, too!"

"Winover! What will the miller think of you?"

"I don't know. I only was inside long enough to see the

shiny things. Next time I'll stay longer and have a closer look about the place!"

My father came outside then and upended the Bowl in the garden. He had been walking about the wee cottage, studying it, measuring it for lumber for the two tiny rooms my mother wanted added at the back for John and me, and for Winover. But now he stood and watched us as we emptied the Bowl.

Something glittered among the roots at the bottom and Winover picked at it. "What in the world!" she said. "A chain—and a whistle on the end. My goodness, we have got something that shines right here in our Bowl!"

My father stooped and took it from her. "It belongs to Young Matt," he said. "And it is something the Over family could just as well do without—if they knew *what* to do with it! It is dangerous to keep—and dangerous to throw away. So we hide it—and forget it!"

"What *is* it?"

"It's the King's Voice!" I told her. "The King's Men blow upon it when they are in need of help, and he who hearkens must obey its summons as if the King himself had called. A King's Man came to our garden in Scrooby the day before —why, it was the very day before I went to Dame Cotter's school and saw you! He threatened my mother and he cut my neck with his lash—and I threw an eel down his doublet! It frightened him so that he plucked the golden whistle forth and threw it far and wide, thinking it was the beastie, you see. But it wasn't. And I found it among the simples. Have it, if you want it!"

"I don't!" she decided promptly. "I can handle my own troubles. I wouldn't blow on a whistle when I was in need. Oh, look here—it says—it says: 'THE KING SPEAKS, RE-

MEMBER!' God's mercy, who does he think he is! Let him speak—what do *we* care, here in Leyden! Give it to 'Memby, it has her name on it!"

"Give it to *me!*" said my mother. And went inside to hang it on a rafter in the little scullery, as we had hidden it in Scrooby.

While she was gone, Winover moistened sand and slapped her rag against the Bowl. "Don't let me forget to tell her about the spinning wheel and loom when she comes back!" she warned.

"What spinning wheel and loom?" my father asked, grinning. The working of the maid's mind was always a rich joke to him. "Are we to have suchlike gear beside our hearth?"

"Aye."

My father stopped grinning and looked at the lass closer. "The Over women know naught of weaving, I suppose you have noticed," he remarked.

"We'll learn. Mevrouw Rembrandt says a spinning wheel and loom are as necessary to the Leyden women as the kettle on their hobs."

My mother was back in the garden, listening. "She's going to teach me to knit, too. And Young Matt!"

Blazes! "Not *me!*" I howled wrathfully. "My goodness!"

"But you *are* to, Young Matt!" she insisted. "All boys hereabouts knit their own warm things. There's a Mevrouw Cort who lives just around the corner—they have a lumber yard——"

"Lumber, did you say, lass?" asked my father, thinking of the two rooms he was to build against the back of the cottage, no doubt. But Winover would not be turned from her first line of thinking.

"Aye," she nodded. "Lumber. This Mevrouw Cort was in the mill and she talked to me, too. She has a little boy named Rudi and he knits all the stockings for the whole family. So you see, Young Matt——"

"No I don't!" I cried.

"What about the spinning wheel and loom?" my mother asked.

"Mevrouw Cort said that more fine cloth was made in Leyden than in any other city and that it was all made in little home kitchens like ours."

"In—in homes? Oh, Winover!"

"She said when the women had made enough for the selling, they took it to the halls."

"What halls?"

"Somewhere near the Stadthuis. There are different halls for fustian, and for baize, and for fine linen—whatever a body makes is taken to the proper hall to be inspected by officials and stamped. And then 'tis sold."

"Winover! Do you really think we could learn?"

"I don't know why not! We're as smart as Mevrouw Cort! She said I should walk along the Oude Vest canal some day and watch the folk scouring their newly made cloth in the water and stretching it on frames to dry. There's something in that particular water that is supposed to benefit the weavings. She asked me if we were Puritans from London-town."

"And you told her——"

"That we were Pilgrims from Scrooby!"

"I wonder why she asked."

"She said there were a lot of Puritans making baize here in Leyden. Especially men. There's work for everybody here —for big and little. Even Young Matt."

"Never mind about *me!*" I warned peevishly. "Why don't you plan for John?"

"John's going to build cities!" she said proudly.

"I'll step around the corner and find that lumber yard," said my father. But Winover was on her feet and had him by the doublet before he could start. "I was almost forgetting!" she cried. "I guess I never would have thought of it again, only for saying what I did about plenty of labor for big and little."

"What now, lass?" He looked down at her curiously. "Am I to knit, along with Young Matt?"

"No. But Mevrouw Cort was talking about her Goodman. He's got a tulip farm outside the walls and he would like to spend all the days in it, only there's so much business here that it's driving him crazy. If he could only get a man to help him—a man with sense, strong arms, and a will to work—but Mevrouw Cort says that the three things don't go together."

"God's mercy!" cried my father. And broke loose from the maid's grasp. "Where did you say this lumber yard was, Winover?"

"Around the corner, where you see the two fat little children. The boy is Rudi, and the maid is Kathi."

"You don't miss much, do you!" grinned my father, approvingly. "I'll take the order for planks along as an excuse. Let me see, what was it again, Goodwife?"

"Timber for two rooms," my mother told him, "and scullery shelves—and——"

"A spinning wheel and loom!" Winover added sharply.

"I couldn't make them, lass!"

"No. But find out from Mevrouw Cort where they are to be had. And get lumber for a cradle."

My father stood and stared. "A—a—for a *what?*" he roared.

"A cradle. Mevrouw Cort said that no kitchen is complete until one swings beside the hearth. I explained to her that we had nothing to put in a cradle, now that 'Memby sleeps on a pallet, but she said it made no difference, the cradle could wait, but the important thing was to have it ready."

My mother jerked at her coif. But before she could speak, I cried: "We've *got* a cradle, Winover!"

"In Scrooby! What good does that do our kitchen, here on the dike? Don't you want our kitchen to look as good as any in Leyden, Young Matt Over?"

"Not if it's got to be done with a Dutch cradle! My mother was rocked in ours, and so was my Uncle Samuel. And my Uncle John. And then it was fetched from Austerfield and *I* was rocked in it. And then 'Memby."

"Lud, it's time we had a new one!"

But my mother agreed with me that none but an Over cradle should swing beside the Over hearth and she promised to tell James Billing to add it to the list of gear he was to send from Scrooby, and after that we all fell to pulling weeds in the border while my father went around the corner in search of Mijnheer Cort.

When he returned, Mijnheer Cort was with him. They sat on two overturned buckets on the grassy bank of the dike and talked until a silvery moon rose above the river Rhine. When they had finished, there was a new lumber business in Leyden, that of Cort & Over.

And so did my father find suitable labor in the Low Country. And so did we find our beloved home and garden on the Weddesteeg. And so did we find the best and truest of friends around the corner.

And when the Over family had freedom and labor, a home and garden, and friends, they asked no more of God.

My mother was busy laying out her garden. Far at the back, where there was a bit of wall that caught and held the sun for the better part of each day, she planted gooseberry bushes from the orchard of the Manor House in a scraggy, prickly row.

Over the wall she draped wild grape vines and pink roses from Elderblow Lane. And against the cottage walls she planted buff honeysuckles.

But in the rich black loam of the borders she planted digitalis roots, lavenders, basil, bergamot, and nep. She planted, too, mints, woad-waxens, ague-weeds, marjoram, rosemary, saffron, felt-wyrts, sullendines, St. John's-wort, ale-hoof, borage, and dill.

And one day while she was making a lovely border of silvery green sage beside the brick wall, with spicy thymes nestled in wherever there was a break between the bricks, she came upon two folded leaves, like two small hands pressed together, uplifted in prayer.

She left them as they were, pushing the thymes and sage sprigs aside to give them room, and she warned us all to have a care of the strange growth. For days on end, while she was grubbing about the spice clumps, she would suddenly leave everything and hurry to the border to question the uplifted fingertips.

"They fret me, Young Matt!" she confessed one day. "Why should these tender green things, more than any others, fold their palms in eternal adoration?"

"Maybe they *don't* worship!" I replied, bending low at her side. "Maybe they fold their hands about something they are to keep hidden for a time, something that is very precious, something that is a secret."

"Why, Young Matt!" she cried. And looked up at me with shining eyes. "The tiny hands are clasped about *buds!* It is just exactly as you say—they are protecting their baby blossoms!"

"Hi!" whooped Rudi Cort, coming into the garden at just that moment. "Mijnheer Kroll's tulips are late, but there they come again!"

"Tulips? Are those tulips, lad?" my mother asked.

"*Ja.* Mijnheer Kroll, who used to live here, bred them; they are later than any others and more beautiful. After he died, my mother and Mevrouw Rembrandt dug up some of the bulbs, but they won't grow anywhere else. So now we leave them here and come to admire them when they bloom. My mother says they love the little cottage on the dike. We call them 'Pride of Cottage Kroll.' "

"I shall love them, too, Rudi!" my mother said.

But I knew what she was thinking when she sat back on her heels and eyed them so curiously. *Tulips,* in an *English* garden!

That night she brought my father to look at the uplifted hands and spoke her thoughts aloud. " 'Tis folly, Goodman Matthew, to raise a barrier between the two bloods, when God Himself allows them, the Dutch and the English, to grow so happily in the one soil!"

"But William Brewster says——"

"My Dutch tulips among the English lavenders speak too, Matthew!" she told him firmly. "And in words that my heart can understand. Hereafter I shall make no objection to a Dutch word on the lips of my children, to a Dutch habit so long as it be sweet, to a Dutch friend so long as the friend be worthy."

A lumber yard is as good as a school for learning and much pleasanter. When Mijnheer Cort seated himself upon a pile of logs and drew his broad thumb along the cut surface of one, I learned the difference between that bit of timber and the one that lay next. I learned of the way the tree stood in its growing, its leaves, its bark, the manner in which it was felled; of fierce inland waterways that floated the lumbermen as well as the logs to the open sea.

"Feel it, Young Matt!" Mijnheer Cort would say and rub my small broad finger behind his. "One is like sand, and one is like satin. Smell it!"

And so I learned that some wood is hard and some is soft and the same plank will not do for every part of a dwelling. Having come thus far in my learning, I went with John down the Breedestraat to have a look at Mijnheer de Key's newest building, and he pointed out to me the curious gable ends—"corbie-stepped," he called them—and I wished that I might climb them to the sky.

And then I saw our workmen bring planks from Cort & Over's lumber yard, and I knew which were hard and which were soft, and what part of the building each was meant for. And I felt prouder of my learning than when I had hunkered on the curb in the Amsterdam fish market and first learned to write my name in full.

One day, hopping about the flatboat that was always tied to the bank in front of the lumber yard, I stumbled and fell into the canal and there again I learned something. I was not half fish, it seemed, as were the lads of the Low Country.

Mijnheer Cort leaned down from the flatboat and had me out by the slack of my breeches—but barely in time.

"Seven thunders, Young Matt!" he puffed and spluttered. "You can't swim?"

I shook my head, wearily. Right at that moment, I had no desire to swim. I never intended to get near enough to water again for that.

"But—but you always lived on that—that Scrooby Water, you call it."

"Only wild fowl swim there!" I told him. "Folks don't swim in mud and quicksand."

"Then in you go—and Rudi with you!" he ordered sternly. "We can't have any lads around this canal that can't handle themselves in the water!"

I howled. But it was too late. I was in—and in a second I realized that Rudi's hand was under my back and Rudi's mouth was at my ear, giving directions. I tried to cling to his neck, but a clip on the ear from Mijnheer's broad fist changed that idea.

Then I said to myself: "If a loon can dip into this stuff and come up again, if a fish can go down and jump out, if Rudi Cort can, well, then, *I* can!" and gave heed to the shouted directions. Soon I felt that I was afloat, with Rudi's hand withdrawn!

That surprised me so that I sank to the canal bottom at once. But I remembered that loons and fish and Rudi did the same upon occasion without evil results, so I scrambled back to the surface and was soon afloat once more. I crawled out to the bank, rested, and then plunged into the water again of my own accord. The miracle held. I floated. And had no fear. My mother would want to know about this!

She was kneeling among her simples, peering at the water

through two clumps of pink basils. And there was no need to tell her what had been taking place.

"I know, Young Matt!" she whispered faintly. "I saw you tumble from the boat. And then Mijnheer Cort—and Rudi. I pressed my head against God's knee and I said: 'Don't take your eye away from him, God! Watch him—help him to conquer fear! And help me, too, to bide among my simples and mind my own business, keeping out of the way of manly matters! But don't forget, God,' I said over and over again, 'don't forget that Young Matt *isn't* a man as yet! He's only seven years of age and small for his years, as are all the Brodes!' As if God didn't know *that* without my telling! But I *had* to prattle, when you dropped out of sight—and when you came up again, laughing, I thought you would find me dead among the basils!"

Winover and John came into the garden just then, and when they learned what the excitement was all about they, too, demanded to be shown how to keep afloat in the water.

"Young Matt can't know anything that *I* don't!" Winover pointed out. "Let's go find Rudi, John!"

"But, Winover, this be man's business!" my mother objected.

"Kathi swims like an eel. We'll have *you* in the canal, next!"

Mevrouw Cort crossed the dike just then and agreed with Winover. "Best encourage her, dear friend!" she said gently. "While the will is hot within her, that is the time! All who dwell in the Low Country must know how to manage on land *and* water in summer, on land and ice in winter. And just see, my dear, the valuable lesson they are learning besides—to watch over each other and help one another!"

So John went into the canal gravely and made no trouble

about learning to swim, as was his custom in all things. But Winover plunged in and before she could catch her breath she came face to face with a dead fish that had drifted in to us from the seafish market and her strangled yell was, I felt certain, the last sound we would ever get from the fiery-headed maid. But Mijnheer Cort dived into the water and got hold of her blazing strand and so hauled her forth. And Rudi went after the fish and got it up on the dike. After that Winover went in again and learned quickly, but it was a long time before she would ever swim without somebody sitting on the dike, watching the waves.

9

NICOLAS

It wasn't long before John found a school where he could prepare himself for work, later, in Mijnheer de Key's studio at the business of building cities, and he was contented and happy. More and more, Winover and I turned to Rudi and Kathi Cort for companionship.

We explored the tree-shaded Breedestraat and we roamed along the shady promenades that ringed the city well within the outer walls. And one day we stopped at a spot where we could face the sea.

"Look!" Rudi pointed outward. "Do you know what happened here, once?"

"You stumbled, the way Young Matt did off the flatboat, only you fell down into tulip fields instead of into water!" Winover guessed promptly.

It seemed that Rudi was not in the habit of stumbling. "Ships landed here!" he told us. "Ships laden with food. To save the Leyden folk from starving to death."

"Don't be silly, fat boy!" Winover sniffed. She never liked untruthful tales. But Rudi insisted he was speaking the truth.

"How could ships climb over those dikes out there?" she asked. "Even if they could sail across tulip fields, ships couldn't climb over dikes!"

We sat down in a row on the high promenade facing the sea and Rudi told us about the terrible war and the siege of Leyden. "Enemies all around the city," he explained. "Nobody could get in—or out!"

"Well, a good thing nobody could get *in,* I should say!" Winover told him.

But when Rudi mentioned the starving people, and that nobody could get into the city with food through the ring of enemies outside, then she began to understand what a very bad thing it might be.

"Right out there in the ocean," Rudi continued, "our folk could see ships laden with food, but they might as well have been in the Seven Seas for all they were doing to the Leyden folk."

"They couldn't sail around to the docks, eh?"

"Of course not—the enemy guarded the way to the docks!"

"Blazes! Then everybody starved to death!" I shouted.

"Not while my grandfather was about!" Rudi told us proudly. "*He* was smart! He figured out a way to get the food. He went across the lowland down there with some men and they broke a great hole in the dike!"

"Broke a hole in the—why, I thought the sea was the worst enemy to the Low Country. I thought the dikes are to keep it far away!"

"The sea was our friend, that day. It rushed in through the hole and flooded the lowland, and in came the ships right after it! Up to these very walls of Leyden, where starving people waited, praying, thanking God for the food that was coming. And so were their lives saved—except those who ate too much and too greedily after having eaten too little for so long. They, many of them, died of too much food that day! But most of the folk were too weak for that. They lay along the wall here, and were fed from the ships and so, slowly, regained their strength."

"And good enough for the enemy!" Winover cried fiercely.

"The cruel beasts! I suppose they slunk away when they saw how your grandfather fooled them."

"They didn't!" Kathi took up the tale. "Even then, they lingered outside the walls."

"What for?"

"Waiting. Just waiting for a chance to get inside."

"Did they?"

"No. They went away after a while, but nobody knows when they went and nobody knows what made them. They went very suddenly."

"How did your people know they *were* gone then?" I asked. The thing puzzled me.

"Well," Rudi carried on with the tale, "there was a lad inside the city here, and he said he had been here too long! He wanted out. He was a daring lad, all right. And curious. He let himself down over the wall and then, nothing would do but he must steal up to the enemy's camp to see what was going on."

"Did they catch him at it?"

"No. The camp was empty!"

"God's mercy!" Winover's cackle rang out over the tulip fields. "Your folks tied up in knots, and nothing to be scared of after all!"

"Not then, as it happened. But if the lad had become impatient but one hour earlier he would have met the enemy in their camp and certain death!"

"We *know* that, for a fact!" Kathi nodded her head solemnly.

"How do you? Did someone tell the lad?"

"Not someone, but some*thing!* In one of the tents, the lad found a huge kettle of hutch-putch and it was still warm. So he knew that the fires had been tended there less than an hour before. The lad took the kettle back to the wall and was hoisted up, and he told what he had found. And they ate of the hutch-putch and it was very good indeed, but cooling rapidly. Something had frighted the enemy away but an hour before, while their dinner was still in the making! We've got the kettle to this day."

"Who has?"

"The city of Leyden. I'll show it to you some day," he promised. "It is in a dwelling over by the fortress. It was on October the third, when the lad found the kettle."

"Do you know why we remember October the third?" Kathi asked happily.

"No."

"Because ever since then it has been Thanksgiving Day! We feast and thank God for His help in time of trouble and we eat hutch-putch."

I knew all about hutch-putch. Every stew pot in the Low Country made the stuff with a different flavor and sometimes it was a brew to thank God with and sometimes it wasn't. The Cliftons in Amsterdam made it with curry, black pepper, and hot red pods so that it took the skin off my gullet and frighted me from dipping into the next bowl that was set before me, at Goodwife Stedman's in Leyden.

The Stedmans, however, seasoned their hutch-putch with English simples and all the left-overs of the larder were to be dipped up from its rich brown depths. It was very good and kept one's interest alive as to what was coming up in the next spoonful, clear to the last drop in the trencher.

My mother had attempted hutch-putch once or twice, but the result was colorless. With barley and rye loaves, soft cheeses, gooseberry and plum jams, hare pasties and chunks of venison roasted with acid and sprinkled with mixed simples—Scrooby cooking, that is—she had a master hand. But she had not as yet been able to accustom herself to the luxuriance of Dutch cookery.

But Mevrouw Cort's hutch-putch would be, indeed, a feast! She put into her kettle some of all the fish, flesh, and fowl to be found in the market, some of all the pungent roots and savory stalks, some of all the dried or fresh simples and pleasant-tasting seeds and pods. And after that, she cleaned up the larder. All left-overs from a spare oily cake to the last smear of stewed plums. I smacked my lips, remembering it.

"You'll come and celebrate Thanksgiving Day with us!" Kathi smiled happily at Winover. "You and Young Matt and 'Memby."

I doubted this almost as soon as I had mentioned the matter to my mother that evening about the supper table. "Thanksgiving Day? What is that?" she asked, puzzled.

Winover and I told her together, but out of our chatter one word caught her ears above another. "Go to thank God?" she repeated. And stopped our voices at that point. "Where do the Corts go to thank God?"

"Why—why, to their church."

"Young Matt"—my father put down his wedge of cheese and wiped his mouth—"Young Matt, you know that it would be most displeasing to——"

"William Brewster!" piped my mother. And shoved at her coif. "More than all else, though, to that worrisome Bell Alley! Just as if a Christian couldn't worship God in *any* place acceptably!"

"Goodwife! Orris!"

"I mean it, Matthew!" she insisted. "I have sacrificed much for the freedom to think—and the freedom to worship.

And I am enjoying them both! Dutch tulips and English pansies—they are growing very pleasantly under God's one sun and one rain! Where is the sin in mingling their fragrance to God in thankfulness? When is this great day to be, Young Matt?"

"On the third day of October."

"Good! Then tell Mevrouw Cort that you will be glad to feast on hutch-putch with her at that time. And thank her for the invitation. And tell her that you will be ready at the proper time to go with her to her church and help her give thanks to God for the deliverance of Leyden from the enemy!"

It was a bleak day, something like eight weeks later, when I stood in the little scullery with my mother.

The new shelves were all in place and filled nicely with jam pots, row on row. There were jugs of essences and cruets of fragrant oils; there were bunches of drying simples pegged to the rafters overhead, knots of pungent roots, and fagots of healing barks. It looked and smelled like the scullery that opened into Elderblow Lane in Scrooby.

We were examining the simples to see if they were dried sufficiently to strip from their stems, powder in the big wooden bowl, and pack away, after they had been well mixed, in the chests that were marked "Strewing," "Farseting Herbes," "Green Wounds," and so on.

Some of the same simples went in different mixtures, I knew. Sage, for instance.

"We couldn't get along without sage, could we, Mother?" I asked, powdering a silvery-green leaf between my fingers.

"Indeed we couldn't! Rosemary, thyme, savoury, fennel,

parsley, and sage make a proper fagot of herbs for the stew pot. Savoury, thyme, and sage are the pudding-grasses for the stuffing of meat and fowl. A brew of sage, alone, is of the greatest help in almost any illness."

"Hyssop, too!" I interrupted. "All by itself, it goes into the chest for 'Green Wounds.' And then, for the 'Strewing Herbes,' we mix balms, mints, lavender, sage again, chamomile, costmary, germander, violets, and hyssop!"

"You remember well, Young Matt!" she praised. "And there's felt-wyrt for coughs and ague-weed for aching joints and—and—what day be this, lad?"

"We've been eleven days in November," I remembered.

She nodded. "Martinmas! The last gentle beauty of summer! Do you know what we would be doing at this time were we back in Scrooby?"

"Powdering simples," I told her, "and packing them in the little wooden chests my Uncle Samuel brought you out of India."

"Oh, no, we wouldn't, my precious widgeon!" she grinned crookedly. "Not on St. Martinmas! We would be getting ready for a great harvest festival—something like the Thanksgiving Day feast you ate with the Corts—and Goodman Matthew, with all the other men of Scrooby, would be killing fatted fowl and salting the meat of cattle for our winter food."

The kitchen door burst open at just that moment and Winover came racing in from the dike, closely followed by Rudi and Kathi. "What do you think," she howled, "the Dutch are going to have *another* feast pretty soon! It's a funny thing *we* don't have good times together—we English folk, I mean!"

"Didn't you *ever* have any St. Nicolas's Day?" Rudi asked sympathetically. "Not even where you came from?"

"*I* didn't, not in Londontown!" Winover told him. "Did you, Young Matt?"

I shook my head. "When is it?" I asked.

"In December."

"Oh, we had that in Scrooby! You mean the Yuletide."

"What did you do?" Kathi wanted to know.

"Oh, we burned the Yule log—and feasted on roast meats and mince pasties. And then we played games around the hearth, like dipping for apples and popping nuts. And then somebody always told stories about the time the King came to Scrooby, and the time the fat Archbishop of York hunted for deer in Nottingham Forest, and the time Margaret, daughter of a King and bride of another King, slept in the Manor House."

"Is that all?" Kathi asked.

"All! Blazes! What more could there be?" I cried.

"But what did *you* do—the children, I mean?"

"St. Nicolas's Day is for the children!" Rudi made haste to explain before we became too confused. "He loved children—good children, that is. *We* have Yuletide too, you know. But first, on December the sixth, we have St. Nicolas's Day, when the good saint himself comes up and down the city looking the children over to see which ones have been good enough to receive a gift at Yuletide."

"Comes up and down the city!" I gasped. "Did you ever see him, Rudi?"

"Oh, sure—every year! He wears a long black cape and a hat like a sugar loaf and he carries a tall, crooked staff. And he has a bag over his shoulder filled with apples and hay."

We had nothing to offer for this astonishing news.

"Every child puts his shoe outside the door," Kathi took up the story while Rudi caught his breath, "and goes to sleep. And during the night, if you have been good, St. Nicolas puts an apple in it. And a gift, too, at our house because we can't wait until Yuletide for ours after we know we are going to get one!"

"Suppose you haven't been good?" Winover asked.

"Hay!"

"Hay!"

"Hay—and no gift!"

"Lud! I wouldn't put my shoe outside the door!" Winover decided promptly. "St. Nicolas might not understand English children. He might think we had sinned when our saint wouldn't, you see."

"Your saint? Who is your saint?" Rudi asked quickly.

Winover choked. "Well, I guess we haven't got any," she confessed. "Unless it would be William Brewster!"

"I wouldn't want to put my shoe out for him!" I cried. She quite agreed. "Neither would I!" she said. "We'd be most sure to get hay. I'm afraid we can't do anything about St. Nicolas's Day!"

She changed her mind, however, and decided to take a chance on the old gentleman in the black cape and sugarloaf hat when Mevrouw Cort invited all of us to the Cort house for St. Nicolas's Eve.

"For all night!" she shouted. "Mevrouw Cort said to tell you that *all* are to come! There will be fun around the fireplace after supper—and then we will all put our shoes outside—and then John, Young Matt, 'Memby, Rudi, Kathi, and I are to sleep in the kitchen on warm mats before the log—and you and Goodman Matthew are to have the spare room. And then in the morning we'll see about the hay and apples!"

"Why—why, that will be wonderful!" My little mother flushed suddenly and sat down upon a stool. "You—will—all have such a merry time——"

"You too, Mother!" I reminded her. But she shook her head. "Not I, Young Matt! Goodman Matthew and I will stay here and wait for you to come back to us in the morning."

"Are you afraid of Bell Alley, Mother?"

"Of course I'm not, widgeon! I—I—well, I think I like my own bed, you see. And, after all, St. Nicolas is for the children. It might embarrass him terribly to find a big shoe like mine on the doorstep. No—Goodman and I will wait. But you are to go, and tell me everything that happens!"

When the time came, I did not want to go and leave her resting on her own bed. I had never seen her there, weary and pale, in the daytime before and it frightened me.

"Nonsense!" she said. "Goodwife Fentry is coming from Bell Alley to spend the night with me, and maybe we'll set our shoes outside, after all, and give old St. Nicolas something to fret about. Lay out plenty of sage on the table and—and—oh, go, lad! Go quickly! Mevrouw Cort will be expecting you!"

For long hours, that wakeful night, I lay on the rug before the warm hearth in the Corts' kitchen, watching the dancing shadows on the wall, caring naught for St. Nicolas and his bag, wishing that I was back in the little cottage on the dike in the wee room that my father had builded next to my mother's sleeping chamber.

But when morning came, I was as excited as the others to

open the door and look upon the miracle of the shoes. John, Winover, Rudi, Kathi, and I—all of us had apples. And each of us had a pair of shining skates with long, upcurved toes. 'Memby had an apple too and, beside it, a Bartholomew baby with golden curls and a feathered bonnet—she was dazed with the glory of it.

I left them, busy with oily cakes and sugar loaves, and blew like a dried leaf across our garden. Goodwife Fentry was bent over a hot brew at one end of the table and my mother was lying on the narrow bed where Winover usually slept, drawn close to the warmth of the blazing fire.

"Happy St. Nicolas's Day, widgeon!" she piped, opening her tired eyes to my horrified stare. "Dump the hay behind the log and we'll both forget it!"

"There was no hay."

"No? I told you St. Nicolas wouldn't know what to make of my shoe if I should set it outside the door! See what he left in it!"

She twiddled a wisp of dried herbs along the linen spread, and as I went to take it from her she caught me by the doublet and drew me to her side. There in the curve of her arm lay something with a tuft of blazing hair, a wrinkled red face, and a balled red fist.

Blazes! Another damp woman child!

I stood like a block of timber. "Come, lad, beam and be proud!" she begged, herself grinning crookedly at my utter amazement. "*I* haven't been prouder since—since the year 1603. You know what happened then, don't you?"

"Aye. The King came to Scrooby."

"He certainly did, lad, *my* king! You, Young Matt! And now we've both got another wee lad to watch over and love."

"Lad!" I burst into words at last. "I thought it was a woman child—a damp one like 'Memby."

"Damp enough, like all wee ones, but a man child like yourself!"

"Not like *me!*" I told her then. "I'm an Over, of the family of Matthew Over, yeoman, of Scrooby, Nottinghamshire, England. And so are Winover and 'Memby. Only Winover is no Brode, like 'Memby and me—and John!"

"God's mercy, lad!" She half raised her pretty head from the bolster to stare at me. "This lad is an Over, too—and a Brode! What did you think?"

"He's Dutch."

"He's as much Scrooby as you are!"

The door banged open just then and Winover, 'Memby, and my Uncle John came into the kitchen on flying feet. Winover was the first to notice the waving balled fist.

"Hi, she *did* it! You did it, Goodwife Orris!" she exclaimed. "You got something to fill our cradle after all! Just wait till I tell Kathi Cort about *this!* Or, wait a bit—" She leaned across the linen spread and looked at the wrinkled red face soberly. "You're sure this *is* our baby, aren't you?" she asked.

"Very sure."

"I'd hate to boast about it, and then make a mistake. Kathi said they were likely to have a baby at their house soon—she's got the cradle all ready. You don't think St. Nicolas got the houses mixed last night, do you?"

"No. This baby belongs to us."

"I believe you—her hair is just like mine."

"It's a man child!" I cried sternly.

"A man—a lad! But look at the hair, Young Matt!"

My mother explained something, then, that I had never

known before. "All the Overs have blazing hair when they are new," she said; "it drops out after a time and brown hair comes in. But the Overs are all red in the beginning. That is how we knew Winover for our very own dear daughter the first time Goodman Matthew and I laid eyes on her lovely strand!"

'Memby crowded to the bedside just then and compared gifts. "Mine—Lunnon baby!" she said. And then, pointing to the one on the bed, she asked: "Who?"

"She means that her doll baby is a Bartholomew baby from Londontown," Winover explained. "Mevrouw Cort told her that St. Nicolas must have been visiting St. Bartholomew's Fair last August in Londontown, and brought the doll baby over to the shop in the Breedestraat just especially for her. She calls it 'Lunnon,' you see, and she wants to know what *your* baby is called?"

My mother shook her head. "He came without a name," she confessed. "I was think of calling him 'Little John.' "

"No!" I cried, even before my Uncle John. "He's not an Austerfield lad—he's Dutch! St. Nicolas——"

"That's it—that's it!" shrilled Winover wildly. "Nicolas! St. Nicolas brought him, so why shouldn't he lend him his name, too? Nicolas is a lovely name—you remember that Nicolas who lived on the Fish Market in Amsterdam, Young Matt?"

I did. I would never forget him. It pleased me to have a Nicolas in my own family. "Nicolas!" I said. Then: "He's a nice baby! John and Rudi and I will take care of him!" And closed my fist about the tiny balled one on the linen cover.

At the proper time, all of us together took the wee lad, wrapped in his best lace petticoats and soft blankets, to Bell

Alley. There he was blessed by Elder Brewster, and christened Nicolas Brode Over.

There were other Pilgrim babies christened in Bell Alley that day, a dozen or more of them, but they were pale, frail, quiet little mites. Not like our Nicolas, who was fat and strong and red and who roared enough to deafen us when Elder Brewster's damp hand was laid upon his brow.

Nicolas was born in 1610. And it was another three years before I visited Bell Alley, save for an hour's worship each Sabbath Day.

The Pilgrims had erected twenty tiny dwellings in the alley up against St. Peter's Church, with a larger dwelling blocking the thoroughfare at the far end. They fancied their English village, as they called it, within the old Dutch city, but the place was chill, sour, dank, and unhealthy, as are all places where the sun never burns.

It may be that some of them regretted the sweet hedgerows of Scrooby, but they dwelt as they must and made no complaint. Bell Alley was conveniently situated for the menfolk, who had found labor about the center of the city as weavers, carders, masons, coopers, cobblers, rope-makers, and the like, and so the women made homes for their families as well as they could. And when they could do no more, were buried in St. Peter's churchyard.

"Jonathan Willet and his mother and his wee sister Nancy slipped away during the past week!" said Goodman Brewster one day, meeting my mother and me in the Breedestraat on our way to the markets along the river Rhine.

"God's mercy!" cried my mother, and stopped to wipe her eyes. "Not Jennie Willet! We'll have no Pilgrims left, William, at this rate! What was it?"

"They took a chill—and were gone in a night."

"The folk in Bell Alley are not ready for any illness—they are weakened by living like bees in a hive. They need the green fields of Scrooby, the blossoming lanes, the hot sun, and the soft loam between their fingers. Thank God I found the little cottage on the Weddesteeg!"

"But—but if all had found cottages on the dikes, Orris, they would have been lost among the Dutch in these three years!" Elder Brewster made answer.

"Better lost among the Dutch than lost in St. Peter's churchyard!"

"We be English folk, Orris, and so must we hold to that belief as long as one of us remains! It may be that you and yours are growing too fond of the Low Country, Goodwife! Your children——"

"My children are fat and healthy. Happy, too!"

"Happily growing as one with the Corts and the Florins and our other good Dutch neighbors! The break will come all the harder for them—if we must move."

"Move? Move away from Leyden, William! Are you trying to warn me against some misfortune?"

"Nothing definite, Orris. Only—only we be Pilgrims, remember! And Pilgrims are wanderers, in search of a home! We have found shelter and safety so far in Leyden, but Leyden is the home of the Dutch, not ours! Well, Young Matt"—he turned to me and closed the conversation with my mother—"it has been a long time since we have seen you in Bell Alley. Walk along back with me for an hour—we shall be alone in the printing shop!"

I looked to my mother and she nodded. "He was only going to the butter market with me," she explained. "You're too much alone these days, William!"

"Aye. Jon has been wed these four years—only sixteen when he went to a dwelling of his own! The children wed young, Orris. And William Bradford lost to me now, since he has taken Dority May beneath his roof. It will be like old days to have Young Matt for an hour."

"How old are you, Young Matt?" he asked, when we were alone, hurrying along the Breedestraat toward Bell Alley. "The years slip by—I seem to forget."

"We are in 1613 now!" I told him. "And I am ten years old. Winover is past twelve, and John is thirteen. Nicolas is close to three, you know!"

"Dear, dear, I should think the time *did* fly! Three years since that fat red lad was brought here for the christening and bellowed as the bulls used to do from the islets in Scrooby Waters. Although I don't suppose you remember anything about that."

Before I could tell him that I remembered *all* about Scrooby Waters, we turned into Bell Alley and entered the printing shop and I forgot all else.

Goodman Brewster, like all the other Scrooby men, had been obliged to find labor of some sort in Leyden, and he, being a man of great learning and wide education, had opened a printing shop. He printed, as I learned much later, pamphlets that set forth the need of men for freedom of mind, body, and soul, and he sent these pamphlets to Londontown and there they came under the notice of the King. And once again the King was fired with a desire to lay violent hands upon the Pilgrims of Scrooby and their leader, William Brewster. But there was no thought of the King in my mind that day when I visited Goodman Brewster in his printing shop in Bell Alley.

I clambered up on a high stool and took the type frame

in my hand. "You said you would show me how to print some day," I reminded him.

He shook his head. "How can you print, lad," he protested, "when you don't reach to the trays yet! I never saw such a lad for remaining squat and thick!"

"The Brodes are like that," I told him contentedly, "all except my mother. She's short but not so very thick. Maybe I could have a wedge of timber atop the stool, to sit on, you know."

He found one and I came within reaching distance of the types. I lifted the longish frame in my pudgy fist and was ready. "Where's Y?" I asked.

We bent above the tray of types. "Yonder, in that small box. But not that way, lad! The types must be set in the frame backward and upside down."

Blazes! "I don't want to make that kind of reading!" I cried indignantly. "I want my father to be proud when he sees how I have printed my name in full. In Amsterdam, I learned to write it—now, in Leyden, I'll print it for him."

"He'll be proud, lad! Once the types are inked and stamped, they appear on the parchment right side up and in the proper order. The letter O is in this box. And U yonder again."

And so, with Elder Brewster's help, spelling laboriously as I toiled, I set up my name in the printer's stick, inked it, and stamped it upon a strip of fair white parchment:

> YOUNG MATT OVER, PILGRIM. SON OF MATTHEW OVER, YEOMAN AND PILGRIM, OF SCROOBY, NOTTINGHAMSHIRE, ENGLAND

Lud! I quivered with the beauty and magic of it. "You take kindly to learning, don't you, lad?" Elder Brewster asked. "A true Brode! I hear that John is making ready to enter the University of Leyden and become a grave scholar."

"No. He's going to build cities with Mijnheer de Key when he's old enough. It won't hurt him to know other things too, he says, just while he's aging."

"And you, Young Matt?"

I grinned crookedly. "All the Brodes aren't scholars like John!" I reminded him. "There's my Uncle Samuel, who takes to the sea, and my mother, who takes to the loam. And Nicolas and I—we——"

"Yes? What of you two?"

"Well, when I grow up I'm going to have a tulip farm with a little brick house and a cow on it, outside the walls in the lowlands. Like Mijnheer Cort's. Were you ever on his tulip farm?"

"No, Young Matt."

"A pity! I'm going to call my tulips 'Pride of Matthew Over,' and Nicolas is going to take care of the cow. That one is crazy about cows!"

Something in Goodman Brewster's tired eyes cut short my prattle. Perhaps the hour was up and the time for my departure long past. I slipped from the stool, abashed. "I'll—I'll be going, now!" I stammered. "My father and John will be coming home to sup. My mother's making hutch-putch with flour balls atop, 'cause John wanted it. She makes pretty good hutch-putch now—she puts more things in it!"

"I'll walk along to the Weddesteeg with thee, lad!" he told me then. "It may be there will be an extra trencher on the table for me, tonight."

10

CITIZEN OF LEYDEN

THAT evening, Elder Brewster sat at the head of our board and prayed for a blessing on our house ere he supped. He had, I remember, two trenchers filled with hutch-putch and declared that he had never tasted a more pleasing concoction.

"The English and the Dutch *do* make a pleasing concoction, when handily blended!" my mother told him, merrily. "Nothing is more beautiful than my Dutch tulips and English pansies, nothing more tasty than my Dutch fish, flesh, and wild fowl brewed with English simples! That mugwort, thyme, and savoury, William, that sage, sorrel, rosemary, and parsley all came from Elderblow Lane!"

The light was still dim outside when we were finished with eating, and there was the silver thread of a new moon reflected in the quiet waters of the Rhine, so we went through my mother's garden and seated ourselves upon the grassy bank of the dike under the great wings of Rembrandt's mill and talked quietly together.

It was very beautiful. There was no song of the nightingale across the water, no call of cuckoos from meadow to meadow, but there was a sweetness from the flowery fields outside the walls, and there were the tulips!

"It isn't Scrooby Waters," I said to myself. "It is much, much better!"

My mother spoke then, softly, of Jonathan Willet and his sweet mother and his little sister Nancy, and my father shook his head sympathetically. "Life is too hard for our Pilgrims," he said. "And their way of living in Bell Alley too unhealthy, William! Orris was right when she insisted upon dwelling in the sun, on the Weddesteeg."

"Goodwife Orris has that wisdom that is above rubies!"

"There is naught that is precious that Orris lacks!"

"Good-man Mat-thew!" warned my mother earnestly, and nodded toward the ring of watchful eyes. "The children!"

" 'Twill not harm the children, Orris, to hear their mother praised!" Goodman Brewster laughed heartily. "And the sight of her bashful beauty will be something for them to remember!"

"Foosh!" She pushed 'Memby's rapt little face away with her elbow and warned the lass to sit up and mind the fresh grass stains on her apron. And then, her ear caught with the last few words of Elder Brewster's speech, she forgot the children and turned toward him with a sharp cry.

"What—what did you say, William?" she asked. "That about the few—the few months——"

"I said that every lovely thing in this kind land should be remembered by the children, for their comfort in years to come. This land that, for a few peaceful months at least, gave us refuge——"

"We have been here almost four years, William!"

"And may be here another four years. But in the end we must wander further. This land can never be our home, Orris—we be English Pilgrims."

"For the Over family it is home!" she told him firmly. "We have rooted into this soil. My garden is here; my gooseberry bushes have begun to bear; my children speak this tongue and are receiving education here—one of them, even, is a Lowlander by right of birth! The Overs bide in Leyden!"

"Matthew——"

"Aye. This be our country now, William!" my father told him in a firm voice. "At the end of the month I go to the Stadthuis with Mijnheer Cort and take the oath of citizenship."

"Young Matt," cried Goodman Brewster, "show thy father the strip of paper that was printed in my dwelling—the paper that was to make him so proud!"

> YOUNG MATT OVER, PILGRIM. SON OF MATTHEW OVER, YEOMAN AND PILGRIM, OF SCROOBY, NOTTINGHAMSHIRE, ENGLAND

He read it through, carefully. And then he took a bit of carpenter's crayon from his breeches pocket and underneath the printing he wrote: CITIZENS OF LEYDEN, BOTH.

And so we knew that my father, of his own accord, had given up his pride of birth and would be born anew, a citizen of another country. It was a solemn thing, we felt, to disown the land of one's birth—to weigh it in the balance and find it utterly lacking in all value.

Elder Brewster made one last attempt at influencing my father. "There is talk in Bell Alley," he said, "of returning to Scrooby, Matthew."

"The Over family will never return to Scrooby!" my father told him, bluntly.

And not long after that, Goodman Brewster rose and wrapped his long black cape about his shoulders and went sorrowfully homeward. And it was many a month before I saw him again.

On one day, my mother laid out my father's new fustians on the bed in her sleeping chamber, new serge doublets and breeches for the Dutch lad Nicolas alongside, fresh array for John and me in our chamber, and stiffened, lace-edged coifs, neckerchiefs, and aprons for Winover, 'Memby, and herself all over the dwelling.

We had basins and buckets of hot water, scouring brushes and thick, soft toweling in the scullery and then, one by one, we bedecked ourselves in glory that surpassed any lily of the field and sat down, primly, in the garden to await the others.

We were to accompany my father to the Stadthuis where he was to "be born anew, a citizen of Leyden." I hoped that he wouldn't become too much like Mijnheer Cort—too short, too red, too round, like the cheeses in the butter market. I expected that he would wear flapping blue breeches, a tight coat with rows of silver buttons running up to either shoulder, a hard, round black hat, and wooden shoes. He was in the habit of dressing like the other Lowlanders when he was at work in the lumber yard; but always, even there, it was easily seen that he was of different birth.

Now, if he was to "be born anew"——

He came out of the cottage and, reaching for a hand of Winover and 'Memby, led the way out of our garden to the Weddesteeg. My mother followed with the Dutch lad and myself on either side. John was to meet us somewhere near the Stadthuis. And we were to call for the Corts as we passed by the lumber yard.

Having allowed ourselves plenty of time, we walked by way of the river bank so that Mevrouw Cort could enjoy herself pinching all the vegetables and fruits in the different markets and punching the fish, flesh, and fowl to judge of the ripeness or richness, while my mother reveled in the beauty and sweetness of the flower market.

I was looking forward to the seafood market myself, but that happened to be nearest the Stadthuis and John was waiting for us there. So we followed him inside at once, inside this newest and most magnificent of Mijnheer de Key's fine buildings.

And there, dropping Winover's hand but not being able to shake loose from 'Memby, my father stood forth upon command and lifting his free hand proclaimed aloud his desire to become a member of the guild and he spoke the oath of citizenship in firm, clear tones. "I vow obedience to the Sovereign Estates of Holland and the Burgomasters of this municipality."

So was he "born anew, a citizen of Leyden." And I rejoiced mightily to discover no change in his appearance whatsoever. He was still as tall and brawny, his shoulders as broad and powerful, he was still as stalwart and unconquerable as when he was Matthew Over, yeoman, of Scrooby.

We left the Stadthuis at once and went back to the lumber yard by way of the Breedestraat, the shortest way, not through the markets this time, because we knew that Mijnheer Cort's flatboat was waiting for us, to take us all to the tulip farm for one long, glorious holiday.

"This is an important day, Mattje, dear friend!" he shouted. "We will make it a day that shall not soon be forgotten!"

My mother fetched a basket of fresh barley loaves, new cheese, and jam pots in plenty from our kitchen; Mevrouw kept bringing out meat puddings of one kind and another, and oily cakes in stacks.

And so we drifted happily away from the lumber yard, along a silver ribbon of quiet water, to the tulip farm in the lowland outside the city walls. And there we helped Mijnheer Cort plant bulbs in rich black muck, we frolicked in the hot sunshine, we ate and ate and ate sitting outside on the turf where we chose, and one by one, each in turn, we tried to lure Nicolas away from Little Darling, the Corts' gentle brown cow. But it couldn't be done. He spent the day nestled as close to her velvety nose as he could get, feeding her greenstuff blade by blade.

"Let him do it!" cried Mijnheer Cort at last. "It is his holiday, too! He should spend it in the way that makes him happiest. Remembering Little Darling and the tulip farm, he will never forget this day that makes of his father an honored citizen of our city, that makes his family and the Corts one!"

And then, reaching for still another oily cake, he looked quizzically at my father and said: "Well, Mattje, *waar zijn wij nu?* As good a time now as another to take stock and make plans for a new life."

"New life?" cried my mother and shoved at her coif. "What do you mean by that, Thoma?"

"Why, Mattje here is a partner in a fine business, he has plenty of money coming in and will make much more, he is a citizen of Leyden—he won't want to live in a tiny cottage on a dike much longer. A man has his pride, you know! The Overs could even begin looking for a fine dwelling on the Hoogewoerd."

"Goodman Matthew."

"Don't fret, Orris!" my father chuckled and helped himself to more meat pudding. "We aren't planning to move tonight."

"Move? We are *never* to move, Goodman! My honeysuckles are just beginning to cover the chimney—and the catmint, costmary, borage, and rue. Why, Thoma Cort, a garden isn't to be left because a man gets a few more coins in his breeches pocket! I would be sorry Matthew ever became a citizen of Leyden if it meant leaving the dike—and the great wings of Rembrandt's mill turning above my head—and Neltje Cort just around the corner."

"Hush!" Mevrouw Cort reached out and patted her little knee comfortingly. "Thoma must have his joke! Of course you are to bide on the Weddesteeg. We'll all grow old together and ripen like purple plums on the same tree."

"Children and all, I suppose!" chuckled Mijnheer Cort.

"The children? Oh, they'll sprout wings and fly away, some time."

"*I* shan't!" I howled indignantly. "I shall dwell right here, and have a tulip farm, and call my tulips 'Pride of Matthew Over'!"

"And I'll dwell alongside!" roared Rudi, choking on a buttered roll but making himself understood, for all that. "I shall marry Winover and——"

"Why, you crazy lad!" Winover broke the bubble of his dream at once. "No such thing! I am to wed with John and help him build cities!"

This was news to John, it was plain to be seen. Unpleasing news. He got to his feet at once and cried: "I shall never wed! But I shall leave this city and dwell far away! This city is old—somebody else has builded it. I shall seek a—a—a wilderness, it may be, some place that is so new that it will be in need of skilled and willing hands, and there I shall erect dwellings and lay out markets and fine gardens—and a stadthuis and school and church and—" He waved his arms as if to say: "Oh, what is the use of spreading dreams before the eyes of those who will not see!" and went inside the little brick house and sat there alone, thinking his own thoughts, until it was time to climb aboard the flatboat and pole slowly back to the Weddesteeg.

And that night, just past the middle of the night, Mijnheer Cort came running along the dike, pounding on the door of our cottage, calling for my mother to come quickly to Mevrouw Cort, who was ill.

I crawled out from under my plaid and crept through the darkness to the scullery door and would have helped her select herbs from the wooden chests and the dried bunches tied to the rafters, but she sent me back to my sleeping chamber with curt words and was gone in a flash.

The next morning there was a damp woman child in the Corts' cradle!

Rudi told me about it at daybreak. "Thunder weather!" he cried. "My father said we should all never forget the day that made your father a citizen of Leyden—and I bet you we won't! We've got a baby to remember it by!"

"Kathi said you were going to fill your cradle away back when Nicolas came to us."

"What of it? We have *now,* haven't we? And a good thing we waited—we might have got a boy like Nicolas, then! A maid is better!"

That is when I learned that this newcomer was another damp woman child. "A maid!" I howled. "Blazes! A maid's not half as good as a lad!"

"When she's beautiful like ours? You're crazy, Young Matt! Nothing ever was so beautiful as our baby! She's only so big, and she has hair like new butter and eyes like pansies, and Mother says she should have the loveliest name in all the world. So what do you think it is?"

I couldn't guess, not having made a study of maids' names.

"Orrje."

"Orrje? Orrje! Do you mean Orris, Rudi Cort?" I shouted angrily. "Why, you can't have that name! That belongs to my mother!"

"Your mother gave it to our baby, herself! She said: 'Do you mean that you would like the little angel to be named after *me,* Neltje?' And when my mother said: 'Yes, because it is the name of the sweetest woman in the world!' why, then your mother said: 'Now we *are* one family, Neltje, and we shall never be separated!' And then she snuggled the baby into her neck and said: 'Orrje, Orrje!' And then I got out from behind the loom and came to tell you about it!"

During the next six years I was too busy putting learning inside my skull and healthy skin over my suddenly shooting bones to think of much else. For I was beginning to grow! God be thanked, I was on the way to becoming an Over, after all! By the time I was sixteen—in the year 1619, that is—I could look down upon my Uncle John, who was three years the better of me in age, and upon Winover, who was more than two years older, and upon my mother, who was like to be left behind in a class with 'Memby and Nicolas, the one eleven years of age and the other going on ten.

"Stand against my thigh!" said my father in June of that year 1619. And when I did, my head whacked his chin and he roared his delight. But my mother feigned grief.

"You are leaving me, Young Matt!" she sighed. "The Brode has been all weeded out of you. But since you have shot so far into the skies, go on a bit more and overtop your father and so put an end to his sinful boasting!"

And he clapped my shoulder and vowed that she was mistaken in her judgment and maintained that it would be a proud day when he could walk along the Breedestraat and look up to a son of his own.

One day that same year—close to St. Nicolas's Day, I remember—I was idling along the tree-shaded street looking at the shops. The leaves were fallen and the bookstalls closed until balmier weather, but the shops were filled with quaint and lovely oddments from the colonies.

A ring of ivory elephants, cleverly carved, caught and held my eye. Each beastie had tight hold of the tail of his neighbor just ahead—there were seven in all—and when they were linked together the whole ring stood firmly upright. But unclasp one trunk from the tail ahead, and the whole ring collapsed.

I bought the trinket for my mother and she was as excited over it as Orrje Cort with a new moppet. She linked the ivory beasties and unlinked them, studying them. Finally she linked them firmly and stood them upon the shelf over the hearth.

"Seven!" she said. "Just like the Over family! And, like the Over family, they are strong to face the world when all are together. But let one fall away, and the whole becomes a worthless mess!"

When my father journeyed to Amsterdam to see about the lading of some teakwood from the Orient, she unlinked the largest elephant and let the whole seven fall where they would until his safe return.

On the day that John, who was working now for Mijnheer

de Key, departed for Delfshaven to sketch the carvings on a new church, the third elephant came unhooked and the ring did not stand upright again until John came through the garden calling loudly for hutch-putch.

When Nicolas fell ill of the fever, the littlest elephant tumbled flat on the shelf and all the rest atop him.

And so, when I swung through the garden on my way home from school one day and on into the kitchen and saw the ivory ring totter this way and that before my very eyes, I was relieved when it tipped over upon the shelf without falling apart. It was shaken from the draft of the open door, I knew, but my mother would have thought it a bad omen and would have turned pale as she did at the sound of plunging hoofbeats along the Great North Road years before. I crossed the kitchen to right the trinket just as Goodwife Fentry came in from the garden and my mother from the scullery.

"Oh, Young Matt—the elephants!" she cried, her hand on her heart.

"I know. I tipped them, banging the door," I told her. And then, knowing how well Goodwife Fentry disliked hearing Dutch words on English lips, I winked mischievously at my mother and cried over my shoulder: *"Goeden dag,* Mevrouw Fentry!"

"Odds blood, I never thought to see the lad so gay!" she boomed and made a wry face enough. "I suppose it is on account of finishing with schooling today. I remember the time, my lad, when you boasted that the Overs desired learning, and your first wish was to write your name in full and read a psalm with your betters!"

"Book learning is all right," I told her gaily, "when you are a titmouse. But when you get muscles like mine you feel the need to use them. My labor is bespoke from tomorrow's morn, did you know it?"

"No!" Goodwife Fentry rested her empty basket on the kitchen table and listened to me with more respect than usual. "A man already! What are you going to do—handle lumber with your father?"

"Not me! I am to manage Mijnheer Cort's tulip farm! I could dance a rigadoon if it wouldn't shock you."

"It would! Remember, if you please, that you are still a Pilgrim, though 'tis hard to believe when your tongue wags in Dutch! What do you know about tulips?"

"Everything. Tomorrow I heap my fustians and other small gear on a flatboat and——"

"Oh, Young Matt!" piped my mother distractedly. "*Now* I know why the elephants fell!"

I howled with laughter. "For *me?*" I shouted. "Well, they didn't come unlinked, anyway, so maybe *all* the Overs are going away in my flatboat together on the morrow."

"God bless children for their light hearts—and their faith in the morrow!" Goodwife Fentry sniffed captiously. "I wish *I* could see the day that is before us as clearly as they can."

"Is your stomach troubling you again, Submit?" my mother asked gently.

"No. But I expect it to be. I've been dreaming again."

"Oh, then you *have* been eating cheese!"

"I have not been eating cheese, and my stomach has nothing to do with it! Not yet, anyway! I've brought my basket for some simples—to make a brew."

"What is the trouble, Submit?"

"Dreams. For three nights running—dreams of wet sheets flapping on a line and myself wandering among their wetness. It's a miserable dream, Orris, but it never failed me yet! It means a move!"

"Do you mean a move like—like from Bell Alley to Nun's Lane? You—you *can't* mean a—a——"

"I mean a move onward, my dear lass! After all, we *are* Pilgrims, in search of a home of our own!"

"Don't joke, Submit!" My mother crooked her elbow and brushed the fluttering cloud of curls from her eyes. "We've been twelve years in Leyden and we could have no better home anywhere on earth! If William Brewster is planning something, and you are trying to break it to me gently, *don't!* Speak out and tell me the worst first!"

"I've told you the worst!" Goodwife Fentry insisted. "Dreams! Dear God, *water* dreams! When Oliver and I moved from Bawtry to Scrooby, there were the dreams of wet, flapping sheets. And there was Scrooby Water! When we moved from Scrooby to the Low Country, sheets and the Ryton! Not to mention the open sea! When we moved from Amsterdam to Leyden, sheets again! And try to get anywhere around this country without tangling with canals! So now, when the sheets begin to flap again of a night, I know that the time has come to prepare that brew of bayberry and hemlock barks, ginger root, red pepper, cloves, and whatnot. And as for William Brewster, he isn't even in Leyden so far as I know!"

"Where is he?"

"Some say in Londontown."

"In Londontown—after that last pamphlet on the subject of free souls and freedom in thought and speech as well as in worship? Why, that would be madness, Submit! The Stuart would have him under his heel and crush him like a cockchafer in the turf."

"William will need to be caught before he can be crushed. And, anyway, the gentry in Londontown have summut more than Scrooby folk to worry them now! There's a war boiling hereabouts, you know!"

I drew up a stool and sat down by the table. This began to interest me. War! I wouldn't want any war to come rolling over our muck lands just as the tulips were set.

"But this war is in Germany, Goodwife!" I pointed out. "It has been going on for more than two years with no harm to us. There is always strife among those German princes!"

"When folk get to fighting, lad, they don't give heed to what or whose land they cover!" she told me solemnly. "They brawl all over the place! This war did start between Protestant and Catholic princes in the eastern part of Germany, but now they are clawing and clinching and bumping along westward. Sweden and France are drawn into the mess already, and the Dutch——"

"But, God's mercy, Submit!" my mother wailed. "The Dutch only finished one war, that with the Spanish people, in 1609, wasn't it? It was while we were in Amsterdam, I remember! And they had been going at that for more than thirty-seven years."

"This is a *new* war, Orris, and they are getting interested all over again!"

"Don't the gentry ever get enough of death and destruction? Can't they live for a time in peace and dig in the loam and make the world beautiful, like us who——"

"Who do you mean by 'us'?" Goodwife Fentry sniffed in disgust. "England is getting into this brawl, too!"

"Into a war that is between German princes? Why should they?"

Goodwife Fentry nodded to me and I went on with the tale as I had heard it along the Breedestraat only that day. "It was a Catholic prince that lost his job as ruler in some little nook in the eastern part of Germany, and the Protestant prince who took his place turns out to be son-in-law to James the First of England! So that is how England is mixing into the stew."

"Son-in-law to the Stuart?"

"The Stuart himself!" Goodwife Fentry replied with a bang of her fist on the table that set the basket to rustling. "See what a chance that sour one has to enjoy himself, now? Lud, if he ever stumbled onto that long nose of his, he'd bleed vinegar instead of blood, that one! They say along the Breedestraat that this war may last from twenty-five to thirty years and draw all the Old World into its fire before the thing is ended. Well, I hope it will keep that lean Stuart's mind off the Scrooby Pilgrims, anyway! You'd think he'd be busy enough with more important things."

The kitchen door banged open, just then, and the elephants rocked and tipped again as my Uncle John blew into the room. "*Ik geloof dat het te laat is!*" he shouted across his shoulder.

And my father, who was following at his heels, agreed. "Aye, lad, too late—too late to keep the secret of our hiding place any longer!"

"What are you talking about, Matthew Over?" boomed Goodwife Fentry. "And hold to the English tongue if you are able!"

"The King's Men have discovered Bell Alley!"

"The—the *King's Men!* Do you mean——"

"Aye. The same, Submit! The ones we used to listen for along the Great North Road."

"But here—in Leyden! Why, it's Scrooby all over again, after twelve years! William Brewster fled no one knows where nor why, and the King's Men lighting on us as pleasantly as a bee in the ear! And now, I suppose, having discovered our hiding place, we can expect to see them every day or so. Can't the Dutch protect us?"

"They have given us refuge. The quarrels of the English among the English are no concern of theirs, just so long as no law of this city be broken." My father shook his great head and sighed. "The King's Men have laid William's home waste. They have broken and scattered all his printing presses, types, and forms. But, having missed William himself, they are content with what they have done for this day, at least, and have blown out to sea again."

My mother trembled and turned white as the pearly snowberry. "We—we are still too near to Londontown, Matthew!" she sighed.

"Was there any other damage done to Bell Alley?" Goodwife Fentry asked suddenly.

"Much! The King's Men tramped through all the dwellings."

"Well, dear heaven, and my kitchen and steps newly scoured!"

Winover tumbled in from the garden, breathless.

"Goodwife Orris!" she gasped. "Such awful things—down in Bell Alley——"

"We know, dear."

"And Elder Brewster told me to tell you to come."

"William Brewster told you! Why, he's in Londontown, child!"

"He just called to me while I was crossing the Breedestraat."

"The man's a flea!" boomed Goodwife Fentry above all our voices. "Nobody but a flea could make the hops that one does! Where did he come from? The regular packet from Amsterdam is not due these three hours!"

"He didn't come on the packet," Winover explained eagerly. "Kathi and I saw him come. It was a big craft, the kind that sails the open seas, and it was poking its slow way up the river, when it drew up to a flatboat and a man climbed down a ladder into the flatboat and was poled ashore. And it was Elder Brewster!"

"Well, God save us all! And you saw him later in the Breedestraat?"

"*Ja.* And he said to tell all the Pilgrims to come to the Big House in Bell Alley at once. That means *all* of us, doesn't it? Only not Nicolas."

"Why not Nicolas?" asked that one for himself, coming in with a rush and throwing his schoolbag on the settle by the hearth. "I heard what you said, Winover!"

"You're Dutch, Nicolas."

"I am not!" The lad shrieked a hot denial. "I'm just as much Pilgrim as you—or 'Memby—or Young Matt!"

"You're as Dutch as oily cakes!" Winover told him calmly. "Run out on the dike and bide with Harmensz at the mill until we come back from Bell Alley!"

However, when we closed the door of the little cottage and went through the garden and out the gate to the Wed-desteeg, my father, my mother, and Goodwife Fentry led the way, and following them came Winover, John, and I. Bringing up the rear were 'Memby and Nicolas, hand in hand.

We took the path alongside the canal to Nun's Lane, and from there we crossed to Bell Alley, and so down the full length of that narrow thoroughfare to the Big House, which closed the far end.

The door was open; the room where we met on the Sabbath Day to worship with Goodman Brewster was filled to overflowing and it buzzed like bees on a sugar loaf.

And standing in the middle of the room, his face to the door, was my Uncle Samuel Brode!

11

"MAYFLOWER–SPEEDWELL! BLOSSOMS!"

"WELL, Samuel," shouted Goodwife Fentry, seeing him as soon as my father and myself, who were the tallest in the room, "what broth hath the Devil brewed for our supping this time?"

"A potful!" he told her at once. "Hatred, war, famine, pestilence, and savagery of one kind and another. Leyden is no longer a safe refuge for the Scrooby folk!"

"You aren't coming here, after so many years, to upset us all again, are you, Samuel Brode?" a rat-like squeak made itself heard. "Just when we are beginning to learn how to deal with these foreigners."

It was James Billing, who had a small odds-and-ends shop in Greenhouse Lane beside the canal, as he once had a shop beside the Great North Road on Scrooby Common.

Before Goodwife Fentry could find words for the blast of rage that parted her lips, 'Lissy Kerry's coral head came between her and the weasel-eyed little man. "I'm ashamed of the drop of English blood in your veins, James Billing!" she cried. "And I welcome the chance to tell you so to your face! The tricks you have used in dealing with these kindly friends——"

"Business is business, my good woman."

"Don't 'good woman' me, please!" she begged. "I could bite you gladly, if I had any taste for worms! Mevrouw

Florin is a friend of mine, I wish to tell you, and I suppose you haven't forgotten the rush-bottomed stool you sold her last week!"

"What about the rush-bottomed stool?" Goodwife Fentry asked boldly. "Mevrouw Florin is a friend of mine, too! I heard she was injured. Did James Billing have anything to do with it, 'Lissy?"

"Everything! He sold her the stool."

"Did I make her buy it?" James Billing squeaked wildly. "Did I? Did I? She came into the shop and chose it out of all."

"And the first time she sat on it," continued Goodwife Kerry, fixing the little man with a cold stare, "she went through the seat to the tiles with her knees slapping her chin. If a leg is broken—and well it may be!—there won't be a whole bone left in James Billing's head this time tomorrow! Herman Florin is a slow man, but exceedingly thorough. He went over that rush-bottomed seat carefully, inch by inch, until he found the place where it had been patched with a bit of reed—and he took the thing to the guild hall to register a complaint. There's talk now of closing a certain shop in Greenhouse Lane, James Billing, in case you haven't heard."

"Well, let's hope they keep it open until we leave Leyden!" Goodwife Fentry's voice boomed out above all others. "I'm ashamed of the man, of hearing him called English and a Pilgrim! He's no Pilgrim—he's a beetle!"

"I'll not be left behind!" screamed James Billing frantically. "You can't do it to me! My lot is cast with the good folk of Scrooby. Where they go, I go!"

"Good folk of Scrooby—huh! The gentle folk, the soft-hearted fools, you mean! They don't flog you away from their skirts as they should, and so you hide behind them—and pick their pockets while they are shielding you from the Dutch."

"Submit—'Lissy—friends!" my Uncle Samuel interrupted the murmur that began to go about the room. "We'll be able to shield nobody from danger very soon; Leyden is not going to be a safe place for any Scrooby Pilgrim! We're hidden here like a bean in the pod, but now the pod is like to burst and cast us forth."

"What's wrong now?"

"War! It draws nearer and nearer to this land. A war that has naught to do with us and a land that is not ours! More than that, we have come again to the attention of the gentry in Londontown."

"God's mercy, that alone is excuse enough for moving!" somebody cried. "But where can we go?"

My Uncle John stood forth then, and I was proud to see the way all heads turned toward the fine young man he had become. "My brother speaks the truth!" he said soberly. "This land is not ours—as yet, we have no home! We left Scrooby to find a home and to find freedom. Really to own and possess a home, one must build it oneself upon land that is truly owned—not merely loaned for a space of time. We have found naught but a refuge in Leyden in a land that is possessed by the Dutch. We have only enjoyed the freedom that was found here—the freedom that the Dutch had fought for. Freedom cannot be reached for like that, grasped from another's hand! Freedom must be earned; it must first be understood and then fought for. It must be forever guarded, lest it slip away. It is the most precious thing in life. Now, what I am trying to say is just this. We of Scrooby must find some unclaimed part of God's earth, there to build homes that shall belong to us alone. Cities, too, in time. And with the homes, we must build laws that shall govern us; we must understand what freedom we desire—freedom of worship, of speech, of thought, in government—and we must be willing to fight and die for that freedom! We have had enough of wandering as Pilgrims—let us cease looking about other cities for a safe, quiet corner in which to hide—let us go forth and build ourselves a home, a country, a way of life that shall be founded on freedom!"

"God love us, how the boys are growing up!" exclaimed Goodwife Fentry almost before John was finished. "And the sense that swells their skulls! I'd rather be English in an English colony than English in a Dutch city, at that! But where——"

"You just said where, Submit!" my Uncle Samuel told her. "In an English colony."

"You—you—you don't mean across the seas, do you, Samuel Brode?"

"Aye."

"In the New World?"

"We must have a new world, for what we have in mind!"

"But—God help us—there be savages there!" whined James Billing and wrung his hands.

"There be savages in Leyden!" Goodwife Fentry told him coldly. "I make no doubt that would be the judgment of Herman Florin. When do we go, Samuel?"

And then, remembering something, she turned and cried to my mother above all the heads: "*Now* I know what those dreams meant, Orris! Didn't I tell you those flapping sheets meant a move—and—and water! Heaven help me, the ocean! I'll need more of those simples, Orris; the brew will have to be twice as strong!"

"William! William Brewster!" Goodman Hughes made

himself heard after a time. "This that has come upon us with such a shock—after what we have seen and endured in Bell Alley already today—must have been well considered by you before you called us to this meeting. If you and Samuel have any plans, tell them to us! We but waste time, going on as we are now doing."

"True enough!" shouted Goodman Roberts. "Are we *all* to leave for the New World, all who now dwell in Bell Alley as well as those who have scattered about the city and those who still bide in Amsterdam? How about it?"

"None are to go," Elder Brewster told us quietly, "but those who volunteer. No persuasion is to be exerted. The undertaking will be a difficult one—only the young and strong will be useful at the start. Later, after the way has been prepared, all who care to join us will be welcomed."

"Who is to choose those who are to go and those who are to remain?"

"The choice is left to each and all of you. You will meet here at the same time tomorrow and tell us of your decision."

"You will stay, William!" somebody interrupted kindly. "You are neither young—nor strong."

"I have watched over this congregation in Scrooby," Elder Brewster replied simply, "and in Amsterdam, and in Leyden. I shall watch over you in the New World!"

My Uncle Samuel stood up then for a last word, as the crowd began to surge toward the door. "Two boats are being prepared!" he shouted. "They will be at Delfshaven some time next week. The *Mayflower* and the *Speedwell.*"

"*Mayflower—Speedwell!* Blossoms!" Goodwife Fentry whirled about and glared at my uncle indignantly. "I would rather hear stauncher names on the craft that are to bear *me* across the waves, my lad!"

"These be staunch craft, Submit! At least, one is! To be frank with you, the smaller craft—the *Speedwell*—has had much to bear in the way of criticism. But I am certain it is only a question of handling. If the *Speedwell* be not over-masted—well, since the rumor is being whispered about the waterfront, I shall elect to go by way of the smaller boat and leave my place on the *Mayflower* for somebody else."

"I thought the New World was pretty well claimed by this time," Goodman Willet, who had kept silence heretofore, spoke suddenly, and most of us stood still to listen. "All of the Old World has reached a hand across the waves to grab a fistful of land, it seems to me. Dutch Colony, English Colony, Swede, French, Spanish——"

"There is no limit to the unclaimed soil!" My uncle answered with certainty. "I cruised along a somewhat northerly coast once with Sir Raleigh and I do promise you that the place is as it fell from God's hand! It is unchanged since the beginning of time—and is a fair spot withal. Sassafras root was growing there in abundance. We took a cargo of it back to England with us and it was sold at great profit. Farther to the south along that coast, there is a colony named in honor of the Virgin Queen—Virginia."

"English?"

"Aye. But they would be friendly. It might be better for us to locate near our own kind, since, when we go to the New World, it will have to be without a charter from the King, without the help or blessing of that lean ruler in Londontown. If we should be in need of protection——"

"What protection could we need, once we were freed from the gentry of Londontown?"

"What's to pay for the craft, the *Mayflower* and the

Speedwell, Samuel? We can look to no help from the King in that respect, either!"

"No. Some of the money will have to be borrowed in Londontown—William Brewster has already attended to that. When the craft return from the New World they will both be laden with sufficient staves (and for that duty must we see that a proper cooper is taken along!) and sufficient sassafras root (and for that *we* must be responsible!) to repay the loan. The rest of the money must be donated by the congregation here in Leyden."

"God's mercy, Samuel! Where shall *we* get money?"

"From every nook and cranny! From the sale of your gold ring and necklace, from the sale of your lace-edged linens. From wherever a penny can be scraped. Many a mickle makes a muckle, you know."

We drifted out of the Big House then. Out of Bell Alley, too. We crossed the Breedestraat and returned to the Weddesteeg by way of Nun's Lane and the bank of the quiet canal. But my mother had nothing to say until we were well within the arms of her garden of spicy simples.

Not then, even, until John said: "Well, Matthew, this doesn't concern you, being a citizen of Leyden, but——"

"I shall always be an Englishman, John!" my father replied gently. "That much I have learned today."

"But, Matthew, you wouldn't leave this home on the dike for the New World! After all, Orris has her garden rooted deep into this soil."

"I have pulled up one garden!" my mother cried shrilly. I had never heard her lilting voice like that before. "What is done once can be done again!"

"But, Orris, you were twelve years younger then! And the King's Men——"

"Don't 'but' so much, my lad!" his sister told him sharply. "And just as much can be said for the King's Men today as then! You said, yourself, that a home must be builded on one's own land; that an English bean can't hide in a Dutch pod forever. That freedom must be won and fought for, not accepted and enjoyed from another's hand."

"But that doesn't apply to you, Orris! The Over family is Dutch now."

"Don't be silly, John Brode! The Over family is Scrooby! When Scrooby is in need, the Over family spends what it has to give aid. Whether it be Matthew Over's mighty strength, or Orris Over's skill with healing herbs, or—or——"

Turning to tread softly through the purple lavenders and silvery artemisia, she caught sight of my face and, reading it correctly, as always, she sang:

"Come, Master Hugo Chillingsworth,
A grin, sir! What's the harm,
With all the rest we leave behind,
To leave a tulip farm?"

"But tomorrow I was to——"

"I know. And tomorrow I was to wash my new fustian in the canal with Neltje Cort! But, you won't, and *I* won't, my lad! Do you remember when we left Scrooby—about the gooseberry jam?"

"Aye."

"Empty out the scullery this afternoon and take all the jam pots around the corner to the Corts! What else did you do, that day?"

"Collected memories."

"Dear God, I'll not ask you to do that again! I mean, when you came back to Elderblow Lane."

"Helped get down the Bowl off the peg by the door."

"Correct! Get it down now, of your own strength, you strapping giant!"

She threw the kitchen door wide open; there was a tinkle, and a soft cry. "Oh, Matthew—oh, Young Matt—oh, everybody!" she moaned. "Look at the elephants! Down in a heap—and all fallen apart!"

That evening, while Winover was setting forth a meal of fresh cheese, meat pudding, rye bread, and stewed plums, Mijnheer Cort stormed into the kitchen. And behind him trailed Rudi, Kathi, Orrje, Mevrouw Cort, and Harmensz Rembrandt.

"What's this I hear, Mattje?" Mijnheer Cort puffed and grew red in the face and almost lost his voice entirely. "Going to leave Leyden? You? But you are a citizen."

"I'm an Englishman, Thoma!"

"Nonsense! Just as we are getting out the lumber for Mijnheer de Key's new building in the Breedestraat——"

"I know. I know."

"And just when Young Matt was to take over the sweet little tulip farm!"

"Don't make it any harder, kind friend!"

"But why, Mattje, why?"

"My people are in trouble. They have need of my strength and Young Matt's youth."

"I heard what happened in Bell Alley today, and was sick for you in my heart. But I did not think it would drive you from your home."

"To find another one, Thoma, where our family may stay! There will be no peace for us here, now that the English King has found us out!"

"Curses on that one, Mattje!" he cried. And went with my father into my small sleeping chamber, where there was quiet, to talk earnestly on business matters and bring to an end the partnership of Cort & Over.

Mevrouw Cort wept with my mother and brought her as a farewell gift twelve tulip bulbs that had been bred on the Cort farm, very precious and costly bulbs that had, as yet, no name.

"Call them 'Remember Leyden,' " she begged. And then she gave her a small, intricately carven ivory box from China to keep her pretties in. To Winover, and 'Memby also, she gave lace coifs as delicate as a spider's frosted web. For the Dutch lad there was a brown cow filled with sweetmeats, and for me a knife, very large and sharp. "To skin a deer—or a savage with!" she said with twinkling eyes.

Harmensz went back to the mill when he saw the gifts. But he soon returned and gave 'Memby a little picture that he had painted himself. It was of our garden. And it showed, too, a bit of the tiny cottage shadowed by the great wings of the Rembrandts' mill. My mother wrapped her head in her apron when she saw it, and disappeared into the scullery with a bang of the door against her heels.

Mevrouw Cort led her brood away then, taking Harmensz with her. "I know how she feels," she explained, "and we will add no more sadness to the hour of parting. Tell her that we will return in the morning for a last word when the sun is shining and the day is at its beginning. There is less time for thoughts then!"

My mother came out of the scullery with her spade when

they were gone. "There's a bright moon over the river tonight," she said, as though nothing more was troubling her attention than the simples in the borders. "We might as well start digging, Winover! I know that brother of mine. He said something about leaving these shores within a week, but if we are ready by tomorrow we'll be barely in time."

"Are you really going to take your garden to the New World, Mother?" asked 'Memby, already prinked out in her lace coif.

"Of course I am. My simples are as good pilgrims as any. With their roots sealed in clay and sunk in dampened peat, the slips, grafts, and clumps will travel around the world if need be. 'Tis fortunate that we have plenty of seeds left in last year's packets—and pungent roots—and——"

"Shall we take all our pots and kettles?"

"Why not? The *Speedwell* should be large enough to carry all our gear. This will not be like the time we fled down Ryton Water, 'Memby! Sometime I'll tell you about that."

"You have—a hundred times!" 'Memby grinned crookedly. "And all about Young Matt calling me a 'damp woman child'—huh!"

"All right. I'll tell the tale to Nicolas, then!"

"I don't care anything about that old country!" said Nicolas, cross with too many sweetmeats. "Are you going to take the silver mug Mijnheer Cort gave me, and the jam pots?"

"The mug. Not the jam pots!"

"Oh, Mother!" 'Memby added her wail to his. "Take the jam and leave the cradle."

"The—the *cradle?*"

"The cradle goes where we go!" Winover insisted calmly.

"John was rocked in it, and Young Matt, and you, 'Memby, and Nicolas! A new home has *got* to have a cradle beside the hearth!"

I left them, boiling with activity as a pot boils into foam over the hottest part of the log, and, slipping through the scullery, sped to Bell Alley without, I hoped, being noticed. And there I found my Uncle Samuel and William Brewster still in earnest conversation.

I laid the golden whistle on the table between them.

"What's this, Young Matt?" my uncle asked, and turned the shining bauble about in his brown fist. " 'Tis soft gold, and prettily cut. There's value in the thing, my lad!"

"I hope so!" I told him. "You said that we were to sell our gold rings, necklaces, lace-edged linens—whatever the Pilgrims might have that was of value to pay our passage to the New World, or for the hire that was still due on the *Mayflower* and *Speedwell.*"

"Aye. But *you* aren't going, Young Matt! Your father is a citizen of——"

"We're *all* going!" I interrupted firmly. "When my father took the oath of citizenship in the Stadthuis, he believed that the Pilgrims would bide in Leyden forever, and he didn't think it quite honest to accept refuge and succor from a community without giving what he could in return. If the Scrooby folk had remained in Bell Alley, my father and I, too, would have striven for Leyden; we would even have gone to war for her against her enemies. But if the Scrooby folk go forth into danger and hardships, our youth and health and strength must be spent for them. My mother feels this also. So we are all going in the *Mayflower* or *Speedwell.*"

"In that case, Young Matt, your father will give what he can toward the debt—it will be enough without this trinket."

"My father has the care of seven!" I told him. "Tomorrow I was to have relieved him of the burden of my support. I was to have taken over the Cort tulip farm. But now—well, I have only the golden whistle with which to pay my way to the New World."

Elder Brewster reached for the trinket, then, and examined it closely. "Isn't this the King's Voice, Young Matt?" he asked. "The whistle you took in exchange for an eel from a King's Man on the day before you fled down Ryton Water?"

"Aye."

"But—but it was not a very safe bauble to have around your gear, lad!"

"We kept it hid in the scullery among the dried ague-weeds. Nobody has ever blown upon it. My mother liked it."

"She would!" he replied gently. "Orris would look upon it and see only her beloved son trying to protect her from danger. It has meant more to her than we know, through all these years. Orris is one to treasure memories!"

"How much value would you put upon the thing, William?" my uncle asked suddenly.

And when he was told, he opened a leathern bag that was bound about his body beneath his doublet and took from it coins to the value of twice the amount. "You have sold the King's Voice, Young Matt," he said, "and can sail the seas with your head up! It has been my pleasure, William," he added, turning to Elder Brewster, "to bring my sister little gifts after each voyage. This time it will be a golden whistle —with still another memory of her first-born lad attached to it!"

We went to the Big House in Bell Alley the next day to volunteer for passage to the New World, and there we learned, as my mother had foreseen, that not a week but scarce a day stood between that hour and the moment of departure.

"Just the way we had to flee down Ryton Water!" wailed Goodwife Kerry. "What's driving us this time, Samuel?"

"I'm afraid it's the same thing, 'Lissy!" he replied. "Those spies that were here yesterday will lose no time in reporting to King James. His fury will flame on high. Then, if he learns that we are all approaching the English coast——"

"Approaching the English coast!" Everybody in the room shouted the words in one mighty voice. "What are you talking about, Samuel Brode? We thought we were to flee the cursed place!"

Elder Brewster raised his hand for silence and, trusting him as we did, we listened thirstily for his words. "It would not be wise for our folk to set forth to establish a colony in the New World," he explained, "without a skilled cooper—Samuel explained the need for him yesterday!—and a trained fighting man who shall guard our safety and teach our young men how to protect themselves and us. We have no such cooper in Leyden, nor a soldier who will throw in his lot with us. But in Londontown Samuel has found two such men. There is a lad named—what is that name, Samuel?"

"John Alden."

"John Alden!" Giles Kerry sputtered into words. "Why, he used to visit in Scrooby when he was a lad—he was—he——"

"He was in our kitchen when the plan was made to escape down Ryton Water!" I added. "Only the woman where he was visiting—a grandmother or something—pulled him back to his stool and later returned him to his folks in London-town!"

"That's the lad!" My Uncle Samuel nodded. "He's a skilled cooper now, and a Puritan. But his heart is with the Pilgrims of Scrooby still, and he is waiting to be taken aboard as we touch the English coast."

"Who's the soldier, Samuel?" asked Oliver Fentry. "Do we know him?"

"Probably not—but a stout man! His name is Miles Standish."

All the Pilgrims of Leyden crowded the canal bank nearest Bell Alley the next morning, and found places on the flatboats that were hired to take us to Delfshaven. Thus far could they accompany us, even the old, the frail, the timid who would venture no further into the unknown.

It was July. And the meadows were sweet. Close to Leyden, the dikes raised the canals to more than fourteen feet above the land level, so for many a mile there was the feeling of riding the air above fields of lovely bloom.

Gradually the dikes lowered until there came a time when water and land lay side by side once more, and there the waterways were edged with linden trees and were shady and cool.

We sat in the flatboats with our faces turned backward toward the home we were leaving. The roofs faded after a while into a veil of mist, but still we strained our eyes for the tulip fields outside the walls. And when the fields were caught in mist, we lifted our eyes to the clouds that hung above Leyden—those clouds that Mijnheer Cort once told me were called "the high hills of Holland."

July 1620. It was a date I would never forget. It was a day I would never forget! We floated down canals for the better of seven hours, a distance of five and twenty miles, and so arrived at Delfshaven only to find there was no accommodation in the place for so many folk.

"No place in the inn, eh?" growled Goodwife Fentry. And then, in gentler tones: "Well, we aren't the only band of travelers to come to a small town on a dark night and find no room in the inn! God and His angels were roundabout, that night, however, so perhaps we'll do all right, too!"

We did. It was very nice on the dock at Delfshaven that night, with the stars bright overhead and the silvery water lapping and slapping at the pierhead. Friend pressed closer to friend, the hum of voices increased with each passing hour, and more than once we knelt upon the planks while our aged pastor, whom we were never to see more after that night, led us in prayer and gave us his blessing, while Elder Brewster, standing at his side, led the congregation in songs of peace and psalms of hope.

Just before the break of dawn, I left my own particular group and, pacing the length of the dock, rounded a pile of stacked gear and so came face to face with a maid who was neither praying, singing, nor whispering farewells to friends soon to be left behind.

She was a neat little maid in a wide blue cape and a trig coif; her hair was smooth and shiny and golden, like a buttercup's petal. She had a kerchief spread across her small knees for drying, but when I looked at her swollen, red eyes, I knew that the kerchief had not been dipped in the sea.

It was Abigail Wain, a maid who had but lately come to Bell Alley from Amsterdam, and she was quite alone. She was weeping bitterly. All this made me forget the warning I had had from other Pilgrim lads that Nabby Wain's face might resemble a flower, but the tongue in it was like the sting of a bee.

"Nabby!" I cried. And popped into view from behind a huge iron pot. "What's wrong?"

She could not restrain the start that flicked her kerchief to the planks, but she sniffed scornfully as she rescued it and tucked it inside her belt.

"Nothing—that *you* could cure!" she said unpleasantly.

"Cure? Are you ill, Nabby?"

"Get along with you, you silly child!"

I grinned crookedly. It had been years before Winover ceased calling me "little boy." But not even Winover had ever called me "child." I could have tucked Nabby Wain into my breeches pocket and lost her there among the odds and ends of my personal gear.

"If it's cramps," I persisted, "my mother has a brew of simples that——"

"Cramps! It's venom! I'm filled to my pate with it!"

I pressed backward against the iron pot, so that it teetered this way and that, finally bounding away in the morning gray unnoticed.

"Did—did a beastie bite you?" I stammered.

"Aye. Your uncle!"

"My uncle! You can't mean John!"

"I mean your Uncle Samuel, ninny! Odds blood, how did that old savage get the right to bite into a body's happiness and bring it to sudden death! You Overs are much too domineering!"

"My Uncle Samuel is not an Over, Nabby!" I explained gently. "He is a Brode—brother to my mother and John. The

Overs are from Scrooby, but the Brodes are from Austerfield in Yorkshire."

"Who cares? I can't think of anything less interesting than instruction concerning your family! And please don't shake any more of our pots into the sea; my Aunt Mercy won't like it! It won't make any difference to her whether a Brode or an Over does it; she won't like it at all!"

I moved away from the pile of stacked gear. But still I could not leave the maid alone to her sorrow and tears. "Where is your Aunt Mercy?" I inquired.

"Kneeling beside William Brewster—and see that you don't disturb her! I don't want her. I don't want anybody on this dock! I came off here to be rid of you Scrooby folk."

Blazes! "I might get some of your own folk, then!" I urged, meekly enough. "Just so you wouldn't be so lonely."

"I haven't any folk, you meddlesome lad! My father died in Bawtry, and my mother in Amsterdam," she told me, staring with cold eyes. "Do you think I would have been sent to my Aunt Mercy else? She never had a lass in all her life—nor wanted one. But she is a saint and believes that God sends bane as well as blessing. I'm her bane!"

"Nabby!" I straightened my broad shoulders and made as though to turn away. "Let me call my mother."

"No!"

"Have you any reason?"

"I've more weeping to do. For—for Leyden."

"I could weep for Leyden, too! And for my tulip farm!" I told her then. "But life rarely works out as we plan it in our youth. There comes another pattern and——"

"There's not likely to come another Klaas Florin so soon!"

I stood still to gape. "You can't mean Klaas Florin whose father owns the bookshop in the Breedestraat!"

"Why can't I? Do you know him?"

"He was friend to Rudi Cort."

"I know—I often saw Rudi at his house."

"Why didn't I see you at Rudi's, then? Weren't you friend to Kathi?"

"Aye. But more to Anntje, Klaas's sister. She was the only *real* friend I ever had! And now—and now—" The tears spurted again and she had a hard time finding the dampened kerchief.

"Your hair is nice, Nabby!" I told her then, with some crazy idea of comforting her grief.

She nodded. "Klaas said so!" she sobbed.

"It's like new butter."

"Klaas said it was like noon sunshine on a field of golden tulips."

"Well, it *is!*" I stood back and judged with a keener eye the lock that was freed from her coif. "When it comes to beauty, there's not much to choose between golden butter and golden tulips."

"Lud! Such—such yeomen as the Scrooby lads are!"

Winover came running up just then and grasped my arm. "Hello, Nabby!" she cried. "Look yonder, Young Matt!"

I turned from Nabby Wain to face the open sea. The pearly mists of morning had thinned and through their vapor two winged boats were edging slowly up to the dock.

The *Mayflower* and the *Speedwell,* out of England!

My mother bustled nearer, sweeping her family before her with outstretched arms and worried chatter. "The Bowl!" she cried. "Young Matt, stir thyself and give Nicolas a hand with the Bowl! And do you, Winover, help 'Memby with the small gear! The *Speedwell* is about ready to take us all on board."

"I want to watch the master take the craft down the Meuse to the open sea!" Nicolas howled, wrathful at being delayed by household duties.

"He'll be some time doing it!" my mother told him calmly. "Hoist the Bowl—and have a care to the contents!"

And then, turning to me and pressing her sweet head to my shoulder for just a second while the bustle was at its worst, she whispered: "Oh, widgeon, I want to turn back like Lot's wife and become a bag of salt and never, never, never leave this beloved land, this blossom-hung Low Land, Leyden!"

But when I patted the back of her coif, she straightened and cried sharply: "Don't pity me, Young Matt! Switch me about to face the open sea! Push me across the waves to a—to a New World and a new life and a new home! I suppose they have loam over there, my lad!"

Nabby freed herself regretfully from our noisy group and turned back to the pile of stacked pots, kettles, and packets that belonged to her Aunt Mercy. "I'll see you again yonder, Goodwife Over," she said gently. "We are to travel aboard the *Mayflower!*"

12

THE SWEET SMELL OF CEDAR

SOUTHAMPTON on the English coast was reached without mishap, and there we took Miles Standish, the soldier, aboard together with John Alden, the cooper, and more of William Bradford's friends. John Alden, I was pleased to see, although five years the better of me in age, was still not my equal in brawn and girth.

I was minded to go in search of him and talk over the happenings between then and Scrooby days, but the *Speedwell* lurched and I was tossed upon a coil of rope.

The *Speedwell* had been reeling and floundering more than seemed needful even before touching at Southampton, but now the complaints were loud and bitter.

"The boat is overmasted!" said my Uncle Samuel, seating himself upon the coil of rope at my side.

"Won't we get to the New World all the sooner—with such a spread of sail?" I asked.

He shook his head. "When we hit the true ocean waves outside, lad, the *Speedwell* will strain and fight; her seams will open and the sea will come seeping in."

Blazes! "So the governors in Londontown hired us an unsafe boat, eh?"

"Either unsafe—no, *not* unsafe!" he corrected himself. "But incorrectly handled."

A seaman passing within hearing distance growled that the lad had the right of the matter. "She be a most unseaworthy craft!" he snarled. "Her hull's rotted—she's fitted only for the ocean bottom!"

"What's to be done about it?"

"A little more of this and then the master will turn back to the nearest port for an overhauling and repair job."

"Southampton?"

"Plymouth, probably. 'Tis closer by."

My uncle rose from the coil of rope and went to seek William Brewster and the ship's master. When he returned, his spirits were no brighter.

" 'Tis the truth we have just heard, Young Matt!" he told me. "Thank God, if we must be landed at all, that it will be at a place far from Londontown, with the moors between us and the King's Men! We may be held in Plymouth for a week."

"But we were to reach the New World while the summer was sweet and warm, so that we could erect shelters before snow begins. A week here may drag on into two weeks—or three."

"Or more!"

"What of the *Mayflower?*" I asked then.

"The *Mayflower* will turn and tie up at Plymouth as long as we do. We were hired to cross the ocean together."

It was July when we turned our backs on the ocean and took refuge in Plymouth harbor. And it was the following September before the patience of the Pilgrims reached the breaking point.

The pleasant summer weather was slipping rapidly away; autumn was closing in, with winter not far behind.

"How many days, William," asked my father one day of Goodman Brewster, "of water must we count upon before we can hope to find land and a spot where we may become established?"

"Sixty, Matthew."

"Sixty! Odds blood, William—why, that will bring us into November!"

"But even November, in Virginia, can't be so very bad!" I thought.

My father was not to be cheered. "The master of neither the *Mayflower* nor the *Speedwell* is sure of laying a correct course to Virginia!" he said. "They will sail as they may—and thank God for a safe landing on some wilderness. It may as well be a bleak northern coast, as far as I can see! We'd best leave Plymouth at once, William!"

"But the *Speedwell* is still not repaired."

"Nor will it be!" growled my Uncle Samuel, coming along the dock to join us. "The master of that craft has no stomach for this journey into the unknown, or I miss my guess!"

"Do you mean he is delaying us on purpose, Samuel?"

"I make no charges. I simply say that the time has come to *go*—if we are going! Take all the gear off the *Mayflower* and the *Speedwell,* leaving it here in Plymouth to be sent after us, then there will be room on the *Mayflower* for most of the *Speedwell's* passengers. Some, of course, will have to wait for later passage—women and children, probably, as when we fled from Scrooby. It is the *men* that the King desires to capture and punish for their preachments concerning freedom—and so the men must go first. It will be the men, too, who are most needed for the first work of preparing the wilderness for habitation."

I left them arguing the matter and ran swiftly in search of my mother. She would be, I very well knew, wandering about the downs gathering wild flowers and simples, but Goodwife Fentry was light on her feet for all her tremendous size, so I sent her in one direction while I took the other. We closed in upon our quarry while she was scooping a bit of borage out of the soil with naught but her slender fingers.

"Look!" she cried. And held the sprig up in triumph. "Borage! It may have escaped from a garden somewhere, but it belongs to nobody but me now. And it is going to the New World in my Bowl!"

"A good omen, Orris!" Goodwife Fentry shouted. "Borage for courage, so I always heard. You are going to need it!"

My mother turned pale. "Have they come for us—the King's Men?" she gasped.

"No, but *we* have, Young Matt and I! We've come to get you in a hurry, my lass! It's sailing time!"

"Is the *Speedwell* repaired?"

"Foosh on the *Speedwell!* She's to be turned back to the governors in Londontown. We are to go on the *Mayflower.*"

"*All* of us? Why, the *Mayflower* is full laden as it is!"

"Her gear is to be left behind with ours. Of course, we can't ask her passengers to give up their places, but all the spare room will be filled with as many of the *Speedwell's* list as can be managed."

"Not—not all are to go, then, Submit?"

"Naturally not. Anybody who wants my place on the *Mayflower* can have it!"

"Does Oliver feel that way?"

"God love us, Oliver Fentry was never known to give up anything he once started in all his life! He'll go to the New World if he has to hang onto the *Mayflower* by a cord and be hauled on behind. I'm easier to get along with."

"You would stay in England—and—*if* Oliver should go?"

"I would stay on land if anybody should sneeze, even!"

"I must go with Matthew!" my mother said sharply. "If the Pilgrims need his strength, they must make place for me!"

"You've got a mess of children, Orris! Their place might better be filled with strong men. You wouldn't leave them, would you?"

"Dear God—come!" cried my mother, and led the way back to the Plymouth waterside.

My father was looking about for her among the women. "Orris—sweet lass!" he whispered, as she came plunging against his arm.

"I know, Goodman!" she told him. "Never mind about the gear—except my Bowl. I must have that! I'm ready to sail any minute now."

"Courage, Orris! It is a good thing we are both so strong. I shall be of value yonder in the wilderness—and you, here with the children."

"*I*—here—oh, Matthew!" I never heard my mother's voice like that before.

"There is no choice, lass! In the spring I will send for thee. There is Nicolas to be considered—and the damp woman child, 'Memby." He tried to bring a smile to her pale lips with the words, but she was looking at me, hardly listening.

"And Young Matt?" she asked.

"I shall go with my father!" I told her quietly. "There will be work for me, protecting and guarding him from savages as he toils in the wilderness."

"Young Matt, son of Matthew Over, yeoman!" she sighed. "God hold you both in the palm of His hand!"

My Uncle John, it was decided, should remain behind to have the broken Over family in charge. "Take Orris and Winover, 'Memby and Nicolas, back to the Weddesteeg, John!" my father begged when we had gone to stand among the men at one side. "Thoma Cort will watch over you all until spring."

I had almost the last word from my mother. "The little ivory elephants, Young Matt!" she shouted, as the *Mayflower* made ready to sail in the midst of much confusion. "They are *down,* lad! Jumbled in a mess in the little box of pretties. And so will they lie until—until——"

I had almost the last glimpse of her, too—standing apart from the women and children who had been left behind, twiddling the sprig of borage between her fingers. Reaching it high above her pretty head, at last, and holding it there with the wind at play with her welling skirts and linen apron until the *Mayflower,* tossed about like a radish in a boiling pot, sank into the valley of a wave deeper than all that had gone before. When we rose once more to the crest of the foam, England was lost to us forever and we were alone with God upon the bosom of His vast deep.

"Young Matt!"

I turned my head wearily at the call and glanced upward. A maid was bending over the spot where I lay upon a bit of dirty fustian, a maid in a long blue cape. A maid with hair like new butter and tulip fields at noon. Nabby!

"Aye. 'Tis myself, Nabby Wain!" she replied pertly in answer to the question of my eyes. "I was aboard the *Mayflower* from the start, you know, and so could not be left behind at Plymouth. But you have seen nobody since we struck the first bit of deep sea! Such misery never was—except when a great giant of a lad falls ill! Shall I help you to the corner where your father tosses on another sour mat?"

"My father? Is he ill, too?"

"Deplorably so! Your Uncle Samuel tends to his needs. A good thing a few of us are able to sway with the planks with no bad effects. Will you come?"

"I would like to, Nabby—but—but I can't keep to my legs, and that's a fact!" I confessed.

"You ate too much meat pudding that first night."

"Oh, Nabby, don't!" I begged. And closed my eyes.

She leaned down and shook my arm. "Make an effort!" she said sternly. "You are not alone in this distress, you know! Nearly everybody on the *Mayflower* is pushed beyond endurance. The women wail, the children complain, the men groan, and the curses of the seamen fill the air. You can't have been too sick to hear all the din!"

"I thought 'twas a gale in the rigging. There was a storm."

"There *was!* Last night. And Giles Kerry just told me you were out here all the time, beaten upon by hail, sleet, rain, and salt spray. Wonderful that there is still life under your doublet!"

"The Overs die hard, I guess."

"Hush!" She cowered in the shadow of a flapping canvas and covered herself completely with her long blue cape. "Here comes that unsavory Piet Billing with his father. Pretend slumber until they have passed!"

She might have been any one of the miserable Pilgrim mothers, or even a heap of discarded gear, wrapped and silent as she made herself. The Billing twain wasted no second glance on her. But they paused beside my ragged fustian mat and Piet scuffed it with his toe. "Here we have Young

Matt Over," he sneered. "Still flat in his puddle! You and I may have a touch of the gripes now and then, but at least we are on our feet and moving about!"

"Oh, Piet!" James Billing clutched at his doublet and groaned. "Why did we ever leave Plymouth?"

"Plymouth? For the matter of that, why did we ever leave Scrooby? We're like the finny beasties down there in the deep, following a ship for the sake of cast-off food. We don't say that, though, you know! We howl for freedom as loud as the next one."

"In a way, you're right, Piet!" James tittered meanly. "The best place for a weed to flourish is in the middle of a garden bed! We do all right among these Pilgrims. Only I don't like the notion of that soldier they've taken aboard. Why should godly folk such as these need a soldier?"

"To fend off savages. To fend off Englishmen, it may be!"

"God save us, lad, is that any way for a pious Pilgrim to talk?"

"Well, Miles Standish isn't crossing the water on the *Mayflower* to plant barley in the New World! You know that as well as the next one."

"They say he is to protect them—and then he begins to drill the women so they can protect themselves! He says there's to be a musket hung over every stew pot. Odds blood! I never saw a woman yet that wasn't quick to make a mistake —and save her sorrow for it until afterward!"

"Don't look so much like a savage, then, or a robber!" Piet snickered and gave the fustian mat another kick. "And watch out about trading pots with cracks in them and rush-bottomed seats that fall out at a touch."

"It was the Dutch that caught me there!" James twitched his head nervously, backward toward Leyden. "These Pilgrims are green as a blade of new grass. Honorable, some might say; gullible is the word *I* use for them! Look what they are up to now—escaping from the King, so they think! And they go right across the water to land that is owned by that same King! Is that bright? Going right to work for the Stuart, clearing a wilderness for him, paying him for it, too, through the nose when the time comes for him to order them to hand over, or I miss my guess! *They* catch the hare—and *he* eats the pasty! Fools, fools, fools!"

"Well, you haven't been able to mow them clean, yet, if they *are* new grass!" Piet told him sharply. "They've got plenty of fine gear and money in their bags. It's the Billing family that eats out of broken trenchers, cooks in cracked pots, and sits on splintered stools."

"Up until now, my lad!" James tittered slyly. "But there's to be a change yonder. William Brewster just had a meeting down in the cabin and he said that when the spot for a colony was selected in the wilderness, the land would be equally divided among the heads of all the families on the *Mayflower.* Moreover, each was to have equal voice in making the laws, in building up a business and carrying it on, in all matters whatsoever. James Billing, my lad, will stand on even footing at last with—with Matthew Over, Oliver Fentry, or even William Brewster himself!"

They rounded the corner and were gone, still talking. But we had heard enough. "God's mercy, did you listen to all that chatter?" asked Nabby, throwing off her cape angrily. "To my mind, the loss would be slight if James Billing were to stub his toe some dark night and miss the rail—taking Piet with him!"

"Did he speak truth about a meeting in the cabin?"

"Aye. But don't fret—your Uncle Samuel was there to

watch over your family's welfare. What we've got to do now, though, is to get you and your father on your legs."

She found me a hard biscuit somewhere, and a jug of ginger cordial from her Aunt Mercy's gear, and she held my head while I gnawed and sipped. The stuff must have skinned my gullet, but its warmth was welcome to my shivering bones for all of that, and after a third or fourth sip I was able to stand and stumble along the deck to where my father lay, and share the last drops with him.

The maid found a plaid somewhere—never *was* such a maid for finding whatever was needful, I was to learn later! —and while we were wrapping my father in it he turned his head and whispered weakly: "Thank God for the Over women, Young Matt! For Orris—and Winover—and Nabby!"

"His mind still wanders!" I apologized to the startled lass. "Big folk like the Over men fall hardest when stricken with fever. If only my mother were here she'd simmer some howsleke in milk and cool his blood in no time—and then she'd brew ague-weed and——"

"The worst of his fever is gone!" Nabby said. And laid her slender fingers along his cheek. "He'll sleep under the warm plaid. But when he wakes, he'll be as famished as you were, Young Matt. So go to the galley while I watch over him and say that Nabby Wain desires two mugs of rich, strong broth—and do you swallow one right there where it is snug and warm! Bring the other here for your father!"

Dawn followed dusk in endless succession. Each day, breaking, showed us naught but a world that was all tumbling water; each day, closing, left us to pallets that slithered about the restless decks and offered little rest.

Though my father and I did little but sit in a quiet corner for days on end, we lacked no attention, since my Uncle Samuel was there to watch over us both. We saw little of Nabby. She kept to the women's end of the deck; and when a wee son was born to Goodwife White during the height of one storm, it was Nabby who took complete charge of the moppet and was seldom seen after that without a wrinkled red face bobbing across her arm.

One day she offered to show the lad to me as a great favor. "Did you ever see a sweeter angel, Young Matt?" she whispered, throwing back a fold of her cape that my view might be unhindered.

"One looks much as another to me," I was forced to confess.

"Why, Young Matt Over! None are alike!"

"How is this one different?"

"He's—he's sweet! It can't be put into words, just how one baby differs from another—it has to be seen and felt. You never saw many, probably!"

Blazes! "Plenty!" I told her. "We had a damp woman child of our own in Scrooby—and a Dutch lad in Leyden—and Orrje Cort was as much with us as anywhere. What name has this one got?"

"Peregrine."

"Peregrine!"

"Aye. Peregrine White. Because he 'travels in a strange land'—that's what Peregrine means. And so he does, bless him!" she added, snuggling the bobbing head into her neck. "And so do all the Pilgrims, for the matter of that."

"I would have named him 'Petrel'—one who walks upon the sea!" I told her. And grinned crookedly. "Do you know, Nabby, I think there is a belt of water that girts the earth and we have happened to be drawn into it! We're like to sail on and on and on until we bump into the Low Country again and——"

"Nonsense!"

"But it is already better than sixty days since we left Plymouth."

"It's more than a hundred and thirty-three days since we left Delfshaven—that's what I remember most!" she told me wearily.

And just then the seaman in the lookout above our heads cried: "Land ahoy!"

"God has brought us to the New World!" shouted my father, running up and pushing me ahead of him to the rail.

Others joined us and we stood in silence for a time, straining our eyes for the welcome sight of land. We knelt and gave thanks to God, with Elder Brewster leading us in the prayer, and then we returned to the rail and scanned the nearing shoreline for sign of habitation or human being.

There was none. We were appalled. But nobody put his disappointment into words, lest a neighbor be made heartsick. We waited for William Brewster to speak, but hours passed and still he was silent, watching the land draw nearer. When he found words, at last, there was but cold comfort in them. "This is Creation as it first fell from the hand of God," he said. "Water teeming with fish, the air clouded with wildfowl on the wing, a pleasantly wooded wilderness——"

"Pine and balsam and juniper, too," I cried, "and a very sweet smell of cedar!"

"The water's thick as hutch-putch with fish!" added Giles Kerry, brightening the gloom for an instant. "Only not a fish hook on the *Mayflower!* All left with our gear on the

Plymouth dock! Lud, Young Matt, if we could only get a bit nearer to that shore, we could drop over the side into the mud and tread a few eels, eh?"

"Not me!" I told him, and drew my doublet closer. "Let the eels bide in their mud! Never was such a cold coast as this!"

"It certainly isn't Virginia!" announced my Uncle Samuel suddenly. "We are close enough now to see that there is no colony hereabouts. It's not that far northern coast I touched upon with Sir Raleigh, either! We've drifted off our course amazingly."

"There was a Dutchman named Block who discovered an island in the New World some six years ago," William Bradford remembered.

But my uncle doubted that this was Block's island. "It is a wilderness," he said over and over again. "If there is any human hiding there it will be a savage."

Blazes! That made some of us draw back from the rail, and no objection was raised when the master of the *Mayflower* decided to cruise further up and down this coast.

We drifted about close to shore, now here, now there, for the better part of a month and still no foot had pressed the soil of that world that lay so enticingly before us. And each day was colder than the one before.

There came a day when the women could endure no longer. They demanded wood for the cabin stove and they demanded pure water for the cleansing of their garments, and so the master, being at that time close to a spit of wooded shore that reached out into the sea like a hook, edged the *Mayflower* cautiously around the hook, away from the wracking waves, and into a pleasant, shallow bay, and there he dropped anchor.

John Alden, Giles Kerry, and I got the craft's shallop over the side and into the water as quickly as the work could be done and, with Miles Standish holding his musket ready, we paddled the short distance to shore and collected a goodly supply of cedar branches. Returning to the *Mayflower,* we set them to blazing merrily and soon the sweet smell of burning cedar rose in a fragrant mist above the shallow bay. If we had not been sickened unto death of boats and tumbling waves before, we would have been then. The cedar smoke whispered to every heart of kitchen and scullery and we longed for the home and the plot of ground that were to be ours in this New World.

The women were especially restless at being held aboard after so long a time afloat. They gathered their soiled linen in great bundles and, binding the loads to their shoulders, leaped from the *Mayflower's* decks into the shallow water of the bay without waiting for the shallop, and so waded ashore and rinsed and beat their clothes as they had so often done in the Oude Vest Canal in Leyden.

PART THREE

A New Country

13

A PACKET OF NEWS FOR MY MOTHER

It was a week or more after that when my father came to me one evening as I sat in the cabin of the *Mayflower,* weary with the toil and the horror of the day just past, and handed me a crayon and a bit of fair parchment. "Too many things are heaping up, these days!" he said. "We cannot hope to carry the memory of all of them until your mother joins us in the springtime. Best begin now and send her a letter."

"A letter!" I had never sent a letter to anybody.

"Aye, a letter." He winked at Nabby, who was loitering near with Peregrine White across her shoulder. "I suppose they drummed the making of a letter into your thick skull at the school in the Breedestraat."

"But—but how send a letter to the Low Country?"

"When we're still hovering over the New Country like a gull on the wing, eh? Well, we'll light some time, my lad! And a way will be found to send a packet to her. Mayhap by this very *Mayflower,* when we have done with her."

"We were almost done with her today!" said Nabby. "Don't tell your mother about today, Young Matt!"

"Tell her about everything!" my father insisted. "As much as we can tonight, then more next week, and more as it happens—until there's opportunity to forward the packet. Tell of the crossing in the *Mayflower*—of the storms and wild waves—of you on a fustian——"

"And you on its mate!" I reminded him.

"That would be of little interest to anybody!" he chuckled and drew the cabin table closer to me. "But tell her of finding land—and not daring to light upon it for week after week. Then the quiet bay, and how our lads brought cedar branches, the first gifts of our new home, back to the boat and burned them, comforting all."

"Shall you tell her about the women who waded ashore to cleanse their linen?" asked Nabby sadly.

After a moment, my father said: "Aye, that too, Young Matt! Sorrowful as it is, it must be told. Of how, drenched to their frail bones, they waded back to the *Mayflower* and could find no warmth for their poor bodies and so fell ill of a dreadful, sudden malady, and passed quickly to their heavenly home without ever having set foot in the one that was promised them in the New World. Tell her that good Doctor Fuller did what he could—as well as all the rest of the men and lads—but it was not enough. And while you are on the subject, tell her how William Bradford's wife, Dority May, tripped and fell from the deck of the *Mayflower* while we were still outside the shallow bay, and was drowned in the sea. And then you can begin on the happenings of today."

"Do you think they would rest her spirit after all that other sad telling?" asked Nabby sharply. "You'll have the woman's heart torn in ribbons."

"Pleasanter writing will follow—I hope!" my father told her quietly. "We will only write of what is past, tonight. She will want to know it to the last detail."

I bit deeply into the crayon.

"The lad doesn't know how to begin a letter!" Nabby giggled and sat down at my side, with Peregrine across her small knees. "First, you put her name on the parchment, Young Matt, and then where she is to be found. And then the date. And then the news."

I drew the table nearer, grasped the crayon stoutly, and wrote:

"Mevrouw Orris Over.
By hand of Thoma Cort.
On the Weddesteeg,
Leyden,
In the Low Country.

"The week after St. Nicolas's Day

"Goodwife Orris.
My sweet Mother,

"We have reached the New World. But we are still on the water. And it is exceedingly cold.

"You on the Weddesteeg will still be feasting on the sugar loaves, oily-cakes, and hutch-putch left over from St. Nicolas's Day. But we here in the New World had our first drink of pure water today and we could have asked for nothing better!

"My father has told me of many things to write you, but that I cannot do. It would take too many words. Fear not that a happening shall be forgotten—it is all fastened in our memory for life. When you cross the sea we will talk it over, over and over again. But now I must begin with today's happenings so that some room shall be left on the parchment for the days that are to come.

"We did not land in Virginia, after all! We did not land anywhere, as yet. But we have before us a wilderness which we shall claim and settle and name as we see fit. Today, my father and I set foot upon it for the first time. (I am not counting the day that Giles and I and some of the lads paddled to the shore in a shallop and gathered cedar branches for a very sweet burning!)

"'Today, Miles Standish chose sixteen men—blazes, I count as a *man,* now!—to make an excursion at a reasonable distance inland, to explore this unknown land. We brought back much that should comfort those who remained on the *Mayflower.*

"First, we found a great iron pot that was filled with maize—a most amazing growth! It has kernels of red, yellow, and blue! The partly buried pot was evidently used as a storehouse by some savage. We took the maize (so my Uncle Samuel named it!) back with us and Miles Standish has it in charge. It is to be saved for seed for our first harvest and will be equally divided among the men.

"Next, we came upon a spring of fresh water, and we took some of that back with us in the iron pot! The water on the *Mayflower* has gone stale weeks ago—we sicken at the sight and smell of it. It seemed as if we could never leave the little spring. Lying full length on our faces before it, we lapped until we were like to burst.

"Only William Bradford, who is sad and restless since the death of Dority May, showed no wish to linger after he had drunk his fill. He wandered away, alone, into the forest and soon we heard him cry out sharply. We feared a savage and hastened to his aid. But it was only a snare that some savage had set for the catching of a deer, and it had caught William instead.

"He was deeply mortified until Miles Standish assured him that he had made the most valuable find of all and to cease struggling lest he harm the snare. We freed him carefully, studying the trap, and now we, too, from materials on the *Mayflower,* can fashion others and so have fresh meat, at last.

"All about us were dried herbs and simples—waiting for you, my sweet mother!—and bushes filled with withered berries. We were gathering what we could when suddenly we were almost deafened by a tremendous blast of gunpowder.

" 'The King's Men!' piped Goodman Morse, who is old and dwells in the past more than the present.

" 'It's the Spaniards!' howled Goodman Crump. You don't know him—we took him aboard at Southampton. He is a Pilgrim from Amsterdam and he was in the Low Country during past wars and if a Water Wagtail crossed his path in the forest he would yelp that it was a Spaniard and fall into the bushes.

" 'The savages have come!" shouted Giles Kerry. And every one of his coral hairs stood on end to have a look for itself.

"But Miles Standish had the right guess. 'It's the *Mayflower!'* he cried. 'The ship's been blown up!'

"Well, it wasn't quite blown up, we discovered as soon as we could get clear of the bushes. The craft was still riding at anchor in the shallow bay, but flames were shooting from her decks most fearsomely. We were downright spent by the time we had reached her decks and conquered the burning. Only then was there time to investigate the cause of the accident.

"It was the fault of a meddlesome lad named Francis Billington—no kin to James Billing's family—and another, Timothy Belt, both Pilgrims from Amsterdam. God knows what the women were doing to allow two such lads the freedom of the cabin with no one to watch over their doings, but such was the case. And one, Francis, 'tis now said, got his paws into our store of gunpowder and scattered it all about the cabin of the *Mayflower.* Trails of the stuff led everywhere. Then, either Timothy helped a spark from the stove on its way or the spark escaped bounds of its own will; nobody really knows. Nor does it matter. It is only by the blessing of God that everybody on the craft wasn't blown heavenward in one terrific blast!

"Nabby Wain says that I should not write you of this happening. But my father says to begin the telling with the story of this day's events. And so I have done. You are not to fret. My father and I are hale. And so is Nabby. She is busied with the care of Peregrine White—oh, yes, I forgot to tell you, we have taken a new Pilgrim aboard the *Mayflower* since leaving Plymouth. One Peregrine White, son to Goodwife White, whose husband is ailing. He is damper than ever 'Memby was at his age, and fatter than our Dutch lad, but otherwise much the same.

"And so I will fold this parchment and put it aside until there is more time, or I am less weary, or some other strange happening makes more writing necessary."

"*December* 22, 1620

"Sweet mother Orris,

"We have ceased hovering over the New World like a gull on the wing, as my father said. We have dropped upon the land and started building our nests.

"It was decided after further exploration that the wooded spit of land which I told you about would be an unsuitable location for a colony, so we lifted anchor, crossed the bay, and there, upon the other side, found a fair spot that pleased us all.

"Somebody has lived here at some time and vanished, because certain fields have been spaded and there are stumps of maize to be seen. It may have been a tribe of restless savages. They move about almost like the Pilgrims, so my Uncle Samuel says.

"This is a fair spot upon which we shall build our first city. A plentiful supply of sweet water flows through it—although, as yet, we have been unable to discover its source. A hill rises in the midst, exactly as the Burcht rises in the center of Leyden.

"We would like to call the settlement 'New Leyden,' but William Brewster holds that we must cling to the fact of our *English* birth. And so we will call the place 'New Plymouth.' The last we saw of the Old World was Plymouth—the first sight of the New World is to be Plymouth!

"Before leaving the *Mayflower* really to study and plot out the site for our colony, we had a meeting in the cabin and there it was agreed—as it had been talked over before!—that each man amongst us should have equal share in the soil and equal voice in the government. I discovered, then, that I do not rate as a man yet! Only when there is labor to be done.

"Goodman John Carver was chosen to be the first Governor of New Plymouth; Miles Standish to head its military; Elder Brewster to care for its souls; and good Doctor Fuller to heal its bodies.

"Thereafter, all together for the first time, we went ashore—men, women, and children. The women and children rambled far and wide, taking pleasure in everything. When they could endure the searching wind and the bitter cold no longer, they were returned to the warmth and comfort of the *Mayflower*. But the men—and lads—remained on land

and began the business of erecting a shelter in this wilderness for all of us.

"The master of the *Mayflower* is anxious to be on his way back to England, so we will not erect separate dwellings until later; first of all, we will build a Big House that shall be a temporary shelter for us all and for our small amount of gear against the elements and possible marauding savages.

"I have chopped logs today until the sleeve is ripped from my doublet. I'm afraid that I have not yet finished growing, either; my garments give at the seams so readily. But that is not the reason for the gash in my breeches—them I snagged on a bit of splintered timber."

"*January* 18, 1621

"My sweet Mother,

"I find that I will be obliged to write you a little of our happenings before the day of the explosion on the *Mayflower,* so that you may understand our latest plans.

"There was a great sickness and many of the women died. Goodwife Kerry has written of it to Goodwife Fentry and from her you will hear more than I could tell. Only this—with the difficulty of building dwellings at this time of year along this coast, and with so many of the women gone, so many homes broken, it was decided to erect as few shelters as possible this winter, dividing the lone men and children among the more fortunate households where a woman is in charge.

"For instance, Nabby Wain's Aunt Mercy was one of those who sickened and died, leaving Nabby quite alone. Goodwife White has an ailing husband and a wee baby, so it was felt that she was doing more than her share when she offered to house Goodman Winslow and care for him. But she insisted upon taking Nabby, too, having grown as fond of the maid as she could be of any daughter.

"It crowds the White dwelling, for there are only two rooms in all and Goodman Winslow is of a breadth and girth and height equal to mine own. Only one other Pilgrim can top us, and that is my father.

"Goodman Winslow brought a brave amount of gear with him from Leyden, so Nabby says. There are boxes of it beside his bed and he never seems to show the wear and tear of labor.

"But *me,* blazes! My father says that he would be obliged to have John Alden make a firkin for me, if it were not for Nabby. She found a strip of fustian in Goodman Winslow's gear and with it she patched the snag where I caught on the bit of splintered timber. She mended the sleeve also, although that was not such a serious matter.

"Since then I have split my breeches the full length! I was bending over, chopping a log, when—pouf! It is because of my growth. I don't know what Nabby can do about this.

"The plan of New Plymouth, as now decided, is to be the plan of Bell Alley in Leyden. We are to build two rows of tiny dwellings; they will face each other—nineteen dwellings in all, running from the shore of the quiet bay inland to the forest—and there will be a fair street between. Closing the street at the forest end will be a Big House, just as there was in Leyden.

"We shall worship in the Big House; there, too, will be our hospital, there we are to store our gear, and there Miles Standish is to have his headquarters, with cannon on the roof that will rake the street to the shore or the forest, from whichever point danger threatens.

"Our congregation consists now of 102 souls, so you can imagine the planning it will take to settle them into nineteen dwellings. My father and I will erect our own dwelling at the fair end of the street against the strand and we will be allowed to occupy it alone, since it is understood that almost as soon as it can be made ready you and John and the Dutch lad and the maids will be here. (Don't forget to bring me extra gear and plenty of fustian strips for patching!)

"More dwellings will be erected, of course, as the ships bring more families from Leyden, Amsterdam, and Londontown.

"I don't know as I made plain to you *why* it takes so long to erect shelters. Of course, the weather is severe, but, aside from that, we have so little time in the day to work on our own log-cutting. You see, we must get out that shipload of staves that the *Mayflower* is to carry back to Londontown with her, to pay for what is still owing for the hire of the craft. John Alden is in charge of this work and he keeps us to it. Although we bend to the labor right willingly. We want to pay the debt. As long as we are under debt to Londontown, just so long are we tied to the English shore. And we would be free!

"Blazes, I've got some breeches! Just as I was writing, Nabby came to where I was sitting (luckily) on a tub and she had a stout pair across her arm.

" 'Goodwife White helped me extract them from Goodman Winslow's box,' she said.

"I objected. But she said: 'You don't think we stole them, do you, silly? We paid for them by extra trenchers of hutchputch. He delights in it and Goodwife White makes it especially rich. When he comes to missing the breeches, he'll be too stout to buckle them around him—and anyway, the ships will be here, by that time, with plenty more garments for him. You can't go about the colony looking like *that,* you know!'

"She went then, and I donned the breeches. And though it felt wonderfully good to be covered again, still I'm worried about log-cutting because I seem to fit even Goodman Winslow's garments snugger than I could wish."

"The next day!

"Dear God, my sweet Mother, we are suffering just one affliction after another! This time it is the Big House! It is gone.

"My father selected and shaped the lumber for it, those who had learned the mason's trade in Leyden laid the foundations, others raised the walls and fitted the roof. But there was none drilled in the art of chimney-laying. Goodman Hughes did his best, but it let fire through to the thatched roof, there was a high gale raging and no water at hand, and that is the tale.

"Inside, we had stored for safe-keeping all the gear we had—the bedding, household effects—everything that had been kept until last week on the *Mayflower.* Inside, too, was Miles Standish's arsenal. Inside, too, were Governor Carver and William Bradford, both sorely ill.

"Thanks be to God, we were able to save these two from a terrible death; and we rescued the muskets and gunpowder. Nothing else.

"My father and I sleep now upon balsam boughs with other boughs to cover our shivering bodies. When you come from Leyden, add plenty of plaids to your gear, and a supply of those down coverlets that the Dutch use for bed-covering.

If there must be a choice, leave the painted trenchers and tulip cups behind and bring these coverings and plaids—and more breeches for me!

"It has been a surprise to us all that no trading ship has appeared at our doors ere this. There certainly must be some other colonies along this coast, but we have had no communication with them.

"The ashes of the Big House were hardly cooled before we began clearing the site and preparing to erect another Big House on the spot."

"Toward the close of January 1621

"My father and I were felling logs for a doorstep this morning and he said: 'Young Matt, were we back in Scrooby, you and I would be sowing oats on the lush land. And your mother would be on her knees, trying to find new growth among the clumps of simples in her garden.'

"It is by memories such as these that we seek to rest our lonely hearts at times.

"A cry rang along Breedestraat just then—some of us call our one fair street 'Breedestraat,' and some call it 'Leyden Street'—that a lad was lost.

"It was that same Francis Billington who, with Timothy Belt, all but blew up the *Mayflower* with spilled gunpowder on the day we made our first excursion on the wooded spit of land.

"He was gone now, and his mother ran this way and that wailing that the savages had stolen him. Few of us would have wasted time from our labor looking for the lad if we could have been sure of that, knowing full well that the savages would have tossed him back of their own accord after a taste of his mischief, but we didn't want the urchin to come to harm of the wolves that have been gravely tormenting us ever since we landed on this coast.

"So we dropped everything and sprang to the search.

"Finally, after we had all but given up ever seeing Francis again, a brother of his thought to climb a tree and from that vantage point he soon located the lost lad inside the forest. He also spied something that was of far more importance to the rest of us, namely a great body of water.

"We had not penetrated any farther into the forest than was necessary, feeling more secure on the open shore, but now Miles Standish and a company of men went in search of the body of water. And it *was* pure and sweet, as we hoped! It was, moreover, the source of that blessed stream that races through our colony to the bay. Now, we know, New Plymouth will never lack for pure, sweet water! Surely God led us to this happy spot in the wilderness!

"We have named the body of water 'Billington's Pond' in honor of the lad who does not deserve such honor, in my poor opinion, but a firmer hand in his upbringing."

"*February* 5

"Well, once again we have a Big House—and today we helped Miles Standish lift his cannon to the roof and plant them, one facing north, one facing south, one facing east, and one west.

"Every family, too, is under a roof and we are able to survey our colony with pride. There are other colonies in the New World that have more—wealth and finer dwellings and a charter from the King!

"But the Pilgrims have no wealth, only strong and willing arms, stout hearts, and a thirst for Freedom. We have no charter from the King! We have fled to escape his hatred.

But we have a Colony founded on Morality, Education, Law, and Freedom. Those, we have decided, shall be the four cornerstones of our building.

"The Overs have a comfortable home of *one* room—later there will be more! We have two narrow beds of balsam boughs, a table, an open hearth, and one slitted window that faces the forest—because it is from that direction that we expect whatever danger may befall us—and one beside the door. The windows are not much more than a crack in the wall, and are unlatticed—covered by sheets of greased parchment against the gales. We dared not make them larger lest a savage or a hungry wolf force entrance. I told you that we have been ceaselessly tormented by wolves. The savages, so far, have been friendly, but the wolves are fierce.

"The floor of our home is of pounded earth—before you come, it will be planked. And we have *no rushes!* Tell Winover that! We sweep ourselves clean as any Leyden kitchen with the besom that stands in the corner where the scullery will be before you come.

"A musket hangs over the hearth—and one over each bed. Although, I must confess to you, I have never yet learned to fire the thing with my eyes open! I do not think that the Overs were meant for shedding blood. My father has no taste for the thing, either. It must be the yeoman strain in us both.

"In the division of the small amount of *Mayflower* gear that was saved after the burning of the Big House, we drew an iron pot, and that now stands on our hob. We will need ladles and trivets, pots, kettles, and spits, when you come. Blazes, you will need to travel to the New World as the fat old Archbishop of York used to travel to Scrooby for the hunting!

"There is a peg beside the door for the Bowl!"

"February 6, 1621

"Sweet mother Orris,

"Just as we were all under shelter and beginning to feel a measure of contentment, the wilderness bared its fangs and showed us what new it had to offer in the way of misery! It was a storm of sleet and ice and it came last night, and never could a worse storm be imagined!

"We are buried to our chimney-pots in snow—Leyden Street to the forest and beyond is level with snow of a depth far more than my father is tall. And over the snow is spread a stout blanket of sheer ice.

"We cannot get about. If we could walk upon the ice we would hardly dare to, for fear of breaking through and smothering in the snow below. And yet we cannot bide inside our dwellings if this storm is to last many more days. Already we are beginning to feel pinched for food.

"There is plenty of fresh meat in the forest, but we dare not, in fact we *cannot,* walk upon the ice to get to it and set the snares. There is fish in the bay, but we have no small craft as yet.

"Now, more than at any other time, do we regret the fact that no other colony along this coast has taken us under its protection. We are so alone——"

"A night and a day later!

"Even as I was writing the above words, my sweet Mother, I heard a noise outside the door where no noise had been for a matter of three days, and, peeping through the slitted window, I saw the arm and shoulder of a savage. Miles Standish has drilled us to spring for our muskets in such an event, but, as I told you, I can't yet turn a musket upon a man. Only on wolves. And not often then, except when one is trapped and suffering torment that is worse than death.

"A human being at the door, even though it be a savage, is to be dealt with differently, I shall always feel. So I unlatched the door and stood ready to guard my father's dwelling with my bare fist, if need be.

"And there stood *my Uncle Samuel!*

"Always, in time of need, there is my Uncle Samuel.

"I forgot to tell you before that he was only with us, after landing on this coast, long enough to get a roof over the first Big House. Feeling then that his usefulness here was spent, he left us to explore the wilderness to the north and west and discover what might be the nature and intentions of the savages who dwell there. Now, as though led by the hand of God Himself, he was returned.

"And with him, a friendly savage.

"And with them both, a slain deer, unbelievably fat!

"There was a second deer outside on the ice. And New Plymouth ate last night! Blazes, there was food for all and to spare! We had hutch-putch in our dwelling, thanks to Nabby Wain, who brought over a pan of sliced pungent roots and groundnut tubers and prepared the meal in our iron pot. The savage ate until he fell asleep with his toes in the ashes. And so we left him, undisturbed, for the rest of the night.

"*Now,* you will be saying, how could Samuel Brode and a savage tramp the forest and kill two fat deer when the Scrooby men were so helpless before the snow and ice?

"It was like this, although I doubt if you will be able

to understand, never having seen anything like the thing which I shall attempt to describe. Both my uncle and the savage were wearing great, flat, curious shoes of latticework that bore them, quite easily, atop the crust of ice. We have studied the things already and shall copy them. Never again will the snow and ice be able to hold us prisoners within our dwellings!

"My Uncle Samuel said that the deer, having no 'snowshoes,' are as helpless in the forest during such a storm as were we on Leyden Street. They try to move about, but their sharp little hoofs cut through the ice, and so are they held by the deep snow below. And so are they easily caught and slain.

"The savage left us today, to return to his tribe in the north. He has promised to tell his chief of our colony here, and that we are a friendly company who wish naught but peace. He says the chief will visit us soon. My Uncle Samuel knows the chief and he assures us that he is a most noble man, and he has warned Miles Standish to hold his fire against the savages until he is certain that some mean harm to us, which he doesn't really believe will be the fact."

"*March*

"Winter is drawing to a close. My father reminded me last night that, were we in Scrooby, we would be rolling the rich meadows across Scrooby Waters and making ready to set hops.

" 'Let's think about Leyden!' I suggested.

"And then he sat down beside me before the blazing log and helped me do it.

" 'In Leyden,' he said, 'the tulip fields will be in bloom. There will be the smell of sweet springtime in the air. Open the door, Young Matt, and see if you can smell a new spring come to New Plymouth!'

"I opened the door. But all I saw was a fog over the bay and a shallop approaching the strand. And then, as it landed, a red man. 'There is a savage coming boldly up the middle of Leyden Street!' I cried to my father.

" 'I hope Miles Standish will remember Samuel's warning!' he said.

"And he did, because the cannon were silent as the red man came nearer. I slammed and latched the door, just as my Uncle Samuel came into the room from the scullery.

" 'God's mercy, open that door, Young Matt!' he shouted. 'And summon all the men of our colony to the Big House! This be the noble chief, Samoset! We must take counsel together and do him honor.'

"The red man passed our dwelling and sauntered onward, proudly and soberly, toward the Big House. And while we were hurrying about summoning the Pilgrims to the meeting, my uncle explained to me that Samoset had been told all about us, that he had watched our accomplishments and trials during the winter, and, since he had come to visit us himself, he meant to be friendly and give us aid.

" 'What kind of aid?' I asked.

" 'We are surrounded by a vast, unknown territory of forests, mountains, and valleys,' he said. 'I have explored some, and been told of more. There are mighty rivers and great inland seas. We but perch on the edge of this New World like a fly on a deer's ear. These forests, mountains, valleys are frequented by red savages—and some white men who are even more savage. Red men lodge all along the banks of the mighty rivers—on the shores of the inland seas. God grant there be no spark of hatred struck when we chance to meet. With that in mind, I have visited Samoset and told him who we of New Plymouth were, of our purpose in coming to the New World, of our suffering in the Old World. That much he could well understand.'

"'What?' I asked. 'Does he, too, know of the lean Stuart?'

"'He knows much about the cruelty of the white man!' my uncle told me soberly. 'A French trader touched some time ago at the coast where his tribe lodge and stole all the fine young men of the tribe, carrying them away to be sold as slaves in the Old World. One by one, they died of their misery. All but one, Squanto by name. Squanto fell into kinder hands, learned the white man's tongue, learned much of the white man's way of life, but always grieved for his tent on the northern coast of the New World. At last he found the means to return to his old chief, Samoset, and has done much to explain the white man to that wise savage. If Samoset is willing to aid us, it will be because Squanto has spoken for us.'

"'But what can this savage do?' I insisted, stupidly no doubt, but the thing had come upon me as a surprise that we could expect any assistance from a red man.

"'He can bind us to peace with the savage tribe who dwell nearest to us. If he *can't* do that, God help us!'

"'Do you know that other—?'

"'The chief of the other tribe? By name only—Massasoit.'

"Well, we met—all the men of New Plymouth—in the Big House to do honor to the red man, Samoset. And after much kindly talk, he left and promised to return with Massasoit.

"And that he did. He brought Massasoit, and Massasoit brought sixty of his braves! And I thought we should pop the walls of the Big House apart when we all crowded inside. We smoked a pipe of peace together—do you remember, long ago when we dwelt in Scrooby, how my Uncle Samuel came back from a voyage one year and brought a bowl that he held between his lips, putting dried leaves in the bowl and setting them on fire with a coal from the fireplace? Smoke came out of his nostrils and we feared that my uncle was ablaze inside. Well, I, too, have put such a bowl to my lips now, and puffed a pipe of peace and friendship with the white and red men, sitting in a circle on the floor of the Big House!

"When the pact between us was concluded, then did we sit and talk a while with these savage folk, and we found them not so unlike Scrooby folk, after all! They take pride in their blood, in their families, in their sons. They can be cruel, but so can a white King! They can be merry and sportive, and the tales they can tell around the campfire are amazing. And they know as much about simples, my sweet Mother, as do you!

"Samoset and Massasoit had much good advice to give us. They suggested that, when the weather warms, we push our settlement more inland, away from the shore that is so bitterly exposed to the gales and sleet storms of winter. And that we will do.

"Before they left—Massasoit and his braves to fade away into the silence of the forest, and Samoset to disappear in his shallop into the fogs of the northland—Samoset promised to send a trading boat to us as soon as possible. Then we shall be able to purchase some bitterly needed gear; and then, too, it will be possible to send this packet of news winging across the sea to find you, in the Low Country.

"Tell Winover that Nabby Wain has tamed a big black

bird that flaps and croaks about her doorstep all the day long. She calls it 'Sooty,' but there are some who call it an evil spirit and fear it. It is a good thing that the Pilgrims hold to no belief in witchcraft. If she were in some places with a black thing like that on her shoulder, whispering into its ear and getting now and then—I give you my word for it!—human words in reply, she would suffer mischief. The first time I heard the bird squawk 'Waugh!' I jumped a foot, fearing a red man in the neighborhood.

"Piet Billing blocked Nabby's way when she was returning to the Whites' kitchen after a ramble in the forest and, although he said he meant nothing more than to steal a kiss, Sooty got between him and Nabby's cheek and all but tore Piet's ear off! It has been a worry to me, those rambles into the forest, but I shall fret no more since Nabby has the bird to protect her.

"Well, the time has been long without you, sweet Mother! In another ten weeks I shall be eighteen years of age. Something important generally happens on my birthday, don't you remember? We went down Ryton Water when I was five—and we left Amsterdam for Leyden on my birthday—and we left Leyden for Delfshaven about that time. Maybe it will be a ship from the Low Country bringing John and the Dutch lad, Winover and 'Memby, and *you!*

"Young Matt, son of Matthew Over, Pilgrim."

14

WISSET

In April I had another pair of breeches from Goodman Winslow's gear and, much as I needed them, I am proud to say that I would have refused them had they not been presented by Goodman Winslow himself.

"Take them, Young Matt!" he said. "Nabby had them half-way out of the box when I discovered her under my bed. I don't blame the lass, either—'tis a disgrace to the whole colony the way you are going about Leyden Street!"

I grinned crookedly. "There's something makes me dig to the bottom of the hutch-putch pot every meal!" I confessed. "And all that goes into me turns into bone and brawn. Blazes, up until I was nine or ten years of age, everybody called me 'little boy,' and my father feared he had another Brode on his hands!"

"I know how you feel!" he sighed. "But Nabby Wain has outsmarted herself. She fed me rich foods with the idea of popping me out of my gear, but she didn't figure when she fed you the same that *you,* too, would soon be too much for their stretch. Look at those breeches—no sag, bag, nor flap! It's the last pair of mine you'll be able to get into. Nabby will be obliged to find a bigger man after this!"

I looked at my legs and bent over to the ground, cautiously. "Lud!" I said. "They won't do through the summer! It's a good thing my mother is coming soon. She'll bring plenty of fustians from Leyden and she'll see that you are well repaid."

That was the day that I first dug spade into the plot of ground that was to serve my father and me for our first crop and harvest in the New World. It was hard work, and the look of the soil did not satisfy me when it was upturned. It was not the soil that would have grown the hops, rye, and barley of Scrooby. It most certainly was not kin to the rich loam of the tulip fields of Leyden. I lifted a clod and examined it closer, pressing it between my fingers.

"Soil very poor," said somebody at my back. "No crop!"

I whirled about. And there stood Samoset. And with him, Squanto, that lad who had been stolen by the French, sold as a slave in Londontown, and learned the tongue and the ways of white men.

"Samoset likes this new colony," Squanto told me then. "He says you are kind and peaceful, that you love freedom as does the red man, that you are very strong and brave, and that you have suffered much. He has brought me to help you. He will return to our tents, but I shall stay as long as I am needed. I will show you how to make this soil rich enough to grow maize."

Blazes! I was so grateful that I was dumb. But both red men must have read my face, because they waited for no words but looked at the clod in my hand wisely.

"Fish!" Squanto explained.

"Fish?" I cried. Surprise loosened my tongue. I broke the clod apart, expecting something live to swim forth, but the savage shook his head.

"The soil must eat before it can produce!" he explained. "It must grow fat on food—now it is too thin. It must be fed fish in large quantities, and then left to rest for a little while, and then it will be ready to grow maize."

It was so reasonable that I wanted my father to hear of

the matter at once and turned to shout a summons to him in our cottage. He was, however, almost at my side and he greeted the two red men courteously. I hoped that he would ask them to bide with us, but he took them to the Big House, and there Squanto made his home with Miles Standish and William Brewster after Samoset was gone back to his tribe in the north.

Squanto taught us all the strange ways of the wilderness. He was a noble lad and a kind friend to the Pilgrims of New Plymouth. Even John Alden, the cooper, learned from Squanto the way to girdle a tree and thus make the cutting easier and the labor of clearing the forest away from our dwellings less arduous.

He taught Giles Kerry and me how to take eels from the mud as the red men do, trampling them; he showed us where the fattest fish ran and how to make fish hooks of bone and nets of fiber, and how to oust clams from the sand of the shore with nothing more than a sharpened stick.

Nabby Wain was at our heels wherever we went, learning of the wilderness with us. She was the only maid that Squanto deigned to notice. Her butter-gold hair fascinated him, and the black bird of evil perched on her shoulder set her above the other women in his eyes. She was a spirit-creature in his thoughts, I very well knew. Nabby felt this, also, and she ordered him about prettily.

"You only teach the lads, Squanto!" she complained one day. "Don't the maids of your tribe know aught of value or interest?"

"Much. Woman's work!"

"Foosh! No matter if it *is* woman's work, you sit right down here and show me some of it!" she cried.

Squanto gathered sweet scented grasses then and showed

her where to find more. And when we had enough, for Giles and I helped with the grasses as Nabby had helped weaving the fiber for our nets, Squanto showed us all how to make mats of them for the greater comfort of our dwellings.

He showed Nabby, too, how to fashion trenchers of wood and adorn them with the juice of certain berries. He made pots of clay for the hearth that served nearly as well as the iron pots which we lacked. And one day he put handfuls of dried beans and a chunk of fat meat in our clay pots, covered the beans with clear water, and sank the pots in hot ashes. We could hardly wait the hours he said we must to uncover the result. But when the ashes were scraped away and the pots dragged forth, an appetizing odor steamed forth that brought all the women of Leyden Street running. And after that it seemed as if we could never get our fill of baked beans.

One day Giles said: "Squanto," and stopped at that.

"Yes, O lad-with-the-head-like-sunset?" Squanto replied.

"Could you make a craft like—like Samoset's?"

"I have made many such."

"You *have?* Thunder weather, Young Matt, hark to that, will you! Could you show us how to do it?"

Right then and there, the three of us set about it to fell a birch tree, while Nabby watched and Sooty squawked "Waugh!" at every blow of the ax. When the tree was down, we peeled it, being very careful to separate bark from bole without a break or hole at any spot.

Squanto then fashioned a framework, while we followed his every move with care; and after that we stretched the birch bark carefully about the framework, sewing the edges with thongs cut from the roots of the cedar tree and covering it, finally, with pitch and gum.

And so we had a shallop that would travel about the quiet bay and along inland waterways like a gull on the wing and was no more burdensome than a couple of muskets to carry on land. It seemed to us too frail for use at first and we tested it with thumping hearts, but we lost all fear of it when we saw the sturdiness with which it withstood the pounding waves outside the bay.

Squanto assured us that it was just such a shallop that had brought him and Samoset from the shores of Maine to our colony; that his tribe made birch craft like this, only somewhat larger, of course, to carry twelve warriors at one and the same time to battle.

Lud! "We don't want anything of battle!" I told him. "But if you think it's safe enough to ride the waters of that bay, it's time we got after some of those fish you were talking about—the kind that are to feed our soil before it can be fat enough to go to work for us and nourish a crop. It's plenty time to get that red, yellow, and blue maize seed under the loam!"

Giles had to be told about the matter, of course, and he was just started on the run after our fish nets when a shot stopped him full in his tracks.

"That's Miles Standish!" he howled.

"The—the cannon!" I yelled.

"That's the danger signal!" Nabby said. And stood to look to the forest.

But Squanto, facing in the opposite direction, warned: "A ship draws near!"

"A ship! A ship!" From mouth to mouth the cry rang out along Leyden Street. The place frothed with excited men, women, and children all heading for the strand.

Only my Uncle Samuel, coming out of the forest where

he had been shaping staves with my father and John Alden, stopped running at the sight of Miles Standish in our midst.

"Who is at the guns, Miles?" he wanted to know.

"Nobody, now! There is no need. This ship is drifting aimlessly—'tis a wreck of some sort. I hoped to see it drift inshore and beach itself before giving the warning, but it seems to have caught on a reef out there in the bay. Something is holding it fast. If we only had a shallop, a small craft of some kind——"

Already, Giles, Squanto, and I were launching the frail thing of birch bark we had but just finished and were cowering inside, with Squanto at the paddle. We skimmed the water like a coot and, making fast to a trailing rope, boarded the wreck without any difficulty.

Not then—and, for the matter of fact, *never*—was the mystery of the wrecked ship solved. We knew nothing more, standing on its heaving decks, than those who watched us from the shore. Nothing, except that the craft was bare of humans. Nothing, except that its decks were piled with boxes of cargo.

We searched above and below decks, in every nook and cranny, finding naught but the boxes on the decks.

"It was a Spanish boat!" said Squanto at last. "I cannot read the story of it."

"I'll wager it was a pirate boat!" cried Giles. "Its crew crossed another craft and came to battle—and boarded the other craft—and this one drifted away—and—and——"

"Blazes, what do we care!" I demanded crisply. "It belongs to the Pilgrims of New Plymouth now!"

So we heaved the boxes into the bay and towed them ashore, and there on the shore we opened them and found them filled with soft silken rugs, with tapestries, and with richly woven stuffs of all kinds. Giles may have been right in his guess, after all.

We made a fair division of the cargo, as we had of the seed maize months before. Miles Standish and William Bradford brought the things to Goodman Brewster, heaping them in a shimmering pile at his feet, and he divided most justly.

My father and I were given three softly beautiful rugs of goodly size. But when we carried them back to our dwelling we had no heart to spread them upon a floor of pounded earth.

"Let Squanto's mats serve us still until we can find time to put a floor of planks between us and the soil of New Plymouth!" said my father.

So we suspended one silken rug from a rafter, where it swung downward across the slitted window, helping to keep the cold and wind outside. And the second we hung in the same manner in front of the door. When not in use, both could be looped aside on stout pegs fastened in the wall. The third rug I spread across my father's bed of balsam boughs.

When all was finished, the Over kitchen had a very snug look. "Waugh!" said Squanto, looking about and nodding with approval.

"Very nobly arrayed!" my father agreed happily.

"The fat Archbishop of York lived in no greater splendor in the Manor House at Scrooby!" I maintained firmly. "Except that he had nine and thirty such rooms! One is enough for the Overs!"

"For now, maybe!" added my father soberly. "But April is gone, Young Matt, and the roof not yet finished over the scullery! We must start that other sleeping chamber, also! And the ell for you and the Dutch lad."

"And a shelf over the hearth!" I reminded him. "My mother will want to set up her ivory elephants as soon as she sets foot in the place!"

"Aye." My father grew thoughtful as he looked about the room. "We'll widen that window tomorrow, lad, and lattice it! Your mother is fond of sunlight in her rooms. And we'll cut another window across the room, facing the bay. She likes the sheen of silvery water in her eyes."

Nabby crossed Leyden Street on the run and, mounting our steps, banged at the door. My father and I knew her footfall and so we stilled our hammers and waited.

"Young Matt!" she called. "Young Matt! What are you doing?"

"My father and I are planking the floor in my mother's sleeping chamber," I told her. "The door is unlatched, as usual."

She came in then and watched us. "Good!" she said. "Your mother will like this. We'll make a grass mat for a covering. Shall you plank Winover and 'Memby's room?"

"Aye."

"Who is to have the ell?"

"My Uncle John and my Uncle Samuel, while he is with us."

"But—but how about you, Young Matt?"

"Oh, the Dutch lad and I will have pallets in the loft."

"There's no need of that," she planned briskly. "Since Goodman White has died, I have moved into the chamber with Goodwife White. That leaves my room vacant. John can have that—the rent would be more than welcome to Goodwife White. Then you and Nicolas can sleep like Christians in the ell."

"And my Uncle Samuel?"

"Let him take the loft—or depart on the next boat. Why should he stay longer? The Pilgrims have no more need of him. Every time I look at him I fear another journey."

"That's a good idea about Goodwife's vacant room for John, Nabby!" my father interrupted hastily. "I'll look into the matter at once. Young Matt and I were going to build on still another ell at the side, but there'll be no need now, and we can spend the time in putting up shelves in the scullery and other odds and ends."

Nabby nodded and, brushing Sooty off her shoulder into the sunshine of Leyden Street, she closed the door on him and crossed the kitchen.

"What I really came over to tell you, Young Matt, was that there is another wolf in your trap!"

"Blazes! Are you sure?"

"I just came out of the forest, and there was a great thrashing around where we set the trap."

"Then the beastie is still alive?"

"Very much so. You'll have to shoot it!"

Lud! She knew how I hated that, as well as I did.

"Come on," she urged. "Fetch the musket and hurry, or James Billing will get there first and rob you again."

"Let him!" I grumbled.

"*Let* him? Why, Young Matt Over! And Plymouth colony needing every pelt it can get so that we can clear off the last of the *Mayflower* debt this month! James Billing doesn't turn his pelts into the fund—he hides them and sells them to Massasoit to his own gain."

"Are you sure of that, Nabby?" My father was worried at the thought.

"Of course I am!" she insisted. "I have seen James meet

a savage of Massasoit's tribe in secret beside the sassafras bush in the trail, and I have held myself still and well hidden while the deal was made."

"Take the musket, lad, and go!" said my father simply.

He knew full well the worth of every single thing we could bring to the red men in trade these days. Later, when the ships came from Leyden, we would have more to offer, but now we would have to depend on pelts, on the barrel staves of John Alden, and on the sassafras roots, to pay the last of our debt in Londontown.

Among themselves the red men used shells as coins, but they would never refuse a good English penny, giving for it four black shells or eight white shells. At the rate they were bringing in beaver skins, our pennies and shells both would be soon gone. James Billing had found a way to sell fine wolf pelts back to them for more shells, but the rest of us would not do that. They were worth more, sold in Londontown. And that was our aim, to sell in Londontown and free ourselves from debt.

We would have another object of trade, once the harvest was reaped—maize. This the red men wanted in quantities, but it was beneath their dignity to till the soil. And, too, being always on the move, they could hardly linger in one spot long enough for a crop to mature. So Massasoit had promised us one pound of beaver skins for each bushel of maize.

Now, however, we could not afford to waste a single pelt. I took the musket from above my bed and turned to Nabby. "Are you coming?" I asked hopefully.

"Indeed I'm not—I don't like the beasts when they are bloody, or any other time!"

"Beside the sassafras bush, you said?"

"Aye, where the underbrush is thickest. Take care you don't go too close—'tis a mammoth critter!"

I went alone into the forest and lost no time finding my trap. There was still a powerful thrashing going on in the shadows of the underbrush. As was my habit, I lifted the musket, aimed, closed my eyes, and fired. Thank God for my dislike of firearms and my lack of skill in handling them.

There was a surprised yelp from the shadows, and a young savage fell on his face from behind the sassafras bush! A jet of red spurted from his ripped shoulder.

The lad's senses were gone when I reached his side, or I would never have got that close. I clinched the gaping wound in my fist and, holding it shut, carried the savage swiftly back to our kitchen and laid him on my own balsam boughs, while my father sped along Leyden Street in search of Doctor Fuller and Nabby took the other direction seeking my Uncle Samuel.

They met together on our doorstep and Doctor Fuller closed the door against us until he and my uncle were finished with the work that had to be done.

Not until then did I get a good look at the wounded lad. He was no older than our Dutch lad, but Nicolas's breeches could have covered two of the size of this one. He had regained his senses, but he made no sound, either of fear or of pain. He simply watched with his sooty eyes as a cornered animal might have, and his velvety skin rippled with horror at every touch of our hands.

Such fright as this could work as much damage as an open wound, so my Uncle Samuel sent me in search of Squanto.

Squanto was on the strand, just returned from a trip across the bay in our frail shallop. He stood in silence to hear the tale I was bringing. And then, still without speaking, he went with me to the sassafras bush and saw the trapped wolf —and killed it with his knife, as he considered the other and more serious matter!—and looked at the spot beyond, where there was a pool of drying blood and a tree clipped by a bullet. And then he stood on the trampled patch of moss where I had kneeled to discharge the musket and sighted carefully across the open space to the underbrush.

At last, he had the picture in his mind and had judged the deed. "Humph!" he said. "Little prying-nose got himself pinched! I know the lad—I have seen him lurking in the shadows often, watching the white lads. He found the wolf and knew you would soon be near—and so he hid and watched. Many surprises are in store for the over-curious one! I will seek this one's tribe and bring understanding to them—no harm will come to New Plymouth because of this accident, I promise it!"

His words were wonderfully comforting, but still I insisted that he return to the cottage with me to talk to the lad and explain to him that we meant him no harm, that what we must do from now on would be done only to hasten his healing.

Squanto called the young savage a name that we never did learn to speak correctly. The nearest we could come to it was "Wisset," and so we called him, although nobody ever said "Wisset" without bringing a flicker of a grin across the smooth bronze face.

Squanto explained the nature of the accident and my grief in it, and the lad, listening in silence, trusted his words and ceased to watch me like a tormented animal.

When Squanto was gone, I drew near the bed of balsam boughs. "Wisset!" I whispered.

The sooty eyes rested on my face in peace. "Here is broth,"

I said. And lifted the trencher to his nose. "Rich broth that you must have if you are to be strong, again, as the young sapling. The medicine man said that you were not to move your arm—and Squanto has said that you could trust me. Do you understand?"

His eyes told me that he understood my meaning, if not all the words. "Sup, then!" I urged, holding the trencher to his lips.

He took the food from my hand without protest, and later fell asleep, trustfully and contentedly.

For days thereafter, my father, my uncle, and myself had only one thought—Wisset. When his fever mounted, we suffered; when the heat withdrew and his flesh became cool and moist, we put fresh meat in the pot and rejoiced.

"You'd never believe the number of savages that lurk hereabouts in the forest!" Nabby told us one day. "Every shadow moves when you are about to step on it!"

"God's mercy! Warriors?" asked Doctor Fuller, who was bathing the lad's wound at the time.

"No-o." Nabby wasn't sure, it seemed. "Some were. But some are squaws. And some are lads like Wisset."

"They are his kin—watching over him from afar!" the good doctor told us then, and went on with his task quietly. "If any harm came to this little rascal, we would hear from it, I make no doubt. But no harm will. It must puzzle those kinfolk of his to see how contented and peaceful he is here among the whites."

"Squanto says he has always been a prying lad," Nabby remembered. "Over-curious concerning the ways of the white man. He says Wisset has trailed behind Young Matt and Giles and me all over the place, just watching us, trying to make out what we were doing and why we did it."

"So he told me," Doctor Fuller laughed comfortably. "And wasn't sorry, if the truth must be told, that the lad was taught to mind his business by Young Matt's musket, since he would learn the lesson in no other way. Now, he hopes, the red lad will be content to return to his tribe and forget about those whose skin is pale."

The red lad had other ideas, however. As he grew stronger, Wisset settled deeper and deeper into our household. His pride in my father's breadth and strength was such as he would have shown in a mighty chief of his own tribe, his delight in my every act was more the admiration of a younger brother. In fact, Wisset became another Nicolas in our home.

He was rather taciturn in front of my Uncle Samuel. And as for Nabby Wain, he lifted his brown palm to her in prayer, the first time he saw her golden head and the black bird riding her shoulder, close to his bed of balsam boughs, the way he had been taught to salute spirits from another world.

Later, when he had touched the smooth goldness under the tiny coif and found it to be hair after all, and been well nipped on the wrist by the bird of evil, he knew them both for what they were and became Nabby's slave.

I was determined that the wolf pelt which had caused all our worry should never go to Londontown. After it was stretched and well dried, I took a beaver pelt, three fat fish, and a bucket of clams to Goodwife White and got, in return, a strip of soft wool weaving, scarlet as the berry of the wild honeysuckle, and with that I lined the wolf pelt most carefully, as Squanto had taught me.

And when it was finished, I threw it across Wisset's bed so that he would lie warm and snug at night.

But he would not have it on his bed. " 'Tis a royal robe—a chief's robe!" he shouted, drawing it about his narrow shoulders.

Nabby made a fastening with a shell and thong to hold it in place. And thereafter, the lad strutted forth into Leyden Street with the long gray tail swishing about his heels.

"God's mercy!" shrieked Goodwife Kerry when she first saw a man-sized wolf come walking toward her on its hind-legs, before a second glance told her that it was Wisset. She wiped her trembling chin with her apron and told him then that the fur was an improvement over his nakedness and to see that he kept the thing well buckled around his neck.

And Wisset did. Not because she told him to, but because the scarlet color pleased him mightily. He would not be parted from it until the sun of late spring caused his skin to prickle under the fur and wool, and then he made a careful folding of the robe and wrapped it in an old doublet which, we learned later, had been filched from a shrub in the Billings' yard where Piet had spread it to dry.

Since it was the only thing he ever stole from anybody in our colony, and since he explained the theft by a careless shrug and the words, "Billing no good!" and since I agreed with him in my own heart, I held my peace when the mystery of a lost doublet was argued hotly up and down Leyden Street. Wisset hid his bundle in the darkness behind our kitchen rafters, until such a time as he would see fit to return to the forest and his own people.

April moved along toward its close, rounding out better than five months that we had survived in a wilderness of the New World.

In Scrooby at this season of the year, there would be a

flurry and bustle going on behind every hedge as gardens were weeded and trimmed and put in shape for the rich crops to follow; bees would be swarming, and Elderblow Lane would be ahum with brisk little birds. In Leyden, right now, the low, lush fields would be green with uplifted tulip palms.

But in New Plymouth we were still surprised by an occasional flurry of snow. "The Great Spirit means no harm by it!" Wisset explained complaisantly. " 'Tis His final gift of winter."

"Gift!" Giles Kerry stared at the lad rudely and sniffed. "We've had plenty of that kind of giving, thank you! A trifle of sunshine and warmth, if you please!"

Wisset ignored Giles, who was mending a net on our step, and turned to me. " 'Tis the sweet snow, Young Matt!" he said.

"I find it no sweeter than the last!" I told him. And grinned crookedly.

"But this is the way of the Great Spirit—after the months of freezing, when all sap is run down to the roots of sweet trees, comes a day of heat. The sap starts upward feebly. Comes more cold—comes more heat—comes more snow—comes more sun——"

"Say, what *is* this?" howled Giles.

But all Wisset would say, then, was: "Come, white lads!"

He took my sharp knife from the kitchen, and a clean bucket. Then he led the way into the forest, cutting a branch from a willow tree as he walked, shaping it into the form of a trough.

He stopped before a lordly maple tree. "Sweet tree!" he explained. And gashed it with my sharp knife, inserting the willow trough in the wound and hanging our bucket beneath.

In the morning the bucket was filled with a sap that was sweet indeed! Giles clung like a huge, bumbling humble bee to the edge of the bucket and wanted to suck his fill, but Wisset would not permit it, promising better things to come.

He boiled the sap in an open pot over a blazing log in our kitchen until it was thick and dark-colored and then he dipped part of the treacle into a bowl and we spread it on thick slabs of bread and it seemed as if I could never get enough of it. Giles, too. And my father, when he came in from the maize field!

"We've been too long without sweets, Young Matt!" he said. "The hunger for jams and sugar loaves needs stilling at times, as well as the meat hunger."

Wisset boiled the rest of the treacle until tiny crystals formed around the edge of the brew and then, twitching the pot quickly away from the blaze, he beat and stirred at the hot sweetness with a paddle. Suddenly, before my very eyes, it was treacle no longer, but brown chunks of a most delicious relish.

"Sugar loaves, too!" Giles howled. "What a tree, my hearties!"

" 'Tis greatly appreciated at the season of sweet snow!" Wisset agreed simply. "When the Great Spirit sends these spring flurries, then do the red men hold their lips to the wounds of trees and give thanks."

We cracked the brown chunks into lesser chunks, heaping them upon a trencher of silvery birch bark, and then we accompanied the lad across Leyden Street while he presented his gift to Nabby. She came out of Goodwife White's cottage with Sooty on her shoulder and after the first small taste she sat down upon the step with us and ate in great contentment.

And Sooty ate too, flapping all over Wisset's bronze knees, begging for crumbs and ever more crumbs from his fist.

With the coming of May, we spent more and more happy hours in the forest. Strange shrubs that had been naught but unsightly twigs heretofore burst into tender foliage, and then into bloom. Some we recognized and hailed as friends. Others I marked in my mind for my mother's study when she should arrive from Leyden. I made a note of the size, form, and color of the bloom and the berry that followed.

One day, Nabby Wain came into the settlement from far-distant wanderings bearing in her arms trailing masses of a most curious little blossom; its delicate pink bloom and slender stems were hooded in a strange, reddish, furry growth; its fragrance was piercing. We did not know what to call the lovely thing and so we just spoke of it as *the* mayflower. Indeed, of all the sweet loveliness May had to offer us that first year in the wilderness, none surpassed the mayflower!

It was Nabby, too, who found the spot where wild earth-berries grew in great profusion. And after that, for weeks the forest was gay with the merry chatter and laughter of lads and lasses on their knees picking trenchers of the tiny, luscious fruit.

We had a new Governor of New Plymouth that May—William Bradford, once of Austerfield, always the dear companion of my Uncle John although the better of him by ten years in age.

"How old *is* William, now?" asked my father as we were sitting before the hearth that night, talking over the events of the past weeks. Of good Governor John Carver's death, mostly, and the strange way he was found, stricken while at labor in a bared field.

"William—William Bradford?" I counted off the years of all the Overs, Brodes, and their friends on my fingers before I came to him. "This be the year 1621. Well, then, Nicolas must be going on twelve. 'Memby would be close to thirteen years of age. Winover—Winover past twenty. And I'm almost done with seventeen!"

"I know about you!" he told me. "Go on with the others!"

"Well, my Uncle John must be one and twenty. Jon Brewster, eight and twenty or thereabouts. And William Bradford, one and thirty!"

"Aye. Time flies faster than a bat on the wing!" my father sighed, and poked the blaze. " 'Tis almost a year since we floated the canals between Leyden and Delfshaven! Almost a year since—since—well, we can look for a ship to come winging in any day now from the Low Country, my lad! Tomorrow we'd better get at that bit of timber we were going to shape for a shelf atop the hearth, here! Your mother will want to set up her ring of elephants as soon as she pokes her pretty little head inside the door."

15

THE *FORTUNE*, OUT OF LEYDEN

IT was in June 1603 that the King and I both came to Scrooby. It was in June 1608 that the Over family left Elderblow Lane and fled down Ryton Water. It was in June 1609 that we left Amsterdam for Leyden. It was in June 1620 that we learned of new wanderings in store for the Pilgrims. It was in June 1621——

I turned over on my pallet and brought my musings to an abrupt finish. June was my month and it had always furnished me with experiences of one kind or another—a golden stranger in my mother's garden, Dame Cotter's Free School, gooseberry jam, the eel market in Amsterdam, Nicolas and the *Halve-Maen,* the Weddesteeg and the Pride of Matthew Over tulips that were never bred.

Always something new in June! A happening, a dream, or, failing everything else, a birthday!

June 1621 could be counted on for the birthday! I stirred on my pallet and sighed. I had so longed for my mother's head in the door of the new sleeping chamber and her cry: "Wake, gogmagog!" (since she could no longer call me widgeon!). "An eighteenth birthday only comes once in a lifetime and is not to be wasted!"

It was, however, my father who pulled aside the tapestries at the slitted window that I might have more of the morning light on an object which he tossed across my legs.

"Very noble raiment, Young Matt—waugh!" he boasted. And Wisset, at his heels, nodded in solemn agreement.

I stared, pop-eyed. Breeches, made of doeskin—sleek, soft, and fine as the new leaf of the mullein pink!

"But—but Goodman Winslow vowed that Nabby had clawed to the bottom of his chest!" I stammered.

"Edward can wear what he has left in peace!" my father shouted in glee. "You've passed him in girth. It was *my* time to begin fretting, and so I consulted with Squanto and he says you have finished growing and will have a hard time to burst *those* seams! God grant he speaks the truth in both respects!"

"I thought you were proud of my size." I grinned crookedly. "I thought you wanted an Over for a son."

"But not *two* Overs in one hide, my lad!" he howled.

Wisset leaned above the pallet and stroked the new breeches enviously. "Very fine!" he said. "Raiment of a chief's son!"

I arose at once and decked myself in the finery. It fell in ample folds, with plenty of sag, bag, and flap. "Blazes!" I yelled. "Now for that sassafras bush beside the trail! It needed felling, all right, but it was a task always remembering to keep my face to Goodwife Kerry's dwelling in case the seams burst while she was on the watch!"

Wisset opened the door and let the June morning into our kitchen. A glorious morning! The sun pointed sharp fingers of light down forest trails, birds sang in frenzied chorus, and children whooped gleefully all up and down Leyden Street.

My father stretched to his full height and stared across the bay to the open sea. "Knowest thou what I would be doing on a morning like this, Wisset, were I back in the Old World?" he asked.

The young savage gazed upon him in admiration but made no answer.

"I would be shearing sheep on my bit of land that lifted out of Scrooby Waters."

"Wisset doesn't know what a sheep is!" I reminded him.

"Odds blood, nor a cow, either!" sighed my father.

" 'Tis from the pelt of a sheep that the scarlet lining to your chief's robe is made, my lad!" I explained.

"Who killed it?"

"Nobody killed it. The pelt is cut while the beastie still lives—lives to grow another pelt for future cuttings! The Old World is filled with just such wonderful things. But if *I* were on the other side of the open sea on such a morning as this, I would be ankle-deep in the muck of a tulip farm. And my mother would be on her knees among her simples. Simples are medicine herbs, Wisset. My mother is a Medicine Woman!"

He nodded arrogantly at that. "My tent also," he declared, "covers Medicine Folk! We all understand the leaves, buds, blossoms, and barks from childhood."

"No!" I turned and stared at the lad in astonishment. "I thought it was beneath the dignity of a brave to potter with plants and growing things. My mother doesn't tramp the forest trails, you know. She grows simples in a garden, close to our cottage steps. There are so many plants, useful and beautiful, in the Old World."

"In the New World, as you call it, also!" he told us quietly. "Come!"

He took a basket of woven reeds from its peg on the wall and led us for a great distance into the shadows of the forest. Nobody in our colony, I knew, had been thus far from the beaten trail unless it might be my Uncle Samuel and Miles Standish.

And still he pointed ahead, and still we followed, until

we lost our bearings entirely and clung to the trail of the young savage as a matter of safety rather than through mere curiosity.

At last the forest came to an end in an open glade where never before had a white man's foot pressed the sod. Balsam trees ringed it darkly, but the fresh green of the open glade was gold-flecked with sunlight. Sweet forest smells rose from it, and little birds sang madly out of sight above our heads.

"Wisset!" I gasped. "Oh, Wisset!"

He accepted my open-mouthed admiration with nothing more than a lifted finger, pointing to a border of bloom that outlined the farther curve of the glade. My father and I crossed to it.

Wild roses grew there in tangled profusion, raggedy white pinks like those that lined the walk in my mother's garden at Scrooby, simples beyond counting that only she could have named, and earthberries of a size never seen under the trees near to Leyden Street.

Wisset squatted among the berries and drew the reed basket between his knees, too proud to demand the apology that he knew was owing. I proffered it freely.

"I'm sorry, Wisset!" I said. "I did not know about this. Your world has as much beauty, as many simples, as the Old World—more! Your world—and *my* world!"

"Do you know the value of all this greenstuff, lad?" my father asked, unable to believe it.

The lad proved it. He brought me a blood-root. "The juice is crimson like blood," he said; "very good for painting a brave's face as well as his tomahawk."

He brought me a bit of shad-bush which ripens in June. "From the crushed fruit my people make a cake!" he said.

An umbrella-like leaf of the mandrake—"The fruit is healing," he said, "but the leaves and root have poison for the eater." The scaly, white Indian Pipe—"Good for sick eyes!" was his terse judgment. Black cohosh—"Healing for the bite of vipers." Leather-wood, a shrub with light yellow blossoms—"My people make very good thongs from the bark."

He brought tansy, milfoil, witch hazel, carpenter's-herb, ague-weed, felt-wyrt, mint, sorrel, monk's rhubarb, and many others, with a word of explanation concerning each.

"This," sighed my father, "would be heaven itself for Goodwife Orris, but I doubt if she could ever stumble thus far through the forest. How about giving us a root or two, Wisset, to carry back in the basket?"

"To make a garden for my mother!" I shouted. "All ready to welcome her when she comes from Leyden. We will never disturb this beautiful spot of yours, Wisset; but couldn't *you* pick and choose here and there from amongst so much growth to give us a few seedlings for planting in Leyden Street?"

He was eager to do this, once he understood what we wanted. We dumped the earthberries out of the reed basket and in their place we tucked plenty of healthy runners, well rooted and wrapped in damp moss. My mother would have fruit for her jam pots next spring.

Wisset gave us also clumps of raggedy white pinks, roots of dusty white milfoil, pale-belled mint, tansy, mayweed, catnip, and yarrow. And more. More and more! Until the reed basket overflowed and my father and I had no other choice but to remove our doublets, knotting them at the corners and using them as extra baskets while we returned to Leyden Street with backs as bare as Wisset's own.

We laid out the garden that very night—my birthday night. I knew that my birthday would bring me something of interest above other days! The plan of the garden was to follow closely the one in Scrooby, and my father and I turned the soil until darkness drove us to our balsam boughs.

Wisset would have nothing to do with tilling the sod during the busy days that followed. Tilling earth was beneath his dignity as a sprouting warrior. But he brought us more roots, plenty of groundnut tubers, and a vine that bore scarlet berries. Also a snowberry bush for the corner. I remembered that my mother told me once that when she was a lass the maids were accustomed to wreathe their dark locks with snowberries and the fruit gleamed and adorned them like rarest pearls.

When the hardest part of the work was finished, my father left me to the planting while he felled lumber beyond our maize field and with it he made a strong paling about the plot as a protection against marauding beasts. We spoke of the plot always as "Mother's Garden"—and my mother's garden was the joy and delight of New Plymouth that summer, even though my mother herself had never as yet set foot in it.

Goodwife Kerry poked her coral head atop the gate one morning and cried: "It's civilized, Young Matt—all the difference between the white man and the red!"

I sat back on my heels and grinned crookedly at her. "It's a mixture of the two," I told her, "and that is what makes it a New World garden. The red man grew the greenstuff wild, in his forest; the white man fetched it in to his dwelling and tamed it in soil of his tilling."

"Did all that stuff come from Wisset?"

"Aye."

"No beans, peas, or sallets in those borders?"

"No. Seed is lacking. When my mother comes from Leyden——"

"Oh, aye—I know all about that! But meanwhile my mouth weeps for a smack of greenstuff. Sassafras root boiled in pottage has a good relish, but it isn't enough! When I think of fennel stewed with eels, or a pot of boiled monk's rhubarb with a marrow bone, or a sallet of crisp kale! God's mercy, Young Matt, we English have eaten sallets of kale ever since the Romans first set foot in Britain!"

"But you aren't in the Old Country now!" I reminded her. "Give thanks for sassafras root and groundnut tubers and——"

"Foosh! I'm going across the street to see Goodwife White and Nabby Wain about this!"

She must have seen every other woman in the colony, also. Because the next time a small trading ship touched at our coast the women were on the shore to meet it with all the bits of bright weaving they could spare, a pelt or two, and extra trenchers of wood, brightly painted, as Squanto had taught them. For this woman's gear they got in trade seeds of peas, beans, pumpkins, carrots, and beets, and lost no time in scratching at the tough sod and baked soil close to their dwellings.

Nabby told me about it. " 'Tis too late in the season for such plantings!" I objected.

"We don't care!" she said boldly. "Goodwife Kerry says if the pods don't fill, or the roots fatten, we'll eat the green tops, anyway! Then next year, we'll plant our foodstuffs early enough."

"Some might come to the harvest, at that!" I mused. "The soil is rich when spread with fish—and we've plenty of them.

And the heat and sun are both stronger than anything we experienced in Scrooby or Leyden."

"Sure, we'll have a harvest!" She turned over a clod and dropped a bean beneath. "We aren't worrying over the harvest—that's in God's hand, once we have finished planting. What worries us is James Billing!"

Aye. What worried all of us right then was James Billing! It angered James, all this stirring of the soil up and down Leyden Street. He feared that it would drive away the wild beasts which he shot and sold with so much profit to himself. When he saw, however, that the hares, squirrels, wolves, and deer were attracted to our gardens, then did he maintain loudly and with utmost satisfaction that there was more profit and less loss in trapping than in shooting and he attempted to set his snares among our tilled rows. We drove him off, of course, as we drove the troublesome beasties away. But the man became well-nigh mad upon the subject. He was never seen any more without a musket under his arm, and sometimes he said he was hunting wolves, at other times Pilgrims. He was not one who jested easily, and so we avoided the Billing property as much as possible.

"Is James Billing about?" I asked Nabby.

"He's always about—James or Piet, one being as bad as the other! Turn over a clump of sod and there's James or Piet underneath, peering and prying!"

It was not as bad as that, of course, but worrisome enough. "I thought all the men were summoned to work in the Big House today," I said. "My father is gone, and I am on my way."

"God's mercy! You *know* James Billing has naught to do with our place of worship, Young Matt! Piet, neither!"

It was true. The place of worship was nearly completed,

but the Billing strength had not been wasted in its behalf. There remained only the stand beside the door where Goodman Gosset would take his place to beat upon the drums when the time had come, each Sabbath Day, to call us to an hour or two with God, and the rack for our stacked muskets, which would be in his care while we knelt and prayed inside. Most of the wooden benches were in place. There was a row of slitted windows all about the room, and between windows was a mammoth wolf's head nailed to the wall.

James Billing would have no thoughts for God with those furry heads before his eyes!

"There will be enough hands to finish the labor at the Big House," I told Nabby. "I was to work with my father on the steps to the lads' gallery, but John Alden will take my place. I'll help you turn sod instead, since you are left here alone."

"Are you fretting about James Billing?"

"Him—or Piet."

She walked with me, then, across Leyden Street to fetch my spade and back again to Goodwife White's garden plot. And there we hacked in peace at the stumps and clumps for the rest of the day.

Summer was come and gone, almost with the startled abruptness of a mouse in the larder—it popped upon us, peered about, and vanished. We thought only of the enormous amount of labor waiting for our hands and measured the days more by the weather than by minutes and hours: so many days of much needed rain, so many days of sunshine and garden growth, so many days of fog when there was naught to do save carpentry, planking the scullery and chambers.

God did indeed bless our gardens, as Nabby had trusted,

and the harvest would be more bountiful than anyone had expected. My father and I left the Big House one Sabbath Day after worship, and William Bradford walked with us.

"The Pilgrims have labored terrifically, Matthew!" Governor Bradford said. And stopped to gaze with pride upon my mother's garden. "They have almost forgotten how to rest and make merry."

"There's been no time for that since we left Delfshaven!" my father told him. "We have been in a race for Life—and only those in New Plymouth today have kept one jump ahead of Death!"

"True!" William Bradford agreed. "But a halt must be made in such a race sometime. A halt to consider what has been accomplished with God's help, and to give thanks to Him for His blessings. A halt for—for—well, for laughter and feasting and pleasantry. Both young and old need a bolus of merriment now and then to keep them in good health."

"It is a busy time—harvest time!"

"After harvest, then! A kind of Thanksgiving Day—as we had in Leyden."

Blazes! "Thanksgiving Day—with hutch-putch!" I yelped.

"God delivered the Dutch from threatened bondage, and they took a kettle of hutch-putch as a sign from Him!" William was thinking aloud. "God has delivered the Pilgrims from the bondage of the Stuart, and our bountiful harvest is a sign of His favor. Why not set aside a day in New Plymouth for prayer and thanks—for feasting on all the fruits of the soil, on all the fish of the bay and shore, on all the meats of the forest—a day for families and friends to gather at one board, and afterward, to frolic and make merry?"

"Waugh!" I interrupted, unable to keep silence longer. "Wisset will like that!"

"Wisset?" My father hesitated and glanced at Governor Bradford. "Wisset is a savage."

"Is there any reason why we shouldn't give thanks to God for some of the savages we found here?" I asked. "Samoset, and Squanto, and Wisset."

"You are right, Young Matt!" William said firmly, after a moment's thought. "Other colonies might have different ideas upon the subject, but, as for us, we are friends with the red men. Explain the matter to Wisset in your own way, lad, and send him forth into the wilderness to find Massasoit and bid him feast and make merry with us!"

Thanksgiving Day! The plan kindled the colony to a blaze of happiness. It was to be early in October, after the harvest was reaped and stored.

A week before the appointed day, Governor Bradford sent men into the forest after plump young turkeys, and in one day they brought back sufficient meat to feed fifty people for a week of feasting.

The women baked and stewed, roasted, simmered, and brewed; there was a continuous reek of fragrant steam above their hearths and bake ovens and the roasting pits that were dug outside in the open. Our trade with the Maine coast had supplied us with plenty of boiled maple sap since that day Wisset had introduced our gullets to its savor, and so the cooking of the women lacked no sweetening, as it did that first dreary winter.

Thanksgiving Day! We were wakened by Goodman Gosset's drums. All New Plymouth obeyed their summons to the Big House to give thanks to God, with Elder Brewster, for this home in a new world, for freedom, for the sustenance that we had been able to draw from the waters roundabout, for the provender of the forest and wilderness, for the harvest of gardens and fields.

Ordinarily, Goodman Gosset, staff in hand, was kept busy walking about us as we knelt or sat at worship, switching small maids who had fallen asleep in dim corners into wakefulness with the fox tail attached to one end of his staff, or cracking the skulls of mischievous lads with the other end, the knobby end. But there was no need for Goodman Gosset's presence on this day. The fragrance of baking kept all small maids awake; the fear of confinement in their homes after the hour of worship as a punishment for misdeeds kept the small lads inoffensive.

When the last prayer was spoken, the last psalm sung, we boiled forth from the Big House, to find Massasoit waiting for us beside the spread tables on the common.

Massasoit—*and ninety of his braves!*

Wisset had made a thorough job of carrying the news of our first Thanksgiving to his tribe!

However, after the first dismay, we remembered that there was plenty of feasting for all and so we made our guests welcome. And then we learned that the red men had not come to us empty-handed. They brought with them five fat deer!

It was like the time when all the folk of Nottinghamshire flocked to Scrooby to see the coming of Margaret, daughter of one King and bride of another. The visitors brought all manner of delicate foods with them, intending to be no burden on Scrooby in their feasting, but rather to leave much behind for the poor of the countryside.

The only difference now was that Massasoit and his braves

had no thought of leaving aught behind; they intended to remain with us until all was eaten! And so our Thanksgiving Day was lengthened to *three full days!*

As I look back upon it through the mist of changing years, I am convinced that there will never be such another Thanksgiving in New Plymouth. We had so much to be thankful for; we had sufficient for our own needs and plenty to share with our red neighbors; it was the first time since leaving Scrooby Village that the Pilgrims had come together as one great family to enjoy hearty cheer, rest, peace, and merry-making upon English soil.

For three days we feasted and sported on the common, although the sports were more in the nature of contests in skill between the whites and the savages. We shot at marks, and there the Pilgrims won easily, until bows and arrows were substituted for muskets. We wrestled, and lost to our guests. It was impossible, we soon found, to get a grip on the red man's oiled skin. We had running races, and Wisset was always far in the lead, to my great joy. We struck heavy bows with axes to test our muscular strength, and again the Pilgrims won.

In endurance of pain, however, the red men were so far superior that there was nothing sporting in the trials and so we discontinued them early in the first afternoon. No torture, however severe, could win a groan from the smallest red lad; but the whites were set to hopping and yelping at the first prick of an arrow. Wisset was utterly amazed at the sight, and more than a little ashamed of our weakness.

Thanksgiving slipped into the past, and with it went the last fine days of a gentle summertime.

Day after day, cold fogs hung about the shallow bay; more surely with each succeeding night did ice film the water bucket in the scullery.

The wild plum tree in a corner of my mother's garden shed its leaves, baring to our curious gaze the tiny nests hanging there, all unsuspected theretofore.

But the birds of New Plymouth were gone—the little birds that had twittered, scratched, and sung about our garden plot all summer, the sail-winged birds that had wheeled and whined above the shallow bay, the troublesome hawks and ravens that had fought our crops and welcome wildfowl. One by one, as at a given signal, flocks of birds had lifted into the air from forest perches and disappeared like puffs of dust driven by a northern gale.

Now, as last November, we were able to determine the location of Wisset's kin by the thin blue fingers of smoke that spiraled upward here and there through the forest trees. A pale haze of burning hung sweetly in the tree-tops as far as we could see.

We had no fear of the savages, however. They knew by this time that the Pilgrims had no evil intentions toward them, and we trusted they were equally minded toward us.

It was on November 19, 1621—so accurately do I recall the date!—that my father and John Alden caught sight of me, as I came out of Goodwife White's after carrying an armload of wood into the kitchen for Nabby, and called to me to join them in the forest.

"Fetch your ax, lad!" my father shouted. "We shape the last staves for Londontown today! After that is our debt cleared, and we shall be a free colony, at last! A colony with no charter—a colony with no frippery and gauds—but a colony of stout hearts and good morals. . . . You will be returning to England, John, now that your task is about completed?"

I fell into step beside them and we moved down Leyden Street, talking.

"No," John answered his question firmly. "I bide with the Pilgrims."

"Well, God bless thee, John!" My father reached out and clipped the cooper heartily on his broad shoulder. "Having sipped of freedom, thou wilt dip thy nose deep into the beaker and drink thy fill, eh?"

"I am as the others. For all their hardships, sorrows, and privations I know none that plan to leave New Plymouth when chance offers."

"Privations!" I resented the term. New Plymouth needed no man's pity! "We may show small beside Londontown, John," I cried, "but what do we lack that we had in Scrooby? We are all housed in warm dwellings with a pot and skillet on each hob, we have trenchers and mugs, woven mats and pelts upon the floor—and all the floors are being rapidly planked, which is more than can be said for Scrooby!—we have greased parchment to close the window openings instead of the open lattice that we had there, we have silken hangings at door and window, thanks to the wrecked ship, and only the Archbishop of York could boast as much yonder! We have plenty of salted fish and tasty roots in our larders also, against the winter that is to come; dried beans, peas, and maize, dried berries and fruits, maple sugar——"

"Waugh!" shouted my father. "Ask Elder Brewster if pride be not a sin, Young Matt! Still, just between the three of us and yonder pine, the lad speaks the truth! There is one family that we could well spare, but none that will leave when the opportunity is given them."

"One family that—oh, yes, James Billing!"

"Aye. God help us, I think the man is becoming wholly evil!"

"There's *one* that will leave when opportunity is given!" I told him. And grinned crookedly.

"One? One family?"

"One man—my Uncle Samuel Brode! He says that he is beginning to feel roots sprout from his toes, and the thought of becoming fastened to one spot of earth for so long a time sickens him. He says we do not need him any more and he longs for the Islands of Spice."

"Where *is* Samuel?" John Alden asked curiously.

"Deep in the forest somewhere."

At that very instant the cannon boomed from atop the Big House, and my Uncle Samuel came down the trail.

"A ship, Matthew!" he cried, pointing ahead to the strand. "Drop the ax and come!"

"For a trader? I have nothing to exchange."

"This is no trader, Matthew! This craft has crossed the seas. I looked from the hill yonder."

It was the *Fortune,* out of Leyden!

And my mother was standing at the rail. My mother!

Beside her were my Uncle John and Nicolas, 'Memby, Winover, the Fentrys, and thirty or forty of our old friends from Bell Alley.

But it was my mother whom I saw most distinctly!

"Winover—John—'Memby—Nicolas—*Mother!*" I shouted, hopping about the strand as crazy as a sand-skipper. "Nabby—Nabby Wain!" I howled, grasping at the first blue cape that came to hand and getting myself well nipped by Sooty without even knowing it. "There is my mother, out of Leyden!"

"I see her. And Winover."

"And 'Memby—and Nicolas—and John—and *my mother!*"

She saw me—of course she saw me!—but she stood quietly, her tiny hands folded on the rail before her, clinging to that pretty dignity which was always hers in public.

"Can that be you, Young Matt?" she piped across the last few ripples of water. "You—you are grown summut! At first I took you for—for—for—oh, Matthew!" she wailed, seeing my father at last and casting dignity to the winds.

"Orris!" roared my father, caring not who might stop to watch or listen. He reached upward as the *Fortune* scraped our jetty and swept my little mother over the rail and into his arms.

"The—the *Bowl,* Matthew!" she cried, embarrassed, striving to collect her shreds of womanly reserve. "After bringing it thus far I would not have it overturned in the confusion."

"Hop over the rail, Young Matt, and sit on that Bowl until——"

"Not *sit* on it, Matthew—Young—Matthew—I declare, I don't know which of you is which!" she pouted. "Where is my Master Hugo Chillingsworth, my squat little Brode lad? You are both Overs, now—God's mercy, I feel lost in a forest of brawn when I stand between you!"

"I'll fetch the Bowl!" I grinned at her crookedly, and she appeared to take comfort in studying my face.

"Have a care to it, lad!" she warned. " 'Tis filled with slips and grafts and pungent roots. But, oh, what a cold journey this has been, Matthew! And wearisome! I hope there is warmth in thy dwelling and a pot of tea boiling on the hob. I have fetched a sight of gear, Matthew!"

Goodwife Fentry leaned down as far as she dared to us then. "Gear!" she sniffed. "Half the cargo belongs to her,

Matthew Over! Scrooby folk will have no more boasting to do about the Archbishop of York and his two hundred laden horses after this; the talk will be all about Orris Over and the stuff she fetched out of Leyden on the good ship *Fortune!* Is that James Billing on the quay?"

The miserable little man glared at her with red eyes but made no answer. She did not wait for one. "It *is!*" she shrilled. "To think I've braved the perils of the deep just to come face to face with that ugly squint again! Well, there's no explaining life! By the way, my man, there still remains a matter of a shilling between us! That besom you sold me as you were getting out of Leyden was worthless—I have plenty of witnesses that the thing fell apart the first time I banged a rat with it in the Alley. Good day to you, 'Lissy Kerry! Cool weather you're having, this side of the world. Now then, my man"—she turned and blasted a hurrying seaman with her scorn—"suppose you cease dawdling and shove a plank out of this tub. I've got business ashore!"

"I'll see to the gear, Orris!" said my father. But he was clutched by the doublet and halted in his tracks before he had even started.

"Wait!" my mother whispered so that only my father and I heard. "Before they come down the plank. Matthew, we have lost a daughter and gained a sister!"

"Lost a—'Memby?"

"Not 'Memby, foolish one! Winover! She and John were wed the evening we sailed from Leyden."

Blazes! Fox-tail—Winnifret—Winover—Win*brode!* I opened my mouth, but before I could fill it with words or close it again on silence, my father had pushed me aside and was folding the fiery-headed lass in his arms. "Always hark to the words of a maid with a blazing strand!" he cried.

"She said she would wed with John—and she has done it! Winover, sweet lass!"

She buried her pretty face against his doublet. But when he called her "sister" she would have none of it. "No!" she begged. "When I needed a father, you were mine; when there was naught I longed for more than a mother, Goodwife Orris became that. Young Matt was my brother, and 'Memby my sweet sister. Can't it be as it was then?"

"Always, daughter!" my father assured her, and kissed the fiery curl that had become loosened from her tight little coif. "John was ever more like a son to me and a brother to Young Matt than not! God's mercy, how we *do* collect sons and daughters, Goodwife—the way a pair of fustian breeches collects cockleburs!"

16

A COLONY IN THE NORTH

MY Uncle Samuel, my Uncle John, my father, Nicolas, and I were busy until afternoon stacking my mother's gear and transporting it from the jetty to our dwelling. When it began to be seen that the task would be hopeless for even our willing hands, John Alden pitched in with all his strength, and then Goodman Winslow, and finally Nabby, Giles Kerry, and 'Memby.

"God's mercy, where did so much furnishing come from?" my father asked once. "Here's fustian enough to clothe all the colonies of the New World!"

"Goodman Winslow must be repaid with interest!" my mother replied primly. "And my family is growing, Matthew! I had boxes of linens, serges, and fustians laid aside when we left Leyden, you remember, to be sent on after us. Well, I've had the better part of a year with nothing to do but weave more. It's all of the best, too—every bit washed in the Oude Vest! Mevrouw Cort helped me, and 'Memby, and Winover, and Kathi, and even little Orrje—we all spun and wove and knitted!"

"But you didn't spin and weave and knit these painted beds and stools, tables, benches, and crickets, these chests of drawers, these pots, kettles, spits, trivets, ladles, and skillets. There are enough iron spiders yonder to frizzle all the fish in the bay!"

"Not all of the things are iron, either!" she boasted prettily. "There's a box or two of trenchers, nappies, cups, and bowls of lovely pewter—'tis something new for us of Scrooby, Matthew, and of great charm! I couldn't resist its charm!"

"But where will we put all the stuff? I'll have to get Young Matt to help me plank up another chamber and an extra ell or two."

"Don't fret about *that!"* she told him, and shoved at her coif. "I wish that it might be as easy and pleasant as all that. But it won't be! I'll have to begin to harden myself to the thought of watching my family divide. It will be a sorrow, but at least I can furnish their new dwellings! I had Winover and John in mind when I brought that painted bed and chest of drawers. There will be a bench or two for them—pots and kettles—some pewter trenchers."

"John and Winover!" My father was aghast. "There's an extra sleeping chamber for the girls, and John has a room prepared at Goodwife White's. We can't talk about other dwellings for our sons and daughters."

"Dear heaven, what a stupid!" My mother fluttered her apron at him impatiently. "We'll be blessed if we can keep ours sons and daughters in the same colony! John and Winover are to have what they wish of the gear. Then, there will be plenty for Young Matt——"

"Blazes!" I yelled. "I don't want any! I've got my balsam boughs in the ell."

"—and 'Memby!" she continued, as though there had been no interruption. "It may be that we can keep Nicolas with us for a time, seeing that he is no more than twelve years of age."

"Lass, you are taking my family away from me just as I have it collected again about my knees!" groaned my father and sat down heavily upon one of the new painted benches.

"Not *I,* Goodman—'tis the years!" she told him gently.

"We didn't bring the cradle, though, Goodman!" Winover came into the kitchen with her arms filled and stopped to listen and giggle. "Don't you remember how I insisted, when we first went to the wee cottage on the Weddesteeg, that no dwelling was furnished without a cradle to swing beside the hearth? I wanted to bring it this time too, for Young Matt, but the poor old thing had stood too much, I guess. Nicolas was a fat child and heavy on the rockers! Anyway, the cradle fell apart and Kathi Cort has the pieces. Mijnheer Cort can mend it, he thinks, and 'twill be a curiosity to them, having come from Londontown so many years ago."

"Still, I don't understand." My father looked about the stacked boxes and shook his head. "Was there hidden treasure on the Weddesteeg?"

"Oh, you mean the quittance! There is no cause for worry there, Matthew! Mijnheer Cort found a huge sum of money still owing to you from the firm."

"There was none! If he gave you money, 'twas a gift out of the tenderness of his great warm heart."

"Well, he *said* it was your due, and he suggested, since money could be of little value to us in the wilderness, that I use it for the purchase of stout, needed gear right there in Leyden. And so I did. And the master of the *Fortune* was fretted enough to find room for the cargo.

"And, dear heaven, there's *more!*" she remembered joyfully. "But not here! Thoma Cort is sending glass for windows, and plenty of bricks for chimneys, on the good ship *Ann.* And he says that he'll send Klaas Florin along with them to see that they are handled properly. But that might be another year."

"Klaas Florin?" I asked stupidly. And was glad that Nabby Wain wasn't in the room to hear. "Klaas Florin who lived on the Breedestraat?"

"Of course. You don't think that *you* could set glass and work with brick stuff, do you? If Klaas comes, Kathi will come with him and——"

"Kathi Cort?"

"Stop standing there and repeating my words like an echo over Scrooby Waters!" she told me then. "Pick up a hammer or a bit of timber and help your father knock those boxes apart!"

She bustled about like a bee in a poppy cup, hanging pots, kettles, skillets, spits, trivets, tined forks, and ladles in the yawning fireplace. "I know where everything goes—you've got the pegs all ready!" she cried happily. "The dwelling is wonderful, lad, more spacious than at Scrooby and yet enough like to be homey."

She turned her bake oven to the heat of the log and slipped inside a pan of maize bread that Nabby had just stirred up. And then, with Nabby's help, she piled the bare pantry shelves with trenchers, mugs, and platters, with pewter trays, bowls, and nappies.

And came upon a little ivory box hidden in a deep bowl. "Oh, look, Young Matt—and everybody!" she cried. Then, taking seven wee elephants from the box, she linked them together, trunk holding firmly to tail, and stood the ring on the new shelf above the hearth. "The Over family is together again, thanks be to God! Seven linked against the world!"

"There should be eight, now!" said Winover, stopping to watch. "Samuel Brode, you know."

"Foosh, that one!" My mother brushed the thought of my

Uncle Samuel away with a fluttering finger. "He's already settled aboard the *Fortune.* When it sails, so will he."

"Well, how about Nabby, then?" Winover laughed. "It seems as if she belonged in the ring somewhere."

"That's what's puzzling me!" my mother replied, shoving her coif with her wrist. "Oh, I know—the King's Voice!" She found a wee golden whistle in the box and dropped it in the middle of the ring of elephants. "So, now we are all fixed. *You* are the golden pretty, Nabby, and get Young Matt to tell you all about it some day. It has never been blown on yet."

"The Overs take care of their own needs!" cried 'Memby from the scullery, where she was hanging knots of dried simples to the rafters.

"Klaas Florin is coming to New Plymouth, Nabby!" I said, as if that was a trouble requiring a golden whistle, if there ever was one.

"I know." She took her cape from a peg and turned to the door. "And Kathi Cort."

My mother turned her attention to the floors of our dwelling. The woven mats and rugs of pelts puzzled her at first, but she accepted them after Nicolas and I had taken them outside and given them a good beating under her direction. But the pelt over my father's bed she refused utterly. She dug deeply into certain boxes and soon all our beds blossomed forth in lace-edged linen, soft woven spreads, and downy coverlets.

"Goodman Matthew and I will take one sleeping chamber," she planned as we all stood about with our arms piled with fluffy pillows and coverings, listening. "And John and Winover, the other. The Dutch lad and Young Matt can stretch themselves on balsam boughs in the ell for the time being, and 'Memby on the settle beside the hearth. Tomorrow we must all see about adding a third small room to the dwelling somewhere. And I shall want more shelves in the scullery. You girls can finish here—I want to go outside with Young Matt and see where I can contrive a garden in the wilderness."

But when we stood outside, in the full bright moonlight of summer's lovely ending, she gasped and could not believe her own eyes. "Why, you have already contrived a garden for me!" she cried. "Already a snowberry bush and wild plum tree—a vine with red berries—what is it called, lad?"

"The trader said it was bittersweet."

"And that shrub with the lovely silvery blue berries?"

"Bayberry. We asked him about that, too, and he said some called it 'candle-berry.' He told us how the maids do in other colonies—they boil the berries and a wax rises to the top of the pot. This is skimmed and melted, they twist milkweed silks into wicks and dip the wicks again and again into the wax. And so a candle is made. I have burned one," I told her, "and the scent of the burning was such as hung about the craft that sailed between the Islands of Spice and Amsterdam."

"Oh, Matt—Young Matt!" she sighed. "I am going to love this new home!"

"There are earthberries in the border yonder," I explained eagerly. "And more simples than you ever grew in the garden at Scrooby! Wisset got them for you."

"Wisset?"

"A young savage."

"Another son, Orris!" shouted my father, coming up Leyden Street with the last packet balanced on his shoulder. "Still another cocklebur for your fustian skirts! Wait until

Young Matt tells what a famous marksman he has become —shooting down prying lads right and left!"

I grinned, abashed, and as we strolled about the frosted but still lovely borders of my mother's garden—lovelier now with its pattern of stalk and shadow in the soft moonlight than it would be later when harsh daylight should expose its faults—I told her of trapping the huge wolf and wounding the hidden lad. And she groaned at the tale, and grieved that I had had no hyssop at hand, it being so wonderfully beneficial in the soothing of green wounds.

Goodwife Fentry sat upon one of the painted benches beside our hearth less than a week later, watching my mother slip a pan of brown spice cake into the bake oven. Winover was beating a bowl of wildfowl eggs at the table, and 'Memby was sitting near, munching some maple sugar that my father and I had stored in quantities in the scullery for winter use. Nicolas had uncovered our supply of nuts and was hunkered close to the blaze, cracking some with a bit of timber and a flat stone. I thought, as I entered the room, what a smell of home there was about the place.

"Only that you've got three rooms in place of nine and thirty, Orris," said Goodwife Fentry, looking around to see that I closed the door against the gale, "your dwelling is even finer than the Manor House at Scrooby. I wish Bell Alley could see it."

"They will!" My mother was comfortably certain of this. "They long for freedom, liberty, and happiness as much as the rest of us. I'm thinking that the good ship *Ann,* next year, will bring the last of them to the New World. The Corts too, or I miss my guess!"

"The Corts? Dutch folk in an English colony?"

"What's to prevent? Weren't we English folk in a Dutch land—and well treated? It might be that they wouldn't care to dwell with us, though; they might prefer to settle with their own kind in the Dutch colony hereabouts somewhere. There are plenty from the Low Country who desire freedom, liberty, and happiness, even though they haven't been ill-treated at home as we were by the Stuart and his gentry."

The door burst open and Nabby and Sooty came in on the gale. "How now, lass!" Goodwife Fentry turned from the blaze with a sharp rebuke on her lips, but forgot to offer it when she saw Nabby's face. "You look as if you had seen the Evil One!" she muttered.

"I have—almost."

"Nabby!" My mother trembled as she used to do when hoofbeats pounded along the Great North Road. "Is anybody outside?"

"Piet Billing's outside!" Nabby leaned against the table and struggled for breath. "But he pushed our door open and trod boldly into the kitchen looking for me—knowing that Goodwife White and Goodman Winslow were away. Only I saw him—and I slipped out the scullery door—and——"

"Piet Billing?" My mother was puzzled. "We want nothing to do with that family, Nabby!"

"I know. I fear him. I think it is because of the musket that's always under his arm—and the blood that stains his breeches."

"God's mercy! We'll have Goodman Matthew speak to the lad; it won't be the first time, either!"

"No!" Nabby shook her head and Sooty waggled his with equal despondency. "The Billings would best be left alone.

They have changed, here in the New World—they act as though they must be forever on guard against us all, to get their share of everything. And Piet somehow seems to feel that I am his share."

Blazes! I started toward the door intending to find Piet Billing and do something, I wasn't yet sure what, when a shriek from the table stopped me. "Nabby! Nabby Wain!" yelled 'Memby. "Send that bird of evil home! He nipped my finger."

"He wants sugar crumbs."

"Call him off!"

"Waugh-h-h!" croaked Sooty, watching Nabby with his beady eye.

Winover stopped beating eggs to watch. "You ought to get rid of that bird, Nabby!" she said firmly. "Sometime the word will spread around that you hold communion with evil spirits, and such whispering is not good. It can grow and grow, until a great wave of sorrow washes across the land. I know, because I lived with a poor old dame in Londontown once who died because of just such wicked tongue-music."

"There be no witches in New Plymouth!"

"There were none in Londontown; but many were so called, and died of it!"

"But we Pilgrims have come from Leyden, and the Dutch pay no heed to witchcraft madness. We have learned much from them!" my mother cried suddenly.

"Aye." Winover agreed to that, but her thoughts still worried her. "But John was in Londontown for some time before we sailed, you know, and he says that the 'bewitchment sickness' is already taking firm hold there again. He says that the Puritans are planning to cross the sea and settle a colony to the north of us."

"The Puritans!" shouted Goodwife Fentry. "What's wrong with them? *They* have never suffered the hatred of a King as have the Pilgrims!"

"I know. But they yearn for freedom, for liberty——"

"Don't tell me that they yearn for happiness, my lass!" sniffed Goodwife Fentry and spread her skirts to the warming blaze. "*They* haven't a chuckle to divide amongst themselves! Such a solemn, stiff-necked lot! Blaming us for not loving England more—and Leyden less! God's truth, I don't care if I *never* see England again!"

"The Puritans aren't likely to come here, are they, Winover?" my mother asked. "Of course, they are Christian folk and noble souls, but, as Submit says, they be not easy in their ways. They look sternly upon life."

"They won't come to New Plymouth!" Winover assured her gently. "John says that they will be given a charter from the King to found a colony to the north of us. The charter will give them all power in their colony—just so long as they do nothing against the English laws—and they will be under the protection of England. As *we* are not! When the Puritans come, they will come proudly. There are wealthy folk among them, highly educated men. When we touched in England before sailing across the open sea, John took me to see some of his friends and I listened to their talk. They are planning to come to the New World on the ship that brought you, Nabby, and Young Matt and the first Pilgrims—the *Mayflower!*"

"I hope they bring some gear and less folk!"

"They'll bring gear enough, and more than one ship to carry it. John said they would even bring bricks and glass and suchlike stuff for the erection of fine buildings. He would like to help build the colony. I only hope they don't catch the 'bewitchment sickness' before they are ready to leave Londontown and bring *that* to the New World with them!"

"Winover! Puritans? God-fearing folk like us?"

"Just the same, I saw plenty of maids among them who were wearing sprigs of ivy twisted in their hair, or bits of mistletoe branches in their pockets, or coral brooches at their necks, or amber buttons. To fend off evil, you know. Evil spirits. Belief in one is the start of the other!"

"Well"—Nabby drew her cape closer and prepared to leave—"I don't expect to dwell among the Puritans—and I shall keep Sooty as long as he cares to perch on my shoulder! And, Goodwife Orris, I forgot to tell you yesterday, when we were grubbing about your garden, that I know a place where rosy milfoil grows. Not the rusty-white kind, but a *rosy* bloom! I'll fetch you a root in a day or so. And some checkerberry creepers. And, oh, yes, some day when the time is right, I want to be the one to show you the floating leaves of the taw-kee."

Goodwife Fentry screeched just then and, leaping from her bench, swept it into her arms for a weapon. "Orris!" she cried. "Orris! The scullery! Don't move—get your musket, Young Matt! I'll bash the critter with this bench if it comes this way!"

We followed her stare to the scullery door which was opening slowly. Slowly, a magnificent wolf's head pushed itself into our kitchen, then a massy, furry body; the huge beast, standing upright, turned about and his elegant tail swished the planks.

Goodwife Fentry raised her bench on high, and I was barely in time to save Wisset's neck. "Don't hit him!" I yelled. "He's my friend!"

"What *is* this? Nabby with her bird, and you with a fierce beastie! Calling him a friend, too!"

"He's my—my brother!"

Before she could put into words the look on her startled face, I turned to the waiting beast and said: "Show her, Wisset!"

He let the wolf's pelt drop to the planks and stood forth, slender, bronze, and bare. "God save us all!" the poor woman shrilled. "Call Miles Standish—a *savage!*" And then: "Find the lad a strip of fustian for his nakedness, Orris!" she begged.

But my little mother rested a kindly hand on the lad's shoulder, pressed him to be seated, thanked him for her garden, gave him a wedge of hot spice cake, and called him "son." And after a spell of silent watchfulness, Wisset walked proudly to the table and helped himself to a second wedge of cake and addressed her as "Medicine Woman." So I knew all was going to be well between them.

"Are you really going to have that savage around your hearth, Orris?" Goodwife Fentry asked nervously.

"It has been his home before it was mine. And I have called him 'son.' "

"Never was such a one for collecting children! Everywhere you add to the lot! Except, maybe, in Amsterdam."

"I never rightly rooted in Amsterdam. I lived, like my grafts and simples, in kegs. This seems like a fine lad, Young Matt," she added, turning to me. "Only he is starved."

"He's not starved. Wisset eats well."

"But so thin—so poor!"

"Forest life keeps him slender, but he is not poor. He's gentry—kin to Massasoit himself!"

"Still, there should be summut of meat on his bones. Why,

he must be three years the better of Nicolas in age—but the Dutch lad would make two of him! Stand out here, lad!"

Nicolas left his nuts and stood forth from the shadows in all his pink and white flesh and pale yellow hair, and Wisset's sooty eyes never wavered once they fell upon him. This, his manner proclaimed to us, was what he had been waiting for! This was an idol worth worshiping. Young Matt was good enough for a brother—but here was a white lad whom he willingly chose as his master. Here was one to be torn away from the tangle of white folk roundabout and kept forever by his side in the vast forest wilderness.

"Come!" he said. "I know where the traps are. We will snare a wolf and fix a pelt for you to wear."

And Nicolas went with a whoop of delight. From that day, he cared less and less for New Plymouth's compactness, more and more for the forest's depth and breadth; less for the colony's white lads, more for the savage, Wisset.

When Wisset left us for his father's lodge that night, he wore a warm little shirt of red weaving that my mother had forced upon him, but when he returned to us in the dawn of the following day, the shirt was left behind and once again he was clad in his chief's robe, in his wolf pelt. He brought with him a fat deer as a gift for the Medicine Woman. And for Nicolas, a suit of white doeskin, soft and beautifully fringed, with beaded footwear to match, and head-gear of a fine beaver pelt with dangling tail.

New Plymouth thrived and spread this way and that like a husky clump of mugwort. Thirty-five Pilgrims arrived on the *Fortune,* out of Leyden, and had to be housed. Early in the following year came the good ship *Ann* with one hundred more. The site that we who came on the *Mayflower* had cleared from the forest began to be a tight fit for so many families.

At first we held the land in common. As one family, we felled trees, tilled, planted, and harvested. Then murmurs began to blow from ear to ear. Goodwife Fentry brought the matter into the open.

"Oliver and I toil from sunup to sunset," she complained, "tilling the maize fields. The Billing folk never open a furrow! Yet when the harvest is divided, I hear their share is to equal ours! Is that just?"

"But we all are to share alike," said my mother, repeating what she had so often heard.

"Then let somebody portion out the labor and make everyone share in that!"

"James Billing won't be forced to till the soil. He traps and hunts and——"

"—eats maize with the rest of us, I suppose!" Goodwife Fentry sniffed angrily. "The thing is all wrong. Now, Oliver and I don't require as much maize as a family like the Hackets, say, with fifteen mouths to feed. We don't feel like working so hard for them, either. We need but a small plot of ground. If we could have our own, separate from the rest——"

Well, it was a murmur added to the others, but a murmur with an idea to give it wings. Most of those who listened, approved. Even James Billing approved the division of land, only he fought for the privilege of dealing with the soil as he saw fit. No maize field for him, he howled. He should use his plot—and it so happened that his plot was up against the forest with his dwelling sunk among the sheltering trees—for the breeding of small game, he declared. For the setting of traps, of snares, for shooting deer—and for shooting any human who planted foot on his domain, thinking to interfere with his will. So he warned us.

A meeting was called in the Big House—this was in the spring of the year 1623—and at that time all the land of New Plymouth was honestly divided, each person receiving one acre to use as he deemed best.

I, Young Matt Over, received my plot with the rest.

"You, Young Matt!" cried my mother when I carried the news home to her. "Why should they give you a building site, a mere lad like you?"

"Twenty years of age come June!" I boasted loudly.

"Who is twenty years of age? Not *you,* Master Hugo Chillingsworth!"

"It was twenty years ago this June that you saw the King come to Scrooby!" I insisted. "Fifteen years since I flung a fat eel down the neck of a golden stranger in your garden of simples. Three years since I sold the King's Voice for passage in the *Mayflower*——"

"Samuel bought it back from William Brewster and gave it to me!"

"—two years since I had my last pair of birthday breeches from Goodman Winslow—or rather, from Nabby—or no, you are mixing me up, Goodwife! Two years since I had the deerskin breeches from my father and Squanto. And that brings me to 1623—twenty years old and a landowner like any other family man!"

"*Family* man—oh, Young Matt!" She turned from the hearth and let her ladle fall in a spatter of hot grease. "Don't leave me, lad!" she begged. "John and Winover are uneasy here. If you go, too——"

"*I* go!" I laughed and spun her around like a top. "How could I leave the roof of my father with no other to cover my pate? My plot of ground is against the forest, at the end of Leyden Street, and there is naught upon it but a fine coverage of stumps. Even if they were cleared, and a dwelling erected, think of the years it will take for me to earn the gear for furnishing."

"God's mercy, what kind of furnishing do you desire, Goodman Gentry!" she taunted swiftly. "Can better furnishings be found in the New World anywhere than those in the home of your father?"

"Why, no—but——"

"Must you have new gear, of your own providing?"

"I have thought so, Mother."

"Then think otherwise! There will be a Spanish tapestry, plenty of woven blankets and soft coverlets, stew pots, skillets, pewter ware, and much more ready for you when the roof is lifted above your walls. Likely Kathi will bring much with her from Leyden."

"Kathi! Kathi who?"

"Cort, of course. Have John plan the building of your new dwelling."

"Blazes!" I howled. "Your thoughts scamper faster than a Water Wagtail over the marshland! I've no thought for a dwelling, having but just received a grant of land. And as for Kathi Cort——"

"What about Kathi Cort?" asked Nabby, poking her sun-gold head into the kitchen. "Is she on the way across the ocean at last?"

"Lud, how should *I* know!" I cried, feeling somehow like a rabbit caught in a snare. "I've no thoughts to waste on Kathi Cort!"

"Why, Young Matt Over!" My mother shoved her coif awry and stared at me with pink cheeks. "Thoma Cort was always desirous, Nabby, that Young Matt—and now that he has land of his own—and——"

"I heard about the land." Nabby came to my aid. "Where does it lie, Young Matt?"

At first I was too flustered to remember, but then I fetched a bit of parchment out of my doublet pocket and read her the location as I had written it down at the Big House: "Beginning at a rock in the stone pile beyond the paling in Leyden Street and running 1 chain and 75 links to a blasted pine, then east 2 chains and 98 links to an oak sapling, thence 1 chain and 12 links to a sassafras bush——"

"Why, that must be the sassafras bush where I found the trapped wolf—and you shot Wisset!" cried Nabby.

"It is. The very same one. I'll never get away from the memory, now."

"You don't want to. Where does the line go from the sassafras bush?"

"One chain and 40 links to the moss-covered rock beside the trail."

"That's pretty far back in the forest—close to James Billing, too."

"Aye. The land can go as far back as one cares to clear ground, I guess. The moss-covered rock will be far enough for me, though. Let James have as much of the wilderness beyond as he likes."

17

ONE BY ONE, INTO THE WILDERNESS

THE summer of 1623 brought toil that taxed even my youthful strength. Besides tilling my father's and my own maize fields in common, I felled trees, shaped the lumber for later use, and stacked it beside my plot of ground to season.

Whenever I could lay hand upon the Dutch lad Nicolas I held to him firmly and saw to it that his strength was added to mine in the labor of forest and field. But the drop from his loft window to the thatched roof of our scullery was slight, and with Wisset calling to him through the fog, and a shallop moored at the foot of Leyden Street, he was as hard to catch as a gnat in the darkness.

He considered that he did his share of the labor anyway, claiming only the right to choose what that share should be, and perhaps he was right. He provided us with a never-failing supply of cod, clams, mussels, and lobsters, with small game, wildfowl, and deer meat.

He and Wisset salted the cod, spread it to dry, and hung it away in a cool place, glistening in its protective coating, for the winter stew kettle. He smoked and dried the deer meat, game, and fowl as Squanto, or Wisset, taught him.

Our dwelling was cozy and ready for winter, that year. Plenty of firewood was cut and stacked against the scullery walls, and the storehouse was filled with salted beef and lamb that we had obtained from the trading post in the north. In the larder were dried peas and beans in plenty, maize, fruits, pumpkins, squash, turnips, parsnips, and onions

—the tender roots buried from the frost in kegs of clean white sand.

Those who came to New Plymouth in the *Fortune* and the good ship *Ann* knew naught of the first winter in the New World and the suffering of those who had traveled to it on the *Mayflower.*

Then, we would have died but for the groundnut tubers that we dug from the forest. Now, however, we feasted on a bountiful variety. We had berry shortcakes, baked beans and sweetened brown bread, pumpkin pies and codfish cakes, hutch-putch made with lobsters, or with deer meat, or with small game, or with wildfowl. We had succotash—a dish that was learned from Wisset's kin—and our bake ovens were always filled with roasting wild turkeys or browning chunks of fresh meat.

"Not even the Archbishop of York!" cried my father, one day, sweeping his mighty hand about the laden board and eying me with a knowing grin. "How does that old boast of yours go, Young Matt?"

"I'd like to see any gentry that live better than we do!" I agreed. "Where's Nicolas?"

"Coming!" said 'Memby. "And I wish you'd look down the street at what he's bringing! Or—or *is* that Nicolas?"

"It's Nicolas, all right!" Winover agreed, putting a dish of stewed plums on the table and joining 'Memby at the slitted window. A first flurry of snow was in the air, clinging to all the stalks, twigs, and drying leaves of my mother's garden in little ridges and puffs. Wisset would have told us that this snow, like the "sweet snow," was just a joke of the Great Spirit's, that after it many pleasant days would follow. But it was far from being as pleasant a joke as the "sweet snow"! After *that,* maple sap would run and the forest would be lovely with the fragrance of hidden mayflowers; after this snow, there would be more drifts, dreadful sleet and ice, and piercing gales.

"That white-headed Dutch lad has lost his pink and white fatness and become a savage entirely!" complained 'Memby while we waited for Nicolas to draw nearer with his burden. "He's as lean and brown as Wisset! Were it not for that floury pate of his that whitens as his skin darkens, 'twould be hard to tell one from the other. . . . What in the world is that beastie in your arms, lad?" She opened the door and shouted out into the gale.

"That nizy of a Wisset brought it out of the wilderness for me." The Dutch lad dropped a gentle little bundle of cozy sleepiness to the floor beside the hearth. We all gathered around to look at the curious thing.

"It's a baby—and almost new-born!" cried my mother. "That's why it shows no fear. What is it, Nicolas?"

"Wisset says it is a cow."

"A *cow!*"

"Not even a calf!" shouted my father. "Tell her what it is, Young Matt!"

" 'Tis a wee deer," I puzzled, "though where Wisset got it at this time of year——"

"That savage can get *any*thing at any time!" Nicolas was both disgruntled and proud. "I was trying to tell him about the sweet, gentle little brown cows roundabout Leyden, and how I was going to have charge of Mijnheer Cort's—lud, do you know how long it has been since we've had a bowl of milk, Mother, or a wedge of cheese, or a layer of butter to our bread?"

"It has been longer for Young Matt and me, my lad!" cried my father. "I never thought a stomach could miss a friend as mine does milk!"

"Wisset never saw a cow!" Nicolas continued. "But when I talked so much about one—its sleekness, brownness, wee horns, and so on, he said that he would fetch me one, fearing that I would climb aboard the next ship that touched the jetty and go back to the Low Country, where they were to be found as thick as gnats, so I told him. Today, the zany came down the trail with *this* in his arms! And he insists it is a 'Dutch cow'!"

"Dutch cow, odds blood!" roared my father. "Well, don't hurt the lad's pride! Take the wee beastie back to him and tell him that Dutch baby cows must always bide with their mothers until their horns be grown. And meanwhile, Nicolas, if you must talk of the past and other lands with the savage, dwell rather upon the tulips of the Low Country—'twill be less embarrassing for all concerned."

We celebrated St. Nicolas's Day that year, to please 'Memby and the Dutch lad. Nabby Wain and a friend of hers by the name of Hope Dale, Giles Kerry and the Fentrys were invited to make merry with us and we spent a long, happy evening before the blazing log, singing the home songs of Scrooby and Leyden—since we knew none, as yet, of New Plymouth!—telling tales, guessing riddles, and playing, again, the games of childhood; we parched corn and roasted nuts in the dying ashes, and we ate trencher after trencher of oily-cakes.

And then, since the weather was too wild outside, we placed our shoes in a half-circle close to the hearth in the kitchen. "Though how St. Nicolas will ever get in here misses my guess!" complained Goodwife Fentry, hobbling across the woven mat on one foot. "I'll have no hay in my shoe, if you please! Tell him that, Goodman Over! And no tricks, my man!"

The women nested in beds in distant rooms as best they might that night, while the men and lads rolled themselves in blankets and stretched on warm pelts before the waning blaze. And so we slept. When morning came, the noise of our merriment rang shrill and clear the full length of Leyden Street.

Because there *was* hay in Goodwife Fentry's shoe! Under the hay, it is true, was a strip of lace as delicate as frostwork for the adorning of her apron or blouse, but it was the hay that caused the shouting. For each of us there was some gay little gift: spice cakes in the shape of Dutch lads with wide breeches and Dutch maids with frilled bonnets, red-cheeked apples, sugared sassafrass root, maple sugar loaves, and knitted coverings for our fists or caps to bind about our ears.

Nabby bound a woven scarf of blue to my shoe buckle, and beside hers I placed a cage made of willow withes and in it a merry little squirrel that I had caught and gentled weeks before.

We feasted at noon on hutch-putch, as we had feasted in Leyden on St. Nicolas's Day. But after that our frolic was such as could only have been found in the New World: John and the Dutch lad packed and smoothed a long border of white, clean snow in my mother's garden, the while I kindled a brisk blaze in the fireplace and Winover and 'Memby set a black pot of maple treacle to boil. When it was thick and brown, we each had a ladleful and, dashing outside to the bank of snow, we dribbled it along, writing with it whatever name we chose, only there must be no break in the writing.

Nabby wrote YOUNGMATT, explaining that she chose that name because of its length and the extra amount of sirup in her ladle; but I wrote NABBY and proffered no explanations to anybody.

When the last drop of hot treacle was dribbled and stiffened against the snowbank, then did we start at the beginning once more, lifting the first sweet bit to our lips; after that, we must eat clear through to the end without breaking the thread of sweetness, without touching it again with our fists. It was a trick not too easily accomplished. But woe to the one who allowed his thread to snap and separate, for there and then he lost all claim to it and the one who finished first fell heir to it. Goodwife Fentry surged along the border an easy victor, but Goodman Fentry broke his chain between the B and M of the word SUBMIT, and so she finished there also, although she proclaimed loudly that she was more in need of a bowl of catnip brew than any more sweets.

We went inside then and drew up to the flaring log to warm and dry ourselves. "Odds blood, I haven't laughed so hard since the first time I saw a fat Mevrouw in ten ruffled petticoats and a starched bonnet going placidly home from the Leyden market with a live eel and a dead hen in a string bag over her arm!" gasped Goodwife Fentry then. "What do you suppose Miles Standish thought was going on down at this end of Leyden Street?"

"Who cares—for once?" giggled Hope Dale, who, it seemed, was friend to more than Nabby, judging by the way she snuggled shoulder to shoulder with Giles Kerry. "Although my mother keeps saying that we will have to mend our ways and grow more sedate now that New Plymouth is on the way to becoming a town."

"We *are* filling up!" sighed my mother. "Elder Brewster is still looking for more and more colonists, but I don't know —we are fairly happy as we are. Other colonies may have more folk and finer dwellings and more impressive churches, but——"

"Other colonies have whipping posts, too, my lass—did you ever think of that?" asked Goodwife Fentry. "New Plymouth has not even stocks on its common! We've no pillory, no ducking stool, no hangman."

"We have no offenders against the law in New Plymouth, Submit!" said my father proudly. "We wish freedom, liberty —and happiness."

"*We* do, and I only hope the others who come to this shore will be of the same mind! How many are we by this time, Matthew?"

"With those who arrived on the *Little James,* one hundred and eighty souls."

"God's mercy, we *are* growing! And only the *Mayflower,* the *Fortune,* the good ship *Ann,* and the *Little James* crossing the open sea to us so far! Wait until one or two craft a year push this way!"

"Then we'll see colonists pushing inland to the Conightecute River!" said my Uncle John dreamily. "William Bradford says that the soil there is particularly fertile. A lovely, sheltered spot."

"You aren't thinking of pushing to the Conightecute, are you, John?" asked 'Memby sharply.

"Not me! That will be for folk who till the soil. My training with Mijnheer de Key points me to places where fine buildings are to be erected—where there is work to be done in brick and carven timber—where fair streets are to be plotted, spacious commons, and suitable formal gardens."

"Blazes! Who's going to do all that in New Plymouth?" I asked.

"Nobody, Young Matt. Not here, where wealth is still reckoned in beads and beaver pelts! But when the *Mayflower* comes again from England, bringing the colonists to that coast north of us——"

"Do you mean those Londontown Puritans, John?" asked Goodwife Fentry sharply.

"Aye. I should like to be there when they arrive. I heard some talk of their plans—spacious and elegant dwellings, schools, government buildings, a Stadthuis, and stately churches. The Puritans are folk of wealth and taste."

"Dear heaven—but dreary souls!" Goodwife Fentry sighed and shook out her skirts to the blaze. "Christians and highly educated, I grant you, seeking freedom and liberty, even as we of Scrooby. But what about happiness, John? There isn't a laugh or a joke or an hour's innocent frolic in a shipload of Puritans! They even criticize us for cutting ourselves off from England—*England,* mind you! That same England that we were forced to flee to save our lives! Why should we love it?"

"Give them time!" my father chuckled comfortably. "The Puritans were persecuted, but not as bitterly as the Pilgrims. So now they take pride in their charter from the King and look forward to becoming a bit of Old England in a new world, eh? Wait until they breathe deeply of our air of freedom! Do you know what I look for, Oliver?"

"No!" Goodman Fentry confessed. "I've not given the Puritans much thought."

"You'd better, man! When they arrive on this coast,

they'll be heard from! I look for them to bite the claws of the grasping hand that reaches across the water from Londontown to their colony."

"Rebellion?"

"They are the men that can do it—I've known some of them! And it may be that our help shall be needed—that Pilgrim will join Puritan—that New Plymouth will become one with the colony of the north and so there will come, in time, to be a New England all along this coast! Maybe in another hundred years—but such is my dream!"

"Well, dear heaven, hark to this dreamer of the Over family!" taunted my mother. "Somebody fetch another log! And let's stop talking about what's to come in a hundred or so years! Today brings pleasure and interest enough for me—tomorrow can stay away as long as it likes!"

The sun was warm, the ground free of its burden of snow, redbreasts and bluewings hopped and trilled and twitched about the brown loam like wind-blown blossoms, and mayflowers were uncurling red-furred tendrils and opening their sweet eyes to peer forth into a new spring.

I stood beside the rock in the stone pile beyond the paling in Leyden Street, whistling monotonously one cuckoo call after another without knowing that my lips had moved. My mind was too busy with problems of its own. I laid off a chain's length, and then added 75 links to the blasted pine. Then I stopped to consult a bit of parchment that was sticking from my doublet pocket most importantly.

"East, 2 chains and 98 links to an oak sapling." I measured the distance and found it correct. "Thence, 1 chain and 12 links to a sassafras bush." This plot of ground was going to show an odd design, but doubtless it was required to do so to avoid running into difficulty with James Billing, who had staked his land to suit his wishes.

"One chain and 40 links to a moss-covered rock beside the trail." And so back in a straight line to the stone pile. I took my spade and turned a narrow furrow all about the plot as I had laid it out—from the rock to the blasted pine, to the oak sapling, to the sassafras bush, to the moss-covered rock in the trail, and then back to the rock in the stone pile. The plot then stood forth before my eyes as though drawn with crayon and parchment. It was enough land. There was a corner sheared away between the oak sapling and the sassafras bush, but that was where James Billing laid most of his traps, and I could erect my dwelling between the stone pile and the blasted pine, thus keeping him at a sufficient distance.

I pulled some logs from my pile of seasoned lumber and laid them along the ground. "Build more spaciously, Young Matt!" a voice warned curtly. It was my Uncle John, standing in the trail, watching me. "There is no haste as when you and Matthew built, you know; you do not have to get a roof over your head in the shortest possible time! Build for the future, lad! Get some beauty into the design!"

Lud! I had only been anxious about getting plenty of lumber and muscle into the labor. Design was something I hadn't figured on, not for a simple New Plymouth dwelling.

"No dwelling is too simple for beauty!" he told me impatiently. "There is a correctness for every need. In buildings, as in garments. Your mother, Winover, 'Memby, Nabby—they are not garbed richly like Margaret, daughter of the King, for instance. Neither are they slovenly. They are neat and trig, fine-lined and beautiful in soft gray weaving and neat linen collars and coifs. You should bear something like that in mind with your building. Not a Stadthuis like the one Mijnheer de Key erected for Leyden; not an earth-floored hut of one room and a shifting chimney like the home James Billing has knocked together; but a low, broad, spacious dwelling, graciously planked and ceiled. There are fine bricks in plenty for your chimneys, fireplaces, and hearths. Thoma Cort sent them over on the good ship *Ann*. Glass, too, for plenty of windows. Take time, lad, and think this thing through before you start hammering."

"I don't know how to begin!" I confessed.

So he sat on the rock at my side and with crayon and parchment sketched his thoughts before my eyes, explaining as he went along, until the vague dream of a dwelling of sorts blew away from my mind, and the picture of my home as it would be stood forth distinctly in all its charm. Long, low, and sturdy, with many twinkling windows and strong blinds of lumber to protect them against the arrows of savages, or the ice and gales of winter; a silvery gray house standing among the green trees of the forest like a silvery birch.

"Blazes, John!" I howled. "Not even the——"

"I know. Not even the Manor House at Scrooby! Well, you're right, for once! Not even the Manor House at Scrooby will be better."

"When will we get at it?"

"*We?* That is what I came along the trail to talk about really, Young Matt. *We* will not be able to do anything together again—Winover and I are leaving for the colony in the north!"

"Winover! You can't do that, John!" I cried.

"She wants to go with me—she has always said that she wanted to help me build cities."

"But—but my mother——"

"That is all that troubles me. I want you to come back to Leyden Street with me and break the news to Orris. She can bear shocks easier when you are near to fall upon."

"But, John, there will be time later when I have grown accustomed to the thought myself."

"Only a few hours of time, lad! A break like this would better be made quickly. A brother of Wisset's has come out of the forest to guide us—we leave in the morning."

And so they did. My mother had no time for weeping. "I shall do that later!" she promised. "But now I want everybody to stand aside while I select plenty of gear to outfit my daughter—my daughter——"

"And your brother, lass!" shouted my father, seeing that she was about to break down after all. It was the right word to stiffen her.

"My brother!" she sniffed. "After bringing the lad up as a son all these years, he steals my sweet maid and carries her forth into the wilderness! He breaks my family circle—God's mercy, Winover!" she shrilled. "That reminds me—the elephants!"

"The elephants?"

"Of course; the ring of Overs that face the world together." She flew to the shelf above the hearth and loosened the third and fourth ivory beasties from their mates. She discovered that which she had not known before, that the remaining five linked easily together, standing firmly upright, although in a much smaller circle. "Look at us—look at us *now!*" she piped. "Such a little family, but brave. You take these two, lass, and stand them above the hearth in your new dwelling in the colony to the north—link them together and never, never, let them fall apart! And think of the five Overs that are left in New Plymouth whenever you look upon them! And now, what else?"

"Winover won't need your fine gear, Orris!" my Uncle John told her quietly.

But she brushed him aside. "I shall give you six of the woven blankets, Winover," she planned. "Six down coverlets and a length of fine linen. There will be several rolls of fustians, and what pots and kettles, skillets, and pewter you wish. There will be more, too; I can send it on by the next boat that touches this coast. We must not let our oldest daughter go to another family empty-handed, if it *is* only the Brode family! Dear heaven, Winover is an Over *and* a Brode, after all! Young Matt used to resent the thought years ago. He said it couldn't be done, but the lass has shown him!"

"I give up!" I told them solemnly. "A red-headed maid with a thought in her mind is hard to turn. One thing, though—Winover may be a Brode, but she can't grin as we do!"

"I shall send you grafts of the Scrooby gooseberries, too!" said my mother when we were tired with laughing at Winover's attempts to grin as the Brodes did, crookedly. "And a root of the buff honeysuckle from Elderblow Lane. Packets of dried simples also, with instructions for their use."

"She'd better go slow on that business!" 'Memby cried sharply. "She's going to live among the Puritans, you know. Witchcraft!"

"God help us—hush!" My mother turned on her sternly. But Winover herself turned us back to merriment by asking: "The Bowl, sweet Goodwife Orris! Do I get the Bowl, too?"

"Indeed you don't!" 'Memby shouted before anybody else could speak. "The Bowl belongs to *me!* I rode in it all the way down Ryton Water."

"And the dampness of you!" I sighed.

"Why, Young Matt Over!"

But the rest agreed with me. And so she was outshouted. And so we rocked with merriment until, what with the noise and confusion of the task that was before her, my mother turned to her packing and found no time to spend in sadness.

Winover and John left New Plymouth on another fine spring morning and I spent the hours that followed digging fish around the roots of the simples in my mother's garden that seemed in need of rich feeding. I had no heart for my own plot beside the trail until well on into the afternoon. Then, stepping out through the scullery, I saw the Dutch lad Nicolas hurrying along Leyden Street and returned to the kitchen to hear what news he might be bringing. My father was already there, to comfort my mother, I knew.

"Nicolas is coming—trotting like a courier along the Great North Road!" I grinned.

"Nicolas? At this time of day?" My mother rose to her feet and blew across the kitchen to the opened door. "Nicolas, where is Wisset?" she called.

"Eating spice cake at Goodwife Fentry's." The lad threw a cooking of plump, small game into a bucket beside the table. "We snared more than was needed this morning and I took a string of this stuff over to her place, and she said that Miles Standish was just back from somewhere or other and had touched the coast just when a trader was coming in with mail bags. Miles brought ours back with him, and she was reading a letter that was in the bag."

"A letter? Where from? Not Leyden!" cried my mother.

"Aye. She said the letter was for you and for her—she is going to bring it over here as soon as she has finished. She told me part of the news."

"Yes? What was it, lad?" my father asked.

"Rudi Cort is coming to New Plymouth."

"Rudi? Rudi Cort—from the Weddesteeg?"

"Well, listen to yourself, Young Matt Over!" 'Memby flounced about to face me, her cheeks burning red. "Is there any other Rudi Cort?"

"But—but crossing the sea! Is he coming alone, Nicolas?"

"Suppose he is!" she continued, giving the lad no chance for further words. "He's old enough, I should hope! Rudi is as old as you are! But, as it happens, the rest of the family are coming, too—only not here. They are going to start a New Amsterdam with some more Dutch folk on the Great River."

"On the Great——"

"The Dutch have a tract of land there and are to start a colony. Every man is to have a plot of ground sixteen miles long, bordering on any stream, and the plot is to run inland as far as the owner likes. Each estate is to be called a 'manor' and the owner is to be called 'Patroon.'"

"Thoma Cort in the New World—a Patroon of a manor!" shouted my father. "Odds blood!"

"And that's not all!" shrilled 'Memby. "The East India Company is going to give every Patroon as many slaves as he needs to work his manor!"

"*Slaves,* 'Memby—oh, no!" cried my mother, horrified.

"Blacks, and plenty of them!" the excited lass replied.

'We came to New Plymouth for freedom, but the Dutch are coming to New Amsterdam for slaves! Odd, isn't it? Winover said that John considered going to New Amsterdam once, but changed his mind in favor of the English colony to the north, because the Patroons, with all their land and slaves to work it, will be apt to remain spread out all over the place. Once a fine dwelling is erected for each, there the building ends. John wants to build schools and a college and churches and a Stadthuis and—and—well, *cities,* you see!"

"Then Thoma and Neltje—they will be gentry!" piped my mother. And shoved at her coif.

"Of course they will!"

"Why isn't Rudi going with them?"

"He *is!*"

"But you said he was coming here! Here, to New Plymouth."

"And how do you know so much about this Dutch business, anyway?" I asked sternly. "Nicolas hasn't had an opening for a word beyond the fact that Rudi was on his way."

"He'll be here any day, now."

"You know that, too? How?"

"It was the plan. Rudi was to come for me this very year."

"Come for—for *you?*" My mother shrieked and tumbled to the bench beside my father. " 'Memby—my *baby*—Matthew—Young Matt——"

"Don't forget me!" grinned Nicolas. "I belong to the family too, you know."

" 'Memby! John and Winover gone into the wilderness—and now my little lass——"

"I'm sixteen years of age, Mother!" said 'Memby proudly.

"Barely, but still, sixteen! And there has never been a lad in my thoughts but Rudi."

"Mevrouw Patrooness—odds blood!" yelped Nicolas suddenly. "Mijnheer the Patroon—I like that! Tell Orrje Cort to wait a year or two for me when you get to New Amsterdam!"

"Hush, you zany!" My mother turned and buried her face against my father's doublet. "The cockleburs are shaking off my skirts, Goodman!" she said, choking. He patted her twitching shoulder tenderly with his mighty fist and shook his head at Nicolas. But the Dutch lad would not be stilled. "Mijnheer Nicolas, the Patroon!" he whooped. "Waugh!"

"First you have to get the land!" 'Memby reminded him.

"Orrje'll see to that. Maybe we won't settle in New Amsterdam, after all! Wisset says that the New Hampshire grants are the place to go for hunting and trapping; he says the rest of this coast is getting too cluttered up with white folk."

"You and Orrje—my word! I suppose you think Orrje Cort would be satisfied with a lodge and a savage for a Goodman."

"*We'll* settle that question, my lass!" he announced in lordly accents. "Odds blood, have a look at the Overs in years to come—John and Winover, fine city folk, dwelling in a splendid brick mansion, afraid to laugh above their breath; 'Memby, fat with oily-cakes, Patrooness of a manor, with two blacks for every fingertip; Orrje and Wisset and me in a lodge on the New Hampshire grants, with naught but a blanket for each and a deer in the stew pot; and Young Matt——"

"Never mind *me!*" I begged. But he did.

"And Young Matt—well, Young Matt sticks to old ways like the gum to a spruce tree! He'll never leave New Plymouth! He and Kathi——"

"That will do, my lad!" I told him firmly. "You've never felt the strength of my fist yet, but any more of that and you will! *Some*body in this family will need to lead you by the scruff to the scullery bucket and duck that prattling tongue until it learns to wag politely!"

He had never heard that tone in my voice before; nor had anybody else. Luckily he met it with a grin and uplifted palm. "Peace!" he grunted, in imitation of Massasoit. "Shall I give the last of my news?"

"Last? Is there any more?"

"Well, 'Memby slopped most of it out of the skillet—but she didn't mention the fact that Klaas Florin is on his way to the New World, too!"

Klaas Florin.

I took up my spade and stepped forth into Leyden Street. And from there into the forest, along the trail to my plot of ground. John's picture of my future dwelling was still in my doublet pocket, but I was not studying about that now. I was not sure that there would ever be a long, low, sturdy dwelling between the stone pile and the blasted pine—a silvery gray dwelling, like a lovely birch among the pine trees; a dwelling with a railed, open room atop the roof where two might walk at sunset and gaze far out across treetops to the open sea.

It might be better for me to tear up John's picture and ship aboard the next craft that touched our jetty in search of my Uncle Samuel. And, having found him in some distant land, to sail the Seven Seas thereafter forever and a day.

And then I crossed the plot of ground drearily to the sassafras bush and found Nabby Wain huddled on the ground below, weeping.

Once before I had found Nabby dripping with tears. That was when—that was when—blazes! "You don't have to cry any more, Nabby!" I told her gently. "Klaas Florin is coming to New Plymouth."

"Not—not to New Plymouth!" she sobbed. "To—to New Amsterdam. It's Kathi—Kathi Cort—that maybe will come to New Plymouth!"

"What for?"

"What for? Don't *you* know?"

We both turned as light feet came flying down the trail and I stood in front of Nabby to hide her tears from Giles Kerry or Piet Billing, as the case might be. It was Nicolas.

"Peace, Young Matt!" he begged, this time humbly. "I'm sorry that I teased you. To pay for my rudeness, I'll tell you first of all some news that was in the letter. Kathi *is* coming to the New World, and so is Klaas Florin."

"So I have heard, lad."

"But did you know that they have wed—and are only coming to New Plymouth to be at 'Memby's wedding? After that, they will settle on a manor in New Amsterdam and—oh, all right, all right, you don't have to sweep me into the bay with that mighty paw of yours! I'm going, Young Matt—going fast!"

I turned about and laid my mighty paw, as the Dutch lad called it, upon the golden head before me. "Well, Nabby," I said, "there's news at last!"

"Good news?"

"The best in the world for me!"

"And for me, too, Young Matt!" she said.

And after that, we walked from the rock in the stone pile to the blasted pine, to the oak sapling, to the sassafras bush, to the moss-covered rock beside the trail, and thence back to the stone pile. I showed her John's picture of the goodly dwelling that would stand there and she was pleased with everything, but most of all with the little railed room atop the roof where two might sit or walk at sunset and look for a white sail at sea.

After that we picked our arms full of mayflowers and came down the trail and out of the forest, down Leyden Street and into our garden, to find my mother.

18

"ALWAYS MORE COCKLEBURS FOR THE OVERS!"

SHE was on the jetty. 'Memby, slamming out of the kitchen as we entered, told us that the Fentrys had just come for her and that everybody in New Plymouth was gathered on the strand.

"There's a sail outside the bay, Young Matt!" she shouted. "A ship is coming in! I had to dash back to shift the bean kettle to the cooler part of the log. You two would better hurry along with me!"

"A ship—a trader?" I asked.

"No! A ship from across the seas! All this time, and only four ships so far! The *Mayflower*, the *Fortune*, the good ship *Ann*, and the *Little James*. And now, out of the fog, comes the—the—I don't know what it is, but it is bringing colonists or it wouldn't touch our coast! Let's see who comes on it!"

Well, it was the *Charity!* Word was already flying from mouth to mouth as we reached the strand that there were sixty colonists aboard. And then, with our own startled eyes, we saw that the *Charity* was bringing us *three cows!*

Three sweet brown heads rested on the rail and stared at land curiously. And there were plenty of young, staring back, who had never seen cows before and clung to their mothers' aprons, howling their terror.

There were other of us, however, who leaped and pranced

with joy at the sight of the three gentle heads and wondered how we had existed thus far without frothing milk, creamy cheese, and golden butter, and how three cows were going to be spread among so many with satisfaction to all. And how marauding wolves could be kept away from the precious beasties. And why not, if cows could cross the ocean, why not sheep and hogs!

Our heads whirled with questions such as these, with bright visions of a future that should find us surrounded by wide, open green fields dotted over with grazing flocks and herds. Scrooby—Leyden—there was no reason why we should lack any of the abundance of the Old World in this, our New World!

And then a savage whoop cut our joy to silence as Wisset leaped in front of the Dutch lad, at the same time fitting an arrow to its tautened string.

"Brother!" he shrilled. "The god of evil rides the waves! I'll hold him off while you fetch your musket—then let a bullet follow my arrow to a spot between the eyes!"

"Wisset!" I bellowed. And fell upon him. Not in time to halt the speeding arrow, but in time to change its course. It buried its nose in the rail of the *Charity* and remained there, quivering.

"You crazy red buck!" Nicolas lifted his angry voice above the uproar. "What do you think you're doing? Trying to damage the first Pilgrim cows that ever——"

"Cows?"

"Of course they are cows! What else?"

"Dutch cows are not like these, my brother."

"Yes, they are, too! What *you* tried to make me think was a Dutch cow was only a baby deer. These be not wild beasties, nizy! These be tame, and of great goodness, and the Great Spirit Himself sent them to us from across the many waters!"

"Drive that young savage back to the forest, Nicolas Over!" boomed Goodwife Fentry above all other outcries. "A nice way to welcome a cow, shooting its eye out before it ever sets hoof on the ground! If I was in their place I'd give nothing but soured curd for the rest of my days! Turn your musket on that redskin if any evil around here is to be marked!"

"None *is!*" I said quietly, and grinned at the staring faces. "Wisset meant no harm—and did none. He was as frightened as these howling moppets, but brave enough to stand forth and try to protect his friend. Once he understands, he is harmless enough."

"Harmless, God's mercy!" Goodwife Fentry sniffed nervously. "Don't tell *me* that heathen is harmless! If I ever heard a war whoop that meant a scalping in the offing, I heard it just now! Get him out of our sight, Young Matt, and keep him away from those cows! I'm warning you."

I pulled Wisset close to my side, between me and Nabby, and grinned crookedly at him. But more than that, I did nothing. Nor was anything more demanded, because the *Charity* was at anchor by that time and the landing plank about to be lowered.

The Dutch lad was the first to spring aboard. He grasped a leading strap and guided the first beastie ashore and up a grassy bank. There he stopped long enough to strip a wisp of greenstuff from the ditch and feed the eager little traveler.

Wisset's lean, bare body tensed when he saw the flicking tongue wrap itself around the Dutch lad's fist, and his brown claw reached for a second arrow. But I held his wrist between my fingers and Nabby whispered: "Waugh!" proudly, and so he stood still and watched silently while his white brother withstood the trial of smoking mouth and devouring teeth.

He was puzzled, and slightly ashamed, when Nicolas cast both arms about the strange beast and hugged it affectionately. The red lad wouldn't have shown his feelings like that toward any living thing. Why should the white men love these cousins to the deer? He stood motionless as a forest trunk until Piet Billing whispered slyly into his ear, taunting him with cowardice. Then Wisset moved stiffly up the grassy bank in the wake of his white brother and holding forth a wisp of green, in imitation, waited for death from the yawning mouth.

The red lad learned quickly. After a second feeding, he squatted gravely in front of the three beasts, thigh to thigh with Nicolas, and would not be parted from them.

"Look at him!" Nabby giggled. "He's ready as always to die for, or with, Nicolas!"

Knowing him better, I was able to read the lad's mind with greater accuracy. "He's composing a tale," I told her, "to be related at the next meeting of young braves around Massasoit's campfire."

"A tale? Of ships that sail the seas?"

"Of *himself,* my butter-headed lass! A tale that will go something like this: 'I, Wisset, am fearless! I met the beasts and gave them look for look. Flame and vapor spouted from their nostrils, but I, Wisset, was unafraid! I strode forward with herbage in my hands and the beasts lowered their heads, widened their mouths, and, although their tongues were like a searing flame, still did I not waver as they seized the offering from my very hand. They ate and, lo, I was passed through the trial of flame, of vapor, of yawning mouths, of searing flame and did live!' "

"Why, the vain little braggart!"

"No!" I told her. "He believes it."

We followed on behind as the cows were led to the common in front of the Big House and there tethered for the night.

"Piet Billing will have them in charge for this night at least," Goodwife Fentry grumbled in my ear. "That family will never miss the chance of being the first to dip their snouts into a bucket of warm milk—see, what did I tell you? There he comes now with a bucket!"

"Grab Wisset, Young Matt!" shrieked Nicolas. But the warning come too late.

Piet Billing, whom the redskin hated, was laying hands upon the sacred beasts of the Pilgrims! It was too much for the lad's strained nerves. He sprang for the bucket, lifted it on high, and brought it down on Piet's head with a crack that stretched Piet quietly along the sod.

"Young Matt! Young Matt!" wailed Nicolas, dropping his rope and leaving the last cow to her own choice between biding beside her mates or strolling off alone into the wilderness. "If Wisset has done any killing——"

"He hasn't—yet!" I assured the panting lad. "It was only a stunning blow, that one. The next may be worse. See if you can't get hold of the bucket!"

"Give it to me, you untamed son of the sun!" the Dutch lad shrilled. "And toss a scoop of water over Piet, somebody!"

"He sought to kill the beasts!" said Wisset coldly. "By torture, that one sought to rid himself of the sacred cows."

"He did not, you fighting wasp!" snapped Nicolas wearily.

"He was only going to milk them—every day they have to be milked so that white folks may get a medicine drink. *I* was going to ask Governor Bradford to let me take charge of them, but now you have spoiled it all. We had to leave Leyden on the very day I was to have charge of Mijnheer Cort's cows, and on the very day cows come to New Plymouth I'll have to leave on account of *you!*"

"We stay!" Wisset told him firmly.

"No we don't—not after what you've done! There'd be war in the colony before morning. I'll have to go with you, to keep free of that Billing tribe; you'll find a place for me in your father's lodge, my brave! And now stick your nose to the forest and beat the gale, unless you want to feel a musket ball against your buttocks—here comes old James Billing, frothing at the mouth!"

The Corts came up the coast from New Amsterdam in a trader for 'Memby's wedding, Klaas Florin and Kathi with them. The two families were so happy at being together again that almost was the purpose of the meeting forgotten. Mijnheer Cort went into the forest with my father to talk lumber until both men were so hoarse that a brewing of feltwyrt had to be made before anything stronger than a whisper could be brought from between their lips.

And Mevrouw Cort looked at my mother's garden, her tulips, her woven grass mats, and her lined pelts—and wanted to see a savage. But Wisset was gone! So, also, was Nicolas. And John and Winover. The manner of their different goings was another hour's tale.

And then our old friends of Scrooby and Bell Alley began to come down Leyden Street, bearing modest gifts of love for 'Memby, crowding our kitchen and garden clear to the palings. And with them, William Bradford the Governor and Elder Brewster.

And so was little 'Memby wed, in a froth of silver tissue and airy lace, in silver slippers and a shimmer of other pretties that had been sent from the country of the French to Leyden to make Kathi lovely when she was wed to Klaas Florin, and were now "being twice blessed," as Kathi vowed, since they had crossed the ocean to adorn another bride.

A gay little crown of myrtle went with the silver lace, but my mother lifted it from 'Memby's soft brown curls as soon as she saw it and put in its stead a crown of green that she wove herself from rosemary, lavender, purple pansies that had come from Elderblow Lane, mugwort, and fennel.

"It was a habit among the old folk of Scrooby to strew fennel in the paths of brides," she explained. "And who wears mugwort can never be harmed!"

'Memby Cort!

Before the bridal party left for New Amsterdam aboard the trader that evening, my mother reached to the shelf above the hearth and loosened two more ivory elephants from the ring.

"Only three left!" she piped merrily, although tears dimmed her eyes. "Goodman Matthew's there—and Young Matt is there—and I am there! Put your little beastie on a shelf in your new kitchen, 'Memby, lass, and think of us in New Plymouth whenever you lift your eyes to it! And give the other to Nicolas when he comes knocking at your manor. Tell him to hold fast to the bit of ivory—tell him never to forget that he is a link in the Over tribe! Some day, God grant that some day our circle may be complete again!"

Kathi and 'Memby called Nabby into my mother's sleeping chamber while the silver tissue and airy lace were being packed into their box, atop the silver slippers and the crown of myrtle.

"I'm leaving it for you, Nabby!" Kathi said, with kindness in the thought. "You shall wear it when you wed with Young Matt. After that, send it to me in New Amsterdam by the first trader and we'll save it for Nicolas's lass."

But Nabby shook her head gently, and called me into the room to judge if she had done wrong in refusing the offer. "It is generous of you, Kathi!" I said. "And Nabby and I both thank you for the thought. But my maid is a Pilgrim."

"So am *I,* silly!" cried 'Memby.

"You are Mevrouw Cort!"

"God's mercy, so I am!" she gasped. Before she could say more, I added: "The first time I really *saw* my maid, she was garbed in soft gray weaving, with linen apron and a blue cape wrapped about her shoulders and a tiny coif atop her butter-colored head. I have never seen her otherwise. I'm not sure that I would recognize her in silver tissue and lace —and I wouldn't like to fail to recognize Nabby on her wedding day!"

"He's silly!" said Nabby. "But his words have sense. You and 'Memby are Mevrouw Patroonesses, or whatever, now. Silver mist and all lovely things befit you. But I shall always be Goodwife—Goodwife Over! I will go to my own home in gray weaving, with fresh linen collar, apron, and coif, wrapped in my long blue cape!"

"And nobody will ever look sweeter!" cried Kathi, kissing her warmly. Nobody ever did!

It seemed as if everybody in New Plymouth had a hand in building my new home that summer. Giles Kerry, William Bradford, Elder Brewster, Oliver Fentry, and John Alden were forever buzzing about my father and me with hammers or with advice, but when it came to lifting the roof, everybody was there, and my mother and Nabby spread a great feast in the open for all.

There was no finer house in the colony. The chimney and fireplaces were stoutly bricked and there was glass in all the windows. The outside was of slabs of shaped lumber, laid one atop the other, stained a silvery birch like the fairest trees of the forest, and the floors were smoothly, warmly planked. The little open room beside the chimney puzzled some, but pleased all when its purpose was explained.

"You shall have the largest of the Spanish tapestries, Nabby, to brighten the best room!" my mother promised. "And as many blankets, coverlets, and strips of linen and fustian as Winover did. Your pick of the kettles, skillets, spits, and trivets, also. And the red tulip dishes from Leyden. And pewter to shine against your kitchen walls. And——"

"Waugh!" I cried. And then: "What will be left to you, sweet blossom?"

"Don't fret about me, widgeon!" she said and tossed her head. "There's all the gear that was to be 'Memby's, you know, besides your own. Thoma Cort brought enough with him to outfit a dozen manors and he said Rudi could find no space for the things I had ready for 'Memby."

We were more than a day getting the stuff up Leyden Street to the new house in the forest. It was almost like the time when my mother arrived from the Low Country on the *Fortune*. When the last bit of gear was under cover, my mother sat on a low bench in front of the fireplace with Nabby at her side and I brought in cedar branches and kindled the first blaze in my own home. And never was there a burning of sweeter fragrance!

Before she left, my mother reached into the pocket of her linen apron and brought forth something which she placed on the shelf high above her head. "Your elephant, Young Matt!" she said. "Now, indeed, *is* the ring broken! Naught but two left, but so long as two are left in the Over home, all is well! With Goodman Matthew to lead the way, and Goodwife Orris to plod sturdily on behind, the Overs will still go forward gaily into the future, strong to face the world since they are together. . . . And this, Nabby, this is for you!" She laid a glittering bauble beside the cocky bit of ivory, but I protested against that.

"That is the King's Voice!" I cried.

"As if I didn't know!"

"But—but it is yours now! Uncle Samuel bought it from Elder Brewster and gave it to you."

"And I give it to Nabby. Is there anything wrong about that? It will have value as a relic in years to come, but to Nabby and me its value will lie in its power to picture to our minds a brave lad who came to the defense of his mother with nothing better than a fat eel. It has never been blown on, Nabby!" she continued, turning her back on me. "And see that you do not blow upon it—the Overs get themselves out of their troubles without help! We do not need to pipe our woe to the winds, that others may come running to our assistance!"

And so she went, proudly, on light feet back to the little dwelling close to the shore, the little dwelling that my father and I had builded, wondering how its roof was to cover all the young, bustling life that would soon fill it, the little dwelling that was now, with its ells and added chambers, like a swollen squash about two lone seeds.

It was less than a week later that a trader came up the coast out of the south and tossed off a packet with a bit of sealed writing for me. Nabby and I took them both to the end of Leyden Street, thinking to comfort my mother in her great loneliness.

"I hope she will not be tearful, grieving by herself!" Nabby fretted.

"My mother is never tearful!" I told her. "But she may be on her knees in the loam, digging about the roots of her simples. And to find her thus, alone and thinking on the past, would be more mournful than downright weeping! I hope Goodwife Fentry has been to see her often."

Blazes! She was busy at the table, preparing a fat hare for the kettle and humming:

"I said to Master Chillingsworth:
'I don't know what we'd do
Without our sage and savouries
To liven up a stew!'

How ever did you get along, Matthew, before I arrived with the Bowl filled with greenstuffs?"

"We missed sweetening and milk foods more than simples!" a booming voice, a happy voice, replied—my father, stretching at his ease on the settle beside the hearth at this time of day! "Odds blood, there was a time when Young Matt and I needed no savouries to liven up *our* stew—all we longed for was the hare!"

"Poor lads! And we in Leyden stuffing ourselves on meat puddings, eels, and oily cakes! Well, it's past and gone now!"

"Aye!" he shouted merrily. "And now, perhaps, I can get a first cut at the delicate eating."

"As if you didn't always!"

"Not me! The best was always slipped aside for Young Matt, or Fox-tail, or that damp woman child, or that fat Dutch lad—don't try to tell me it wasn't! I had eyes, even if I kept them shut to all your goings-on!"

It was more than enough. Merry as titmice, the two of them, when I had come to comfort! I pushed open the door and stood before them. "Well, Young Matt!" my father cried contentedly. "That nose of yours can still smell out stewed hare in the making, I see! Welcome, daughter. Are you returning our lad to us? I know his value is small, but I hoped——"

"A trader just touched at the jetty," I interrupted his banter sharply. "There was a letter and a packet for me from the south."

"A letter?" cried my mother softly. "From—from——"

"Aye, from Nicolas. Nabby said to bring everything here so we might read the letter and open the packet together. She thought it might comfort you."

"Thank God for such a sweet lass! Open the letter first, Young Matt!"

We sat about the table as I read aloud.

" 'Young Matt:

" 'Wisset and I have come down out of the New Hampshire grants and we are here for a time with Rudi and 'Memby.

" 'Rudi tells me that Piet Billing has come to no harm from the crack on the skull Wisset gave him with the bucket —too bad!

" 'Rudi says there is no reason why we shouldn't return to New Plymouth, but there *is*. In the first place, I like it here in the forest better than in New Plymouth. Our colony is becoming overcrowded—a body can't move without jogging elbows with his neighbor. It's not like that here on the Great River. There's *room!* And the second reason is—Orrje Cort!

" 'Lud! The oily-cakes and hutch-putch that one can make! I'm thinking of taking a manor not far from Rudi's, and Wisset will build him a lodge back in the wilderness close by. Of course Orrje and I are young, but Mijnheer Cort says New Amsterdam needs young settlers and the more Overs he has in his family the better pleased he will be.

" 'Mijnheer Nicolas, the Patroon of the manor, waugh!

" 'The New World is doing odd things to the Overs: Winover and John, Puritans; Young Matt, a Pilgrim; and 'Memby and I, Dutch! And Wisset, a savage as ever!

" 'Bid sweet Nabby and evil Sooty welcome to the family from me, the young savage Nicolas! Wisset and I are sending to her the first fruits of our manor. We lift the hand and bow the head in loving greeting to our "golden-headed sister."

" 'You will hear from Orrje and me as often as a trader passes by. Take my mother alone into the scullery, Young Matt, where she will not be embarrassed before onlookers, and kiss her roundly for the lad who loves her! Tell her I've got the ivory elephant in my pocket. To my father, also, my honest love.

" 'Nicolas.' "

"What's in the packet?" asked my mother, smoothing her apron and looking proudly and happily about her family circle. "I'm afraid to look at what those two wild lads may be sending. It might be a porcupine—you never can tell!"

It was a long cape of finest beaver, lined throughout with a white deerskin that was fine and supple as any silken weaving. With the cape was a tiny coif of beaver, also lined with soft white deer and clasped by two pearly shells; and with the cape and the coif were boots of beaver made as the red men like them, high and furry and warm inside.

It was a gift for a princess! For Nabby!

The next five years are blurred in my mind—like the early morning hour beside our quiet bay—leaving but a handful of events to stand forth sharply from the fog. The first of these was the arrival of a bundle of goods from Thoma Cort. When the lumber and fustian were pulled aside, there was the cradle of the Over family! The same cradle that had swung beside the hearth in Austerfield for my mother and my Uncle Samuel and John; the same cradle that had been borrowed to bed my father. The same cradle that had traveled to Scrooby, in the same year that the King did, for me, and remained there for that damp woman child, 'Memby. The same cradle that had crossed the sea to the Low Country and welcomed the Dutch lad Nicolas and been kicked to pieces by him.

Now, Mijnheer Cort had mended it as new as ever, stouter in fact, and had brought it across the ocean to New Amsterdam. And here it was, ready to stand beside the fireplace in the silvery house beside the trail in the forest of New Plymouth, and lull small Matthew to slumber.

Small Matthew himself was the second event of those first five years that no fog of forgetfulness could blur. And after him, before he was freed from gruels, came the twins Dearlove and Dearborn. And then, indeed, was the cradle filled to bursting!

All her friends in the colony had hoped that my little mother would take her ease, now that my father's house was swept clear of young, and learn the joy of sitting for a peaceful hour in the sunshine with folded hands. Goodwife Fentry made no secret of the wish.

"You've worn yourself out over children, Orris!" she boomed one day, sipping a cup of hot tea and nibbling a fresh cake in my mother's kitchen. "Always a mess of children hanging on your care! Puritan children (if Winover can be called that—anyway, she came from Londontown!), Pilgrim children, Dutch, and, God help us, a savage! Besides soothing the ills of a whole community with your simples. Why don't you take your shoes off and learn to rest?"

"Small Matthew's the worst one for colic ever seen!" my mother told her happily, and went on shredding dried leaves into a skillet of boiling water. "And he won't take his catnip tea from anybody but me! Then, too, there's the spice cakes!"

There *were* the spice cakes! More than that, all manner of baked, brewed, stewed, and boiled stuffs. My mother could not break herself of cooking for eight, now that there was only my father to sit at the end of the table. He did his best by her efforts, but his best was not enough. So she kept our larder filled.

"I never get a chance to bake you a spice cake!" Nabby complained gently one day. "How can a woman keep a proper house when there is naught for her to do in it?"

"The house is proper!" I told her with great contentment. "And don't fret—your turn at the bake oven will come! Wait until Small Matthew learns more about his legs—and the twins begin to sprout teeth and there's gold-thread, high-tapers, felt-wyrt, and catnip to be brewed all over again for their troubles! Are you ready for important news, woman?"

"Aye. If it be pleasing."

"Judge for yourself. Goodwife Over, we are to have a cow!"

"A cow? All for us alone? Oh, Young Matt!"

"All for us alone! And it will be the proudest moment of my life—well, *almost* the proudest moment of my wedded life, anyway, since Small Matthew and Dearborn and Dearlove arrived—when a cow is tethered to the paling outside our door."

"But—but where will you get it?"

"William Bradford has arranged for a trader—" I turned at a noise outside and saw a magnificent savage stalk through Nabby's garden of bright blossoms. Behind him were my father, my mother, and Goodwife Fentry, with Small Matthew streaming out behind them. Each woman held firmly to a wrist of the lad, making his legs of no more use to him than two tails to a rabbit. I crossed the room in a bound.

"Wisset!" I cried.

"Young Matt—brother!" he replied with great dignity.

A grand man, this! It might be that he was three and twenty years of age, straight, handsome as a forest tree.

"Wisset—you're a lad no longer! You're a—a great chief!"

"God's mercy, give Small Matthew a seed cake to quiet his howling, Nabby, and give Young Matt one, too!" cried Goodwife Fentry impatiently. "We want to hear Wisset's voice, not theirs! Five years since that Dutch lad drove you into the wilderness at the point of a musket, lad."

"Almost five years since we've heard from either of you!" sighed my little mother, seating herself on a bench and gathering Small Matthew to her side. "Not a word since the wedding gift of beaver to Nabby! Are you still dwelling near to Nicolas, Wisset?"

"Mijnheer the Patroon Over sent me to——"

"Who?"

"My white brother Nicolas."

"That's better, lad!" shouted my father. "Now, then, let's hear about Nicolas!"

"Has he prospered?" asked Nabby.

"The Patroon has much land. His land is wide, his land is deep. Great forests stand upon it and it borders a river. Nicolas and Mevrouw Orrje and the small Johann dwell in the Manor House close to the river. At the other end of the estate, within the depths of the forest, in a lodge of our own, dwell Wisset, Sweet Wind, and Little Beaver."

"Sweet Wind? You have wed, Wisset? It must have been outside your own tribe, then."

He bowed gravely. "Even as did my brother Nicolas. Sweet Wind is a Sinneka. But she makes hutch-putch!" A flicker of laughter lightened his eyes.

"You have done well, lad!" said my father.

"Very well. Nicolas and I are wealthy men, each in the eyes of his own people. We trap and hunt and share alike. We are content."

"I should think you would be!"

"Only, lately I did begin to feel a restlessness of spirit. 'It is time,' I said to my brother, 'for my father's tribe to see Sweet Wind and Little Beaver. We will travel northward through the wilderness.' "

"You came all this way through the forest!" shrilled Goodwife Fentry.

"It is the red man's way. Nicolas will come by water."

"Nicolas! When?" gasped my mother.

"When John arrives, to accompany him."

"John? Do you mean my brother, Wisset? John Brode and Winover?"

"There was business on the Conightecute River, and from there John and the fiery-headed one traveled to New Amsterdam. I was to go ahead and tell you that, traveling homeward to the colony in the north, they would stop off here. And with them will come my brother Nicolas, as I said, and Mevrouw 'Memby with Mijnheer the Patroon Cort. And Mevrouw Kathi. And others."

"*Others*—God's mercy!" piped my mother. And shoved her coif awry with her crooked elbow.

"Steady on, lass!" My father beamed heartily on us all. "It looks like a big visit!"

My mind still hung on certain of Wisset's words. "Business on the Conightecute," I repeated. "What business could John have there? Are they building cities that far into the wilderness?"

"There is trouble!" Wisset replied quietly.

"Between the red men——"

"Between the white men! Between the white chiefs of the colony to the north and the white chiefs of New Amsterdam," he began. And then was silent. He drew forth a bit of rolled parchment from his quiver and held it out to me. "It is written better than I can speak!" he said.

"Dear heaven, a letter!" shrilled Goodwife Fentry. "Whom is it from, Young Matt?"

I looked. "John."

"Read it out, lad, read it out!"

19

THE RING OF IVORY ELEPHANTS

" 'YOUNG Matt,

" 'The English and the Dutch have burst into a flame of rage over colonizing the Conightecute and I have been sent along the river to New Amsterdam by our Governor Winthrop to see what can be done about settling the dispute.' "

"John has!" interrupted my mother, aghast. "Umph, the lad must have risen high in the esteem of the Puritans!"

" 'I shall take the opportunity on my way home,' " I continued reading, " 'to visit with you, Nicolas, and 'Memby. Wisset will tell you about that and our plans.

" 'God has prospered me greatly since coming to this colony. I have been granted 75 acres on the west side of a wide river in Newtowne and upon it I have erected a splendid dwelling of brick, timber, and tile that were brought from England.' "

"Odds blood, John must be gentry!" cried Goodwife Fentry.

" 'The dwelling is shaded in front by a magnificent elm tree and is surrounded by high palings for protection. The savages hereabouts are friendly for the most part, but it has been decided to erect this high fence between their lodges and our settlement; each landowner will be responsible for the care of the fence along his own property. My part is a matter of six rods.

" 'In our Commonwealth, all grants of land must be

certified by a committee of Deacons, and I have already been elected a Deacon.' "

"God's mercy, John *is* gentry!" wailed my mother. "Our living will never suit him now!"

"Our living will always suit him—and Winover!" my father insisted pleasantly. "We'll have Wisset fetch a deer to roast—and you and Nabby can make hare pasties and spice cakes to your hearts' delight!"

"I mean—I mean—bricks and elms and Deacons and——"

"Tush!" said Goodwife Fentry. "Go on, Young Matt!"

I found the place and read further. " 'I have taken the Oath of Freeman. When I took that Oath, Young Matt, I was minded of the time we went to the Stadthuis in Leyden and watched Matthew become a citizen of Leyden. Just as solemnly did I take my oath:

> "I, John Brode, being by the Almighty's most wise disposition become a member of this body consisting of the Governor, Deputy Governor, Assistants, and Commonalty of the Massachusetts in New England, do freely and sincerely acknowledge that I am justly and lawfully subject to the Governor of the same, etc.

When it was all said and done, I was become Deacon John Brode, Freeman.

" 'Never shall I cease being thankful for the instruction in land surveying I had at the hands of Mijnheer de Key. Because of it, I have been chosen to lay off boundary lines between Watertown and Concord, Dedham and Newton. I have also laid out some military land for the Commonwealth.

" 'The Puritans are much more concerned about education than the Pilgrims of New Plymouth. A first Public School is already under consideration—and funds are being raised for a College! I have given 70 pounds toward that institution.

" 'There is much more to tell, but something must be left for the time when we shall meet again. I wonder if you will be able to get our party under one roof—it seems to grow with each new day. Now the Corts insist upon joining us! And 'Memby and Kathi cannot manage their finery and children without their blacks! And, of course, Wisset must be included. As I figure it, we will come to call on you and Orris in the following numbers!

John, Winover, and two children	4
'Memby, Rudi, two children, two blacks	6
Nicolas, Orrje, and little Johann	3
Kathi, Klaas, two children, two blacks	6
Wisset, Sweet Wind, Little Beaver	3
Mijnheer and Mevrouw Cort	2

and to that, must be added:

Young Matt, Nabby, and three children	5
Orris and Matthew Over	2

Thirty-one mouths to feed! Thirty-one to bed at nightfall! Will it be possible?' "

"He shouldn't fret!" said my mother with a toss of her pretty head. "Some dwellings—some *brick* dwellings might find themselves strained, but we will take care of our own, here in New Plymouth!"

" 'Winover says that she is afraid you will blow on the

King's Voice when you see us all get off the trader. She stretches her arms toward Leyden Street and wraps the Overs in her embrace.

" 'Ever your loving,

" 'John.' "

"Thirty-one souls!" gasped Goodwife Fentry when I had finished reading. "Heaven above!"

"I," said Wisset with great dignity, "shall bide in the lodge of my father."

"No, you won't!" my mother told him firmly. "We should never see aught of the Dutch lad if you were in the forest; and, besides, you have a place in the family with the rest. Of course, if you could just sleep nights with your kin——"

"That, certainly, we will do!"

"Then—then—my goodness, I don't know how to *think!*"

"I'll do it for you!" shouted Goodwife Fentry willingly. "You take John, Winover, and their two children in with you and Matthew. The two older Corts can find a bed here with Nabby. I'll take 'Memby, Rudi, and their two. 'Lissy Kerry will be glad to have Nicolas, Orrje, the little Johann, and a couple of the blacks. She's got lots of room, now that Giles has built a house for himself and Hope Dale."

"But that leaves Kathi, Klaas, their children, and two more blacks."

"I'm coming to them. Goodwife White has plenty of room. Anybody in Leyden Street, for that matter, would be proud to help in the Overs' come-together! Of course, when you think of feeding thirty-one mouths——"

"Nicolas and I will bring food!" Wisset spoke firmly. "None know the forest as we! We will bring deer. We will bring small game. We will bring turkey. We will bring water fowl. We will bring fish, lobsters, and shellfish. We will bring eels. We will bring——"

"Glory on us, Wisset, don't bring anything else!" Goodwife Fentry cried, and pulled Small Matthew away from the trencher of seed cakes. "The way you talk about the forest, and game! A good thing for you James Billing isn't living hereabouts any more!"

"I have no fear of James Billing."

"I believe you. But haven't you any curiosity about the worm?"

"He is an evil man."

"*Was,* Wisset; he may be now, of course, but at least we of New Plymouth don't know about it. To think that we had to set up our first stocks on the common for James Billing! After all our boasting of the wickedness in other colonies and the goodness in ours! Well, we got our sinner at last."

"He should have been burned by fire."

"God love us, lad, we don't go in for torture, you know!"

"What did he do, that evil one?"

"Oh, he got to thinking he owned all the wild life hereabouts and most of the forest. Let anybody set a trap—or start down the trail—and he went crazy! One day when Goodman Morse bent over his snare, James shot at him from behind a tree."

"Killed him?"

"Well, no! But an old man can't run *that* hard and far and do any good to himself! William Bradford set up the stocks and fastened James inside. Dear, dear, after all these years! They took away James's musket, too."

"He was cured? No!"

"No is right! The very day he got loose from the stocks he grabbed Piet's musket and shot the Norton lad, who was short-cutting it homeward across a corner of the Billings' property. When James and Piet heard Miles Standish and his men coming for them, they simply disappeared into the forest and have never been heard of since. Their land lies idle yonder—it will have to be divided. A good thing for Young Matt here—he'll get enough of it to straighten out that line between the oak sapling and the sassafras bush."

"Thirty-one!" cried my mother suddenly, as though she heard the number for the first time. "Can it be possible that we add up to thirty-one? I don't believe it!"

"You don't? And you drawing children into your household at every turn?" laughed Goodwife Fentry boisterously. "I'm only surprised it isn't a hundred and thirty-one!"

"Give them a few more years, Submit!" begged my father. But my mother asked: "When are they coming?"

"Toward the end of November."

"November, eh? So soon? Well, 'twill be another Thanksgiving Day, no matter the month."

"Thanksgiving Day? In November? Did you hear that, folks? Always something new whirling about this Goodwife's pretty head! I suppose we feast, too."

"Of course we do! Thanksgiving Day can be at *any* time when you've got enough to be thankful for."

"Wait until Elder Brewster and William Bradford hear of this!"

"Why, of course—why, to be sure!" She stood up from the low bench and clapped her hands. "You go right away and see them, Matthew!" she ordered prettily. "And bid them to the feast with us. And we'll want you and Oliver, Submit!"

Blazes! Thirty-one weren't enough for her. In a breath, she had added four to the list. "There'll be snow to the chimneypots along Leyden Street in November!" I reminded her. " 'Twill be impossible to set a board for five and thirty in the open in November!"

"Then we'll feast inside, my lad! You and Matthew shall fetch planks and stretch them on braces the length of the kitchen and into the chamber beyond. Once again, the Over family and their guests will sit at one board and give thanks to God for His eternal goodness!"

The very air of Leyden Street was spicy with the fragrance of good food during the days that followed. There was a constant clatter among my mother's black pots and Nabby's swinging kettles. There was even a tantalizing odor of spices about the fustians of anyone who so much as lingered near our kitchens; and as for my father, he complained that he smelled so viciously of sage and savoury that the wild turkeys fled into the forest ahead of his coming down the trail.

Goodwife Fentry and my mother covered the long, smooth planks of the table with strips of fair linen and Nabby set the Bowl in the middle. " 'Tis as much a part of the Over family as any of us!" she vowed. "It carried a part of Old England from Scrooby down Ryton Water to the Low Country, and from the Low Country along the canals to the open sea and across to a New England! Come, and be an honored guest at the Overs' home-coming, sweet Bowl!" she cried merrily.

And then she heaped it to overflowing with ripe brown nuts and rusty-brown apples and chunks of sugared maple sap; and in and between all the lovely brown that spilled over upon the fair linen, she placed lumps of dusty amber spruce gum. And trailing outward from the brown and gold to reach all four corners of the long board and drip adown the sides were delicate tendrils of that ivy-like vine that always bore scarlet berries in great profusion at this season of the year.

"Waugh!" shouted my father when he came into the kitchen and saw the splendid array.

And then it was time for him to follow Wisset to the jetty to meet the trader, while I brought a last load of cedar branches into the kitchen and Nabby and my mother and Goodwife Fentry and Sweet Wind bent above the pots and stirred among the steaming skillets and shifted the bake ovens before the blazing logs.

With shrieks of delight they came trailing up Leyden Street—Winover, 'Memby, and Kathi with their men, their young, their kin, and their blacks. New Plymouth had never seen such a merry gathering before and every shining pane held a watchful head, all up and down the street.

'Memby led the throng. "Mother! Mother!" she shrilled before she was even with the garden gate. And then: "Hurry, Family, do just what I told you!"

We were ready, each one of us. As the kitchen filled with shouting, snowy, wool-wrapped humans, eight of us somehow parted from the rest and, standing in front of the shelf above the hearth, solemnly lifted a bit of ivory to 'Memby and watched her link trunk to tail in a firm ring.

"There we are!" she cried then. "Here we are, sweet Mother! Matthew, Orris, John, Winover, Young Matt, 'Memby, and Nicolas! The Over family against the world! Hold on a minute—where's Nabby?"

"Here!" said the butter-headed lass, and dropped a golden bauble in the center of the ring. "The King's Voice!"

We thought my mother would dance and prance and make merry with the rest of us, but she couldn't. Not just then. She stood in front of the ring of ivory beasties and clasped her little hands.

"Now, God be thanked!" she whispered. "My—my family!"

A great stamping in the snow outside the door brought her back to her old brisk, anxious self and she flew to welcome Elder Brewster and William Bradford. And while they were greeting our guests, the women covered the fair linen of the long board with smoking food.

First, four enormous pans were spaced along the length, each pan being a huge pasty of small game, tender hare, fat squirrel meat, and such. Between the pans were turkeys, five of them, stuffed to bursting with crumbs of maize bread, pungent roots, and pudding-grasses, such as sage, thyme, fennel, savoury, and parsley. And scattered about wherever room could be found were trenchers of roasted deer meat, bowls of thickened gravies, nappies of boiled and baked vegetables, and pretty woven baskets of snowy parched maize.

There were, too, beans baked in clay pots in the hot ashes; and steamed breads and baked breads of golden maize stuffed with dried huckleberries as thick as plums in a pudding; and spice cakes beyond counting; and a string of jam pots from one end of the kitchen to the other.

But we began the feast with bowls of hutch-putch made of lobsters and mussels and I know not what else. It was a dish thick with richness and every dip of the spoon brought up something new and choice from the bottom of the bowl. The children, I remember, ravenous with the food smells about them and excited by the strangeness of everything, were as hard to keep under control as a hill of disturbed ants until they were set before the hutch-putch and promised as much as they could hold. After that, they lost interest in the rest of the feast and we had no more trouble from them. They were bundled back into their woolen wrappings and sent forth to frolic in the snow of Leyden Street, leaving their parents to a long afternoon of peace and enjoyment.

Elder Brewster and William Bradford sat side by side at the head of our board; and next to William were Jon Brewster and my Uncle John, those three dear friends of Scrooby days. We spoke long and affectionately of Scrooby. My mother told about when the King came to the Manor House there, in the very year I was born; and she told about the visit of Margaret, daughter of one King and bride of another; and she told about the fat Archbishop of York and his 200 horses laden with rich gear for the Manor House; and she told about the time a King's Man came into her garden of simples and went away without his golden whistle.

And then Nabby ran to fetch the bauble and it passed from hand to hand while my mother told of how I had come by it, exchanging it for the fattest eel that was ever drawn from Scrooby Waters, and how, later, it had traveled down Ryton Water in the Bowl and tinkled under the very nose of the pompous bailiff of Hull, and how, still later, I had sold it to pay for our passage in the *Speedwell* to a new world—only the *Speedwell* had never sailed beyond the English coast and the journey was finished in the *Mayflower*. And the King's Voice was forced to return to Leyden for a dreary while before it was again bedded among simples, grafts, and slips and so transported to a new and kinder England.

"Speaking of the *Mayflower*," cried Winover suddenly above the din, "*there's* a craft that won't soon be forgotten along this coast! It fetched the Pilgrims in safety to New Plymouth, and the Puritans to Salem Bay! They speak of it with honor and love as much in the colony to the north as you do here."

"The *Mayflower*—tush!" sniffed 'Memby before anybody else could speak. "Who cares for that old tub! The good ship *Fortune,* out of Leyden, for me!"

"Or the *Charity*—with its three cows!" yelled Nicolas.

"Puritans—Pilgrims—after all, we are but children of the same household!" Governor Bradford spoke thoughtfully. "We should be under one roof."

"We will be—we will be!" my Uncle John told him—and us. "The talk is already going around. Salem Bay and New Plymouth should be one, it is said, joined under a new name, such as the Massachusetts Bay Colony, or something like that!"

"It won't work!" Goodwife Fentry cracked a nut in her strong teeth and shook her head against the plan. "We *aren't* children of the same household, William! Don't think it! We Pilgrims are the poor relations in the household of the wealthy Puritans, and who wants poor relations underfoot at every turn? How can there be any pleasant union betwixt folk who have had too much and folk who have had too little?"

"Still, there will be!"

"Besides, the Puritans cling too easily to the King who rules in Londontown—and over them, too!"

"Not too easily, and not too closely—not any more!" my Uncle John told her unhesitatingly. "There is some flavor in the air of this new world, and the Puritans have tasted it. Freedom! The rights of common people! Fruits they would never have considered nibbling at in Old England. But here, in the wilderness, they have *had* to think for themselves; they have been obliged to wrest homes from the forest, cities and communities for their own comfort and protection, laws for their own safeguarding. These things will not be easily given up if the time ever comes when the King in Londontown casts covetous eyes this way; and it *may* come, that time, for all that the Puritans hold a charter. Each day I believe more and more firmly that the Puritans would defend their freedom as fiercely as the Pilgrims against *any* hand, no matter whose, which may be lifted against it!"

"Any hand lifted against *them,* huh!" Mijnheer Cort grunted his displeasure. "But they can lift what hands they like against others! Let them stop sending colonies down along the Conightecute! The Conightecute belongs to *us* of New Amsterdam! There'll be blood shed around that river before long, mark my words!"

None feared that more than my Uncle John, but this was not the time nor was it the place to tell all that he had recently learned in his journeying through the wilderness. He kept silence, while Nabby pressed more spice cake on Mijnheer Cort and William Bradford turned thoughts to pleasanter fields in his own way.

"I like the emphasis the English of Salem Bay are putting on education, John!" he said. "Did you know that we in New Plymouth will have a school before long?"

Blazes! This was news to all of us!

"How's the cost of a school to be met?" cried Nabby, startled at the thought.

"You and Young Matt will pay part of it!" William told her. "All families with children are to be taxed, whether the children attend the school or not. At least, that is the plan that is being considered."

"Are all the folk of New Plymouth able to be taxed?"

"If not, the town will attend to it. And the tax need not be paid in money, you know. Corn, beans, wheat, or beaver skins will do quite as well. One thing, though: all parents will be obliged to cut wood for the heating of the school during the winter months or their children will be sent home!"

"Corn, wheat, beaver skins—will that provide for the upkeep of a school?" asked Winover. "To me that sounds more like Dame Cotter's Free School of Scrooby!"

"Well, other ideas are being considered," William told her then. "For instance, school-meadows will be set apart and rented, the rental going for the upkeep of the school. You'll want part of a meadow, Young Matt, for that cow of yours! We're going to take James Billing's plot of land for the first school-meadow. It has been vacant and idle, you know, ever since the family fled into the wilderness."

"Well, bless my soul, some good comes from that old rascal after all!" boomed Goodwife Fentry above the hubbub. "If he's alive and ever hears of it, though, he'll drop dead; and if he's already in his grave, which God grant, he'll turn in it like a haunch of deer meat on the spit!"

A piercing whistle interrupted her words and she gripped the edge of the board. "God's mercy, speak of the evil one!" she gasped. But I sprang across the room and pushed the door to the scullery wide open.

My mother was seated on an overturned bucket. And in front of her, still wrapped in his outdoor woolens but with his breeches dropped, one hand clutching at the fat of his buttocks and the other a tight fist, stood Small Matthew. The scullery was a jumble.

"Young Matt, lad!" sighed my mother as soon as she spied me. "I have need of help. I cannot handle this thing alone."

"Did you blow on the King's Voice?"

"No. My need wasn't *that* great! But *his* was!"

"His? Small Matthew's?"

"Aye. He's got the thing in his closed fist. I saw him reach for it on the shelf when nobody was looking, but I thought, let him have it, likely he's always wanted to get his paws on it and Nabby wouldn't let him. I didn't even know that the lad *knew* it was a whistle! But when he came in here—and I heard my jam pots crash——"

"Was he after gooseberry jam again?"

"Just as fond of it as you used to be! Only when I saw that he had pulled down most of my simples getting to it, I lost my temper and took him across my knee and warmed his buttocks good for him."

"Fair enough!"

"That's not blood all over him, Young Matt; it's jam! And while I was smacking him, he got the King's Voice between his lips and blew on it! God's mercy, lad, the first time I ever heard the sound since Scrooby days!"

"The first Over that's been in need of help, like as not—a need that he couldn't handle by himself!" I grinned crookedly. "And stop trembling, sweet blossom, there are no hoofbeats pounding along the Great North Road, you know! We're far from all that, and this one who blew is your own wicked grandson. Give me that bauble, small one!"

"No!" Small Matthew let loose of the handful of fat and held the whistle in both clutching fists. "No! No!"

"Only it's aye, aye, my lad!" I told him firmly, opening his bent fingers and taking the shining pretty away from him. "And now you are to be swabbed off with a pot cloth and spend the rest of the afternoon on a pallet in the loft, to make up for the trouble you have caused!"

"No! No! No! No!"

"Mercy, do something about that racket, Young Matt!" said Nabby, pushing her golden head in at the scullery door for no more than a glance.

"I'm doing it!" I told her cheerfully. "A bucket of water and a besom."

"No! No! No! No!"

"All right, some more of *this,* then!" I agreed. And lifted the spunky lad to my thigh and raised my hand. My mother came between his jam-soaked breeches and my palm like a pettish bee.

"Enough of that, Young Matt!" she buzzed. "The lad is ill of too much sweets and too many kinfolk! What he needs is to be made clean and have a sup of catnip brew and a nap on Grandmother's own bed with her arm snuggled about him to keep all strangers away. Do you give that golden bauble back to Nabby and tell her to keep it under lock and key—I never want to hear its call again—and then keep our guests talking over schools and war and whatnot for an hour while I nap with this baby. Dear heaven, thirty-five souls underfoot at once is a chore, after all! I must be aging, lad!"

In the morning, the Overs and their kinfolk parted, and all New Plymouth gathered on the jetty to watch their going. The traders crossed the shallow bay side by side, but when they were come to the tumbling waters of the open sea they parted and one soon vanished into the fogs of the north, while one was lost to view in the mists of the south.

Then did I turn with words of comfort for my little mother, but she was not among the watching women. "She disappeared as soon as the traders cast off!" Goodwife Kerry told me. "I don't know where she went."

There was only one place. I hurried up Leyden Street, through the withered stalks and snow-covered clumps of her garden, and lifted the latch to her kitchen door.

She was sitting upon a low stool before the blazing log, her skirt neatly folded back across her knees, her little legs stretched to the comforting warmth. Her blue cape hung on its peg beside the Bowl, her spinning wheel was back in place beside the hearth, the kitchen table was shrunk to its normal size, and every pewter plate and nappy was silvery and quiet in its rack along the wall. My mother's house was at peace.

She turned with a crooked grin on her pretty little face as the latch clicked. "I thought it would be you, Young Matt!" she piped. "The wind across the bay had too much bite in it for me. Well, lad, it's all over! They had beds under them, every one! And food enough to burst them. Maybe in another twelve months I could look forward to another homecoming of the Overs, but now I keep thinking of the words of the Psalmist: 'Let peace be to this house!' It needs it!"

Blazes! The woman never did what I expected. "I thought to find thee sunk in gloom," I said gently.

"Tush!" She shifted about briskly so that another surface of her leg might share the heat. "And don't whisper, lad! There's no death in the house, you know."

"But you grieved so when your children went into the wilderness, one by one, that now when they went——"

"Thirty-one at a time, eh? Well, Young Matt, I suppose every redbreast grieves when its young tumbles out of the nest, but they're soon pulling worms from the sod as gaily as ever. And eating them *themselves,* for a change! Thirty-one, ho hummmmmm! What a wildcat that small Johann is! I'm afeard Orrje will spare the rod with that one—and regret it!"

"You never lifted the rod to me."

"*You*—foosh! You were quicker than most to learn, my lad—and you had the lesson of a King's Man's lash and Dame Cotter's birch rather early in life, remember!"

"The rest didn't, though—and they've done pretty well for themselves! Even Nicolas. And if there ever was a wildcat, he was one! Johann is a mild lad to that one."

She chuckled softly. And poked the log to a quicker heat. "A grand family!" she said proudly. "John and Winover, honored and happy among the Puritans; Nicolas and 'Memby prominent and satisfied among the Dutch; and you, Young Matt Over, *Pilgrim* still, poorer than the others, it may be, but helping to build a new, a better world. Building schools, making just laws. This, I said to myself while I was looking you all over on the jetty a while ago, this is the way a family can grow in a land where there is freedom! Put a handful of catnip in the pot, lad, the kettle is on the boil. I need a calming drink when I have been doing overmuch thinking."

I started for the scullery, but she called me back before I had opened the door. "*That* was the kernel of my thinking, lad—freedom!" she said. And shoved her coif to the back of her curly pate. "We who fled down Ryton Water knew the value of freedom—we suffered much for it! And now we think to hand it over to Small Matthew and Johann and their generation as a *gift*. God's mercy, that is not the way with freedom, lad! It must be constantly *fought* for. Somebody is always ready to steal it away. If Small Matthew should lose this thing that we have suffered so bitterly to give to him——"

"He won't!" I assured her. "Little chance of *that* one letting go his hold on anything of value that falls his way!"

She laughed aloud. "The way he squeezed that King's Voice!" she remembered. "It all but shrieked of its own accord. Add a few elder blossoms to the brew, Young Matt!"

"The elder is a cursed tree!" I warned her.

She half rose from her little stool. "Why, Young Matt Over!" she cried, shocked. "Of all the herbs God put upon this earth for the healing of mankind, none has more value than the elder!"

"You aren't forgetting how the English maids brought elder branches to the place of death—and about Judas and the elder tree!"

"Foosh! I'm not forgetting, either, that even when you were a baby in the cradle there were many who looked upon water as a cursed thing and forbade the bathing of children in it, or overmuch drinking of it."

"That didn't keep me out of the Bowl, or free from your scrubbings, did it?"

"It did not! Put a bit of the elder bark into the brew with the blossoms, lad! And a handful of hop tassels. And a scraping of valerian root. With some pennyroyal and mint."

"Blazes! You *do* need calming!" I came out of the scullery with my hands full.

"I do!" she agreed happily. "I have seen my family spreading over the New World like gill-over-the-ground in a garden bed and 'tis exciting to the fancy. God's mercy, lad, list to that racket!"

"I've heard it before!" I told her. And poured the hot brew into two bowls. "It was always the boast of the Overs that they could handle their troubles themselves without spilling the news to the world. Small Matthew is different. He believes in summoning aid wherever it may be found."

"Is that only *one* lad?"

"But an angry one! He is coming to find me with his mouth stretched to the full." I handed her a bowl and supped deeply of the second one, myself. "Drink quickly!" I urged. "We'll both need calming, now!"